The Man Who Fell in Love
with the Moon

Tom Spanbauer is the author
of one other novel, *Faraway Places.*
He lives in Portland, Oregon.

Tom Spanbauer

The Man Who Fell in Love with the Moon

Minerva

A Minerva Paperback

THE MAN WHO FELL IN LOVE

WITH THE MOON

First published in Great Britain 1992
by Martin Secker & Warburg Limited
This Minerva edition published 1996
by Mandarin Paperbacks
an imprint of Reed International Books Ltd
Michelin House, 81 Fulham Road, London SW3 6RB
and Auckland, Melbourne, Singapore and Toronto

Reprinted 1996

Copyright © 1991 by Tom Spanbauer

A CIP catalogue record for this book
is available from the British Library

ISBN 0 7493 9567 2

Printed and bound in Great Britain
by Cox & Wyman Ltd, Reading, Berkshire

To Mike Taylor,

to Mutt and Jeff, Dellwood and Shed,

the altar boys, Ida and Alma; a family,

with all my love

My heartfelt thanks: Anton Mueller, Eric Ashworth, Peter Christopher.

And to you: Mendy Graves, Kally Thurman, Jim Erdman, Ellie Covan (Dixon Place), Clyde Hall, Charles Lawrence, Hazel Truchot, Kerry Moosman, Paulette Osborne, Kay Oswald, Bob Waring, Judith Waring, and Laura Zigman.

And to you: Susan Anderson, Antonia's (Key West), Eve Baron, Kate Brandt, Mary L. Bryan, L.M.T., Ira Chelnik (Chef Ivan), Stacey Creamer, Howard Crook, Will Docherty, J. D. Dolan, Jack Fought, Roger Finney, Ruth Füglistaller, Bob Gamblin, Martha Gamblin, Joe Garamella, Eva Gasteazoro, Osvaldo Gomariz, Dr. Stuart Grayson, Bob Green, Leo Gulik, Helen Gundlach, Johanna Hays, Ms. Jasmine, Kip Katzen, Joanna Knapp, Stephen Koch, Tom Law, Lana Lynx, Jutta Meyer, Ellen Michaelson, Mick Newham, Gaetha Pace, Harold Richards, Atul Shah, Lillian Shah, Aiden Shea, Ken Shores, Matt Slater, Rose Taylor, Chris Taylor, Jennifer Taylor, Bill Tester, Tom Trusky, Robert Vasquez, Diana Verlain, Sam Verlain, Joe Wheat, and Gay Whitesides.

Special thanks to Len Steinbach.

And to the Columbia Fiction Program.

Also, thanks to Joel Weinstein and *Mississippi Mud*.

In loving memory: Carl Tallberg, Silvio Zignazo, Anthony Badalucco, Ethyl Eichelberger. Bless your hearts, you guys.

Contents

Book One

There was a Time: Killdeer

If you're the devil, then it's not me telling this story. Not me being Out-In-The-Shed. That's the name she gave me not even knowing. She being Ida Richilieu, and later, after what happened up on Devil's Pass, they called her Peg-Leg Ida.

Hey-You and Come-Over-Here Boy were also what I thought were my names. First ten years or so, I thought I was who those *tybo* words were saying. *Tybo* being 'white man' in my language. My language being some words I still can remember.

My mother was a Bannock and she worked for Ida, cleaning, and whenever a man took a fancy for a breed. That's how I came about – or so I thought. My mother called me Duivichi-un-Dua which means something, which means I was somebody to have a name like that – not like Out-In-The-Shed.

Took me a long time to find out what my Indian name means. One of the reasons why is because my name's not Bannock but Shoshone, so none of the Bannock could ever tell me when I asked. Always thought my mother was Bannock. Guess she was Shoshone. Why else would she give me a Shoshone name?

My mother died when I was a kid just ten or eleven years old. Murdered by a man named Billy Blizzard. One of the things I remember about my mother is that she gave me my name and that I was never to answer to my name because it might be the devil asking. If somebody called me by my name, I had to say that it wasn't me first off. Another thing I remember about my mother is just before I sleep and then she's only a smell and a feeling I don't have any words for.

After my mother died, I took her place at Ida's, cleaning and doing the odd jobs. Some nights, out in the shed, when the moon got too bright, and things got too still, when all I could hear was my heart beating and the breath coming fast in and out of me, I'd tiptoe up the back steps to the second story of Ida's Place and look in Ida's window. Ida Richilieu would be sitting in her room in her circle of light, the kerosene lamp making her room look the rose color. If it was winter, Ida'd be all bundled up in her quilts. If it was summer, Ida'd hardly have anything on. Winter or summer, though, you could always find Ida in her circle of light late at night, when the work was done, writing in her diaries about life and about being mayor.

Watching Ida in her circle of light, with her pen and ink, putting words down on paper, telling her human-being stories — always made you feel good. Made you feel that there were secrets you needed to find out about — or stories that you just had to hear. Made the awful pounding inside you stop.

Then there was the time I almost froze to death. Just fell asleep standing outside Ida's window looking in. Guess I fell asleep — didn't feel like sleep. I wasn't cold anymore, wasn't looking in the window, was in Ida's circle of light, the rose color on my skin, and I was lying in Ida's feather bed.

I stayed in Ida's feather bed. Me awake sometimes, Ida at the desk writing in her circle of light. Me not awake sometimes, not knowing where I was, me gone to the somewhere else you go when you go to sleep.

When I woke up for good from somewhere else, when I wasn't sick with fever anymore, sometimes Ida'd let me sleep with her in her fancy room in her feather bed. I wasn't supposed to tell anybody and I never did. With Ida, if she made you promise, then that was it. I always had to wash up good first though.

One night I was sleeping with Ida and I woke her up with what was going on. Ida always said she couldn't sleep if there was a hard-on in the room.

After the night Ida couldn't sleep, and after she saw my dick hard – well, knowing the rest of my story – even though I was no more than twelve years old – Ida figured I'd like the job. So I ended up taking on the rest of my mother's duties; that is, whenever a man took a fancy for a breed.

Berdache is what the Indian word for it is. First time I heard the word *Berdache* was the first time I met Dellwood Barker. He told me the word, along with the story of the Berdache named Foolish Woman, and how Foolish Woman had healed Dellwood Barker, then taught him how to fuck.

I don't know if *Berdache* is a Bannock word or a Shoshone word or just Indian. Heard tell it was a French word, but I don't know French, so I'm not the one to say.

What's important is that's the word: *Berdache*. 'B . . E . . R . . D . . A . . C . . H . . E,' Dellwood Barker spelled, 'means holy man who fucks with men.'

The only tybo words I know for out in the shed, for how I am, for fucking with men, are words now that I don't use. Used to use them, though. Thought they were just more names for who I was.

Dellwood Barker changed all that, though. Came back into my life after two years of not being in my life and changed all that – what I called myself, who I thought I was. He knocked on the door of the shed. Stepped in the door. There he was, Dellwood Barker, the man who I thought was my father. Everything was different. I was different. I was somebody who had fallen in love.

I loved him hard and fast and right off and forever.

Forever had been one of Ida's words. Was one of the first words she made me learn.

'F..O..R..E..V..E..R,' Ida had spelled. 'Means always,' she said.

Me, I didn't figure I'd ever fall in love with anybody, let alone a white man, let alone my father, let alone forever.

Dellwood told me he was in love too. But it wasn't me, not me, that he was in love with. It wasn't Alma Hatch either – the pink-nippled, rose water-smelling beautiful bird woman who one day walked into Ida's Place out of the blue and, in front of all the men in the bar, paid cash for an afternoon with Ida's breed boy, out in the shed, paid cash for a fuck with me, fucked me, then sent me off, not a wing to fly.

Wasn't with any one of us – not Ida Richilieu, not Alma Hatch, not me.

You see, Dellwood Barker was the man who fell in love with the moon.

Excellent, Idaho, is where this all happened; that is, in Excellent and Gold Bar and in between. Those both being towns up here just north of the Sawtooths. Excellent is in the valley of the north fork of the Payette River, and Gold Bar is a full day's ride in good weather from Excellent over Devil's Pass, where it gets so high the trees stop growing and there's snow til midsummer.

Both Excellent and Gold Bar had other names during their leaner days; that is, before the gold rush of '63 in Excellent and '72 in Gold Bar. The name for Excellent was an Indian name I forget, which meant Good-Hot-Water-Out-Of-The-Ground. Gold Bar was just plain old Rock Creek. Names got changed during the first gold strike. Wasn't just the names though. Just about everything changed. Tybos were crawling all over these mountains, digging, blasting, getting drunk, shooting each other, and getting rich. That lasted for a while, and then the gold got harder to find and then impossible. Within ten years after the first gold strike, you couldn't find more than a hundred people in both Excellent and Gold Bar. At least that's how Ida told it, and she should know because she was the mayor of Excellent for quite some time – before the Mormons, that is – during the time what folks around here call the Second Coming, from '82 to '02.

Ida, besides being a whore and the mayor, was also the town historian and she wrote all these things down, everything she had ever heard, or experienced her own self about this area, she wrote down in her diaries. Told me to burn her diaries just before she died. Didn't do it, though. Me and Doc Heyburn pulled a ruse on her and saved the diaries. So now people know these things as fact and not just somebody talking talking, which is all that most people up here know how to do.

'That's just how people are,' Ida'd say. 'They just got to talk. You can't stop people from talking. They talk and pretty soon you got a story, and what's a human being without a story?'

Like a lot of things that Ida said, I thought about what she'd said about human beings and stories, and like a lot of things that Ida said, she was right. That's just how people are – tybo or Indian.

The only difference between tybo stories and the stories *we* tell is what those stories are about.

We being Indians, which I was only half of.

The half I liked to call the me part of not me.

Indian people talk about how the world is. Their stories are about how wolf got the name wolf. How mosquitoes got to be such nasty little things. How elk got antlers, what bears say to bees when they want the honey, how river sings a song to trees and how trees sing back.

The Man Who Fell in Love with the Moon

Indian people talk about the mountain that Excellent, Idaho, is built in the shadow of – the mountain the morning sun rises behind – how it is the reason why we're acting the way we are. Indian stories say the mountain has powered us here – snagged us. We may think we're here for this reason or for that reason. We may think that what we're doing is what we're doing, but really what we're doing is being snagged by the spirit of the mountain. Its name in tybo is Indian Head, but its name in Indian is something you can't say out loud.

Since it's not me telling this story, though, I'll tell you.

I don't know how you say it in Indian, but this is what it means: Not-Really-A-Mountain. It can also mean 'forever,' but don't ask me why it works out that way.

What tybos talk about is: gold, money, dollars and dollars, but even though that's what they're saying, that's not what they're talking about. Dellwood Barker pointed this out to me years ago: what tybos are talking about is how they're going to be – somewhere down the line and around the corner – talking about themselves as if they weren't even living yet.

'Almost all of them – hardly an exception,' Dellwood Barker always said, 'afraid of being who they are right now.'

Ida Richilieu was tybo too, but she didn't talk tybo. She used tybo words but what she said wasn't tybo. That was the case, too, with Alma Hatch, and as I have said, with Dellwood Barker: three tybos, not tybos.

What Ida Richilieu talked about was the Sawtooth Mountains and Indian Head in particular. She talked about this river valley and about Devil's Pass and Excellent and Gold Bar. She talked about business. Talked about whiskey and opium and locoweed and fucking. She talked about keeping clean, keeping promises, and keeping going. She talked about dicks that were big, dicks that were little. Ida talked about Dellwood Barker's dick. Talked about my dick – Ida loved to talk about dicks. Was nothing she liked talking about more than dicks except for Mormons and especially at the end.

Ida talked about Alma Hatch, about Dellwood Barker, and me. What she loved most, though, she never talked about. That was that old ink pen of hers and her bottle of ink, and her leather-bound diaries with gold edges on the pages that she kept locked in her big wood desk, and the light she sat in at night when she wrote.

Alma Hatch talked about love. She talked about hearts that were full of love. She talked about the hot springs and about whiskey and opium and locoweed and fucking. Alma talked about birds and flying birds and dragonflies and just about everything with wings. Alma talked about Ida, about Dellwood, and me. Alma talked about her hair. She also made strange animal and bird sounds and not just when she was fucking. You never could tell when that woman would start in yelling.

Dellwood Barker talked about whiskey and opium and locoweed and fucking. Talked about me and Ida and Alma. Talked about Berdaches. Talked about how most people all they do is tell themselves the story of who they are. Talked about his horse, Abraham Lincoln, and his dog, Metaphor. Most always, though, what Dellwood Barker talked about was the moon.

You'd have to ask them what I talked about and it's too late for that. I mostly didn't talk, I think, unless we were drinking or smoking opium – Dellwood called it stardust, so we all started calling opium stardust – and when I was drinking and smoking stardust, they tell me I could talk the hind leg off a mule and you couldn't understand one damn word I was saying. They called me Out-Of-The-World or Out-Of-His-Fucking-Mind instead of Out-In-The-Shed when I got that way.

Everybody else in the valley, and even those over in Gold Bar – tybos – when they weren't talking about how they were going to be, talked about Ida Richilieu, and about Alma Hatch, and

Dellwood Barker, and me. They didn't talk just stories, either. They talked legends.

Even myself, I have heard them. Stories about me I have heard, legends, I mean.

One I heard said I was as good as any woman in pleasing a man out in the shed, and I'll tell you right now that's a damn lie. Ain't no woman could do what I could do out there and anybody who tells you different's a Mormon.

Another legend goes that some nights when the moon is right, Ida Richilieu's legs go walking around trying to find the rest of her. The rest of her that's singing her favorite song: *Come take a trip in my airship and we'll visit the man in the moon.*

There's the one about the Mormon church – the new brick one they built – the one nobody will go into because it's haunted.

The legend of Billy Blizzard – that he would never die.

Ida's twins – how they're half Ida and half something else.

Another legend I heard said that Alma Hatch was the most beautiful woman with the most beautiful hair in the whole world. Was so beautiful that when she froze to death up on Devil's Pass that night, the buzzards, when they went to light onto her and peck her eyes out, couldn't do it. Her eyes were froze open and the way her eyes were so beautiful no bird would go near her because what was in her eyes was how flying was to them.

There's the one too about Alma's animal and bird screams at night. Even myself, I have heard them. They're just about the saddest sound ever.

Heard tell too that Dellwood Barker was as crazy a cowboy as ever was, a titched-in-the-head, not-all-there, half-baked, hare-brained, foolhardy, moonstruck drunk of a man.

You can believe that if you want to. Like most of these stories up here, it's part truth. In my case, I've already told you how Dellwood Barker was for me. Besides that, I think he was just about the kindest man I ever knew, Indian or tybo.

As Ida said about such stories going around: 'You got to consider the source,' she said, 'a story about a crazy man told by crazy people should only make you wonder.'

Then there's the legend of William B. Merrillee, one of the twelve apostles of the Church of Jesus Christ of Latter-day Saints who had a vision that his people should move to Excellent, Idaho, and own a gold mine.

Ida's Place burning down and those who went with it.

The open season on the Wisdom Brothers.

The Mormon bishop tybo and the sheriff tybo who were found hanged soon after Ida's Place burned down – their heads pierced through ear to ear with a bayonet.

One more I heard was that some nights you can hear us all laughing. Our fool heads off the way we used to do because we were a family. Even myself, I have heard it, and no matter what, I always end up laughing, my fool head off. Sometimes I think that what everybody hears when they say they hear the laughing is me.

Then there's the legend about that night. The night it was payday in Gold Bar and we were still in Excellent. The legend about our contest to see who could have the most fun: men or women. How much we drank. How much we smoked. How hard we laughed. How Alma Hatch started in on eagle sounds. How Ida danced on the bar – what was left of it after the fire, still on her legs in her white dress in all that black. How Dellwood Barker hitched up the mule backwards. How hitching up the mule backwards means death.

The strange cloud on Devil's Pass that night and how hard it snowed inside the cloud.

Who won the contest.

I guess it was Ida who won. She just lost her legs. Alma Hatch lost her whole life. Dellwood Barker lost his mind.

Me, in the end, I lost them all.

All that's left of them is this story and me telling this story.

Wasn't til I lost them all, that I heard the story I had forever needed to hear, and I found out things weren't the way I thought they were, which meant: what I was doing wasn't what I thought I was doing, and me, in the end, who I thought I was, wasn't at all who I was.

Wasn't til I lost them all that things being how they were or not being how they were didn't matter. As Ida always said, *best stories are the true stories,* and, truth is, no matter what, we were always a family – better than any Mormon family – Dellwood Barker, Ida Richilieu, Alma Hatch, and me.

A family.

*

My earliest memories are of playing a game I called killdeer. I played killdeer so long, got so I couldn't tell the difference between the game and me. Truth is, I'm still playing killdeer.

The game started when you got up in the morning. You had to be quiet because the girls and the customers were still sleeping, especially Ida who was a light sleeper. The hardest part was getting out of room 11 where me and my mother lived. The door to room 11 made the sound of the devil coming after you. Either you opened the door slow or you opened the door fast in one big sound that Ida sleeping would think was the wind or snow falling off the tin roof. It was better to open the door slow, but in the mornings, I always had to pee, and opening the door slow was just too excruciating.

'E..X..C..R..U..C..I..A..T..I..N..G,' Ida spelled, 'means too painful, and sometimes that's good.'

The chores I had to do were chop the wood, start the fire in the kitchen stove, and then start the fire in the potbellied stove in the bar. The kitchen stove had *Kalamazoo* written across the oven door. The stove in the bar didn't have a name written across it. Ida called that stove the Thord Hurdlika, though, because Thord Hurdlika, the blacksmith, had made the stove up special for Ida. Instead of payment, Thord Hurdlika took his work out in trade. Had a lifetime free fuck at Ida's Place, and Saturdays half price on whiskey.

Another chore was carrying water up to the rooms. I'd pump the water from out of the red spigot next to the horse trough, then pack the two buckets of water across Pine Street, up the stairs, then pour the water out into the white porcelain pitchers without spilling any, one of those white pitchers in every room, five rooms and five pitchers all together.

Another chore was taking out the thunder mugs and dumping the thunder mugs into the shit hole in the outhouse, then me rinsing the thunder mugs out, sometimes having to take the horsehair brush to the stains.

I called the game killdeer because of the bird. Heard my mother tell a customer once that she liked the killdeer bird because killdeer played a trick on you. Trick was, killdeer acted like her wing was broke so that fox or coyote would follow her away from her nest.

One day I found a killdeer bird and followed her. That's just what she did – played as if her wing was broke so I'd follow her away from her nest.

Thought that bird was pretty smart to do that.

I was a lot like that bird.

The killdeer game was I was looking for something, but I didn't know what I was looking for. Was killdeer I was looking for.

Trick was, though, if you acted like you were looking for killdeer, you'd never find killdeer.

You had to be killdeer.

Something else with the killdeer game – if you didn't want somebody to see you, they couldn't see you.

Couldn't catch the bird, couldn't find the nest, couldn't see me.

Killdeer started after chores. I'd push against the screen door on the back porch ever so slightly. When the screen door made the stretching sound – that was it – you had to be out of there fast.

I ran past the outhouse, past the ash pile, past the shed, through the gate, and headed toward Chinatown along the old wire fence until Hot Creek. Three jumps to cross Hot Creek – always on the same three rocks. Put the rocks in the creekbed just so myself so they'd be right. Then on up running past the jailhouse with the door always open and nobody in the jail except on Saturday night, running up to Dr. Ah Fong's house, where he lived in Chinatown – a place that looked like a bunch of wooden boxes set on top of each other. Dr. Ah Fong's house was the wood box closest to the road, which was the start of Chinatown. The other Chinatown wood boxes followed the curve of the earth down to Hot Creek and then up the side of the hill.

Killdeer in Chinatown was big. I'd sneak in, looking, scrutinizing.

'S . . C . . R . . U . . T . . I . . N . . I . . Z . . I . . N . . G,' Dellwood Barker spelled, 'means touching what you're looking at with your eyes.'

Scrutinizing: the gunnysacks stretched from wood box to wood box across the sky, fish bones in the street, the smell of Chinese cooking mixed with burning incense, and sometimes their music.

Wasn't til I was older, though, that I knew what it was in Chinatown, what the big killdeer was, down the steps to the smoky room and the beds, not til after my mother died, and I was older.

What I remember most as a kid, though, was the ice cream.

Killdeer

Dr. Ah Fong had ice cream on Sundays. My mother would take me to Dr. Ah Fong's, and we'd have that Sunday's flavor. My favorite was cherry. Hers too. One spring I remember especially, Ida Richilieu, Gracie Hammer, Ellen Finton, and all the rest of them women were at Dr. Ah Fong's too. We were all sitting in the sun, it being too cool in the shade, and all of us were eating cherry ice cream, the cherry ice cream pink – those women in their dresses, tits bouncing up and down, pink as cherry ice cream – those females laughing and talking and eating ice cream.

Past Chinatown I'd run to the cemetery. Killdeer in the cemetery was my favorite. The forest had been cleared and only the big virgin trees left – eleven lodgepole pines going up straight to the sky. The light falling down onto the grave markers was the closest to the killdeer feeling you could get except for fire and at the hot springs and up at the Dry House.

There were two parts to the cemetery – the part where the tybos were buried with fences around their graves, and the gravestones with their names carved in them – then there was the other part where the Chinese were buried and the prostitutes and the murderers and the ne'er-do-wells. Ida Richilieu called that part of the cemetery *her* part. Was my part too.

The cemetery was the best place to sit and scrutinize Not-Really-A-Mountain. Nothing in your way. Was just you looking and the mountain.

After the cemetery was more running – to the open field. There was a big old fir tree that you could lean against. In the field was June grass, green for no more than a week and the rest of the time it was golden, especially in the late afternoon. Facing west, the sun going low, all you could see was gold. Not gold the way tybos thought gold, but the light of gold, the killdeer, that could touch back your scrutinizing eyes.

The river was always a different color – blue or green or grey. In the spring the river was brown and dark. Sometimes it was black and sometimes so clear that when you put your face down you could see all the rocks in the bottom and the fish and your own face looking.

That water was cold. Even when the season was so damn August your balls smelled of pine sap that water was cold. Standing in the river, your feet and legs screaming, your blood would run up in you fast as blood could run, putting as much distance between itself and river as blood could get.

Up at where I called the nest, I'd just throw myself off the big granite rock into the air, flying through the blue sky and into the deep blue green grey black clear water, into the hole in the river, and then get out fast and stand naked in the sun, panting and breathing, heart beating.

More than anywhere, though, it was up at the hot springs that the killdeer bird played its broken-wing trick on you. When you came to the edge of the riverbank, where the earth went down to the river, you could see the river, but you couldn't see the hot springs. But if you just took one step the right way and looked over a little – there, before your eyes, was the most beautiful sight good eyes could see: hot water falling down out of the side, running down the rocks, splashing big onto the one big rock in the middle, then down into the pool. When the sun was hitting the water everything sparkled, making rainbows. Hard to beat a rainbow for killdeer.

Dragonflies and water skippers.

At night, the moon made everything different.

Truth is, the moon is the sun playing the trick on you.

Sometimes, when room 11 was full, I'd stay out on the river for days and nights at a time. Camp out and make fires, staying in the stretch of river by the hot springs where the hot water came out of the bank, walking along the river, in the river, catching fish, playing the game. You could see every animal there was to see: cougar, mountain lion, bob cat, ocelot, beaver, wolverine, badger, white-tailed deer, antelope, elk, even moose – skunk, fox, coyote, wolf, jack rabbit – bear – all of them. Even the animals that only come out at night and in the fog in the mornings.

Running back into town, still looking for killdeer, the first building was the school where the Mormon kids went. I couldn't go to that school. Not that I wanted to. My mother had tried but they told her I could only go to the school if I started living with a Mormon family. That was how my mother had been raised and she said the hell with it. Said she'd rather have a dumb Indian for a kid than a Mormon.

I didn't know any of the tybo kids. There was only four or five of them and they all looked alike except some of them were boys and some of them were girls and they were always gawking at me – when my killdeer let them see me, that is.

Next to the Mormon school was the Mormon church. Both the school and the church were painted white and had a fence like around some of the graves – *picket* fence, painted white too.

After the Mormon school and church, next what you came to, just past Moosman's farm, was where Pine Street started. First off, on the left, was Hot Creek and then the Indian Head Hotel – Ida's Place. Ida's Place was painted white too – the only other building in town besides the Mormons' that was painted. In front of Ida's Place was why Pine Street was called that: one big old solitary ponderosa, the trunk as big around as four men standing in a circle holding on to each other's outstretched arms. Across the street was the barbershop where most of the men in the town met and told stories to each other. They'd all sit around the potbellied stove inside the barbershop in the winter, and in the summer they'd sit on the bench outside. Next to the bench was a pole that was painted blue and red and white – those colors going around and around down the pole. Outside the barbershop was the horse trough and the well with the red spigot and pump handle. There was a wood walkway in front of the barbershop that went all the way to the front of where the stagecoach stopped. That was the post office. American flag hanging in front of it.

Over in Ida's Place, whenever you looked out the window of room 11, that's what you saw first – the flag.

The pole the flag was hanging off of was the pole I'd shinny up to feel killdeer. The pole, not the flag, was where the killdeer was.

Mail was brought in twice a week from Owyhee City and Mountain Home by stage in the summertime. In the winter, the mail was carried by a mail carrier on skis over Devil's Pass.

Fern Hurdlika, Thord Hurdlika's wife, was both the postmaster and the barber. Story goes that between Thord blacksmithing for the town and Fern cutting everybody's hair and opening everybody's mail, Thord Hurdlika and Fern Hurdlika knew everything there was to know about everybody in the whole valley.

After the post office was Stein's Mercantile and then North's Grocery. Neither one of those places was I allowed in. Had to go around the back and so did my mother because we were Indians. Stein and North were rich men and didn't live in Excellent anymore. Lived in Boise City. Just had people working for them in Excellent. Every spring, Stein and North would come up with a bunch of wagons with provisions and everybody'd rush over there and buy new stuff.

Once, my mother got all dressed up like a white woman and pulled her hair up and wore one of those hats and went over to Stein's Mercantile. Walked right inside. Old Stein had my mother by the hair right off and took her outside, and right there between Stein's and North's Grocery – where the runoff from

Pine Street stands in the spring – threw her in the muddy water and everybody stood around and laughed. Stein was smarting, though – my mother had got him at least one good one in the balls – Stein was trying to act normal but the way he was standing, you could tell.

Wasn't long and Ida Richilieu was walking down the street with her shotgun – walking straight for Stein and Stein knew it. He tried talking to Ida but everybody knows there's no talking to Ida when she gets that way. North stepped out of his grocery right then with his shotgun and I let him have it with a rock about the size of my fist. He went down, that shotgun going off and blowing a hole in his screen door. Stein started running then and Ida blew him a load of buckshot into his ass. Couldn't sit down for six months, or so they say.

Stein signed a complaint against Ida Richilieu, and Sheriff Archibald Rooney from Sawtooth rode over here and asked everybody questions. Sheriff Rooney didn't do a thing to Ida, though, because he had free whiskey with her and free girls, plus like everybody else in Excellent, Sheriff Archibald Rooney didn't like Stein because he was one of those tybo tribes they called Jew.

Ida Richilieu was one of that tybo tribe too. She was Jew too.

'Which gave me every right in the world to blow that old bastard a new asshole,' Ida always said.

Sometimes killdeer would lead you around the corner past Stein's Mercantile. Down the road a piece, just before you got to Thord Hurdlika's blacksmith shop, was where Doc Heyburn had his office.

You could always see people sitting in his office – mostly women, waiting to see the doctor. Most of the time, though, they were waiting for nothing because Doc Heyburn was always up at Ida's Place drunk as a skunk. Never seen a man who could drink as much as him and still keep standing – and that's including Ida Richilieu. Never could figure that Doc out. Hardly ever talked until he was so drunk you could barely understand him – but then Doc Heyburn didn't ever give a damn if you understood him or not, him always standing at the bar talking out loud to himself, weaving back and forth, telling folks how one day he was going to be.

Down the street was the only stone building in town. It was Thord Hurdlika's blacksmith shop. Spent a lot of time killdeering with the rocks in the south wall of Thord Hurdlika's. The rocks were all smooth from the river and most of them were about the size of my head and lighter than my skin. The wall facing south was the best place to sit in Excellent in the spring on a sunny day. The stones soaked up the sun, and if you sat in front of the stones with your eyes closed, being a rock, so did you.

Whenever I'd run by his stone building, usually Thord Hurdlika would be out front, shoeing a horse or banging on steel. Sometimes, I'd go inside, sit and work the bellows, and scrutinize. Thord Hurdlika's feet were as big as my whole body. Same way with his arms.

Was plenty of killdeer inside in his shop with the fire going in the forge and him sweating and bending iron around. What hair was left on his head was sticking up all over.

Thord Hurdlika didn't talk much to me, or to anybody – not anybody except himself, that is. Scrutinized him many a time and this is what he'd do: all of a sudden, he'd stop what he was doing, wave his arms, and move his lips as if he was talking to a bunch of people who were standing around him listening – but there wasn't a soul. Figured Thord Hurdlika was trying to work something out. Dellwood Barker said Thord Hurdlika was a perfect example of a man being how he is because he's always telling himself the story of how he is.

Thord Hurdlika always wore leather gloves when he worked and never took them off, even way before he got married he wore those gloves. Story goes he kept petroleum jelly inside the leather gloves – inside in each one of the fingers – so his hands would always be soft for his wife when she came along. Then, when I was about ten years old, Thord Hurdlika up and married a woman named Fern Thurman from Idaho City, in the summer on the front porch of his house, Fern Thurman becoming Fern Hurdlika.

Always wondered about the story of Thord's hands. Thought a couple of times of asking Fern if it was true. Never did though.

Then, when I was older, the night that Thord Hurdlika came out in the shed – first thing I took a hold of was his big hands.

'Best stories are the true stories,' Ida Richilieu said.

When Pine Street makes the S curve – just past Thord Hurdlika's – at that corner was Damn Dave's livery stable. Killdeer was always big at Damn Dave's. Don't know how Damn Dave started getting called that. Ever since I knew him he was called Damn Dave. Damn Dave and his Damn Dog. His dog being one of them mutt dogs, black and white with floppy ears that are happy and wag their tails, smiling with his tongue hanging out, always wanting to play.

'Only creature alive besides his own mother who could love Damn Dave that much would have to be a mutt dog,' Ida said.

They were always together, Damn Dave and his Damn Dog, whenever you saw them. Damn Dave with his ears and that nose of his and his black hair turning silver and his skinny body. Skinny Damn Dog with his ears and nose and black and silver hair. Hard to tell them apart sometimes.

'Is what tybos call retarded,' my mother said about Damn Dave. 'And that's not good,' she said, ' – far as tybos are concerned. In Indian, though – a man like Damn Dave would be considered holy,' she said. 'Damn tybos,' my mother said, 'can't stand anything that isn't like everything else.'

Damn Dave never talked once; that is, not til the end. Was always polite and kind, never causing any trouble – him or his dog. Did a good job at the livery, always keeping a change of fresh horses for the stage.

There was one thing, though, that you never wanted to do to Damn Dave, or his Damn Dog – and that was get them drunk. What would happen was that Damn Dave would start laughing. Sounded like cats fucking when Damn Dave laughed. And him laughing always got Damn Dog going then too – howling.

Two of them drunk one night laughing and howling probably was how they got the names.

What got Damn Dave to laughing when he was drunk was that he'd get a hard-on, and unlike most men, who take that very seriously, Damn Dave was just the opposite. He'd hold onto his dick and laugh his ass off – Damn Dog howling and howling. Took all night for them to shut up.

Besides having the livery stable, Damn Dave also had a wagon and he hauled things around for people. He was a beekeeper too, and whenever there was a swarm, Damn Dave was the one you called. He smoked meat too, in a smokehouse out back of the stables – hauled applewood up from the valley and smoked hams with the applewood. Some days you could smell Damn Dave's smoked ham all the way over to Gold Bar.

As far as the town is concerned, that was it for the running and the killdeer. Wasn't any more of a town to run in but what I've told you about. Every once in a while, though, when I wanted to stay out for more than a day, and I was getting a taste for something new, I'd run up Gold Hill – same hill that Devil's Pass is on only on the other side. Things were a lot different on Gold Hill and you had to be careful. Tybos up on Gold Hill were serious about their gold and you could get shot for just stepping on the earth in the wrong place.

There were holes in the side of the mountains and men would walk inside the holes and not come out all day. There were big wood buildings with tin roofs, big fires in the buildings and the smoke coming out. In the spring, the placer mines ran from dawn to dark. Tybos running water through wooden boxes, *sluice boxes* they called them, sluice boxes on legs of timber, rocks always clogging up the boxes, tybos crawling up, cussing, throwing rocks every which way. In the winter, they'd go up and shovel snow out of the flumes.

Whenever I'd go to Gold Hill and sit and watch them work, every time I knew for sure that tybos were plumb crazy.

'Six hundred thousand tons,' Ida said once, 'by the time they were through digging at that mountain. Six hundred thousand tons of gold ore.'

Then there was the Dry House. That's where the miners'd go to change their clothes. They'd walk up the hill every morning, or pay two bits for a ride, up to the Dry House where they'd change into their mining clothes. After they were done working, they'd come back to the Dry House and shower in the big long shower, all the naked miners standing in a line in the shower and walking around. Every kind of tybo man you'd want to see. Killdeer big in the Dry House too. Sometimes too big. Left me dizzy, my heart pounding and only the sound of my breath.

There was a window you could look in where the men took their clothes off, and a window you could look in where the men showered. Steam would be on the inside. Loved looking at the white backs and the white asses on those men. Not because I wanted to fuck them – I didn't know about fucking then – but because they were so beautiful.

You could crawl under the Dry House too and listen. Men undressing and dressing together always talk the same.

There was a couple times, through the smudge in the steam on the window where the men took their clothes off, I saw and heard more than I figured anybody but those two doing what I saw and heard should know. Me, just a kid, maybe eight or nine, me and night outside looking inside, through the smudge in the steam on the window, watching — inside the Dry House a kerosene lamp, a circle of light, and two grown men trembling, touching, two men talking of love.

So, that was it. That was how you played killdeer. You ran all over the valley and looked in on things that couldn't see you looking, for what it was out there that you didn't know and needed to know — scrutinizing people, the world, for the best story, for the truth.

All the while, Not-Really-A-Mountain, the mountain the morning sun rises behind, playing killdeer with me. Making me think that what I was looking for was what I was looking for.

The trick, the broken-wing trick: out there. Me looking for me out there.

A crazy story about crazy people told by a crazy.

Should only make you wonder.

*

Ida Richilieu bought the Indian Head Hotel in 1882, but she had lived in the valley since 1872, when she arrived with her new husband, Vinitio Luchese. Ida was fourteen years old when she married Vinitio Luchese, a baker, in New York City. After her marriage, she was Ida Luchese, and she and her husband came to this valley looking to bake bread and looking for gold. Least she thought she was looking for gold. What she was really doing was being snagged by the spirit of the mountain.

Vinitio and Ida bought a cookstove in Boise City, hauled the cookstove up to Excellent in their wagon, and set up a bakery in the back of North's Grocery. Vinitio Luchese baked his bread, put his bread in the back window — along with a picture of the Sacred Heart of Jesus — and waited for customers. Customers never came though.

That was before Excellent was called Excellent, after the first gold rush, and before the Second Coming when there wasn't one nugget of gold in sight. Folks were either owing the bank or were destitute or were clearing out of the country.

Mormons were the only ones with any money.

Thing was, though, Mormons don't buy Catholic bread.

Vinitio Luchese was a big bear of a man, story goes, with a little dick, and was given to fits of depression and Italian opera. One day after selling no bread, he just hiked up Indian Head and jumped off. Sang a bunch of opera before he jumped off – naked. Story goes he was a tenor and no bigger than a normal man's pinkie finger.

When I was older, I asked Ida about her husband one night because we were smoking stardust down in Chinatown. I don't remember all that Ida said. But I do remember the look she got in her eyes when I asked her.

'Big heart filled with too much loving pain. You could taste it in his bread and you could hear it in his voice when he sang. Break your heart listening to him sing,' Ida said.

Ida was sitting in the shadows on one of Dr. Ah Fong's beds. Stardust smoke was hanging around her head, a cloud around a mountaintop.

'Only fell in love twice in my life,' Ida said. 'First time it was a big man who baked bread, with a beautiful voice, a troubled soul, and a little dick. Not a good thing to have if you're Italian,' Ida said, 'a little dick.

'I have hated Mormons ever since the day I picked my husband's body off the rocks,' Ida said. 'As if you need an excuse to hate those cussed people – latter-day saints – of all the gall!' Ida said, 'Decided right then that I was going to get even. Even if it killed me.

'That's just the way I am,' Ida said. 'Don't ask me to change.

'Second time I fell in love the soul was even more troubled and

25

the man was only a child. Didn't even know he had a dick, he was that young.

'Crazy men and their dicks,' Ida said. 'Paul Bunyan and his big blue ox. I'll never understand. How a man is, is how his dick is. Woman hasn't a thing to compare to that – no part on her body that is so blessed important and takes up so much time. Closest thing would be her hair, and that ain't close at all.

'Oh! The humanity! I swear I wouldn't have a dick hanging on me for the world!' Ida said.

Vinitio Luchese left Ida fifteen hundred dollars after funeral costs. She had Dr. Ah Fong cremate her husband and then had him buried over in Naples, Italy. Vinitio also left her the wagon and the mule team and all his mining tools.

Ida started making her way – only way she said an uneducated woman can make her way – on her back, in the wagon, making special deliveries.

Story goes it was ten years to the day that Ida'd shipped off Vinitio's ashes to Naples, Italy, when Ida up and changed her name back to her Richilieu self, sold Vinitio's tools at auction, bought that hotel from the township of Excellent before they even called it Excellent, kept the wagon and the mule team for deliveries, spruced the place up, and didn't waste any time getting down to work.

The hotel was the Indian Head Hotel, but everybody called it Ida's Place. Was the only hotel in Excellent. You couldn't miss it because, like I said, it was one of the three buildings in town that was painted and the only one painted that wasn't Mormon. It was right next to Hot Creek, was made of wood clapboard, two stories high with a porch on each floor front and back. There were banisters around the porches and round supporting posts. Seven wood steps up from Pine Street to the front porch. The double front doors had an oval window in each door – those doors always closed in winter, always open in summer – leading to the main saloon. The windows of the hotel all had louvered shutters that at one time were green.

Above the second-story porch in the front was the sign, *Indian Head Hotel*, that needed painting.

Ida didn't want no dirty men getting into her clean bed sheets so, sometime during the Second Coming, Ida had Dr. Ah Fong get some of his folks together and they built the bathhouse off the side of the hotel right over Hot Creek. In the bathhouse, there was a big tin tub and the floor was river rocks with slats of wood over them. The walls were wood too – board-and-batt – and the roof was tin.

Ida moved in to the Indian Head just six months before the discovery of the Excellent Lode up on Gold Hill.

That was when they started in on what folks around here call the Second Coming.

Six hundred million tons of gold ore.

Ida Richilieu right there supplying the goods.

That's just how Ida was. Different from any other tybo I've ever known, tybo woman or tybo man – except for Alma Hatch and Dellwood Barker. Maybe it was because she was from the tybo tribe Jew. I don't think so, though. Think it's just the way she was.

Ida never went out of her way to tell people she was different – being Jew, that is – but never denied it either. Said it was nobody's business. Said some things were private and best left unsaid.

Story goes the way you could tell she was Jew right off was because she handled money so well and she bought commercial property and always thought of herself as good as any man living or dead – and that's Jew, for a woman, or so they tell me.

Ida'd be the first to tell you, 'That's just how I am.'

Ida Richilieu was always saying that's just how I am, along with, 'Don't ask me to change.'

And, 'Oh! The humanity!'

And, 'The deck's stacked against you – just figure on that.'

And, 'A woman's got her pride.'

Not to mention, 'Keep your promises, keep clean, and keep going.'

And, 'Best stories are the true stories.'

One thing was for sure: getting along with Ida Richilieu wasn't easy. Was excruciating. Was something I always tried to do, though, right up until the end.

There's a word, it was Dellwood's word.

'P . . E . . N . . E . . T . . R . . A . . T . . E,' Dellwood spelled, 'means putting your dick in a hole, or discovering the inner contents or meaning of, or entering by overcoming resistance.'

That's what I did with Ida, all my life with Ida; not me trying to penetrate her woman's hole, but me trying to discover the inner contents of – the inner contents of Ida, that is, by overcoming her resistance. Resistance, though, was something Ida Richilieu always had a lot of, and not just resistance to me. Believe me, there are stories, long before I was ever born, about Ida Richilieu – legends, I mean, of how cantankerous and full of resistance she could be. Wasn't a man, woman, or beast in this valley that wasn't afraid of her; that is except for one human being who was every bit as cantankerous and full of resistance.

My mother wasn't scared of Ida Richilieu.

I got the story to prove it: the mud fight. According to Ida, this story never happened, was me just talking talking.

I looked around the corner of the outhouse. Ida and my mother were hanging out wash.

'There's a customer waiting for the Princess,' Ida Richilieu said to my mother. 'And since the Princess don't have that many customers, I think maybe the Princess should step lively and get her ass up to room 11 as soon as possible.'

My mother's real name, her Indian name, was Buffalo Sweets,

but at Ida's Place everybody called her the Princess, which is short for the Indian Princess.

My mother – who I think in her own Indian kind of way was a little Jew herself – did not step lively at all, but just kept hanging up wash as if Ida Richilieu had just been flapping her gums.

The sky was real blue with big white clouds in the sky and the ground was just starting to thaw and there were puddles of water. Mud was everywhere and snowdrifts on the north side of things or where there was mostly shade. The bed sheets that my mother and Ida were hanging out were white too, white as clouds. So white with the sun on them that it made your eyes sore. There was the smell of the outhouse and the pile of stove ashes, but you could smell the sheets too. My hand was against the grey wood of the outhouse, me standing, my two eyes watching those two women.

Never will forget how my mother looked that day in the sun in front of the bed sheets hanging up, and how Ida looked too. Surprised me how Ida looked – Ida Richilieu a little bit of a thing next to my mother. Ida always wore what she called 'a good dress' for cleaning during the day with an apron over the dress and always her petticoats and always her lipstick. She'd scrub the stairs in her good dress, the sleeves rolled up. Ida was always cleaning, dusting, sweeping, doing the wash, ironing. Worked harder than any one human being I ever saw. Expected you to work that hard too, even me.

Ida was damn chintzy when it came to paying out a good wage, or at least that's what the girls who worked for her said. *Damn chintzy* – which was another reason you were supposed to be able to tell that she was from the tybo Jew tribe.

'C . . H . . I . . N . . T . . Z . . Y,' my mother spelled, 'means cheap.'

Chintzy was the reason my mother wasn't stepping lively.

So when the Princess didn't listen to Ida that sunny day with the white sheets in the backyard, when my mother just kept on hanging up the bed sheets instead of stepping lively upstairs to the customer the way Ida'd told her to do, and then when Ida walked over and boxed my mother's ears — that's when the Princess grabbed Ida by the combs in her hair and pulled her down right into the mud.

There was nothing new about my mother being mad, but every time before, when my mother was mad, it had always been at me. My two eyes never looked up at my mother — just down at the ground, when she was mad. The day, though, that my mother threw Ida Richilieu in the mud, what was new was my mother was mad — but not at me — so my eyes didn't have to be afraid because the mad they'd be seeing wasn't at me, so they could go ahead and look.

I'd never seen buffalo, but knew that was how buffalo looked: my mother's long black hair, her eyes dark buffalo eyes; her shoulders, her thighs, her legs, her head held high was buffalo. My mother big as buffalo.

Ida Richilieu looked like something you'd laugh at — the petticoats of her good dress sticking out, Ida sitting in the mud, staring up at my mother who was buffalo.

Wasn't long, and the whole town had gathered around. Stein was there, so was North. Saw Stein make a bet with North. Doc Heyburn put a dollar bill on the fence too. Thord Hurdlika came running, his lips going faster than his feet.

'What's all the hell-raising about?' he was shouting.

When Thord got to the clothesline he saw, and when he saw, he knew what it was, and placed his bet. Wasn't long before Ellen Finton and Gracie Hammer had their heads sticking out their second-story windows. Their money was on Ida. Sounded like magpies, those two, yelling down.

Ida managed to get to her feet again and when she did, she wound up and socked the Princess square in the jaw. My heart stopped beating. The Princess blinked and stepped back a bit but didn't fall. Then Ida hit her the same way again.

That's when my mother turned into mountain lion and Ida Richilieu turned into mountain lion too. They kept on that way, the both of them screaming and yelling and howling and clawing at each other for a time – rolling around in the mud puddles. Ida was yelling tybo things I had never heard before, probably from her own tribe of tybo language, and my mother was letting Ida have it in Shoshone or Bannock or whatever Indian she was. The white sheets had big mud wipes on them and some of the sheets had come down off the line and were in the mud too.

Even Mormons started gathering. Got to be quite a crowd of folks. Next time I looked, Ida Richilieu and the Princess had stopped and were staring at each other, them breathing hard, looking like who you'd never tell your name to – dresses, hair, face, hands, shoes covered in mud.

Was Ida who started laughing. Pretty soon the screaming mountain lion women were both laughing their fool heads off – mouths wide open not making a sound laughing, holding on to each other.

Ida and the Princess went into the bar after that, two mud-covered wagons in a ditch, and even though Indians weren't allowed in bars then, Ida bought the Princess a whiskey and they kept on laughing and carrying on in the bar way on into the evening hours with all the tybo men staring.

That night Ida and the Princess washed each other off out in the bathhouse in the bathtub in lots of bubbles, the hot water steaming up the window. In Ida's room, they slept together in the same bed.

Slept together regular from then on.

We never talked about it. Certain things were private and best left unsaid.

I had room 11 all to myself – when the Princess didn't have an all-night customer, that is.

*

Ida's stories were always the truth and nothing but the truth.

'The gospel truth,' as Dellwood Barker put it, 'the gospel according to Ida.'

The feathered-boa story is one story in particular Ida always told. Can't tell you how many times I've heard that story. Truth is, though, every time I've heard it, it's been different.

But you never could tell Ida that.

The story's about the test my mother gave me when I was still a baby – the test to find out which way I would be. It's Indian and goes like this: You lay the baby down on a bed on his or her stomach. You put a bow and a feather on one side of the baby, and on the other side of the baby you put a gourd and a basket. If the baby is a boy, and he reaches for the bow and feather – then you've got a boy, the way tybos figure, whose human-being sex story is the way every boy's sex story had better be. If the baby is a girl, and she reaches for the gourd and basket – then you got a girl whose human-being sex story is the way every girl's sex story had better be.

But if the boy reaches for the gourd and basket, or if the girl reaches for the bow and feather, then in tybo, you got a boy or you got a girl whose human-being sex story is a sex story you got to shut up about.

In Indian there are words for you if you choose the way most babies don't choose. I don't know how you say them in Indian, but I know they're not at all like the tybo words. In Indian, they mean either 'basket-man' or 'bow-woman.' There's the word *Berdache*, too.

Ida told the story of my test this way:

'The Princess got all the girls together in her room, me and Ellen Finton, Gracie Hammer, and herself.

'There we were, the four excellent whores of Excellent, Idaho, and this baby boy. The Princess puts a feather and bow on one side of the kid on the bed. She puts a gourd and a basket on the other side of him. Then she says to us, "Watch!" So, we watch. The kid does nothing but lay there. We watch some more. He lays there some more. I'm about ready to give up on this test when the kid rolls over. First time in his life he's rolled over! We all gasp and cheer and talk baby talk. Then, you'll never believe it – what this kid did, you'll never believe: he reaches up to me! To me! He grabs a hold of my feathers – my feathered boa!'

Whenever Ida got to this point of the story, she always had to stop and laugh and slap her knee and cough and laugh some more. She'd try to tell the end but couldn't because she'd be laughing her fool head off.

What she'd finally say is this: 'He didn't reach for the bow and the feather – he reached for the *feathered boa.*'

*

My mother died this way: Billy Blizzard beat her to death. That's how I figure it. Hard to tell what happened from what was left of her up on Not-Really-A-Mountain, where he lived, where I found my mother's body, the following spring.

He came to town four times, Billy Blizzard. That first time, when he hooked up with Ida Richilieu, in 1884, I wasn't alive yet. The second time, around 1889, he'd found religion and was spouting off the Book of Mormon and called himself Brother William. The third time, about five years later, he was after Ida again. Third time was when he raped me and killed my mother. The fourth time he came, he was supposed to be dead. Fourth

time he came, he wasn't who he was. The fourth time, Billy
Blizzard was somebody else.

First time Ida Richilieu set eyes on Billy Blizzard, she was
wearing the blue dress. Ever since that day, whenever Ida was
fixing to fall in love again, that's the one she'd wear – the blue
one.

He was just a boy of about thirteen years. It was April and
spring was early the year of 1884. Billy Blizzard blew in from
Boise City to Ida's door and wanted to pay. Ida took one look at
him and fell in love. Anyway, that's what she told me – when me
and her were down in Chinatown, after I was older, my ears
listening up good even though we were smoking stardust. Only
time Ida talked about Billy was in Chinatown, laying on the bed
with the red sheets and red pillows smoking stardust. Rest of the
time it was just too private. Was something best left unsaid.

'Can't say what it was about him,' Ida said. 'He was a wild-
looking kid, sexy, looked like he had some Jew in him, or Italian –
maybe that was it. Always have gone for dark men.

'But it wasn't just how he looked,' Ida said. 'Was something
else about him. Hard to say what it was. Looked like he'd stood
himself too close to the fire. Didn't have anything to lose so he
wasn't afraid of a thing. Wasn't afraid of *me*. Looked at me
straight, not a blink in his eye. I knew for sure I was in trouble.
My knees went weak and I was sweating like a pig in heat.

'Oh! The humanity!' Ida said.

After she set eyes on Billy Blizzard, Ida said, she had needed
some time to compose herself, so she told my mother, the
Princess, to help the young man with his bath.

I often think of my mother in the bathhouse scrubbing on the
man who would be the death of her.

When the Princess was finished, she brought Billy Blizzard to
Ida Richilieu. The rest is downhill after that.

'Fucked myself sore and that's quite a feat,' Ida said. 'Was like being with a woman with a dick, that boy. Never anything like it. His dick wasn't even all growed out yet. Hardly any hair on his balls. Tasted like young boy too, and you better believe I tasted all of him.'

The way Ida told it, Billy Blizzard would lay in her bed, while Ida'd get up early as usual, put on her good dress, and clean all day. Then they'd fuck all night. That went on for over a week.

The whole town was talking. The most time Ida Richilieu had spent with a man, besides her husband, was twenty minutes.

Wasn't long, though, that Billy and Ida started fighting.

'At sixes and sevens,' Ida said. 'Like cats and dogs.'

Ida yelling, *Hey you, come over here, boy!*' – taking a broom after Billy, Billy with a bottle of whiskey, and a bottle of glue, glue on his nose and that crazy on his face.

'Was a blessing for all that Billy Blizzard's father showed up in Excellent looking for his son when he did,' Ida said.

'One day, I was just looking out the window and a fancy surrey drove right up to the front door, and out stepped a distinguished gentleman. When he walked into the bar, I put my white dress on, and my face on real quick, rushed to the stairs, then descended the stairs gracefully, like a lady.

'The judge introduced himself to me, said he was Judge Parker Blizzard of Boise City and was looking for his son, Billy.

'You can always tell when you're meeting a gentleman,' Ida said. 'And Judge Parker Blizzard was a gentleman. Soon as he walked in the saloon door I knew he was a gentleman. Bought him a whiskey right off. After he told me who he was, I told him I'd get his son for him – wasn't no inconvenience at all. I went up to my room thinking I'd find the little rat in there, but he wasn't. Then I heard the commotion in Gracie's room. I could always tell a mile away if that boy was in rut. Even if I was on one side of the Snake River and he was on the other, I could tell – instinct, I guess. And sure enough there they were – Gracie and Billy in Gracie's bed.

'Instead of murdering the both of them, I went straight to my room, packed up the boy's stuff, and it wasn't an hour later and Billy Blizzard was gone out of here with his father back to Boise City for good.

'Or so I thought,' Ida said.

Wasn't more than a year later that Thord Hurdlika read in the Boise City paper that Mrs. Diana Blizzard, wife of the Honorable Judge Parker Blizzard, had fallen to her death in her Boise City home.

There was a photograph of Mrs. Diana Blizzard.

If you scrutinized, she didn't look anything like her son.

A year after Mrs. Diana Blizzard fell to her death, the Boise paper reported that Judge Parker Blizzard did the same thing – fell down the stairs and broke his neck.

Surviving the death was an only son, Billy.

There was a photograph of the Honorable Judge.

Scrutinizing, the judge didn't look like his son either.

'That's because he was adopted,' Ida said. 'Billy told me that the first night. Told me too that he didn't know for sure who his real parents was, but he believed that his adopted parents – the judge and his wife – had killed his real parents.'

'Who were his real parents?' I asked.

'Indians,' she said. 'Or so he thought. Thought the judge had killed his parents in an Indian raid and carried him off and then named him Billy Blizzard.'

'Indians?' I said.

'Indians!' Ida said.

'Is it true? Was his parents Indians?' I asked.

'Nobody knows for sure,' Ida said. 'Heard it told, though, that he was Big Foot's son.'

'Big Foot?' I asked.

'Big Foot,' Ida said. 'Haven't you ever heard the legend of Big Foot?'

I'd heard the legend of Big Foot, but wanted to hear it again.

Here's how Ida told it to me – the legend of Big Foot – in Chinatown on the red pillows smoking stardust:

'Story goes that Big Foot was a breed: mostly Cherokee, with some Negro and white. Had every kind of blood there was to have almost. He left Nebraska when he was nineteen years old because he was afraid he'd kill somebody for making fun of his big feet.

'At Goose Creek, Big Foot fell in love with a beautiful black-haired girl they called Spanish Roberta who was traveling with her mother and father in a wagon train. Spanish Roberta, though, was already in love with a man named Wheat. One night, the wagon train lost some horses, so Big Foot and Wheat set out to get the horses back. Out on the prairie, when those two were alone, story goes Wheat called Big Foot a big-foot nigger, and Big Foot shot Wheat between the eyes and then threw Wheat into the Snake River.

'After that, Big Foot jumped in the Snake River himself and swum across. Then he got in with the Indians.

'The next year or so, Spanish Roberta and her folks came down to where the Boise River and the Snake River come together. Spanish Roberta had a baby by then – Big Foot's baby – or that's what they say. Big Foot took a mob of Indians and went in and killed them all and took their horses and all their stuff. Said the only thing he was sorry for was that he'd killed Spanish Roberta but if he didn't kill her the Indians would.

'They put out a reward of one thousand dollars for Big Foot and there was a man named Wheeler who was after the thousand dollars.

'Nobody living now knows where the spot is for sure where Wheeler caught up with Big Foot. Up on Indian Head, they say.

'This Wheeler saw Big Foot coming and he hid behind a rock and he shot Big Foot and got him down. Then, Wheeler said that Big Foot gave three big war whoops and came right after him. Shot him sixteen times before Wheeler downed him good.

' "Give me a drink before I die," Big Foot said.

'Then Wheeler shot Big Foot again and then gave him a drink of water. Big Foot said then, "Give me a drink of whiskey."

'Wheeler had a pint and gave him that. Big Foot drank that and said, "Wash this Indian paint off me, and you'll see I'm a white man."

'Wheeler washed the paint off him, and Big Foot was a nice-looking white man. His feet were seventeen inches long – no telling how big his dick was – and he was seven feet four inches tall. Just skin and bones and muscle on him. No fat at all. They used to say that Big Foot could run so fast that they couldn't catch him with a horse. He would beat them to the Snake River and swim it with one hand, holding his gun up with the other.

' "Now all I ask is that you don't cut my feet off when I die and I'll tell you my whole story. I've been an awful bad man," Big Foot said.

'Wheeler told him he wouldn't cut his feet off and buried him in the rocks up on Indian Head.

'But the story doesn't end there,' Ida said. 'Big Foot's baby lived. Judge Blizzard, when he heard about the baby, took the boy and adopted him – since him and his wife couldn't have kids – and they took this little baby boy and called him Billy – Billy Blizzard.'

Nobody saw or heard from Billy Blizzard until maybe five or six years later, when Brother William came into town – the second time – preaching the Book of Mormon with the Latter-day Saints, all straitlaced and talking Brigham Young.

Billy Blizzard was the first person I remember seeing who

wasn't my mother or Ida. He was like Dellwood Barker in the fact that he wasn't there, and then he was, then after him nothing was the same. Billy Blizzard and Dellwood Barker were the same in another way, too: they were both crazy. Not the same brand of crazy, though, not the same at all.

Saw Billy Blizzard's crazy first time I ever laid eyes on him. I was four or maybe five. Was the day before the night Billy Blizzard sang the man-in-the-moon song with Ida in the bar.

I was in room 11 and heard something outside. I looked out the window, moved the curtain back, moved the geranium in the pot over, and looked out into the street. It was hot August and sunny. Below, I saw a dark, youthful man dressed in black and wearing a black hat. Dust was flying everywhere. The horse he was beating was making a terrible noise, and Brother William was cussing Bible talk, sweat coming off him in buckets. The look on Brother William's face was the crazy that he was. The horse was covered in foam, blood coming out his nose and from an open wound on his shoulder. Red blood flowing down the horse's side, down his leg, into the dust. The horse was fighting back with everything a horse knows how to do – rared up and knocked Brother William over, Brother William flying against the horse trough, water in the trough splashing when he hit it, Brother William sprawling into the dust.

Brother William pulled his gun and shot the horse in the eye – the left eye.

Later, I went over to the place where the horse had fallen. Took my toe and made a circle in the dust around the horse and the wet bloody spot. My eyes stared at the circle, at the horse laying big and dead in the street, dust and flies, his brown rolling muscles foamed up, blood coming out, still saddled, bridled.

Only what was left, that horse, killdeer everywhere.

Damn Dave and his Damn Dog hauled the horse away in his

wagon. Damn Dave cried the whole time he loaded the horse up. Damn Dog sitting next to him on the wagon seat, howling.

That night after he killed the horse, Brother William bought himself some glue and a pint of whiskey and became Billy Blizzard again, walked into Ida's Place while Ida was at the piano playing the man-in-the-moon song, and started singing with the voice of a Christian angel.

I was sitting at the bottom of the stairs next to the bar, killdeer big in me, Ida at the piano, her wearing the blue dress, playing the song about the man in the moon. Ida's voice wasn't much of a voice to be singing, but when she sang the man-in-the-moon song, story goes, whoever heard her, no matter who, heard what was sore, what was excruciating, inside the human heart.

That night, when Ida started singing, Billy Blizzard started singing too. He was standing in the doorway to the bar, his black hat on crooked, his black jacket covered with dust and straw.

When I saw that it was Billy Blizzard, what my eyes saw next was his dead horse laying in the street. My feet wanted to run as fast as they could in another direction – but then, there was Billy Blizzard singing, him making the rafters shake, him singing to Ida, him walking across the bar to her, eyes on fire, walking toward Ida as if she was doing something to him to make him walk that way. He walked right up to the piano and looked his eyes into her eyes and sang to her. Wasn't hard to see – even for a kid – that Billy Blizzard's heart was big with loving pain.

Ida, when she heard his voice singing, jumped as if a stick of dynamite had just gone off inside her. Then, when she looked up at him, all the trouble that had always been in Ida's face left. Didn't even know there was trouble in Ida's face til when the trouble left her face that night.

'Come take a trip in my airship and we'll visit the man in the moon,' Ida sang, and Billy sang.

Wasn't a sound in Ida's Place except for them two singing.

Killdeer

When the song was over, Billy Blizzard threw himself down at Ida's feet, crying. I'd never seen a man cry before. He was saying all sorts of things – he couldn't live without her, he wanted her to have his baby, and without her he wanted to die. Ida stepped away from him, then got some men to help her get Billy Blizzard to the bathhouse.

When they brought Billy Blizzard to the bathhouse, he was screaming and crying and threatening to kill himself. I was looking in the window and saw Ida give my mother some money. My mother took off over to Dr. Ah Fong's and I followed. My mother was inside Dr. Ah Fong's for a while and then came back out. When she got back to the bathhouse, through the window I saw that Ida had Billy Blizzard tied up naked against the wall and she was spanking him with a willow. Billy was yelling and crying. My mother walked right in on them. Gave Ida a triangle-shaped piece of red paper, and then cleared out.

Ida turned up the wick on the lamp that was setting on the table in front of the window. She took the white powder out of the red triangle and poured the powder out onto tobacco that she rolled into a cigarette. Ida lit it, smoked some of the cigarette, then gave the cigarette to Billy Blizzard, holding it for him. When they finished smoking, Ida took her blue dress off, and her underthings. Stood just in her boots whipping Billy Blizzard, him screaming and crying and cussing Bible talk. *Sin*, he'd yell. *Everlasting damnation and fire*, he'd yell. *Hell*.

My mother's Billy Blizzard story, I wasn't supposed to hear. I was under the bed when she told Ellen Finton. Heard it all.

'Billy Blizzard is how the devil is,' my mother said. 'What you're seeing when you see him, and what you're feeling when you see him are two different things.

'That's how the devil is: how he is looking to you isn't how he is. Your eyes see one thing while your heart is seeing another.

The Man Who Fell in Love with the Moon

'That first time I saw him,' my mother said, 'a cold wind blew through me. He was only a boy of twelve years or so. He came out to bathe before going in to Ida. A cold wind. I damned near jumped right out the window when I saw him. But I couldn't move.

'Billy was a tall, broad, strong young man, with dark hair and skin like my own. Eyes that were two burning coals in his head – looking at everything. Those eyes not missing a thing.

'While I was washing him was when I saw the ring on his right hand middle finger. Looked like the devil's ring – stars and a moon setting on top of a set of horns. I wanted to look closer, but he wouldn't let me.

'Then I saw them bruises. The boy was covered with bruises. Especially on his backside, along his crack there.

'That boy wasn't here more than two or three days that first time and he had Ida spanking him – spanking him, and more. Then, the second time Billy Blizzard came to town – after he killed his horse and sang to her, after he was opiumed up – he had her doing more than just spanking him. Wanted her to hurt him – tie his balls up and shove things up his ass.

'Started right back up that night after eight whole years,' my mother said, 'him begging Ida to hurt him. Ida really didn't like it, but she did it. Pretty soon he'd be spouting all sorts of Bible – evil Bible, you know, the kind Bible folks like him talk: flesh and sin and body parts and desire and eternal damnation in hell, him all tied up, Ida switching away at him with that willow, or sticking carrots or whatever up his bunghole – the whole time Ida scolding him like he was a naughty boy. But he was a grown man by then. Wasn't long and he'd be ejaculating and squirming and crying too. Telling Ida and the Lord that he was sorry.

'Went on for almost a year. He just kept coming back for more. And more. Said it was love.

'After a while, you could tell that Ida'd started like it as much as him. Ida'd never say that out loud, but it's the God's truth.

'And that's also how the devil is,' my mother said, 'makes you like things and want things you wouldn't usually. Gets you so that you like them a lot.'

The third time Billy Blizzard came to town it was 1894. Me – I'm the best one to tell the story. Nobody knows the story of the third time like I do.

Ida Richilieu wouldn't have Billy Blizzard back. Told him she was done with him and his ways for good. Wasn't going to have another thing to do with him.

Billy Blizzard hung around town for a couple of weeks, staying where he could, but he wasn't welcome. That was the time when Billy Blizzard got Damn Dave drunk on purpose. Story goes, Ida wouldn't sell Billy a bottle of whiskey, so Billy found a bottle of his own. Billy Blizzard took his bottle over to Damn Dave's, got Damn Dave so drunk that he could barely walk or stand, then took Damn Dave to Pine Street in front of Ida's Place at two in the morning on a Saturday night. Damn Dave was laughing because he had a hard-on and Billy Blizzard got Damn Dave to take his dick out and that really made Damn Dave start laughing and Damn Dog howling. Everybody in Ida's Place came out onto the street.

I was sitting in the window of room 11 that night. I was laughing too, at first, looking down at Damn Dave with his dick out laughing under the ponderosa pine and the American flag, Damn Dog howling away. After a while, though, you couldn't tell if Damn Dave was laughing or crying, him holding onto his dick as if his dick was something sore. Billy Blizzard kept egging him on – kept pouring whiskey into him.

Damn Dave started humping the air, the way dogs do sometimes when they're glad to see you, when they're pink and hard and sticking out of their skin and can't get back in. Humping and humping, tears rolling down Damn Dave's cheeks, Billy Blizzard pointing at Damn Dave's dick, laughing.

Then, there she was, Ida Richilieu, walking down the seven steps and onto Pine Street. Things got quiet. Ida Richilieu walked up to Billy Blizzard and doubled up her fist and hit Billy Blizzard the way tybo men hit other men. She hit him again, then kicked him in the balls. Billy Blizzard doubled up but kept standing. Didn't try to fight back. Ida spit in Billy's face.

Ida Richilieu took hold of Damn Dave then and drew him near her. He still had the humps going through him. Ida took him and Damn Dog inside up to her room and closed the door. Heard Damn Dave in there crying all night, Damn Dog whining.

Was a week before anybody saw Billy Blizzard again. When they saw him, they only heard him. Heard him singing the man-in-the-moon song.

Come take a trip in my airship and we'll visit the man in the moon.

I was in room 11 when I heard him singing. Then I heard the shotgun blast. When I got to Ida's room, she was still pointing the gun out the window. I looked out but couldn't see a soul.

He was out there though, somewhere.

It went on that way for a couple of weeks. I'd wake up and hear him singing and then Ida blasting at him out the window with her shotgun. Still, nobody saw him.

Story started going around that Billy Blizzard was dead and it was his ghost come to haunt Ida.

Ida said she didn't have time for such stories. What she did have time for, and what she *was* worried about, though, was the flesh and blood of him, of Billy Blizzard.

As usual, Ida was right.

About two weeks later, my mother had an all-night customer in room 11, and I was out in the shed. It was late and the moon was bright the way it scares you.

Killdeer

Billy Blizzard called me by name but I didn't answer. Said it was not me.

He was inside the shed. He grabbed me by the back of my neck and brought me to the window in the moonlight. Showed me his devil's ring. Said he'd give it to me, if I'd come with him. I jumped for the door, but he caught me. Put his hand on my mouth and dragged me out the door. Stood me in front of him and started singing. Cocked his six-shooter and put the gun aside my head and started singing. We were right under Ida's window.

Come take a trip in my airship and we'll visit the man in the moon.

Wasn't long and I saw Ida's shotgun slide out her window. She didn't shoot though, not this time, thank God, or else I'd be dead and buried.

Instead of shooting, Ida started talking to Billy Blizzard, him talking back, over my head, all the while Billy Blizzard holding his gun to my head with his one hand while with the other he was raising my nightshirt and looking for the place in me to put himself in. Then him spouting Bible – sin, fire, eternal damnation, and hell. I was looking down at Billy Blizzard's red boots. I was thinking about that dead horse in the street when he spread me open. I was thinking about that day that Ida and my mother were fighting in the mud and the sheets were bright with sun. Was thinking about Not-Really-A-Mountain looking down at me and those red boots. Was thinking about the devil. How I hadn't told him my name. How he had found me anyway. Had found me and was splitting me up the middle – two parts from that time on always trying to get back together again, forever trying, me and not me. The devil had found me and was pounding my ass down, my breath coming fast in me and the sound of my heart beating in my ears.

Then Billy Blizzard started crying and asking the Lord for forgiveness and I was upside down, face against red boots, bent over, broken inside deep.

What I remember next, was Ida slapping Billy hard across the face, and the shotgun going off. Then I heard him hit her back. I saw Ida fall. He kicked her hard in the stomach. The awful sound of breath leaving her body.

Then, I heard a scream that didn't come from Ida or from me – the likes of which you could hear only once in your life – or so I thought – until I heard the scream again, years later, out of my own mouth, the night I found out the whole truth and nothing but. I was laying on the ground and so was Ida. Then I wasn't here anymore. Don't know where I was, but wasn't here.

Later on, Ellen Finton told me that after I fell, Billy Blizzard ran to Pine Street and stole a horse that was tethered to the horse trough. My mother ran out the back door, and my mother, when she saw Ida and me laying on the ground, let out a scream – a war whoop – took off on foot, running down Pine Street after Billy Blizzard. My mother couldn't keep up with him, so she ran back, and jumped into Ida's wagon that was setting out front. Ellen said she looked up, out of the window of the shed, where she had carried me, and saw the Princess, hair all flying back, Ida's shotgun in the crook of her arm, heading out of town in Ida's wagon, hot on the trail of Billy Blizzard.

Wasn't anybody ever saw my mother alive again after that night.

*

I spent most of that winter in a fever. By spring, I was back to being me and walking around and thinking things. Least I thought I was me. What I was, was not me, though.

The posse they'd got together that went after Billy Blizzard never found him. Or my mother. They spent all that fall season looking. Winter came and they had to stop. Thord Hurdlika said *they left no stone unturned.* Doc Heyburn said *it was the damnedest thing — just disappeared.*

Was sometime in April, one morning I just woke up and knew where my mother was. My eyes scrutinized where she was. Guess it was a dream. I took my snowshoes along but not my skis. I crossed the river just below town. There still wasn't much runoff, so it was easy crossing. Walked up to Not-Really-A-Mountain and started climbing on it.

You had to make your way between the rocks and pull yourself up. Sometimes, it was so steep that when you reached straight out in front of you, there was the mountain. But I was young and had been cooped up inside all winter. The wind on my face was cold but the sun was coming down strong. After a while, things started leveling off. The trees were getting thin and I was close to the ridge that, when you were standing back down in Excellent looking east, made up most of the horizon: a slope going up the way a man's back is when he's laying on his belly and leaning against his arms. I would have kept traveling along that ridge, if the wind hadn't just then blowed my hat off. I went running after my hat, down toward the face of the mountain, not really a mountain, jumping from rock to rock, my hat almost in my hands a couple of times, but just as I got to the hat — the hat was off again. Chased my hat for a good part of the day. Then I understood. It was killdeer. If I quit chasing after my hat, I'd get it. So that's what I did.

Wasn't long and I just walked right up to my hat. I followed a trail down, trail getting wider and wider as I went. Pretty soon it was a wagon trail — two trails with grass growing in between. Then I saw the wagon — Ida's wagon — on its side, wheels all busted up. Couple of dead mules.

I turned around then and followed the trail back up, my mother getting closer and closer. Trail ended at a big outcrop of granite rocks. Climbed up the rocks and looked over the side and there it was – the most beautiful meadow my two eyes or yours would ever want to see. The grass was green, and in some places very green and growing all over were yellow and white flowers, and the orange Indian paintbrush flower, and the purple ones that stick up.

The meadow stretched out all the way to the edge, to where there wasn't anything anymore but sky and forever. A circle of high rocks went all the way around the meadow except for at the ledge. Right at the base of the rocks, to the north, was three ponderosas.

I crawled down the rocks, walked to the ponderosas, and found a broken-down old cabin.

Big Foot's cabin.

That's where I found her.

What was left of her. And Billy Blizzard.

My heart knew right off it was her before my eyes even started looking. Then, when my eyes looked, they saw that she was just some leather on a skeleton with hair. There was her red blouse and winter deerskin skirt. Pieces of them. Her skull was all pushed in and there was Ida Richilieu's shotgun laying next to her.

All that was left of him was his red boots. I knew them was his boots. When he was hard at my ass and had me down, I had got a good look at the red boots.

I kicked the red boots. Kicked them around for a good long time. Pissed on the red boots.

The ring was gone. No devil's ring on the hand on the dead man who was laying next to my mother.

When I went back to her, the wind came down and blew on the grass around me, blew on my ears and eyes, smelling of her. Behind me, over in what was left of the cabin, the wind was scratching, making Big Foot sounds. The wind went up, shaking the three ponderosas, and then the wind was gone.

My mother was only a lump on the earth in a patch of sun, an old log soon to become the ground it was laying on.

I made a fire bed for her. She was not one piece to pick up, but I picked her up and put her on her fire bed. Started the fire the way she'd showed me how without matches. I watched the flames and the smoke, wondering what fire was, what smoke was. Her hair up in smoke, her buckskin skirt, her red blouse, her bones up in smoke.

I walked to the edge, where you could see out forever, forever to the setting sun. There was a rock that stuck out the farthest and I walked right out as far as you can go, and sat down.

My mother's favorite story, which was my favorite story, was about buffalo and how my mother got her name.

When she was a girl, her woman time not yet come, my mother was called Beautiful Third Daughter. One morning – she was living with her people then, not with the Mormons – my mother woke up with a thundering in her ears. She got up and ran outside the tipi.

'The sound was everywhere,' my mother said.

She called out to her mother and her cousins to come out and listen to the huge sound in the air, but no one else, not one other person, left the tipi – same with the other tipis in the camp too – nobody would come out even though my mother was yelling her fool head off.

My mother ran toward the direction where the sound was the loudest – just over a hill above where they had their tipis – and when she went over the rise, the sight that greeted her eyes made her send down roots.

'As if I was a tree,' my mother said.

Only a few feet away from her, thousands of buffalo were running.

'Right there in front of me, big dark animals stampeding, wild and loud, louder than you could ever think loud was, like it was the earth exploding,' my mother said. 'Never anything like it — the power and the freedom — like my people before the white man.'

She said she just wanted to start running with them, or jump on one of them and ride to where we don't know yet.

'I started yelling and screaming and making them deep grunt sounds and the next thing I knew, I was laying down on the ground and my mother and my cousins were gathered around me. They helped me to stand up and right then my woman time flowed down my legs.'

The buffalo were gone. No one besides my mother had seen or heard them.

Ever since that day she had that name: Buffalo Sweets.

Sitting up in my meadow that first time on Not-Really-A-Mountain — on the jut of rock, the sun almost down, the smoke of my mother gone into the air and the fire only red under black — when I looked down I could see Excellent. Could see Ida's Place down there, couldn't make out but knew where the window to room 11 was.

The last time I had seen my mother was the day before the night that he had come. The door to room 11 was open and she was sitting on the bed. She had her buckskin skirt on and her red blouse. She got up and walked to the window. She pulled the curtain back and touched one of the leaves of the geranium plant in the pot. Then she looked out the window — more at the sky that at the street. The way she looked, I figured she'd be taking off for a while again, for a couple of days, up to the hills, maybe to Indian Head — just to walk around and listen to the animals and make a fire and live the way her people did. Sometimes, she'd take me with her. But sometimes – most of the time – she said there was no place for me in her and that she had to go alone.

That place in me that doesn't forget has my mother always looking out that window with the fall light on her face.

Years later, when I'd tell Dellwood Barker about sitting on the rock that jutted out, at sunset, my mother smoke and fire behind me, he'd listen – Dellwood would listen. Then he'd say this:

'Smoke and wind and fire are all things you can feel but can't touch. Memories and dreams are like that too. They're what this world is made up of. There's really only a very short time that we get hair and teeth and put on red cloth and have bones and skin and look out eyes. Not for long. Some folks longer than others. If you're lucky, you'll get to be the one who tells the story: how the eyes have seen, the hair has blown, the caress the skin has felt, how the bones have ached.

'What the human heart is like,' he said.

'How the devil called and we did not answer.

'How we answered.'

Just as the sun was setting, while there was still light, I reached in my pocket and pulled out the photograph of my mother. The one she had taken of her when she was in Cody, Wyoming. The tybo photographer had dressed her up as an Indian princess with all sorts of feathers and blankets and shells and beads.

There she was, Buffalo Sweets, dressed up by a tybo to be what she already was: a princess, a young girl smiling.

The sun went down and the sky still held on to the colors. The kerosene lamps down in Excellent made tiny windows in the dark.

After all my mother had told me about the devil, I still let him get me.

Since he got me, he got my mother too.

She had gone without me. Once again, there hadn't been

room enough for me in her where she was going, and my mother had gone alone.

*

The winter after Billy Blizzard, the winter I was in fever, what I remember was the sound of my breathing and my heart beating. I remember dreams I didn't know were dreams, me flying high and graceful, not a sound but wind and if blue was a sound. Then I'd wake up from the dream, from the somewhere else, and I'd be laying out in the shed, or I'd be shitting blood in the outhouse, and somebody would be attending to me: Thord Hurdlika, Fern Hurdlika, Ellen Finton, Gracie Hammer – once it was Damn Dave and Damn Dog.

Ida took to her bed too and, story goes, was as far out in the blue as I was. Three broken ribs and a collapsed lung.

I often wondered why me and Ida didn't bump into each other, us being both out in the blue. I asked Dellwood Barker once why I hadn't bumped into Ida, and he said, 'Did you call out for her?'

I said, 'Nope.'

'All you had to do was call out,' Dellwood said. 'Why didn't you?'

'Don't know,' I said, but what I meant was that I wasn't ever me enough to be calling anything out, me being just flying around and wind and blue.

When I asked Ida why we hadn't bumped into each other, she gave me one of her looks.

'Quit talking nonsense,' Ida said. 'It was the fever. Your mind was playing tricks on you,' she said. 'The deck was stacked against you, that's all,' she said. 'But that's all in the past now. Just forget it. Keep your promises, keep clean, and keep going.'

Then there was the night I woke up in room 11, and all there was, was the terrible sound of my heart. Of my breath in and out. I got up out of bed, wrapped my Hudson Bay around me, walked down the hallway, past the rose light coming out from under Ida's door, out the door onto the porch, then to Ida's window. The moon was pumped full of light, full like blood to balls when you're next to what you want. The snow was moon too. There she was, Ida Richilieu in her circle of light, wrapped up in her quilts. Her hair was undone, a basket of black curls on her head. She was smoking and writing, dipping the pen in the inkwell, bringing the pen to the page, writing words down on paper.

Me standing outside, thinking I was inside Ida's circle of rose-colored light with Ida writing down words. With the human-being story of her words. Secrets I needed to know. Stories I had to hear.

As it turned out, that was a story itself, me standing and watching Ida — killdeer, me thinking I was standing and watching, but what I was doing was not what I thought I was doing. What I was doing was freezing to death.

Woke up a couple of days later in Ida's big feather bed and she was standing over me with her hand on my forehead. My eyes couldn't believe what they were seeing and my forehead was burning because she was touching it. I jumped up and ran out of her room as fast as my two legs and two feet could run, Ida running after me, the skirts of her dress and the petticoats sounding the same as my breath going fast in and out.

'Like a chicken with its head cut off,' Ida'd say, 'running amok through this town.'

Ida loved to tell the story of her chasing after me that day. Every time she told it, I'd be running faster. Every time there'd be at least one more whore chasing after me. Was almost as favorite a story as her feathered-boa story. Heard both those stories so many times, even I started to believe them.

Ida's story goes this way: The cowboy with the crooked dick

lassoed me in Chinatown. Then Ida and the other whores put me back into Ida's bed, and Doc Heyburn gave me a shot of something so I'd settle down. When I settled down, I opened my eyes and looked right at Ida and said, meaning my mother, 'She was my spirit of things.'

Story goes that was the first time Ida Richilieu'd ever cried.

Story goes too that that was the first time I ever spoke.

Everybody thought I was one of them who couldn't speak: Indian or tybo.

That is, except for my mother.

Guess I talked to my mother. Maybe I didn't. I remember talking. Maybe it was her talking and me listening that I remember.

Makes you wonder.

I stayed in Ida's bed for about a week. After that I moved out of room 11 and into the shed for good.

'A man needs his own space,' Ida said.

There was already a bed out in the shed. Ida bought me a braid rug for the floor and hung up one of her old petticoats over a broom handle for a curtain over the window. She gave me a kerosene lantern, and a mirror too.

I put the photograph of my mother taken in Cody, Wyoming, behind the mirror. Every day I'd turn the mirror around and look at my mother.

The stove in the shed was a pretty good one, but there were chinks in the walls where the wind came through. I stuffed some paper and old sheets in the chinks.

Wasn't long before things at Ida's Place went back to being pretty much the same – chores, and me back to running killdeer.

Ida started acting like her old self again. She'd put a good dress on in the daytime and scrub everything in sight. Even started up yelling at me again, *'Hey you, come over here, boy,'* with those painted red lips of hers.

One thing that was different was that since I was older there were more chores to do.

Another thing different was that Ellen Finton and Gracie Hammer had left Ida's Place, left Excellent, because they were afraid that Billy Blizzard wasn't dead and that he'd be back.

Something else that was different: now and then, when the moon scared me, and only if I washed up good, Ida would let me sleep with her in her big feather bed.

Another thing different was now that Ida knew I could talk, Ida started teaching me how to read words and write words, and spell words. Tybo words. Every weekday, after one o'clock and before her bath at three, Ida Richilieu would sit down with me in her room with one of her four books.

When she first started teaching me, Ida would read to me. After a while, I started reading with her. Then, in the end, I was the one reading to her. Took me just two years to learn how to read and write, and spell.

Had a good head on my shoulders.

The books we read were these: *Paul Bunyan and His Blue Ox, Catholic Martyrs, Sinners in the Hands of an Angry God*, and *Lean Hard on Me* – but mostly we just read the Paul Bunyan one and the *Lean Hard on Me*.

When we read the one about the Catholic saints, Ida told me to just pay attention to the words – not what they were saying. Mostly I liked the pictures in that book of people with circles of light around their heads talking to animals and getting murdered with arrows, and hung upside down on trees.

We read the book about the sinners and the angry God mostly because it had some good words in it. Ida also said it was good for me to know that people could actually think that way.

'Know what you're up against,' Ida'd say.

Lean Hard on Me was poetry, not regular tybo English.

'Paints a picture rather than tells a story,' Ida said.

The pictures that *Lean Hard on Me* painted were of lonely men and women up in the hills with their human-being sex story going wild on them.

That one was my favorite.

After I learned to read and write, Ida quit our afternoon lesson. Said I was on my own and if I wanted to keep going it was up to me. We kept on spelling, though.

Got to be so that day and night she'd yell words across the room, across the yard, across town at me.

'Rendezvous!' she'd yell.

'Chandelier!' she'd yell.

'Rhinoceros!' she'd yell.

That's just the way she was.

Now that I was older, eleven or twelve, one of my new chores was to help Ida with her bath, the way my mother had helped Ida before my mother died. What I'd do was go down to the bathhouse in the afternoon – usually just after her and me got done reading and writing. I'd dip the copper bucket of hers into Hot Creek and carry the bucket up the back stairs, and dump the water into the copper tub she had in her room. After the fourth trip up with the copper bucket, I'd take some rosemary leaves and thyme leaves that Ida kept on her dresser and put them in the water. Sometimes, she'd want the bubbles that came out of the brown bottle that she kept on the windowsill. I'd lay her soaps out and creams on the corner of her dressing table. Then there were the towels she needed.

The tub was right next to her dressing table and the tub looked more like a chair made out of a bucket than anything else. When she took a bath, Ida'd sit in the bucket part of the chair, in the water, and lean up against the back.

Ida'd take off her good dress and petticoats and slip and corset and underthings. Sometimes she'd wash out her underthings and hang them up on the line on the south side of her room, by the windows.

Ida'd sit naked on the chair in front of her dresser that had the mirrors that went all around. When it was sunny, the sun would come in and lay window shapes on her body. Her skin would look so white – the way sheets were when they were hanging on the line. If it was cloudy or raining, you could see the blue in the blood of her stick through. You could see how cold she could get. In the winter, when it was dark, she'd light the lamp, close the curtain, and her skin was that rose color from the flame.

I always made some kind of excuse to go over to the dresser by her – to lay down a brush, or take a towel over or something. It never seemed to bother her that I got near. Ida never paid any attention to me during her bath time. Might as well not even have been in the room as far as she was concerned. I'm not saying Ida Richilieu was being mean to me. That's just the way Ida was. Figure that's the way most women are, though. Sometimes there's no room in them for you and they got to be alone.

Ida Richilieu needed her time and her cigarettes in front of her mirror between her day chores and her night chores. Needed to look at herself. Needed to drink on her glass of whiskey and look at herself. Sometimes, Ida in front of her mirror, what was staring her back was the liquor and the cigarettes and the hard face of an old woman. Sometimes what was staring her back was the damned skinny arms and bony legs of an ornery little girl. Ida Richilieu wasn't an old woman, though, and she wasn't a little girl. When she raised her arms up to pull her hair back – that's when you could tell. She was a woman – full-smelling of sulphur springs or places on the earth deep with topsoil. The curve of her arm down to the black hair in her armpits, down to her breasts, always gave me a feeling. Her dark, round, big nipples slapped at my heart same way the black hair at her woman's hole did – slapped my heart when I saw her, smelled her.

Something else, too. Those places on Ida – nipples, woman's hole, ass, armpits – never quite seemed to belong to her. Seemed more that those parts were an outfit – a corset she'd step into and strap onto herself when she was going to work at night. During the day was the real Ida – washing, cleaning, scrubbing, Ida the white and the smooth of her running her business, shouting orders out to get things done. Then, in the afternoon, Ida would step into her sex, into those parts of her, strapping them on, the same way Thord Hurdlika put his petroleum jelly gloves on – both Thord and Ida, hard at work, trying to keep something soft.

After Ida's bath, I'd watch Ida put her face on. She'd turn the lamp up high even in summer and she'd put some powder on her face and color on her eyes – blue or purple – then she'd finish up with the lips red.

The dresses in the evening she called her *working dresses*. They were all shiny; a white one, a red one, and a blue one. Each one had a story. Each one a secret.

Ida told me the secret to each one of her dresses, and, as I have said before, a secret to Ida wasn't something you treated lightly.

Before she reached into her closet, Ida always went out to the corridor and looked down into the bar and scrutinized the men, Ida deciding what the business was, and consequently what dress she would wear. She wore the white one when there were lots of young men in the bar.

'Callow young fellows looking for a bride,' Ida'd say.

Then she'd put the white dress on, let her hair down, and start acting the virgin bride, walking down the stairs, holding her dress up. Every eye in that place on her ankles.

Callow young fellows never had a chance.

The white dress was the dress that she married Vinitio Luchese in.

'Altered some,' she said.

It was shiny and smooth like the moon on still water.

'Silk,' Ida said. 'Pure silk.'

Secret about that dress was that she wasn't a virgin the first time she wore it.

The white one was the longest. Went clear to the floor, covering up even her shoes. That's why, when she walked down the stairs, she had to hold it up in the front. Ida liked to do that though – walk down the stairs and into the bar, for her *debut*, as she called it.

The white dress didn't show her tits much.

'After all, I got married in it,' she said. 'Left the scoop neck like it was, just took off the lace and crap and sash and took the bustle out.'

'Unencumbered it,' was how Ida put it. 'A working girl's got to be unencumbered. Got to move about freely as possible.'

When she wore the white dress, she usually let her hair down and wore it plain, hardly any combs, like a bride.

The white dress was my favorite. That black hair and her skin white and those living red lips of hers in that white dress was definitely my favorite.

The red dress was shiny because it was velvet and had beads all across the top. That one barely covered her nipples, pushed her tits up, and flattened them out so that they looked like they were growing almost right up underneath her chin. The skirt part of the dress went down to just above her ankles. With the red dress, she wore the red slippers that she called her *ballerinas*, her hair pulled up with the set of combs, and the long earrings – *the rhinestones* – that she got from Franz Bieberkopf, an admirer of hers from Germany with a skinny *Schwangstücke*.

'S . . C . . H . . W . . A . . N . . G . . S . . T . . U with two dots on it . . C . . K . . E,' Ida spelled, 'means dick in German.'

The secret to the red dress was that Ida never wore any underthings under it. After scrutinizing, she only wore that dress when it was a bar full of horny men looking for a fuck.

Should have seen her walk down the stairs in that one. Was my favorite. Ida in the red dress, red lips, her ballerinas, rhinestones, tits up high, was my favorite.

The blue one made a sound when she walked.

The *taffeta*, Ida called it. She only wore the blue dress when she wanted to fall in love. Usually once a month when she was ovulating.

'Always want to fall in love when I ovulate,' Ida said.

Ida was wearing the blue dress the night she fell in love with Billy Blizzard. Wore it the night Alma Hatch came to town. Wore it that time when she scrutinized the bar and her eyes bugged out with Dellwood Barker.

She'd put blue ribbons in her hair and wear a strand of pearls *from the ocean* and a pearl in one of her ears, and the blue feathered boa wrapped around her. Ida walking down the stairs that way was quite a sight. Her skin was the way the moon is when you can see the moon up in the blue during the day.

The blue one was my favorite.

Truth is, the blue one was the one.

*

The last time I slept in Ida's bed I didn't have any idea it was going to be the last time.

I took a good long bath and cleaned underneath my finernails and behind my ears good. Went up to Ida's window and stood outside and watched her in her rose-colored room in her circle of light writing. Wasn't long before she saw me and motioned me to come on in. I walked around through the back door, into the corridor, over the flowered carpet, up to Ida's door, and knocked. She had the white nightshirt waiting for me all folded up and smelling nice. She checked my fingernails and behind my ears. We didn't say much, we never did. I changed into the nightshirt behind Ida's screen and jumped into her big soft cold feather bed that I figured felt like clouds, and let my body sink down. She tucked me in. The room had that hazy look about it from the kerosene lamp and her tobacco and the other kind of smoke. It smelled like soap and clean things and kerosene and tobacco and her. Ida went back to writing and I fell asleep. Dreamed about flying and clouds and white things floating.

When Ida came to bed, I woke up but pretended not to. I stayed in the same position and counted to one thousand even though I couldn't count that high. I always knew when it was right. And it was always one thousand when I'd roll over and lay myself against her.

I was back to flying. Then I woke up because Ida had jumped out of bed. She lit the kerosene lamp, turned the wick up, and lifted the covers.

Then she lifted up the nightshirt.

Ida looked under my nightshirt for a while and said, 'Look at the size of that one, would you?'

No more sleeping with Ida.

She told that story about as much as she told the feathered-boa story, and the whores-chasing-me-around-Excellent story.

'Never could sleep if there was a hard-on in the room,' she always said. Then she'd say, 'When I lifted that boy's nightshirt – there it was. Needed a double mule team to drive that thing home.' Then she'd laugh and cough and laugh some more.

Every time Ida told that story, my dick got bigger. To listen to her tell it, my dick was bigger that a grizzly bear's. Bigger than Paul Bunyan's. Bigger than his blue ox's. Big as the state of Idaho.

That's how I got my other name, the name that all of us – Ida Richilieu, Alma Hatch, Dellwood Barker, and me – used to laugh at: Out-Of-His-Pants. Dellwood Barker was the first one to come up with the name. After that, whenever one of them would say my name that way, we'd all laugh — them first, then me. I couldn't help it. No matter what, I always ended up laughing too.

'*Way*-Out-Of-His-Pants,' Dellwood Barker used to say. Then we'd laugh. Our fool heads off.

I loved them all so much.

*

The summer after the spring that I'd found my mother dead up on Not-Really-A-Mountain, and not long after I had woke Ida up with my hard-on — about the middle of August — Ida decided it was time for me to have a customer.

'Going through the change,' Ida said. 'Horny as a two-peckered billy goat.'

Ida figured since I had reached for the feathered boa, since I had a big dick, since my ass wasn't virgin — that naturally I'd be needing sexual gratification, and a lot of it, because of what I was half of, namely *Indian*, which, according to Ida Richilieu, as far as my human-being sex story goes, meant just two things: noble and savage.

Ida also figured that since sooner or later I'd be getting gratification one way or another, her and me — and mostly chintzy her — might as well make some money off it.

'G . . R . . A . . T . . I . . F . . I . . C . . A . . T . . I . . O . . N,' Ida spelled. 'Means getting what you're looking for.'

One afternoon, before her bath, Ida told me that I'd be having a customer out in the shed that evening, and that I should be especially nice to him, as he had been a good customer of hers for many years, and since this man had expressed a sexual interest in me, Ida had felt obliged to provide my services, and expected a good job out of me.

'Fucking's the easiest thing in the world,' Ida said. 'Easy as falling off a log.'

Then she stopped and looked at me.

'You ain't been fucking, yet, have you?' Ida asked.

'Fucked Billy Blizzard,' I said. 'Case you forgot.'

'Ain't forgot,' Ida said. 'Some things are just best left unsaid,' she said, 'and I plain don't want to hear them.'

'No, I ain't been fucking,' I said.

'Good!' she said. 'You're going to love it. Only thing you got to remember is that even if you're not having a good time, you got to act like you are. The rest comes natural.

'Another thing is you got to be clean – unless he wants you dirty. Whoever wants to stick his dick in the other is your business. I don't want nothing to do with which dick goes where.

'Customer gives *me* the money,' Ida said. 'Starting off I'll give you a dollar for every customer – only I won't give the dollar right to you – I'll put it someplace safe until you're old enough to handle your own finances.

'Your first customer will be out in the shed at eight o'clock. His name's Stoney and he'll be crocked. He'll probably have a bottle and he'll offer you some, but you're not allowed, hear? There's no whiskey or smoke for you until you're old enough. Understood?'

The afternoon before my first customer, I remember as clear as if it was yesterday. The world was the same but looked different. Couldn't put my finger on how things could be the same and different at the same time. Was a bright sunny day, dust rolling up around your feet as you walked, everything sweating. The trees sweating, the rocks, even the shade was hot. All the windows in the bar were open and Ida had sprinkled down the wood floor twice already and it smelled wet.

I spent a lot of time in the bathhouse, scrubbing, getting my fingernails clean, and behind my ears. Cleaned up the shed. Got the last of the yellow daisies that were growing on Hot Creek near where Chinatown started and put them in a jar on the table by the window.

Paid a visit to Dr. Ah Fong and asked him if he had anything that smelled nice for a man. He shuffled into the back room and got me a bottle of something he said came from bulls' balls.

For the longest time, with the way Dr. Ah Fong talked tybo, I couldn't understand he was trying to say 'bulls' balls.'

So Dr. Ah Fong tried to show me what he meant. He put his two hands by his head to look like horns. He started making bull sounds, snorting and mooing and all. Then he cupped one hand around his own balls and kept up with the bull sounds.

Both of us got to laughing hard with Dr. Ah Fong acting that way. Told me since I'd made him laugh so hard, he'd give me the bottle of bulls' balls free.

'Flee,' Dr. Ah Fong said.

When I got the bottle home, I smelled the stuff and Oh! The humanity! Was no way I was going to put that stuff on me.

The rest of the afternoon I thought I'd play some killdeer but couldn't get interested. Every time I looked at the bar clock only the big hand had moved and not much. I was hungry but then I wasn't hungry. Didn't know whether to eat a lot or not eat at all. Ended up not eating. Stole some tobacco from Ida and smoked all day. Almost made myself sick.

When it came eight o'clock that evening, I was sitting on my bed, acting like I was sitting on my bed, but I wasn't. Was ready to hightail it out of there like a farting steer with heel flies. Then I heard the knock on the door.

Stoney was a skinny old guy. I'd seen him in and out of Ida's Place and Excellent a couple of times over the years. He was all scrubbed up, clean pair of pants, boots shined, his red underwear rolled up at the sleeves. Smelled like bulls' balls.

Ida'd been right. He was crocked. His blue eyes got bluer with every drink he took. He'd take a big swig and wipe his mustache and offer me some and I'd say no. We stood looking at each other for a long time before I asked him in. I finally got my mouth to move, and I said, 'Come on in, Stoney.'

He came in and I closed the door behind him.

'Flowers're pretty,' Stoney said.

We stood and looked at each other some more, him taking swigs and wiping his mustache and them blue eyes of his. I didn't know what else to do, so I stepped up to him and put my arms around him. Just made things easier, reaching over and touching someone else.

Touching a man for the first time was warm wind blowing spring to cabin fever. With that embrace, with the reaching out, deep inside your muscles didn't have to hold you up anymore, and you could relax, you could lean, lean hard onto.

Stoney's dick was hard and stayed hard but not for long, him coming fast the first time, and after that didn't get hard at all. Said he had to eat between and sleep some. I told him that I could fry him up a piece of beef if he wanted, but he said no. Said he didn't want to break this up, meaning us laying, him next to me.

He put his head on my chest, looking down, ear to my heart, and listened. Said there wasn't a better sound than that. Or a better sight.

Stoney put his hand around my dick.

'Lordy boy, you got a whole life of fucking ahead of you,' he said. 'Don't know if I feel sorry for you or if I'm just plain jealous.'

The next thing he said made him tremble.

'Dig it in,' he said, lifting his leg, showing me what that was.

So I dug it in.

Easy as falling off a log.

Didn't have to act like I was having a good time. I was.

Next morning, Ida Richilieu tried not to act curious. Spent the whole day acting not curious. She cooked some steak and peas that night – something Ida didn't do much – cook. Hollered at me to come and eat. I didn't know if I was hearing right, so I walked into the kitchen and sure enough – there was two plates on the table and a steak on each plate. Two bowls too, filled with peas. Ida had a whiskey too. We ate and I didn't say anything and she didn't say anything. Ida was acting pissed off, the way she always acted when she wanted to get something out of you – her making it seem as if it was your fault she was pissed off, so that you'd tell her what she wanted to know. Finally, she just blurted it out:

'Cat got your tongue?' she said. 'Is this the way I get treated after all I've done for you? Just remember you're a dollar richer because of me, young man!'

I finished up the last bite of steak and poured the peas down my throat before I said anything. Told my legs and feet to get ready to run. Then I said it:

'Certain things are private and best left unsaid,' I said. 'A man's got his pride, you know.'

Ida was looking for something to throw at me.

'That's just how I am. Don't ask me to change,' I said.

I ducked the frying pan, and her bowl full of peas, and was halfway up to the hot springs before my ears couldn't hear Ida Richilieu yelling at me anymore.

The next day, Ida did manage to sit me down, though. Said it was *imperative*. She knew if she used a new word, she could get me.

'I . . M . . P . . E . . R . . A . . T . . I . . V . . E,' Ida spelled. 'Means do it or else.'

Ida always was a good talker. More than that, she was a good teller. What Ida wasn't good at, though, was explaining. She'd be the first to admit it. Hated it. Whenever she had to explain something, she'd get to acting again like it was your fault that she was having to explain something to you.

That's the way it was that day that she had to explain about the trouble I could get myself into having sex with men in a Christian society. Had to explain that I had better watch my ass, and the best way to do it.

'You're *never* to find a customer yourself,' she said. 'Or even act like you're interested. Even if you are.

'No matter how wild and uncontrollable that Injun dick of yours gets, first thing is scrutinizing – *me* scrutinizing,' Ida said. 'Then after scrutinizing, it'll be *me*, Ida Richilieu, and only *me*, who decides upon the customer, and when, and where.'

Said she'd leave the how up to me.

Then Ida Richilieu made me swear, made me promise, that was the way things were going to be: me doing the fucking, her doing the telling me who to fuck.

I promised.

This is how me and Ida would do it:

If Ida herself, or one of Ida's girls, had a customer that expressed any interest for more than the usual, or if they didn't express it but Ida scrutinized it, or if the guy had trouble getting hard, Ida would send for me to bring up some towels or soap or a bottle of whiskey. Sometimes, she'd have me help the customer with his bath, like my mother used to do. Scrubbing those miners' backs was always a surefire way of telling. Ida had me wear what she called *the outfit*, which in the winter was a wool felt shirt with no collar and wool felt pants gathered with a drawstring, no underwear, and my boots. In the summer it was just shirt and pants, cotton ones.

So, if the guy was in a room, I'd come walking into the room just after the girl had excused herself to go to the outhouse. I'd ask the guy something like:

'Sir, do you know where I should put these towels?' Or: 'Sir, did you order a bottle of whiskey?'

Then I'd pull up the drawstring part of the pants so that he could see how I was down there, or I'd bend over, or rub myself against him accidentally.

If the guy was interested, I'd let him grab on to me and I'd act like I was shocked that he'd do such a thing.

It was Ida's rule that man-to-man sex was done only out in the shed. So, when the human-being sex story started happening, I always broke it off with:

'Your girlfriend is coming back!' Or: 'Here comes Ida!'

Then I'd make a time to meet him out in the shed later on. In the meantime, Ida would talk to the guy, and collect the money.

Ida was pleased with my work, you could tell, though she'd never say.

Then: 'What does he do out there?' Ida said. 'I might as well retire. All of us might as well retire. Hang up my corset for good and just be his bookkeeper.'

I was getting to be a rich man – or boy, anyway. Got so popular, Ida had to put another door in the shed. So there was a door for the customers coming in and one for the customers going out.

Never once had a problem because, I figure, I was good at what I did and because Ida made the men promise never to say a word – for their sakes as well as mine. Meaning hers.

You know what Ida thought about promises. Those men knew too.

*

The following spring just about everything changed. Started with Ida going plumb crazy on spring cleaning. Then spring cleaning turned into hotel painting.

Pink.

Painted Ida's Place pink.

That whole fucking hotel pink.

That's what brought Alma Hatch here, I'm sure – all that pink on Ida's hotel – along with getting snagged by Not-Really-A-Mountain, that is. Between the two of them, was no way in hell Alma Hatch could keep herself away.

Spring cleaning started first with ripping up the carpets. Each one of the carpets was tacked down. Ida's room was first, then all the other rooms. The carpets weighed a ton and had to be drug through the corridor and down the stairs and through the bar and around to the side and hung over the clothesline.

Was my job to beat those carpets. Had to haul the carpets back up too, and tack them back down again – rotated.

Every spring each carpet had to be rotated.

Then there was repainting the ceilings and repapering the walls. Painting ceilings wasn't so bad, except for in the bar because the ceiling was so high. Had to stand on the very top of the ladder and even then had to reach.

Papering the walls was the one, though, that could drive you crazy. Had to tear the old paper off first – without ripping the lining off the wall, which cost money. Then mixing flour and water just right so it wasn't lumpy and not runny. Then there was getting the new paper on without any wrinkles.

Ida Richilieu hated wrinkles in her wallpaper.

She had to have all the windows cleaned too. Ida Richilieu didn't like wrinkles in her windows either. I'd hang my ass out the second-story windows, one hand gripping the windowsill, the other wiping the window glass, both hands near to freezing because spring here is sometimes cold as winter.

Everything was scrubbed twice as hard as it was usually scrubbed. Even scrubbed the bar floor. I swear, there were places on the floor that had been scrubbed as thin as the paper I'd been pasting on the walls. Had a skunk under the floor one winter. Nearly killed business. Had to get Damn Dave and his Damn Dog to finally get the skunk out. That part of the bar still smelled skunk on certain days.

The bar mirror was another chore. I'd wipe and Ida'd walk to different places around the bar looking at the mirror, trying to see if there was smudges. One whole day there was smudges. Ida Richilieu and her smudges and wrinkles.

Bar glasses were washed special in boiling water along with the kitchen dishes and silverware. Swept and scrubbed under the bar and swept and scrubbed the kitchen. Same with the back porches and the back stairs.

Then there was the sign, *Indian Head Hotel*. Ida told me to scrub it and I scrubbed it so good most of the paint came off. Sign said *Ind He Ho* when I got done.

That's when Ida decided to paint the place. Not just the sign, the whole place. As I told you, there was only three buildings in Excellent that were painted and two of them were Mormon.

None of them had ever been *re*painted.

Any color.

Let alone pink.

Ida Richilieu always did like being the first person to do something.

She bought the pink paint from Stein's Mercantile, who had to order it from Boise City. Took over two weeks for that paint to get here. When it did, the whole town gathered to watch it get unloaded off the stage. Whole town kept on watching too, watching me that is, as I started in to paint. Me painting and Ida telling me how.

The first day I opened the can of paint, Thord Hurdlika was there, and Doc Heyburn, and Damn Dave and his Damn Dog, and the whores. At first, I thought they'd sent the wrong paint because the paint looked shit brindle to me.

Ida said, 'Stir it!'

So I did.

I swear right in front of my eyes that paint turned pink. It was so pink that it smelled pink. People clean over on the other side of Pine Street came running over because they'd smelled the pink.

Started in the back. Ida figured I could make my mistakes back there where nobody could see them, then I could do the sides. By the time I got to the front, I'd know what I was doing.

I picked up the can of pink and started climbing up the ladder, every eye in town on me. At the top, I got the can steadied, stuck the paintbrush into the paint, and put a swath of pink onto the backside of Ida's hotel.

Some folks gasped and covered their mouths. Children started crying. Damn Dave's Damn Dog started howling.

Mormons stampeded out of there as if pink was some kind of sin.

Ida loved it.

I ended up spending May, June, July, and part of August painting things pink – when I wasn't doing my regular chores, that is, and taking customers out in the shed.

Wasn't easy, that summer. Got to thinking that pink *was* the devil's color. Wouldn't just stay on the walls and in the bucket, that pink. No matter how hard I tried.

Pink was on everything. The ground around Ida's Place was pink. The grass was pink. The ladder was pink. Window glasses – the ones I'd spent my time cleaning – were pink. Pink on dishes and knives and forks and spoons. Pink on the red spigot and well pump. Pink water up at the hot springs. Pink splotches on horses – pink Appaloosas. Pink under my fingernails – no way to get it out. Even had me some pink pubic hairs. Don't ask me how.

Later, 'All he had to do was touch something and it'd turn pink,' Ida would say. 'You could tell who each and every one of his customers was, because when he got done with them, they always had some pink on them somewhere. One guy had to buy himself a whole new set of false teeth.

'Pinkest smile I ever saw,' she'd say, and then she'd laugh, cough, and laugh some more.

When I got done painting, though, I swear, Ida's Place was a sight to behold. Was the prettiest building in Excellent, Idaho. As soon as you came over the rise into town, Ida's Place was the first thing you saw. Couldn't help but see it – a big pink clapboard two-story hotel with double porches and the new sign up top that said *Indian Head Hotel*.

People have talked about that hotel for years. Talked about the pink of that hotel for years. Couldn't stop talking about it. More a legend than a story.

*

Alma Hatch walked into Ida's Place just three days after I was done painting it pink.

Surprised it took her that long.

It was late summer going into fall. Pine Street was a dusty damned road going to nowhere but hot. Day after day, the American flag in front of the post office hung down on the pole, not a trace of breeze. Nighttime, if you slept, if you could get to sleep, you dreamed of wind and things getting rained on. Only thing cool besides the river was the wine bottle with the basket weave around it on the second shelf in the kitchen cupboard. When you took the cork out and poured the drinking water into a glass, when you held the glass of water in your hands, something in you just loved water so much then. Wanted to speak water language and say thank you to how water sounded getting poured into the glass, thank you to how water looked sitting on the table waiting for you to drink it, thank you to the liquid of it, the cool of it on your skin, but most of all what was thankful was your thirst.

I was spending as much time as I could on the river. Up at the nest, the water was still over my head. You could jump off the granite rock, fly through the hot, dry air, and splash deep into water that was still too cold. Took your breath away on the hottest of days.

That day, I was just coming back from a swim, was just at the Mormon church at the picket fence, when I saw the stage roll in. The sun was high and made me squint. Damn Dave opened the stable doors and walked out to the stage, Damn Dog following. The men, who were sitting outside on the barbershop bench, had pulled their hats up and were looking over in that direction. When I got to the front door of Ida's Place, I looked over just as Thord Hurdlika got up and walked to the horse trough, wetted a red bandanna, squeezed it out, and laid the bandanna onto his head. All the windows were open, and just outside Ida had the white sheets hanging on the line. You could smell the soap. Other things you could smell were the wet wood floor, and something like pine tar boiling, which was bodies sweating – the bar was full of men.

Ida was behind the bar. She was wiping bar glasses dry. I walked back next to her and started helping. Neither one of us said anything. I hunkered down and stacked some bar glasses under the counter. That's when Alma Hatch walked in.

I didn't actually see her walk in, but it's hard to believe that there was ever a time when I didn't know Alma Hatch or what she looked like. So now, when I remember that first day, even though I was hunkered down below the bar and only heard her voice, I see Alma Hatch, her long hair pulled up from her face and piled high on her head under her hat. I see her dark eyebrows, thick like a man's, and underneath, eyes as brown as dirt.

'Alma Hatch floated in,' Ida'd say, 'beautiful like you'd only heard tell of.'

Of course, Ida Richilieu, at the time, didn't let on to any of her feelings. Some things are best left unsaid. She didn't even look up when Alma Hatch walked in, even with Alma walking the way she did – the way hummingbirds fly, straight to sugar.

When she got to the bar where we were, she said, 'My name's Alma Hatch.'

Knowing Ida, she'd probably been studying Alma Hatch since five miles down the road before the stagecoach even got to town. But right then, when Alma Hatch introduced herself, that was the first time Ida'd actually put her eyes on her.

'I'm looking for the proprietress of the Indian Head Hotel,' Alma Hatch said. 'I believe her name is Ida Richilieu.'

Ida just kept wiping the bar glass she was holding, and said, 'You're looking at her.'

'Well, then, Ida Richilieu,' Alma Hatch said, 'I'm glad to make your acquaintance. I understand that you have a real prize of a good fuck in your back shed – a breed boy by the name of Mr. Shed. I'd like to have him for the rest of the afternoon and maybe for the night if he suits me.'

Everybody in the bar stopped what he was doing. I asked my ears if they were hearing right. Then Alma Hatch said, 'Just how much am I going to pay for this Mr. Shed and his place out back there?'

That's when I looked at Alma Hatch. I slowly raised up. My eyes saw her hat first. Looked like a big bird of prey sitting on her head. Then I saw her eyes, my eyes level to the bar.

I can't remember ever hearing the world or the people in it so quiet. Even late on a winter night with moon on the snow, it doesn't get that quiet. Every man in the bar looked like a photograph of himself standing in the bar. Ida dropped the glass and it broke. I went to pick up the pieces, but Ida motioned me away with her

leg. When I stood up, I was surprised that I was looking down at
them, at those women, at Ida Richilieu and Alma Hatch.

'This here's Mr. Shed,' Ida said. I watched Ida's lips say 'Mr.
Shed.' Then Ida said, 'And Mr. Shed, this is Alma Hatch.'

I looked Alma Hatch straight in the eye, every eye in the room
looking at me looking at her.

'Five dollars,' Ida said, and someone whistled, and, like
everybody was looking, everybody stopped breathing even more
than they had not been breathing before, including me.

'Here's six,' Alma Hatch said. 'What percentage does he get?'

'Dollar for the room. Fifty cents for sheets. Dollar for the
house. In this case, I'd say Mr. Shed gets the rest. Plus you get ten
percent off on a bottle of whiskey, and the glasses.'

'Bath included?' Alma Hatch asked.

'Bath included,' Ida Richilieu said.

'Fifty cents cover the towels?' Alma Hatch asked.

'Towels're included in the fifty cents,' Ida Richilieu said.

'You charge extra if he bathes with me?' Alma Hatch asked.

'That's up to Mr. Shed,' Ida said, and then she looked at me
and said, 'Mr. Shed, will you be charging extra for bathing with
Miss Hatch?'

'. . . Mrs.,' Alma Hatch said.

'. . . *Mrs.* Hatch,' Ida corrected herself.

I looked at Mrs. Alma Hatch and then at Mrs. Ida Richilieu,
then back to Mrs. Alma Hatch, then back to Mrs. Ida Richilieu.

'No,' I said, 'I won't be charging extra.'

I walked around the bar figuring I'd pick up the bags the way I
usually did.

Ida said, 'I'll attend to the luggage.'

I said, 'What?' because I didn't know those words yet: *attend*
and *luggage*.

'I'll get the bags,' Ida said.

So then I went to walk out through the kitchen to the back

door and then out into the shed, when Ida said, 'Use the front door, Mr. Shed, and then around to the side.'

So I did as I was told and walked around the bar to where Alma Hatch was standing. There was no getting around her. I didn't know what to do, so I took her arm the way I had seen tybo men do, and then we walked out that way, Alma Hatch and me, through the bar, through the men in the bar, and out the front door. Thord Hurdlika with the red bandanna on his head and the men sitting in front of the barbershop just across the street were squinting and gawking. Alma Hatch and me turned the corner to the side, and walked through the lines of white sheets hanging, their shadows like real things moving on the pink-covered ground, to the front door of the back shed.

Alma Hatch sat on my bed with her hat on, holding her purse.

While we were waiting for Ida to bring the bags, Alma Hatch asked me why there were two doors in such a small building.

'Coming and going,' I said, because I didn't know what else to say.

All of a sudden, there was a smile on Alma Hatch's face that she didn't want me to see. Was having herself a hell of a time. Didn't know it then, but that was going to be Alma Hatch's favorite story about me.

'First time I met old Out-Of-His-Pants,' Alma Hatch would say, 'we called him Mr. Shed.'

Then she'd laugh, and Ida'd laugh, and Dellwood. 'Was all downhill after that,' Ida'd say.

Always started that way, that story.

Ida brought in Alma's bags. There was two of them. The small one had Alma's oils and perfumes and feminine things in it. I found out later that the other bag had a white dress, a red dress, and a blue dress in it, her underthings and jewelry, and a pair of high-heeled shoes. And there was something else: it was a large leather-bound book that said on it in gold letters, *Ornithological Studies in the Pacific Northwest.*

I didn't get the *ornithological* part of what it said on the book for some time, but the pictures in the book of those birds were hand painted, all in color, some of them of birds sitting on branches, some birds flying, and all of them showing how the female looked and how the male looked, and what kind of eggs they laid, and where they laid them.

Ida put Alma's bags down at the foot of my bed. Put that bottle of whiskey and *two* glasses down on the table. Then Ida walked around Alma and smoothed out the wrinkles of the Hudson Bay that was laying on my bed.

When she walked out the door, Ida turned to us and said, 'Bathwater's hot and ready to go!'

There are all kinds of stories about that afternoon. Every man in that bar and every man on the barbershop bench had a different one. Some of them had Alma Hatch and me fucking right there on the bar as soon as she walked in.

One of the stories goes that Alma Hatch had a tail that you could actually see sticking up from the back of her – especially when she was horny – and that thing was always sticking up.

There's even one story that goes this way: Alma Hatch really had a dick, and that's the only reason why I agreed to fuck her.

Then there was the sounds she was making. Ida said it sounded like there was a herd of holsteins out there out in the shed and all of them was giving birth.

Here's my side to the story: Alma Hatch brought the bottle of whiskey with her to the bathhouse. She had some hemp, she called it locoweed, rolled up into cigarettes. Well, we smoked some of that stuff, and then we drank each of us a shot of whiskey – which was my first time for either of those things along with me being with a woman. First time, too, for me getting into that bathtub with another person – male or female.

We kept smoking that stuff, and Alma Hatch started taking off more and more of her clothes. Was taking off mine. Both of us having another shot of whiskey. Alma letting down her hair. Testing the water. Trying to keep the locoweed dry. Me holding my balls as I lowered myself into the water. Alma plopping herself down in the water. Me trying to get my legs around Alma Hatch's in the tub – water sloshing all over. Keeping the whiskey bottle and the glasses in reach. Then there was the bubbles and the whiskey and another puff on the locoweed, me pressed up tight against Alma Hatch.

Wasn't long before there was water and bubbles all over creation. Alma was hollering geese going south and me talking in languages I'd never heard before. My eyes talking. My ears, my skin talking – big words coming up in me: *ornithological, attend,* and *luggage*. Fingers talking, feet and toes. Me hard in Alma Hatch, slipped up inside in her, a salmon swum home against the current, the tip of me at the place where there ain't no further.

Alma coming and coming, and screaming and coming. Me coming then, too. No words left, only not-talking passing through me into her. Through her, my body pulled up sweet to her sweet, to sunlight on a white bird way up high in the blue, flying.

Alma Hatch's body was sarsaparilla or hard candy in a dish or an all-day sucker. Something so sweet and pink and sticky you got it all over yourself. Something once you started in on you couldn't stop til you made yourself sick. Always smelled of roses, too – roses mixed with woman smell. Alma Hatch was always putting rosewater on her. Behind her ears, under her arms, on her wrists. Sometimes, she'd just sit her ass down in a puddle of that stuff and suck rosewater up inside her. If you walked into a room and Alma Hatch had been in there during the last twenty-four hours, you'd know it by the roses. Pink roses. Not red, white, or yellow – pink. Nipples were pink, woman's hole was pink, lips pink. I swear Alma Hatch was no white woman. She was a pink woman.

'Best whore in the state,' Ida Richilieu would say about Alma years later. 'What makes Alma so good is that she looks like a rose, smells like a rose, and then fucks your thorns loose.'

Alma Hatch stayed with me out in the shed for the rest of the afternoon – then, for the night again – both of us just wanting to feel the same way as that first fuck.

All the while out in the shed fucking I'd catch myself talking to Alma Hatch about things my brain didn't know anything about. But still the words came off my tongue and my lips knew how to speak them.

One time, sitting face to face, Alma Hatch sitting on me, riding me like a horse, I watched her lips, her tongue, her teeth – the muscles inside her mouth wet – stretching out sounds. I could see it – language – coming up to her mouth from down inside her deep. My eyes were right there looking into her mouth, into where she made her words. Wondered if she knew any more about what she was saying than I did. Could only make out a word or two.

But I understood: killdeer.

When I woke up the next morning, figured I was in love. I had reached for the feathered boa, but there I was in love with Alma Hatch.

Alma Hatch, though, said it wasn't love. Said it was the locoweed.

But I just couldn't get the smell of her, the smell of roses, and the taste of her out of my way – the remembering of it. Her words were left all over on me, them becoming my new language. My new language loud in me. Excruciating, though I was looking for some quiet.

Usually, I made my own breakfast. Sometimes, I made mine and Ida's too. But that morning it was different.

Ida had Rocky Mountain oysters for me, scrambled with eggs, coffee, and baked bread waiting for me.

I was eating alone.

That is, not with Alma Hatch.

Alma had said that she was done with me and thanks.

Alma paid me, closed the door behind her, and before I knew it, I was standing in the shed bare naked, holding on to three dollars and fifty cents, and a couple of them rolled-up locoweed cigarettes. Alma Hatch had her own room rented by nine o'clock, and just wanted tea and a slice of corn bread buttered on both sides brought up.

I asked Ida please kindly for me not to be the one who did the bringing.

Ida sat at the other end of the kitchen table not saying much. Mostly just feeling the warm of the coffee cup on the palms of her hands. She was acting pissed off because she thought she was going to have to explain.

I started crying somewhere between my first oyster and my first bite of baked bread. I kept crying the whole while until I had slicked my plate clean and was finished with my second cup of coffee.

Ida washed my plate and fork. She wiped her hands on her apron when she was done. I just sat at the table, didn't know what else to do. There wasn't anywhere to go. All the places had Alma Hatch in them. So I just sat, my dick wanting to get hard again with her, my eyes crying, and my fingers touching one another across my two hands.

Ida came over and leaned herself against the back of me.

'Consider the source, Shed,' Ida said. 'Your mother is dead, and she will never come back.'

Then she said, 'Your customer tonight's at ten o'clock.'

'I won't be there,' I said.

'Suit yourself,' she said. 'He'll be waiting for you out in the shed if you change your mind.'

*

The only place left to go was up on Not-Really-A-Mountain – to Big Foot's cabin, in the meadow, where Billy Blizzard had killed my mother.

That day I was as much drawn to him as I was to her.

I crossed the spit of water trickling down that was the river. Then I was standing face to face with the mountain. I started, pulling myself up between the first of the rocks. The sun was right above me. As I inched my way up though, the sun was inching its way too. Wasn't long, and it was behind me, and my shadow was in front of me. Every rock I pulled myself up to, there was my shadow, crawling up with me.

I got to thinking that if I wasn't me, then there wouldn't be a shadow of me. Mostly, though, I didn't think of anything but Alma Hatch. And Billy Blizzard. And my mother. Wished my mother was with me so she could tell me a story, or we could go off together and live like her people for a couple days. When the ground started leveling off, and the trees started getting thin, I thought I was lost. Had to cut back to where I remembered the wagon was. Took me all morning to find that trail again. Wasn't wearing no hat this time, so the wind couldn't blow it off and show me the way.

When I got to that big outcrop of granite rocks, I wasn't lost no more. Climbed up, looked over the side, and there it was – my meadow. The grass wasn't green, was gold and brown, except for where there was underground water. In those places, the grass was still green. Weren't no flowers this time. Too damned hot for any flower, except for a cactus flower maybe, and there wasn't no cactus.

I walked over to Big Foot's cabin – to Billy Blizzard's cabin – past where I had made the fire bed for my mother. Sat down under one of the three ponderosas and started crying again. Cried for all the times I never cried. Cried like my mother used to, when she'd get filled up with crying.

Then, sitting under the ponderosas, there was a flash of light, and somebody was standing next to me. I turned to look, but my eyes couldn't see. What my eyes saw was me flying, the way you do when you're in fever, or when you dream.

Then I knew. The spirit of that mountain had snagged me. Was making me think that what I was doing was what I thought I was doing.

What I thought I was doing was hating Billy Blizzard because he'd killed my mother, all the while wanting to kill me one Alma Hatch.

What I thought I was doing was trying to find my mother, but where she had gone there was no place for me in her, and she had gone alone.

What I thought I was doing was being in love. What I was doing was just like every other sorry man I'd ever known. Running from one woman to another. Running from mother to wife. Head still up one woman's cunt while stuck like a dog's dick fucking in the other.

At the edge, where the rock stuck out the furthest, as far as you can go, the wind came down to me and blew on the grass around me, blew on my ears and my eyes. I could smell the wind. Smelled of me. I picked up a sharp piece of granite. Took the granite and scratched a circle all the way around me. I stood in the center of the circle and made it known, loud and clear, to the spirit of the mountain, Not-Really-A-Mountain, and to anybody else who wanted to hear, that from then on I was free of woman's hole. That I had pulled my head out. I had pulled my dick out. I was free, unencumbered.

And if, in fact, a man needed a woman, then I'd make a part of myself that woman for me.

I was back down in Excellent by ten o'clock. My customer was in the shed waiting. The night was clear, and the air was on your skin the way you can't tell where air ends and you begin. The moon and the stars were things I could reach up and grab and hold.

I took a rolled-up locoweed cigarette from my pocket. Lit it and pulled the smoke into my lungs.

Ida Richilieu was at her window looking down. My heart got big with longing for the rose color of her room, her deep feather bed, for her smell.

She'd have to get her own bath from then on.

At the other end of the hotel, Alma Hatch was standing at her window looking down. She waved. Easy as that.

The two women, in their windows, floating ovals above me in the night sky.

From deep inside me, language started coming up. Didn't know what it was I was going to say. Wanted to say something big to them, something that after saying it, nothing could be the same.

'Duivichi-un-Dua,' I said my Indian name out loud.

I opened the door to the shed. The man inside stood up. His face was in the shadows. But I knew who he was. For a dark while out in the shed, he was going to be me.

*

Ida Richilieu gave Alma Hatch room 11, my mother's room, and Alma started taking on customers right after that.

Screamed for every one of them.

Seems everybody wanted to fuck the wild woman who'd walked into the bar and bought herself a boy. Business picked up. For a while, men were standing in line all the way down the corridor.

'Even more popular at the beginning than you were,' Ida said to me.

Ida had started wearing her blue dress almost every night. Some sort of record in ovulating. When things were slow, Ida and Alma would sit up on the veranda, under the Indian Head Hotel sign, and talk like magpies making a nest, laughing their fool heads off, cussing, smoking locoweed, smoking stardust, drinking right out of the bottle. Men walking by would holler up. Sometimes Ida and Alma would holler back, leaning over the railing showing tit. Mostly they didn't holler back, though.

From the very first with those two, you could tell that Ida and Alma had something. And what they had, you didn't.

Hardest part, though, was when they sang the man-in-the-moon song together, at the piano, looking into one another's eyes.

The way those two carried on.

Mornings, when I'd make breakfast for me, sometimes they'd come stumbling down, hair all over the place, hardly anything on, the both of them waking up from the same bed. They'd plunk themselves down at the table, drink cup after cup of coffee, and smoke cigarettes the same way – each of them staring straight ahead, not mattering where.

That promise that I'd made on Not-Really-A-Mountain about being free of woman's hole hadn't been as easy to keep the next day after I woke up.

Truth was, I was still stuck in them both. They knew it, too. Knew I was theirs.

Killdeer

Story goes that Mrs. Alma Hatch was the Mrs. to a Mr. Aloisius Hatch, a Bible salesman from Minneapolis, Minnesota. She just married him to get away from her father, a scientist who took brains out of dead people and studied them under magnifying glasses.

Story goes that Aloisius Hatch was a big, barrel-chested man with hair covering his entire body except for his head. He did not drink or smoke. Did not take the Lord's name in vain.

Aloisius Hatch did have a weakness for women, though, especially when traveling, and especially in the afternoon when he'd knock on the door and only the lady of the house was home.

Story goes that the day the maiden Alma opened the front door of her scientific, godless home, it was in the afternoon. Her father was in the basement with bottles of things soaking and bubbling, cracking open human skulls.

When Aloisius Hatch saw the beautiful Alma – her long brown hair and those eyes – and when Alma looked down and saw Aloisius Hatch in his traveling, afternoon condition, it wasn't no time at all that the two of them were on the parlor floor.

'After all those years, I finally found the Lord,' is what Alma Hatch said.

They got married in Minneapolis, Minnesota – in a church. Wasn't long and Alma was selling Bibles herself. City to city and door to door.

Story goes, traveling had the same effect on Alma.

One day in Cincinnati, Ohio, with Aloisius Hatch door to door in the evens on the north side of the street, and Alma Hatch in the odds, on the south, Alma finished the block first and went looking for her husband. Looking through a window, she found him fucking with what the mailbox said was Notary Public. Upon seeing her Aloisius on top of Mrs. Public, Alma Hatch went back to the odds, found herself a bachelor gentleman at home with influenza, and set right in to curing his ills.

'From then on we had divided territories,' Alma Hatch said.

Last she'd heard of him was in Omaha, Nebraska. Sold him back her part in the business – two dozen Bibles with gold-leaf lettering – and, on the very same day, joined the National Audubon Society. Then joined the circus. Circus took her to Seattle, Washington, where Alma Hatch danced on the stage as Phoenicia – half bird, half woman.

'In front of an audience of thousands,' Alma Hatch said. 'Me up there on the stage, free as a bird, undulating my hips like Arabia.'

The town of Excellent, Idaho, couldn't talk about anything else but Alma Hatch – Alma Hatch and Ida Richilieu, that is. Thord Hurdlika, Doc Heyburn – every one of them at one time or another – tried to get me aside to hear the whole story.

I just told them it was all true – whatever they'd heard was true.

One day, Alma Hatch up and turned her hair blond – the color of white straw. Every man in that town lined up again for Alma Hatch. Had to fuck that white straw hair. Lines of them standing in the corridor. Sheriff Archibald Rooney came all the way from Sawtooth to investigate some damned thing. Or so he said. What he was doing was not what he thought he was doing. What he was doing was wanting to fuck Alma Hatch's new hair.

For me, trouble was – the biggest trouble was – I wanted to fuck that hair too.

*

The day I left Excellent, Idaho, was the day after the night that I woke up again with my heart pounding and my breath fast in and out.

It was early September and the evenings were still warm. I got up and walked straight to Ida's window so I could look at her sitting in her circle of light.

Ida was in her room with Alma Hatch. The two of them were laying on Ida's feather bed in the rose color. Both of them were naked and smoking and talking. There was no room in them for me and they had to be alone. They were touching each other nice, telling stories, talking secrets, talking things I didn't know about, needed to know about, and didn't.

Later on that night, when they were sleeping, I walked in Ida's room and stood by their bed. My promise to be free of woman's hole was a curse stuck in my throat. Went to where Ida kept her money in the wall. Took out what she owed me. Wrote a note that said I took what she owed me. Just signed it 'Mr. Shed.'

Put the money in a leather pouch and hung the pouch around my neck.

Out in the shed, I looked around. Wasn't nothing to take but me. I left my mother's photograph behind the mirror. Straightened everything out, smoothed the wrinkles out of the Hudson Bay on my bed. Closed the door behind me.

Didn't start the morning fires.

Wasn't daylight yet, but the sky wasn't black, was dark blue. Stars were tiny pieces of broken glass.

I started at the back porch. Walked on the rocks over Hot Creek, up past Dr. Ah Fong's and Chinatown, to the cemetery, to the fir tree in the field. Went up to the Dry House next. Came back around to the hot springs. Sat by the hot springs for a good long while. Then up to the nest, then down alongside the river and back into town, past the Mormon school and the Mormon church and the picket fence, past Moosman's farm, down Pine Street, past the ponderosa, and Ida's Place, and the barbershop, the American flag, the post office, Stein's Mercantile and North's Grocery, past Doc Heyburn's, Thord Hurdlika's, and Damn Dave's stables.

The Man Who Fell in Love with the Moon

Last of all I looked up at Not-Really-A-Mountain. I could stay or I could go, as far as that mountain was concerned.

I said goodbye.

Killdeer everywhere.

Book Two

There was a Time: Journey

Part One

Dellwood Barker

The sun was just starting up as I came to the crossroads to Gold Bar. Down the road, some miles, some hours later, I flagged the stage to Owyhee City. Had to ride on top because I was Indian. I attended to the luggage.

The road went back and forth onto itself all the way down. On a couple of switchbacks, the stagecoach swaying and groaning, I'd look over the edge down into forever, me gripping onto whatever I could. Truth is, though, I liked that I didn't have to sit inside with tybos. Liked sitting up on top. Liked looking over the edge.

I was Indian to me too.

At the halfway house, the stage stopped, and the four tybos in the coach got out to piss. I just stayed on top, laying on the luggage, and looked up at the sky.

By late afternoon, after we crossed Kally's River, the road started straightening out. Flat-topped mountains sloped their big dirt bodies down to trees that stood in families along the river. Mostly, though, there was space. Long, dry, empty space. And sky. Earth arms, earth legs rolled up to meet sky. Thighs, sloping valleys, breasts, elbows, hills – a heap of one big unmade bed as far as eyes could see.

The day was hot, and the farther down we went, the more sun

there was. Things smelled of hot pine tar, dust, sagebrush, horses running and sweating, and my own self sweating.

No doubt about it, I was meeting sky for the first time.

Changed horses at Five Corners. There was a trading post with a house behind it, a barn, a bunch of wild-looking tybo kids, and five roads that all came together for some damned reason right in the middle of the plain.

When I went to get off the stage, the driver told me to jump, but I wouldn't. Wasn't sure after I got myself into all that sky, I'd ever hit the ground. Might just float off.

Once I *was* on the ground, when I was walking, I made sure my one foot was all the way down on the ground before I lifted the other one up.

Walked that way all the way to the barn. By then, I was feeling better connected to the solid below me. Out behind the barn, I pissed on a corral post. Some of the other men were pissing too. A couple stood themselves so I could see. I knew who they were. Now and then, they'd look over to me as if I was just another corral post. Then they'd look at me hoping I'd catch them looking, them thinking my name was Behind-The-Barn as well as Out-In-The-Shed. The way the sun was – as far as I could tell in all the bright and no shadow – was around the time that Ida'd start her bath. She was probably sitting in front of the mirror right then. Those skinny bones of hers looking back at her. She'd be wondering which dress it was that night, smoking, deep-inhaling on her cigarette, swirling whiskey around in the shot glass.

Me, I was pissing on a corral post, somewhere – somewhere that wasn't there. Couldn't even tell if there had ever been a mountain, let alone a town called Excellent with a woman sitting in it, in her room in front of her mirror in a pink hotel.

She'd wear the blue one. She'd think I was coming back and she'd wear the blue one.

When I went to get a drink of water in the trading post, I was an Indian again, and had to drink out of the spigot in the back. The water tasted the way everything else looked: flat. No chokecherry bushes, no pine trees or spruce or fir, no up and down, and no big granite boulders in that water. I splashed the water on my face and wet back my hair. At my feet, the dusty ground had big dark wet spots.

I settled back into my place on top of the stage. The driver yelled, 'Giddyap!' and snapped the reins. The fresh horses pointed down a road you could see for as far as there was ahead. At sunset, the horses headed right into the sun. The flat-topped mountains, somewhere along the way, had sunk into the ground, leaving only the flat. Flat, sagebrush, jackrabbits, and bitterroot – not one tree.

I was a bird flying low, an Alma Hatch bird flying into the place ahead, to the edge, where things hadn't happened yet.

Purple and pink and red and yellow in the sky, the earth dark. It was my face, those colors; my hair, my eyes, the dark. Me the breathing wind.

Before the sun had set, before my face rolled back into my hair and all there was was my dark eyes, I knew. Knew what I had to do.

Had to find my mother's people.

And the buffalo.

Find out what my Indian name, Duivichi-un-Dua, meant.

Who I was to have this name.

*

The Syringa, in Owyhee City, the first town we stopped in, was twice as big as Ida's Place, full of people – men, some women not even whores in the saloon drinking, too. It was a big, bright place with a chandelier made out of a wagon wheel with oil lamps on

93

the spokes hanging from the ceiling. I knew it was a chandelier, even though I'd never set eyes on one, because I'd learned to spell the word. Ida Richilieu had taught me to spell *chandelier* even though it was a French word, because Ida planned to buy one some day.

'A big French chandelier with crystals hanging all over on it,' she said. 'And since a chandelier's going to be hanging above your head every day, you got to know how to spell it.'

While I was standing on the front porch of the Syringa scrutinizing, a cowboy came out of the swinging doors and ran into me. Nearly knocked him over. His hand went straight to his six-shooter.

My feet started in on the runs, but I didn't run. I looked my eyes into his eyes. They were green. Nice big green eyes on the cowboy, him looking otherwise tired, dirty, and whiskey for breath.

Then my ears heard my mouth asking him this: 'Is that chandelier inside there a French chandelier?'

The cowboy looked at me like I wasn't speaking English, his hand still on the handle of his gun, his eyes getting greener and greener.

Devil.

My feet turned and pointed in the best direction of getting out quick, and I was already on my first step when all of a sudden my body started getting bigger. Me standing on a saloon porch in some town called Owyhee City in the early evening – my legs, my arms, my head and hands – my whole body, bigger and bigger, more and more Indian, and more in this cowboy's way.

I was wishing hard that I was back in Excellent, that I wasn't getting bigger and I was back out in the shed in Excellent, behind the pink hotel on a mountain you couldn't even see from where I stood.

The cowboy kept his eyes on my eyes, pulled his shoulders back, and said, 'Salt Lake City.'

'Salt Lake City?' I said.

'The chandelier,' he said.

'The chandelier?' I said.

'Comes from Salt Lake City,' he said, and with that, gave me a wink, turned, and walked down the street.

I watched the cowboy until I couldn't watch him no more. When I looked back at my own self, I was my usual size.

I stepped out of the way of the swinging doors, but kept on scrutinizing. The working girls in the Syringa were all wearing the same kind of dress – black and red with red feathers. There was a stage, too. While I was watching, seven of them got up on stage and started dancing and kicking up, shaking their skirts – sticking their butts out to the audience – the men hooting and hollering, grabbing themselves.

Then, what my eyes saw the rest of me couldn't believe – Gracie Hammer and Ellen Finton – the both of them up on the stage, singing and dancing.

I started hollering and jumping up and down, waving at Ellen Finton and Gracie Hammer. Wasn't long before a tybo with a big mustache and several other mean-looking tybos came out the door. One of them grabbed me from behind and pushed me off the porch. Then there were tybos everywhere on me – one on each arm, a couple at my legs, another with his arm wrapped around my neck. Carried me to the back of the Syringa. They weren't especially rough about handling me. Didn't call me any names or hit me. Was more like I was like a cow out of pasture, or a dog that needed training – a chore for them, an interruption – and they wanted to get me over with so they could go back to the bar.

The tybos put me down behind the Syringa.

'Where people like you,' the one with the mustache said, 'are supposed to drink.'

'But me and Ellen Finton and Gracie Hammer are friends,' I said. 'Old friends,' I said.

The tybos acted as if there wasn't one word coming out of my mouth, them just talking to each other, only hearing each other, not me. I could feel my body starting to disappear, so I quick brushed myself off, walked up to the back window, laid my money down, and bought me a pint of whiskey. It wasn't the whiskey, it was buying the whiskey that kept me from disappearing.

The tybos left me alone after that, me sitting by the back door of a saloon on the ground under some trees with a pint of whiskey. I sat and drank and started thinking that maybe I was *thinking* I was talking language but really wasn't, the way I was before I was older, before my mother died, before I said, 'She was my spirit of things.'

So I made some words for my ears to hear, and truth was, I was talking just fine – unless my ears were in cahoots with my mouth.

What I figured was this: it wasn't me that was not talking. It was the tybos who were not listening.

Wasn't no different from anywhere else.

Folks not listening being what was no different.

Excellent, Idaho, being anywhere else.

I took another swig on the whiskey. A big black stink bug, heading west, held up its hind end and walked in front of my two feet. I asked the stink bug what you had to do to get yourself listened to. Asked why sometimes my body wouldn't stay its size, and why sometimes my body got so big and other times you couldn't even see me.

Stink bug kept walking. I kept watching – stink bug going west until I couldn't see stink bug no more, until all I could see was sunset. I bought another pint and swigged on it until my eyes saw something new: lights on the street.

If you stood on the front porch of the Syringa – which I was doing after the first half of the second pint of whiskey – where Union Street comes together with Grant Street, you could see lampposts on Grant Street go five of them straight ahead to the north of you, and on Union Street, five of them go to the west of you, then five more of them going east.

The lampposts in each direction were standing in rows all of them the same distance from each other one two three four five. The way the light was from the lampposts made it look like you were in one big room, the outside walls of the buildings on the street being the inside walls of the one big room. Then when you looked up, the ceiling was the huge sky.

Beyond the last lamppost, in each direction, where the light stopped, in the darkness, it was huge too, waiting for you: sky.

I walked to the end of each of the three rows of lampposts, counting to five every time, taking a swig at each lamppost, every time the houses and stores gathering themselves up close to the edge of the light.

When I started seeing double of the lampposts – ten instead of five in every direction that you looked – and when I started having a couple extra arms and legs too, I figured it was time to lay down.

At the edge of light on Union Street at both ends were Mormon churches. At the edge of light at the end of Grant Street was a Catholic church. I decided to sleep behind the Catholic church because it was the closest to the Syringa.

When I first walked out of the light and into the darkness, I thought I'd disappeared. Took me a while, but I found a gully. The gully wasn't that deep but at least you had something to lean your head against. I drank the rest of the whiskey in the dark looking to where you could see things on Grant Street in the light. There were crickets and wind in the grass, but mostly what you could hear was the Syringa – how people, mostly men, sound in bars. I was feeling pretty good. There was grass at my ears, and once my eyes got used to the darkness, they saw a tree right in front of me. Made me feel all the better. Tree stopped the sky some.

Then I heard a piano playing and a woman singing. The men-in-bars sound stopped. The wind stopped too, and the crickets. Her song was about her broken heart. She sang better than Ida Richilieu, her having those kinds of waves in her voice when she hit the high notes. But it was a dumb song about tybos kissing and fainting and carrying on.

Then, what my ears heard wasn't the woman singing. Was Ida Richilieu singing the man-in-the-moon song, in her blue dress in her pink hotel, singing all the way down to me.

Took me a long time to hear other things again – wind in the grass, wind in the tree, crickets, birds, ants in the grass digging dirt. I waited to hear my heart, for my breath in and out, but they were silent as the moon and big things that are far away.

I was just about asleep when a bell started ringing. Folks in the Syringa walked out into the lighted street; some got on their horses and rode off, a couple of them stood in the street talking. Two guys tried to hold one another steady as they walked, but they both ended up falling down, getting back up again, falling down.

The people in the light of the lampposts – I scrutinized their human-being stories, tried to hear what words they were saying to each other. Ida would have known about each one of them, known what dress to wear for them, what to write down in her book about them.

Wasn't long before the street was empty. Some people left together, some alone – out of the light and into darkness. Where there had been human beings now there weren't.

Made you wonder.

I closed my eyes then, and told myself that I would dream somebody back into the light – somebody special – so I could watch them and know their story. My mother, Buffalo Sweets, walked into the lighted street. Her long black hair and red blouse, barefoot, her leather skirt. Ida Richilieu walked into the light wearing the blue dress. Alma Hatch glowing pink, smelling of roses. Billy Blizzard walked into the light all in black, wearing his red boots, wearing his devil ring.

I opened my eyes. I saw a man step out from the back door of the Syringa. When he opened the door there was a piece of light the size of the door in the darkness. He was talking to a woman. Ellen Finton, Gracie Hammer, maybe. He kissed the woman and closed the door, walked along the building to the front porch of the Syringa, lit a cigarette, looked both ways, and then stepped into the street.

My ears heard running horses behind me. I threw myself out flat in the gully, breathing dirt. They almost ran over the top of me, horse running horse feet, horse breathing all around, me covering my head, keeping my ass low.

Just as quick as the horses had come up behind me, they were gone in front of me. Then it was just me and the gully again. I looked up.

The man who had come out of the back door of the Syringa was the green-eyed cowboy who knew about the chandelier. He was running hell-bent up Union Street toward the Catholic church and me. The two men on horses were riding up fast behind him. One of the riders – the big one on the roan – reached down with his rolled-up lariat and smacked green eyes aside the head and knocked him down into the dirt of the street. Both the men jumped off their horses, horses not knowing which way to go, stirring up dust. They jumped on green eyes and beat him. I ran out, past the church, to the edge of the light. That's when I saw their badges – the big man the sheriff, the other man the deputy.

When the sheriff and the deputy got up from him, they stood and talked to one another, looking down at green eyes laying bloody in the street.

Then they threw green eyes over the saddle of the deputy's horse. The deputy led his horse, the sheriff rode his horse down Union Street, them following the lampposts, past the Syringa, down to the last lamppost to the edge of light and then into the darkness.

Back in the gully, what I was doing was wishing for more whiskey, and promising myself I would never dream up another person ever again, no matter what.

When I finally got my eyes to close again, when I finally went to sleep, what I dreamed was it was my own self the sheriff and his deputy were murdering.

Then what happened next.

What was staring me in the eyes when I opened them was the devil crossed over from the other side – bright and loud out of darkness, sun coming straight at me in the middle of the night, smoking fire.

The wheels of the iron horse went by my head no further than the length of a man not even my size. The ground was shaking, fire and brimstone coming up. Steam engine locomotive didn't even stop – just screamed through Owyhee City, through every muscle in my body, leaving me shaking from the devil and my pants full of shit.

I laid in the gully shaking and tried to think how Ida Richilieu or Alma Hatch would have handled my situation, but that only made me laugh thinking of either of them women having a load in their petticoats. I sat for a while, then I stood for a while.

I took the locoweed out of my pocket, took the leather pouch from around my neck with my money in it, and dug a hole in the gully and buried it all for safekeeping. Put a river rock over the buried place.

I walked, pretending I was just normal, to the horse trough in front of the Syringa. There wasn't a person on the street, but I knew that behind each window there were folks peering out at me, watching me walk like a man with his pants full of shit down their bright street in the middle of the night. I didn't know what I was going to do when I got to the horse trough. Seemed like my feet knew what they were doing, so I followed along. What my feet were doing was what any normal pair of feet would do – trying to get as far away from the shit in my pants as they could.

There was a damn lamppost bright as ever could be at the horse trough. Weren't any horses around to hide behind. Stood for a while looking into the water. Finally I figured I'd do things the way Ida Richilieu'd do them. I took down my pants, stepped out of them, and sat my ass down into the water. When I got that done, I stood up, dried off some, and then started scrubbing out my pants.

That's how I was standing – bare-assed, ringing out my pants – when the sheriff came up behind me.

At first, when I looked, I thought I was looking into the eyes of Billy Blizzard.

Sheriff didn't look anything like Billy Blizzard but my body thought so.

He was the devil, alright – my eyes seeing one thing, my heart another.

When he asked me my name I told him Aloisius Hatch. I was holding my pants in front of me. The sheriff was holding his gun in front of him.

'Hands in the air!' he said. I put my hands up. He pointed his gun at me down there and cocked it.

'Let's go!' he said.

Let's go was to jail on a side street off Union past the one

Mormon church. We walked, me ahead holding my wet pants, sheriff behind me with the cold steel barrel up against my ass cheek, through the light into darkness, down a hill, over the railroad tracks, to the jailhouse.

There was a kerosene lamp on his desk. The sheriff lit it once we were inside. Then he locked the door.

'Aloisius Hatch,' he said.

'Aloisius Hatch,' I said.

'Where you from, Aloisius Hatch?' he asked.

'Minneapolis, Minnesota,' I said.

'What's your occupation?' he asked.

'I don't know that word: *occupation*,' I said.

'Where you work,' he said.

'How do you spell it?' I asked.

'Don't fuck around with me,' he said.

'Bible salesman,' I said.

'Bibles?' he said.

'Bibles,' I said.

Sheriff told me to take everything out of my wet pants pockets. There wasn't anything in them so I pulled nothing out.

'No identification?' he asked.

I didn't know that word either, but I didn't ask him how you spelled it.

'Papers telling me who you are,' he said.

'No papers,' I said.

'Where's your ration ticket?' he asked.

Occupation, identification, ration.

'I don't know what that is,' I said.

'You're Injun, ain't you?' he asked.

'Irish,' I said.

'Irish,' he said.

'Irish,' I said.

'Any money, Aloisius?' he asked.

'Just ran out,' I said.

'Any Bibles?' he asked.

'Sold them all,' I said.

'What you doing in Owyhee City?' he asked.

'Passing through,' I said.

'Don't you know a curfew when you hear one, Aloisius Hatch? Don't they have curfews in Minneapolis, Minnesota?' he asked.

'No,' I said.

Sheriff told me to take my shirt off. I did. There I was standing in my boots. Then he told me to take them off. I took my boots off. He stood looking at me standing.

'There's a Bible in the cell right behind you,' he said, motioning me into the cell with his gun. 'I'm sure it'll make you feel right at home.'

'Can I have my clothes back?' I asked.

He slapped my chest with his open hand.

I thought maybe I'd kill the sheriff right then.

'You like that, don't you?' he said.

I didn't say anything.

'Get in there!' he said.

I walked into the cell. Sheriff turned the key in the lock of the cell door, put the key in his pocket, went to his desk, and blew the light out. He stood in the dark for some time, for a long time, breathing hard.

'You smell like shit, Aloisius Hatch,' the sheriff said. 'Injun shit!'

He unlocked the front door, walked outside, slammed the door, and locked the door behind him.

*

It was hot and dark and I was naked. I walked back and forth in front of the window, wishing the window was Ida's and I could look in on Ida and watch her writing in her circle of rose-colored light.

This time, it was the moon looking in the window. Moon outside watching me.

I sat in the corner, knees against my chest, and watched the window of moonlight move across the floor. When the window was just so, I fit my two feet and my two hands into the moonlight, no edge of dark touching.

The next morning, the sheriff hollered, 'Twelve o'clock!' when he walked in the jailhouse. The deputy was following the sheriff, carrying a tray.

'Deputy Jones, like you to meet Aloisius Hatch – Bible Salesman!' the sheriff said, and unlocked the cell door.

I couldn't tell if the sheriff was as big as I thought, or if the deputy was as little.

'He's Irish,' the sheriff said.

'That a fact?' the deputy said.

There was a piece of bread on the tray and a bowl of soup.

'Stand up, boy!' the deputy said. 'Let's see all that Irish of yours.'

I stood up. Three more men came in the jailhouse then. The sheriff introduced them: O'Reilly, O'Casey, and O'Brady.

'They're Irish, too,' he said.

'Can you do an Irish jig?' O'Brady asked.

More men came in the door. Wasn't long and the whole place was filled with men. When my mouth asked if I could have my pants back, my ears didn't know who was talking. The men laughed the way men laugh in bars. I had no idea what my body was going to do next, so I told my body I'd rather disappear than get big.

My body stayed the same. Everybody else changed, though. The men laughing changed into dogs barking.

'Ain't Irishmen got hair on their chests?' the sheriff asked.

O'Brady opened his shirt to a mass of red hair.

'Turn around, boy!' the sheriff said.

I turned around.

'No hair on his ass, either. Must be a bleeding Englishman,' one of them said.

'. . . English*woman*,' someone said.

'He still ain't answered me!' O'Brady said. 'Show us how you do an Irish jig!'

I jumped up and down some the way I'd seen Irishmen do drunk at Ida's Place, holding onto my balls.

'He got the feet right, but not the arms!' one of them yelled.

The deputy threw the bowl of soup in my face. 'Get the arms right!' he said.

I danced the Irish jig with my arms right.

'That sure as hell ain't Irish!' O'Casey said to O'Reilly, pointing at me bouncing up and down.

Dogs and dogs barking.

'Is he an Irish tenor?'

'No, he's an Irish setter, can't you tell!'

'Bark for us!'

'Sing us a song! Sing us a song!'

When I started singing, I didn't know what was going to come out, me never singing tybo out loud before. I closed my eyes and wrapped my heart around the song, same way the moon had wrapped my feet and hands the night before. Sang as if the song was my last singing, for Ida Richilieu, for Alma Hatch, for my dead mother, for me.

'Come take a trip in my airship and we'll visit the man in the moon.'

When I finished singing, it was so quiet. Wondered if I had been dreaming, things were so quiet. I opened my eyes. It was no dream. The men were standing, staring at me. They weren't dogs anymore, weren't barking. Just men standing and looking.

The sheriff came through the crowd and hit me square in the face. I fell to the floor. Then he kicked me in the stomach the way Billy Blizzard had kicked Ida Richilieu in the stomach.

I thought about the green-eyed cowboy getting beat up in the street the night before.

Maybe he *was* me.

Maybe this was a dream and all I had to know was how to wake up.

When I woke up I wasn't sure if I was woke up until I started feeling where the sheriff had hit me. I knew I couldn't be sleeping because if I was, then it was a nightmare, and nightmares – when they get that bad – always wake you up. I touched my face. My lips and nose were all crusty. I rolled myself into a ball, hands between my legs. The window of moonlight was on my knees and on the floor.

A hand reached into the moon on the floor.

Took me a while to believe my eyes. Took me a while to believe my ears:

'Fucking moon's getting full. Making folks crazy tonight. Sheriff's moon crazy as I've ever seen him. Full in the balls this month, the moon – and that's not good for you and me, us being in here, and him being out there and needing a man as bad as he does. If he don't get him one soon, he'll kill us for sure – well, *you* for sure, and maybe me too – course, the sheriff has no idea that he needs what he needs. He just hates Indians and loves guns and his Irish whiskey and his buddies because he thinks that's normal. Which, if you think about it, it is.

'Next month the moon's in the hips. We'd be better off if we was in here during the hips, but we're not and you got to begin where you are because before you take off on any wild-ass wishing you got to ground yourself, firm, in the dynamics of your situation.

'The situation is: we're in here, and he's out there. He's normal and the sheriff and we're not – that about sums it up.

'After that, moon's in the knees. When it's in the knees I'm always climbing rocks. Don't plan it that way, but always do – lava rocks – cold hard things that used to be hot and sticky. That's how sperm starts out. Put your hand down on your balls sometime and breathe up. You'll see. Starts cold in the balls but comes out hot. Last month moon was in the kidneys. Hard as hell to stay for any time on a horse. Good time to eat asparagus and piss every chance you get.

'I checked on the chandelier. Chandelier *is* from Salt Lake City. That's what it says on it on the bottom: Salt Lake City, Utah. You got a name? My name's Dellwood Barker.'

While the voice of him was talking at me, the face of him out of the darkness slowly took on the green-eyed cowboy I thought was beat to death the day before.

Every one of my muscles was telling me to turn snake through the bars, bird through the window, or turn gopher into the floor and out of there because, I figured for sure, who was talking to me was a ghost. Figured then that I was a ghost too.

'I was in the next cell today when they started in on you. Thought for sure you was lynched, you singing so pretty. Then tonight when they threw me in here with you, looked like you was dead. Figured they were going to pin you being dead on me. Now, I figure he wants us to fuck so he can watch. In any case, he's got something up his sleeve.

'You know you're lucky you're still alive, him hating Injuns like he does. Guess I'm lucky too – course we ain't out of here yet. You never can tell about Sheriff Ronald R. Blumenfeld.

'All kinds of stories about Sheriff Ronald R. Blumenfeld. Myself, I can vouch that most of them are true.'

I was hoping the stories about Sheriff Ronald R. Blumenfeld were only crazy stories told by crazy people.

'Let me see your face,' Dellwood Barker said.

I didn't move. Didn't want to show him anything. Then Dellwood Barker laid his face down into the window of moonlight on the floor. His shoulder touched my knee. He was warm – or cool – I mean he didn't feel dead; that is, unless I was dead too – the both of us dead. Figured if we both were dead, it'd be hard to tell what dead was.

I sat up and moved away from him touching my knee. I looked at Dellwood Barker then, his whole face laying in the window of moonlight. The only place on him that wasn't bruised, bloody, or hanging open was right up by his hairline.

Then, as I was looking at him, I scrutinized something was wrong. I put my hand in front of my left eye and closed my right eye. Couldn't see a thing. I was looking through one eye not two.

'Are we dead?' I asked.

His face in the window of moonlight looking at me said, 'No more than usual. All this stuff around us is just a dream we're dreaming anyway – a story we're telling ourselves.'

The face smiled. 'But we're alive, alright. I mean I'm the one here who's dreaming this dream. So, if I'm me then you must still be you.'

'I think maybe I'm you,' I said.

'No, *I'm* me,' he said. 'That's a basic dynamic of this situation and we got to keep that straight.'

'D . . Y . . N . . A . . M . . I . . C,' Dellwood spelled when I asked him, 'means how things are coming together.'

'I dreamed you up last night,' I said, 'and put you out in the light, but I didn't figure the sheriff and the deputy would beat you up like that. Really – I had nothing to do with that,' I said. 'Then today, while they were beating me, I thought maybe I was you last night only today.'

'Who *are* you?' he asked.

'Hard to say,' I said. 'Mostly I'm not me.'

'You mean if you're not you, then you're me?' he asked.

'No,' I said. 'The only me I know is not me. I must have been born that way, and so far living hasn't helped out any.'

Then I said it: 'Half-breed,' I said. Never said that word aloud before. Didn't know why I said the word then.

'Heard you was Irish,' Dellwood Barker said.

'Might be,' I said. 'Half of me. Your guess is as good as mine. All I know is it's tybo. Other half's Indian, alright – Bannock.'

'I should've figured,' he said.

'Figured what?' I said.

'That's what you're doing here,' he said.

'What's that?' I asked.

'Moon's got a hold on you. That Indian side of you's gotta figure out who the hell it is so you can figure out who it is you really are who's trying to figure it all out,' he said.

I thought for a while and then I said, 'Makes sense.' Then I said, 'It starts with a name.'

'Which name is that?' he asked.

'Got two of them,' I said. 'One that I know ain't me and that's the tybo one. Left that one back up on the mountain. Then there's the other one that *is* me, the Indian one, but I don't know what it means that I am.'

'What's the names?' he asked.

'Can't tell you,' I said.

'Why's that?' he asked.

'You might be the devil,' I said.

The whole time he was talking to me, Dellwood Barker was laying with his face in the window of moonlight, looking up at me. He looked away when I said that about him maybe being the devil, then looked back. Even though I could see his face clear, I couldn't tell what he looked like except beat up. I saw he was naked, too. Ida Richilieu would have called him parlor-sized.

'I'll just call you Aloisius, then,' he said.

'What's a curfew?' I asked.

'That bell you heard ringing last night. Means you got to be off the street and in your house, or inside somewhere, within a half an hour,' he said.

'C . . U . . R . . F . . E . . W,' Dellwood spelled.

'Why did *you* come out after the curfew?' I asked.

Dellwood Barker shrugged his shoulders. 'It was time to go,' he said. 'Don't much believe in other people telling me when things're right and when things're wrong. That's something that's always got me in trouble,' he said, and stopped for a while to think about what he had said. He let out a big sigh then. 'Oh, well,' he said. 'That's all water under the damned bridge. Now it's all up to Ellen and Gracie.'

'You kissed her in the back doorway after the curfew,' I said.

'That's her,' he said. 'Where was you?'

'In the gully,' I said. 'Ellen or Gracie?' I asked.

'Ellen,' he said. 'Know her?'

'No,' I said.

'Well, the plan is' – Dellwood Barker moved himself over closer and started whispering – 'Ellen and Gracie are going to break me out of here. Now that you're in here too, they're breaking the both of us out – but they don't know about you yet.'

'Why?' I asked.

'Why what?' he said.

'Why me too?' I asked.

'Need all the help we can get. Besides, the moon told me to,' he said.

'Told you what?' I asked.

'About you,' he said.

'What'd it tell you?' I asked.

'. . . *She*,' he said. 'Moon's not an it, she's a *she*.'

'What did she tell you about me?' I asked.

'Don't know yet, but it's a humdinger,' he said.

'When did she tell you?' I asked.

'Same time she was telling you about me,' he said. 'Just about killed the both of us though, hasn't she?'

'She sure has,' I said.

'That's a woman for you,' he said.

'Yeh,' I said, 'that's a woman for you.'

'Either Ellen or Gracie, or the both of them together's going to sneak out between customers sometime tonight and get my horse, Abraham Lincoln, and my dog, Metaphor, and be waiting out back with my gear. We're going to have to be ready for anything. You'd better get up and move around some. Pretty soon we're going to be running.'

'How're they going to get these doors unlocked?' I asked.

'Woman's intuition,' Dellwood said. 'Don't worry, they'll think of something.'

'Why's the sheriff hate you so much?' I asked, my legs trying to get up, my arms trying to help my legs.

'I'm just more me than most folks are, I guess. Sheriff Ronald R. Blumenfeld can't stand that. He's a Republican and Mormon to boot. Plays everything by the book. But what really did it was the painting.'

'The painting?' I asked.

'The one I painted of the moon that used to hang above the bar in the Syringa. Now and then I paint pictures – usually of the moon on the prairie. Well, this one I painted was of a bunch of buck-naked cowboys dancing drunk and crazy in the moonlight around a campfire. One of them cowboys – the one playing the fiddle with his own little fiddle hanging out – looked a lot like old Blumenfeld himself.'

'Why'd you come back to Owyhee City, then?' I asked.

'Was time to see my friends Ellen and Gracie again,' he said.

'Moon tell you to do that, too?' I asked.

'Yup,' he said.

'Just how *does* the moon go about telling you these things?' I asked.

'Moon language,' he said. 'Comes up from the heart. Sometimes from the balls. Either case, you just got to know how to listen.'

'What's the moon sound like when she's talking to you?' I asked.

'Like breathing,' he said, 'like your own heart beating.'

Then: 'Come here and I'll show you,' he said. 'Listen!'

When his hand touched the back of my neck, I was slow going down to him, his hand guiding me down, my face to the hair on his belly. I rolled my head over, my ear firm against his chest – ear skin to chest skin. In front of my good eye was his nipple, him slow breathing my head up and down. My own breath going through me fast, heart fast too, blood going down to balls and back up. After a while, though, the rhythm of my breathing and beating was same as him.

My ear pressed against him, I heard her – the moon. The full, gentle sound of the heart, of someone else there.

When I woke up, I was wishing I was back to sleep. In front of my good eye, just beyond Dellwood Barker's nipple, was Sheriff Ronald R. Blumenfeld.

'Shit-smelling Injun is a cocksucking Injun too, huh?' the sheriff said.

Although my head laying on Dellwood Barker had only to do with heart-listening and not cocksucking, I didn't try to explain. Dellwood didn't do any explaining either. He didn't stand up or try and cover himself. Dellwood just kept laying, stretched, his arms behind him, propping his head up.

'Cocksuckers!' the sheriff said. 'Obscene perverts,' the sheriff said.

'O . . B . . S . . C . . E . . N . . E,' Dellwood Barker spelled. 'Means something that gives you a hard-on when you hate hard-ons.

'P . . E . . R . . V . . E . . R . . T,' Dellwood spelled. 'Means being different – meaning not being Ronald R. Blumenfeld.'

Sheriff Blumenfeld walked to his desk, put the lantern on the desk, got some handcuffs out of the drawer, and threw the handcuffs into the cell. They landed at Dellwood Barker's feet.

'Handcuff the Injun to a bar on the window,' the sheriff said, pulling his gun out and cocking it.

Dellwood Barker got up and turned toward me. 'Trust me,' he said so only I could hear.

It was dark in that part of the jail, but I could see his green eyes. Dellwood started putting the handcuffs onto my wrist.

Trust.

I was handcuffed to the bars of the window.

I thought for sure that any second I was going to hear the big loud of a gun, but what I heard instead was the moon talking to me: my breathing, my own heart beating.

Dellwood Barker walked straight for the sheriff, no hesitation. Sheriff Ronald R. Blumenfeld started shaking and sweating. Dellwood Barker knelt down, grabbed the sheriff by the belt, and pulled him close to the bars. The sheriff pointed the gun barrel right at Dellwood's head – the gun still cocked – ready to blow red all over.

'A dying man's one last request,' Dellwood Barker said. 'You can't deny that, can you, Sheriff?'

Dellwood was undoing the sheriff's fly – and the sheriff was letting him – that is, until Dellwood got his hand in the sheriff's pants. That's when the sheriff pulled away – or started to.

'Come on, Sheriff, we've done this before,' Dellwood said. 'You can't stop now!'

Then, what I saw, I couldn't believe what I saw: Dellwood

Barker being an obscene pervert – doing the best job of cocksucking my good eye had ever seen. Was so good I wished my bad eye wasn't, so I could see more.

The sheriff's gun barrel started pointing every which way, but mostly at me. In fact, the sheriff fixed his eyes right on me, him moaning something about a big naked Indian. I figured it was me he was talking about, so I stepped out of the shadow and into the light coming from the lantern on the desk, to give the sheriff a better view of what he was moaning about.

Then, from out of nowhere, Ellen Finton was standing right next to the sheriff.

'Sheriff Ronald R. Blumenfeld!' Ellen cried. 'Folks are murdering each other at the saloon. You must come quick!'

Coming quick was what the sheriff was doing.

Ellen reached right over and took the gun out of his hand.

'You men!' Ellen cried. 'How can you think of sex at a moment like this? Innocent people are suffering sorely from the lack of law and order, and here you are taking sexual advantage of helpless prisoners!'

Ellen pulled a hanky out from between her tits, wiped the sheriff off, and had him back in his pants and buttoned up before you could say, 'Praise the Lord.'

Sheriff Blumenfeld ran for the door. That was when Ellen slipped the keys to Dellwood.

'Handcuff key's on there too,' she said. 'Should've bought you some clothes, but I just didn't think about it. God bless!'

Ellen Finton looked right at me then. 'Shed,' her lips moved my name but did not speak it. Big tears came up in her eyes. She winked and threw her head back, and didn't stop to take a breath.

'How could you do a thing like that, Sheriff?' Ellen Finton yelled after the sheriff, who was running up Union Street. 'With a *man*, no less, right when your community needed you most!'

Dellwood was out the door first, me following. Sure enough, Abraham Lincoln was waiting for us out back, and Dellwood's dog, Metaphor. Dellwood jumped on Abraham Lincoln, then gave me a hand up.

As we passed by the window of the jail, Dellwood reined up on Abraham Lincoln and started searching through the bedroll lashed to the saddle. Dellwood pulled a coin out of the bedroll, a shiny dime, and threw it into the jail window.

'Always got to thank the place where you've been,' Dellwood said. 'Got to give it a gift, whether the place was good for you or not. Dime's usually my gift. Dime to me is like the moon.'

We ran down Union Street, lampposts going by one two three four five, to the gully behind the Catholic church for my locoweed and leather pouch of money, then us riding out of the light altogether, me and Dellwood Barker on Abraham Lincoln and Metaphor running into the night, the moon putting her light on things, making them shine: silver on the bridle, the horse sweat soaping up, Metaphor's eyes, and the skin of Dellwood Barker's back and arms. There were rocks that were shining too, and long empty flat places. Shadows – sagebrush and bitterroot, boulders, now and then a tree: they were all dark strangers waiting for us, watching us run.

Forever we ran, caught up by the sky, rolled into something round, far away, silent, reflecting light, passing through darkness.

*

Just before dawn we smelled the river. My good eye could make out some foothills. Dellwood started reining in and we finally got Abraham Lincoln stopped. I fell off more than got off. My whole body was sore – especially my ass from riding bare against horseflesh and saddle blanket.

Dellwood Barker pulled the saddle off Abraham Lincoln, and the bridle, tied the reins loosely around the horse's neck, and led Abraham Lincoln through a stand of willows.

'Kally's River,' Dellwood said.

While Abraham Lincoln drank, Dellwood Barker scooped river onto the horse and talked as if he was talking to a person, thanking Abraham Lincoln for doing a good job of running with such a heavy load. Metaphor sat patiently near, waiting for Dellwood to notice him, whining a little, and moving closer to Dellwood.

The moon was big in the sky, a fruit so ripe it was dripping. The sky was more dark blue than black and the stars were specks of fool's gold up in that dark water. I walked to a place on the river where the moonlight was headed straight for me. I sat down on a rock and put my feet in. The river running over the rocks was the best sound I'd ever heard. I put that sound in my head instead of what was in my head – a lot of complaining about my sore body and bad situation.

Once my feet got used to the river, the rest of my body wanted in too, so I waded to a place I could sit in up to my armpits. I laid my head back ear deep and listened to the river and the rocks in the river.

On the bank, Metaphor was lapping up a drink. Dellwood knelt next to Metaphor, bent down, lapped up river same way as his dog, then stood, waded in, and sat himself down right next to me.

The thing about Dellwood was his skin – so white, and his black hair, some grey, growing out of his white skin. I didn't look at his eyes – they were too big for me, too green.

I already knew a lot about his body. He was, I figured, a good forty years old. Hard living was on him in the lines of his face, knife scars on his belly, and a whip that had got to his back. His long cowboy arms and big shoulders needed fattening up. His legs were big and big muscles in his butt. Down the front of him was black hair that went all the way down to where there was lots of hair, that dick of his poking out now and then into the moonlight.

Something else about Dellwood's body – I'd forgotten with all the commotion – and sitting leg to leg with him in Kally's River, my nose reminded me what that was.

Being the business I was in, men smelling wasn't news to me, but Dellwood Barker's smell was. As it is with most men, his smell was mostly his breath and his sweat – the cigarettes he rolled and whiskey, and beer when he drank beer. As it is with most men, his sweat smelled of come and asshole, even after a good wash.

How Dellwood Barker smelled was the same as most men only, with him, it was more – a cellar full of rotten apples or spuds, or the insides of a deer when you cut the deer open. Horse's breath after the horse eats pears. Strong the way moss smells when you pull moss out of a spring.

Smelled how I figure a bull felt wrinkling up his nose for a cow in heat – something so raunchy you just had to go back again.

Wasn't long before Dellwood's smell and me thinking of Dellwood's smell, Dellwood's leg against my leg, and moon on the flow of river over us got to be too much for me. I managed to get myself up and back to the riverbank, where I stood, and then Dellwood stood, until the shivering stopped.

Dellwood threw a dime in the river, and once we got back in the saddle, Abraham Lincoln wasn't running anymore – in fact, he was barely walking. Still, it was all me and Dellwood could do to hang on. Metaphor still had plenty of energy, though. He'd run ahead or take off after a jackrabbit.

'Only time that dog gets tired is when he's bored,' Dellwood Barker said. 'He sure ain't bored tonight.'

We stayed with the river. Sometimes I was asleep, both arms around Dellwood Barker, my mouth open slobbering down his back. Sometimes Dellwood was asleep, leaning forward, me holding the reins, keeping him from falling off. Sometimes Abraham Lincoln was asleep. There was a couple times I woke up and all three of us were snoring, standing out in all that flat I had no idea where.

When I woke up, we were at a dogleg in the river. Dellwood was awake too. We were all awake. I dismounted first and then helped Dellwood off. We walked through some tulies to a sandy place by the side of a hot spring not far from the river. The sun was just starting over a hill and things were pink and gold with morning. Dellwood unsaddled and unbridled Abraham Lincoln again, took his lariat and made a loose wrap around the horse's neck, and set Abraham Lincoln to grazing. He pulled a leg bone of a sheep out of his pack and gave it to Metaphor. That dog set right to eating, growling while he ate. I stretched out on the sand, my muscles feeling good, not all cramped up.

'I got some friends over on the other side of that hill,' Dellwood said. 'I'm going to see if I can get us some food and clothes from them. I figure it's best for you to stay here. Easier to explain one naked man than two.'

'Need any money?' I asked.

Dellwood smiled a little bit. 'Well, the folks on the other side of the hill are generous, but maybe I could get you a horse outfitted if I had some.'

I figured it was time.

'They call me Out-In-The-Shed,' I said. 'My Indian name is Duivichi-un-Dua. Is thirty dollars enough?'

Dellwood hunkered down and started moving his finger through the sand. It was getting light and more and more I was thinking about him and me being naked. I was feeling better, so that meant my dick was feeling better too. I was afraid my dick would start feeling better too much. I pulled my legs up and put my arms around my knees.

'Out-In-The-Shed,' he said. 'Nice name, although it's kind of long. The other one's real nice too, but it's too difficult for me. How about if I just call you Shed?'

'Shed's fine,' I said.

'Thirty's probably enough,' he said.

I counted forty from my pouch.

'Maybe I should call you "sir" with all that money of yours,' he said.

'Sir Shed,' I said.

'Mind if I ask you how you got all that money?' he asked.

'Earned it,' I said.

'How'd you do that?' he asked.

'Out in the shed,' I said.

'Oh,' he said. 'Out in the shed.'

The sun was up full by the time Dellwood Barker walked his white ass over the side of the hill. Abraham Lincoln stayed behind and so did Metaphor, even though Metaphor didn't want to. I walked over to get acquainted with the dog a little better, but Metaphor just grabbed onto his sheep bone, showed his teeth, and growled.

The sound of the river was telling me to walk closer, so I did. On the opposite bank, at the base of the hill, was a family of pine trees – friends of mine I had sorely missed – didn't know how much until right then when the wind blew through them.

I jumped into the river – a narrow channel, and deep. I swam to the bottom, my good eye open, watching my arms move in front of me, watching the sunlight in the water, the colors, down to the mud, then back up to where the warm water flowed in from the spring.

On the bank, I crouched on a big white round rock. The sun

was in my eye, the way the moon had been the night before when me and Dellwood sat in the same river. I was gooseflesh, shivering again, my nose running, me breathing hard, rounding my body like a rock, sitting on a rock.

That's when my good eye saw the trout in the shallows. Soon as I saw the trout, I grabbed a rock and threw it. Stunned him the first time, with the second rock I killed the trout.

I hadn't eaten for a time I hadn't counted, but when I did count, it had been three days and back in Excellent.

'Three days!' I said out loud. Seemed more like three months.

I held the trout up like maybe my grandfather had, or my grandmother, on my mother's side, and I thanked the Great Mystery, for the trout, my food, using words I wasn't sure the Great Mystery listened to – tybo words.

When I finished my prayer, there was only me alive and the trout dead standing in the river. I told the trout that I was sorry and that someday I was going to be dead too. I packed mud around the trout and pine needles like I'd seen my mother do, started the fire like she started fires.

When the trout was cooked, I ate the trout, enjoying the eating – gave Metaphor a couple bites. The bones and guts I gave back to the river.

I fell asleep and dreamed of the trout. I was the trout swimming.

Abraham Lincoln started nudging me and I woke up. He was at the end of the lariat, looking for more grass. I moved him upriver – I mean, *her* upriver. Abraham Lincoln was a mare. I wondered why a man would call his mare horse a man's name – a president's name like Abraham Lincoln.

Then I'd heard tell crazier stories.

I jumped in the water again and swam to the other side. Metaphor jumped in after me, finally taking a shine to me the way I had to him. We climbed the hill together, and when we reached the top – where I had last seen Dellwood Barker's white ass go over – there was a big lava rock sticking out of the earth. I climbed the rock, helping Metaphor up, and we sat down.

There, just below me in the valley, surrounded by a brick wall, were three large brick buildings – two houses and a church with a cross on it.

Saint Francis of Assisi is what I could read written above the church door. The river flowed around the hill in front of the Saint Francis of Assisi, and started into white water and spray going down over the side into a big waterfall making a rainbow.

Around the outside of the Saint Francis of Assisi's wall were square patches of green things growing. Was green around the river too, especially by the waterfall. Everything else was the color of the earth – red to brown – except for where the sagebrush was silver-grey and rust.

As far as I could see in every direction, the mountain valley spread out flat and the flat was big. Along the horizon, purple buttes stuck up, fingernails or teeth. Nothing was as big, though, as the sky hanging blue – big blue – above it all.

The whole time we sat on the hill, though, we didn't see one soul stick his head out of the buildings or walk outside the wall.

Was something else we didn't see.

No buffalo – only the empty sloping earth, the white water, the wind, Metaphor panting, and moon talk: myself breathing, my own heart beating.

Abraham Lincoln was laying next to the water and looking at the water as if she was thinking about something when we got back. I sat next to her and Metaphor sat next to both of us. Dellwood's gear was laying rolled up next to Abraham Lincoln.

I thought, what the hell – maybe I could get to know his human-being story better if I looked inside, so I opened up his bedroll and took a look.

His bedroll was a piece of canvas with sewn-in pockets. In the pockets was a bowie knife, a bar of soap, a coffeepot, a tin cup, a frying pan, a tin plate, a can of coffee, tobacco, tobacco papers, and stick matches.

Then I found something I knew right off what it was: his medicine bag – an eagle feather, an owl feather, a rattle, an eagle-bone whistle, and a leather bag filled with dimes.

Besides his bedroll, there was also a bag of oats, a canteen of water, his .22 rifle, his six-gun and his holster.

Then I saw the book.

The book was all beat up and barely hanging together. Had a piece of string tied around it. On the cover was a diagram of the moon. The name of the book was *Secrets of the Moon*. I undid the string and turned the pages. Each page had something different about the moon on it: phases of the moon, eclipses of the moon, moon in Scorpio, moon in Cancer, moon in Pisces, moon in the rest of them – twelve altogether – one for each month. The book had things to eat, things not to eat, when to eat them and not eat them. When to have sexual intercourse and when not to. When the moon was right to take an enema, when to plant root vegetables, cut your hair, and even when to clean your ears.

Another part of the book was called 'Lunar Lunacy' and that meant that the moon could even make you crazy sometimes, and during those times – which were a lot of times – you had to stay away from strong drink and the company of women who were having their period.

I was busy reading about the times not to have sexual intercourse – as far as I could tell, that day that I was reading wasn't one of them – when something fell out from the pages.

I picked it up. It was a photograph. It was a photograph of a woman. It was a photograph of an Indian woman.

It was the photograph of my mother.

My mother, inside Dellwood Barker's book about the moon, looking up out at him.

First thought I had was Dellwood Barker had gone to behind the mirror out in the shed back of Ida's pink hotel in Excellent, Idaho, and stole the photograph.

Then I turned the photograph over. From what I could read with my good eye, the writing said: *To my loving husband, 1881.*

The sun was setting by the time Dellwood Barker got back. Metaphor and Abraham Lincoln heard him before I did. What I heard was a horse crossing downriver, then a high whistle.

'Ain't you a sight for sore eyes,' he said.

Dellwood was a sight for my sore eye too – full of life, wearing pants and boots and a straw hat. 'This here's your horse,' he said to me, and then to the horse he said, 'Horse, this is . . . Can I tell him your name?' he asked.

'Sure,' I said.

'. . . this here's Shed, horse. Later on he'll tell you all the rest of his names,' Dellwood said.

I looked into the horse's eyes. Loved him right off. Never knew I could be so good as to have a horse beautiful as that – a big black stallion with devil eyes.

'Half Morgan, half quarter. Twenty-seven dollars and four bits including blanket and bridle. Those Franciscans drive a hard deal. Here's your change – twelve dollars and fifty cents.'

He put the money in my hand. 'Count it!' he said. 'They gave me some boots and a pair of pants and a hat – a shirt too. I figure you can wear the shirt and the hat too if you want it. I doubt if the boots or the pants'll fit you. You're a damn big boy,' Dellwood said, looking me up and down.

'What you going to call your new horse?' he asked.

'Princess,' I said.

'But he's a stallion,' Dellwood said.

'Abraham Lincoln's a mare,' I said.

'Fair enough,' Dellwood said.

The black of the horse was almost blue. I walked over to him, put my hand on his neck, and laid my head on his shoulder. Ear flesh to horseflesh, you could hear his horse heart beating. I knew right off he was going to love me too.

Was a lot to handle, being loved and loving back somebody as big and blue and wild as that.

I led Princess over to Abraham Lincoln and those two had a little round at first, Abraham Lincoln pulling her ears back and farting some, Princess prancing around, showing off, Abraham Lincoln baring her teeth and kicking up. Metaphor wasn't ever far away, taking it all in, sitting in one place not moving, his tail beating the dirt.

'Those two horses are going to fuck like crazy someday,' Dellwood said, looking green eyes straight into my good eye. 'They both know it. It's simple – what makes you hard you go after,' Dellwood said. 'All they're waiting for is the right time.'

'Simple,' I said.

'Ain't it the truth!' Dellwood said.

The truth wasn't simple, though: I thought Dellwood Barker was my father.

What I was doing was making him hard, and what my father was going after was me.

Then I thought: If Dellwood Barker really was my father, he wouldn't be going after me. Sons don't make fathers hard – besides, not one single part of Dellwood Barker's body looked like me – hair, eyes, skin, dick – nothing. Probably what happened was him and my mother had ended up getting a divorce.

Truth was, though – no matter what I thought, what my heart was saying was Dellwood Barker was my father.

Truth was, the light coming out his green eyes was making me hard too.

We both knew it. Me and Dellwood Barker were going to fuck like crazy. All we were waiting for was the right time.

I tied Princess alongside of Abraham Lincoln while Dellwood Barker started undoing his bedroll. He pulled out the coffeepot and the frying pan, leaving the piece of canvas with sewn-in pockets laying open. I could see just the top of *Secrets of the Moon* sticking out of the one pocket.

'Throw me over the side meat from out of that gunnysack, would you?' Dellwood yelled.

I opened the sack and there were two big loaves of bread, a couple of tomatoes, a dozen or so of potatoes, a big hunk of cheese, and some apples. I ate one of those apples in no time and then I ate another. At the bottom of the sack, I found the side meat, and a corked green bottle with a brown-looking liquid in it.

'Bring that bottle over here too, would you?' he said.

I brought him the side meat and the bottle. Dellwood took a swig, but didn't offer me any. I thought, what the hell – took the locoweed from out of my pouch and rolled it up, lit it, smoked some, and then gave it to Dellwood Barker. He took the cigarette, looked at me first, and then inhaled. We smoked it down without talking. When the burning part got too close down to our fingers, Dellwood ate it.

The locoweed kicked in powerful and things got the way they get when it's good smoke and a clear quiet night. Besides the sound of the side meat frying, there was the sound of the horses, the river, and a coyote howling now and then. There was the sound of the moon talking; my breath, my heart.

I put on the shirt. It wasn't a shirt but a nightshirt – the kind Ida Richilieu made her customers wear if they were spending the night and not wearing long johns. The nightshirt was white, and went all the way down to my knees. The sleeves were too long so I rolled them up. Moon was all over that shirt, making it glow.

I walked over to the river, bent down, splashed river onto my face, cupped my hands and brought river and moon to my lips and drank. I stuck my head in the river.

'Soup's on!' Dellwood Barker yelled.

When I got to the fire, 'You look like a ghost,' is what Dellwood said. He swigged on the bottle then handed it to me.

'Brandy,' he said. 'Best you can get. Those guys at the Saint Francis of Assisi ain't dumb.'

I took a drink of the best-you-could-get brandy and what my throat said was: *firewater*. I tried not to look too dumb choking on that stuff, so I took another drink.

When I was done coughing, Dellwood handed me the plate heaped up with spuds, tomatoes, and the side meat. He ate out of the frying pan, dipping hunks of bread into the grease. We shared the cup with coffee in it like we were sharing the best-ever firewater in the green bottle. I was finished eating first, so Dellwood gave me some more of his food.

'Is that Catholic?' I asked.

'What's that?' he asked.

'The Saint Francis of Assisi,' I said.

'Yup,' he said. 'Saint Francis of Assisi was a Catholic saint. He could talk to animals and they'd talk back.'

'Can all Catholics do that?' I asked.

'Nope,' he said. 'Only Saint Francis.'

'They seem like nice friends to have,' I said.

'Yup,' he laughed. 'You should have seen the faces on them this morning when I knocked on their door. They were the Good Samaritan right off. Father Jack, who's the head one of them down there, took one look at me and announced that I should be taken to his room immediately for his own personal care.'

'Have you known those Franciscans long?' I asked.

'Yup, we're friends from way back when I showed them how to keep jackrabbits and deer out of their fruit trees and vegetable garden. Of course, those Franciscans thought there was some sort of scientific explanation for what I was doing, but there wasn't. I was just doing what Saint Francis used to do – talking to the animals, giving them presents, asking them to kindly stay away from the Franciscans' fruit trees and vegetable garden.

'After about a week, the animals finally listened to me. Takes a while to express yourself just right so that you can get yourself heard.

'When Father Jack saw what I had done, he was strongly taken to me because of the success of my efforts.

' "Is there any way I can repay you, Dellwood?" he asked – Father Jack's this big lumbering guy with a red beard and beautiful feet. I thought for a while and then said, "Sure, Jack" – I just call him Jack – then I told him what I wanted.

'He had to pray some first – what I wanted being a sin and all for him – but, as it turned out, a little sinning was just what Jack needed. Then there was the chastisement. Did him a world of good.

'C . . H . . A . . S . . T . . I . . S . . E . . M . . E . . N . . T,' Dellwood spelled, 'means getting spanked for liking to fuck.

'Ever since then,' Dellwood said, 'you might say that me and Jack have had a real fine and special kind of friendship two or three times a year.'

The whole time Dellwood was talking, I was watching his mouth. Figured that any kind of words could be coming out of his mouth, but it was those particular words that were coming out of his mouth. Figured the words he was using were those words because he was who he was.

Dellwood Barker's human-being story, and the words he used to tell his story, were pretty much the same as with other tybo folks. How Dellwood Barker put his words and his story together, though, was another story altogether.

I didn't know what to ask him first – to just flat out ask him if he was my father, or to ask him where he'd learned to suck cock like he'd done Sheriff Ronald R. Blumenfeld – because I was the only one out in the shed I'd ever known. Then too I wanted to ask him if talking to animals was the same thing as moon talk. Wanted to tell him that the moon had always talked to me. Wanted to tell him about killdeer. Wanted to ask him how you spelled *Metaphor* and what *Metaphor* meant.

Dellwood Barker pulled out some of his own locoweed, rolled it up, lit it, sucked on it, and then handed the cigarette to me.

When it got time to ask him one of the questions I had wanted to ask, I had forgotten all of them. When I woke up, the fire was almost out and the dishes were cleaned up, the moon was low on the horizon, Metaphor was sleeping with his head on his paws, I was laying on my saddle blanket, and Dellwood Barker was laying on his saddle blanket next to me. This time his ear skin on my nightshirt, the both of us breathing, hearts beating. I had a powerful urge for a manly hard-to-hard with him. My dick was standing up the nightshirt and waving *please* to me from over on the other side of Dellwood's head.

Father.

Dellwood Barker then took a deep snoring breath and turned over, snuggling into me. His face was a child sleeping. A child – human being same as me. What was beating his heart was beating mine: *brother.*

That's how I spent the rest of the night: my dick waving please, my head saying father, my heart laying up to his heart beating brother, brother.

More than anything, though, what my feet were telling me to do was run.

Next morning, the first thing I heard was Dellwood Barker whistling while he made the fire. I pretended to be asleep, wishing I had a blanket to cover me up. When the coffee was ready he brought me the cup.

'Can't sleep all day,' he said. 'We sure as hell got a posse after us!'

I sat up and drank the coffee, me trying to get myself into one body that I could recognize, when Dellwood Barker said all at once:

'You ought to come with me to the ranch where I work in Montana – the Sage Hill Ranch over near Livingston. I'm the foreman. Big Injun buck like you'd be a good hand. You could stay until things cool down with the law and all. There's some nice folks up there, and I'd enjoy the company.'

*

We rode through country that sloped up and down, big piles of lava rock sticking themselves up out of the slopes, the very tops of mountains. The farther we traveled south and east the piles got bigger and higher and more of them.

'Craters of the Moon dead ahead,' Dellwood yelled. 'They'll never find us here.'

That whole day, wind beat the hell out of us. Me and Dellwood had to wrap up into ourselves, and when we needed to, cupped our hands to holler back and forth, him mostly at me about where we were going.

I liked not having to talk, though, because I had some thinking to do about Dellwood Barker, about how I was feeling about Dellwood Barker being my father. The wind, the sunny blue sky, the dirt and sand flying against me, all made it a perfect day for thinking.

We stopped around noon at a place Dellwood called Dry Creek. After we filled the canteens, there wasn't much water left in the creekbed at all – was that dry. We sat in the shade of one of the piles of lava rock, shielded from the wind. That's when I told

Dellwood about the buffalo and my Indian name and that I had to find out what it meant.

'Watch for rattlers,' is what Dellwood Barker said first. 'You want to carry my rifle?'

'No,' I said.

Then he said, 'There ain't no buffalo.' He spit dry when he said it, then wiped his sore mouth tenderly with the red bandanna he had around his neck. 'Disappeared fifteen or twenty years ago,' Dellwood said. 'White man killed them all.'

'Got to be some somewhere,' I said. 'You couldn't kill a thousand buffalo.'

'A thousand! Hell, it's more like a million!' Dellwood said.

'A million?' I said.

'Maybe more,' he said. 'There were herds that were ten miles wide and twenty-five miles long.'

A million buffalo.

'Heard tell of two places, though, where you can still find the buffalo. One of them's Fort Lincoln.'

'Where's that?' I asked.

'Might just be the place where you can kill two birds with one stone,' he said. 'Just south of here four or five days' ride on the Bannock Shoshone reservation.'

'That's where I'm going, then!' I said. 'Where's the other place?'

'We'll be there tonight,' he said.

'Craters of the Moon?' I asked.

'Yup,' he said. 'There's a special breed of buffalo there. Most times they're hard to see.'

'Hard to see?' I said.

'Hard to see,' he said.

'How many times have you seen them?' I asked.

'Only once,' he said, 'a long time ago.'

The sun was at about three o'clock when I pulled Princess to a stop on a high place. I took a look around. Far as you could see was big bubbles of black hard lava rock going up high as mountains, some caved in deep down the way the other ones had exploded up. You could see how, when the lava was hot, it had flowed over the land, rivers of the stuff – red-hot rivers now dark and hard like scabs on a big burn wound – cliffs of scabs, of valleys – forever.

Dellwood Barker brought Abraham Lincoln up next to me and Princess, stood up in the stirrups, stretched his back, and said as if it was his own: 'Craters of the Moon! Most beautiful place in the whole world. Only rattlesnakes and bugs live here and an occasional jackrabbit – nobody else can.'

'How about the buffalo?' I asked. 'The special breed of buffalo?'

'Them too,' he said, and then he said, 'You got to be careful. You can get up and walk ten feet away and get yourself lost forever. There's skeletons all over in here of folks trying to get themselves out. Me and Abraham Lincoln know it like the back of our hand.'

My eyes were watching Dellwood Barker's mouth move again, watching his lips make his words.

The woman in the photograph is my mother, were the words on my tongue, on my lips. The truth, *Father,* just about ready to jump out my mouth to his ears.

'Where we're going I call Buffalo Head,' Dellwood said. 'Nobody's seen this place besides me, Abraham Lincoln, Metaphor, and Berdache Indians in the old times.'

'Berdache Indians?' I said.

'B . . E . . R . . D . . A . . C . . H . . E,' Dellwood spelled. 'Tell you what it means later.'

We struck out onto a trail, in and out of rocks, trail no wider than Abraham Lincoln in front of me. Wasn't a trail at all, except that we were following it — a mountain on one side and on the other side forever down just below my dangling foot.

Wasn't one green thing to see besides Dellwood Barker's eyes: not a tree, not a bush, not a stick of grass.

At a place on the trail where there wasn't room to fart, Abraham Lincoln suddenly shied. I thought the both of them were going over for good, Dellwood headfirst into sky. Abraham Lincoln got her footing though, and when Dellwood was back in the saddle and Abraham Lincoln had settled down, Dellwood pointed to a nest of diamondbacks just off the trail — snakes squirming and wiggling and rattling, a hole full of tails switching flies.

Metaphor came creeping up to the hole. When Dellwood saw that dog doing that, he let out a ferocious yell, and Metaphor put his tail between his legs and made tracks in the opposite direction.

It was a steady climb for the rest of the day. When the sun was at its hottest, we came to a high chaparral that stretched out bright and flat. Dellwood pulled up alongside again, and shading his eyes with one hand pointed east with the other.

'Buffalo Head,' he said.

I shaded my good eye too and squinted. In the distance was a rock that sat on the heat waves of the chaparral, a huge head of something frying in a pan. Dellwood spurred Abraham Lincoln and started off running. Princess jumped to catch up.

My body didn't like what my good eye was seeing at all. Closer we got, the more I wanted to go the other way.

The trail wound down and through an arroyo. We rounded a lava outcropping and started climbing again. When I looked up I saw the full dark head of a horned buffalo staring down at me.

Looked more devil than anything else.

Every step closer we took from then on, the more Buffalo

Head didn't look like a buffalo head but the biggest pile of lava rocks I'd seen so far.

This pile of rocks was different, though.

This pile of rocks had been piled up – someone big's big hands had piled the rocks up – setting the rocks one by one on top of each other, just so.

More and more, Abraham Lincoln and Princess were talking horse talk to each other and stamping the ground. Metaphor was behind us, slinking low. Princess rared up and I had to quick grab around his neck. Abraham Lincoln switched her tail back and forth, dancing.

'This is my place,' Dellwood yelled over to me. 'Buffalo Head.'

We rode right up to the pile of rocks, circled the rocks clockwise to the point farthest east. There was an opening that was a mouth, a place that you'd never want to go into. We went into the mouth.

Inside it was only dark. Dark pitch black. Dark my good eye still in the bright chaparral. Could barely see Dellwood and Abraham Lincoln right in front of me.

My ears were still hearing the wind. I asked Dellwood if Metaphor was alright and my voice was a hundred voices.

'Metaphor's fine,' Dellwood said.

Fine. Fine. Fine. Fine.

Light began to filter down through the rocks. Big pieces of light, Ida Richilieu's sheets on the washline in the sun. Dust hanging in the light.

Dellwood, passing through one patch of light, waved his arms and moved the dust in circles. Blue and green and rose-colored dust moving the way his arms had moved.

We were climbing again, but not steep, circling slowly through shadows and light.

'This is what I call the Round House,' Dellwood said.

We were in a space so big you could have put all of Ida's Place in it. Light was shooting down all around. You could walk up to the light and touch the light, lean hard against it.

On one side of the Round House, sun was coming in ground level through an opening. Dellwood rode over to the opening, dismounted, and started to take the saddle and bridle off Abraham Lincoln. I did the same with Princess. We let the horses loose, and put the saddle, the bridles, the blankets, and our gear next to a pile of hay and a stack of wood.

'Where'd you get all this hay and wood?' I asked, but Dellwood was already through the opening. Then I heard something I hadn't figured on hearing: water running.

I walked out the opening and into the bright again. The sun was in the west and all over my body. So was the wind.

Metaphor was at the pool lapping up water. I asked my good eye if it was just seeing things. Walked over next to Metaphor, and sure enough, what I cupped my hands into was water – warm water from a spring coming out of a crack between two rocks about shoulder high to a tall man. It was just enough to stand under. Green moss was on the rocks, and grass was growing – green grass – down around the pool. Dellwood had rocked up the pool so the water was knee-deep. I don't think anything has ever looked so good.

Dellwood was smiling like a fool, so proud of his place. He took me by the arm and we stood arm in arm.

As far as my good eye could tell, me and Dellwood were standing on a ledge near the top of the pile of rocks that was Buffalo Head. Over the side, to the west, you could see as far as the bright world went. On each side of where you could see, rocks stuck up out of the ground, Buffalo Arms coming out of the Buffalo Head reaching for sunset.

Above us, a smooth jut of rock covered our heads, and the rock we were standing on was wind-, rain-, and snow-rubbed flat.

I walked to the edge and looked over. It was down to an expanse of flat reddish brown and silver-grey that rolled west to where it all stopped: to that edge, to the horizon. Then it was over the horizon, over the edge, over the side into millions of blue to where the someone big one day had reached out from and piled the rocks, big hands setting the rocks on top of each other just so for Berdache Indians in the old times, for Dellwood Barker, and now for me.

'When the time comes, this is where I'm coming to die,' Dellwood said. 'Story goes if you live your life being true to your heart, you'll find a place like this where you can come to when you die, and you can tell the story of your life out loud to all of nature listening. Death has got to wait until you're done with your singing and dancing and whatever else you got to do to get your story told.

'By telling your story, the knowledge you have will become understanding. And *that* – knowledge becoming understanding – is better than anything there is to feel.'

You never knew what was going to come out of Dellwood Barker's mouth. That's why I liked him so much. Probably why my mother had liked him too. Most of all, though, I liked that a tybo could be a man like him, and that a man like him could be my father.

Truth was, I couldn't imagine a better way of dying. I knew right then that was the only way for me, but I wasn't quite sure of what that way was exactly – with that talk of knowledge becoming understanding and all.

Most important, though, was that I knew that I already had my place. The meadow up on Not-Really-A-Mountain back in Excellent was calling me, loud and clear.

'I got to tell you some things, though, about this place,' Dellwood Barker said. 'You know it's no ordinary place, especially at sunset and around the time of the full moon like it is now.'

The sun was pushing the shade back into the head of the buffalo and the wind was whipping around us.

I waited for him to tell me why this was no ordinary place. Dellwood Barker just looked at me with his green eyes.

Dellwood took off his hat, and undid the gunnysack from around his shoulders. Then he walked into the shade, through the opening, and back into what he called the Round House. He came back out leading the horses. Abraham Lincoln went right to the pool and drank. Princess wouldn't drink at first, the water was so warm, but after watching Abraham Lincoln get her fill, he wasn't about to stay thirsty.

The sun was beating down strong and it was going to get hotter than hell. When the horses were done drinking, Dellwood led them back to the Round House. I went to the waterfall and was about to strip for a shower. I looked over to Dellwood. He was standing on the ledge, pretending he wasn't watching me.

I had met Dellwood Barker naked, traveled on a horse with Dellwood Barker naked, sat in a river with Dellwood Barker naked, laid next to Dellwood Barker twice, had already memorized his body right down to where most of the grey in his head of hair was – and there I was too shy to take my shirt off.

I took the nightshirt off. I stepped under the water and let the water come down over me. I stayed in the pool, under the waterfall, because the water felt so good, but mostly because I didn't know what to do with myself once I got out.

I washed out the nightshirt, got out of the pool, and spread the nightshirt out in the sun. I sat down in what little shade was left and closed my eyes. Wasn't long before I heard Dellwood Barker taking off his boots, then taking off his pants. Heard him getting into the water.

I went inside the Round House where it was cooler, but not much. Abraham Lincoln and Princess were standing in a sandy place facing each other neck to neck, nibbling on each other, quivering themselves to keep off the flies. I took my saddle blanket and laid it down on the sand, then laid down myself. Metaphor laid down next to me. Princess shook himself and the dust of him hung in the air in the patches of light. Mostly it was dark – not dark night anymore but shade.

What I told myself I was doing wasn't what I was doing. Told myself I was sleeping. What I was doing was still thinking.

Buffalo Head.

No ordinary place.

Old Berdache Indians.

Special breed of buffalo.

Hole full of rattlesnakes.

Dynamics of the situation.

Father.

Knowledge becoming understanding.

Going to your special place to die and death waiting for you to tell your story.

Moon language; breath, heartbeat.

When I woke up, things were gold and shining from the insides of them. Dellwood Barker was sitting on his saddle blanket by the pool. Next to him, the kindling was stacked up, a little tipi, dry wood ready for fire.

I wished for a window to look at Dellwood Barker through. Wished to lay down in his big feather bed in a cold room. When he finally came to bed, I'd count to a thousand and roll against him.

I walked to the pool and splashed water on my face, someone big's big hand rising up inside me.

'Sun's setting,' Dellwood Barker said.

My bad eye started opening up.

The Man Who Fell in Love with the Moon

'It's a great place for healing,' he said. 'Come here, let me look at you.'

I sat down next to Dellwood Barker. His human-being sex story was getting him hard.

Dellwood's nose and lip weren't as swollen and his black eye was blue. His cuts were nearly healed. 'You'll be fine and dandy in no time,' he said. 'I doubt if your face will ever be the same, though. Probably have a sleepy eye. The girls'll all call it your bedroom eye,' he said.

The someone big in me was piling rocks. My arms, legs, belly, my thighs and head piled higher, and higher.

'The sleepy eye's your left eye. The eye of your soul. Most people say it's both eyes are the window to your soul, but it's only the left. Right one only sees what it's not afraid of. But don't worry, you'll still be one beautiful man,' he said.

Dellwood Barker put his hand on my hand.

I pulled my hand away.

'Have you seen any buffalo?' I asked.

'Not yet,' he said. 'Maybe tonight.'

My stomach was big as the Round House. My whole body was bigger than the state of Idaho – arms and legs and dick and head – mountain ranges going every which way.

'Shed, are you feeling alright?' Dellwood asked.

'I'm feeling fine,' I said.

'That's one of those things that's not ordinary about this place,' Dellwood said. 'Here, no matter what, you got to tell the truth.'

'Truth,' I said.

There was snow on my mountaintop, on my ears, on my head, cold winds getting colder.

'Yes, truth!' Dellwood said, his hand on my forehead.

Truth was his hand hurt.

Father, it hurts.

138

'You said there was buffalo,' I said.

'They'll be here,' Dellwood said. 'Tell me the truth, Shed,' he said.

I spread Dellwood's legs, and rested his legs on my shoulders.

'Take it easy with me, son,' he said.

I put the head of my cock against him, held myself firm until I was in the fold of him and he opened for me. What had been between us wasn't anymore. Slowly in, up to all the way, taking it easy, excruciating the slow in and out. When he was all mine, the dynamics of the situation was just me and him, just the gratification of two human beings fucking good, snakes squirming in a hole, the something big inside us both too big, skin to sweaty skin, left eye to left eye, mouth and mouth, the language – one word only: truth.

*

First thing I learned by my own self, without Ida or Dellwood or Alma or anybody else telling me, my own first truth was this: fucking was the same way as with everything else – what you thought you were doing was not what you were doing. What you thought you were doing was sucking and penetrating and kissing, holding, and ejaculating. What you were doing, though, was telling a story.

First off, thing is, you got to know you got a story. Then you got to have to tell it. Knowing how to tell your story good is important, but the secret to good fucking is how well you can listen. Fucking only gets good when the two stories start being the same story – the human-being sex story – when the two bodies stop being two bodies and start being the big excruciating, the one heart beating.

Most men, most sorry men, always tell the same old hard-dick ejaculation story, and always got to be the one who leans hard onto. Most women, sorry women, tell this story – which really isn't a story: you talk, I'll listen, tell me when you're done. They always end up being the one who gets leaned hard on. Doesn't work that way when you're fucking. Good fucking is bartering, wrestling, swapping tales back and forth, and telling lies til you get to the truth. Up on Buffalo Head, when I leaned hard on Dellwood Barker, on the man I thought was my father, I was a boy whose business it was to fuck, and so I fucked – even though the devil knew, even though I knew, you didn't fuck your father.

At first, I was no different from every sorry man – telling him the story I thought he wanted to hear – telling it hard – leaning hard into him. At first, what I was doing was what I thought I was doing: fucking a man who happened to be my father, fucking the father who had left me. At times I hurt him, didn't take it easy with him like he'd asked, and hurt him – pushed his ass down, my father's ass down, same way Billy Blizzard had pushed mine.

Wasn't long, though, before things were different. Wasn't long before everything changed. I started listening. It was his green eyes, his skin, a kindness in his touch – Dellwood Barker telling a story I'd never heard spoke so true. Him in my arms going past where you don't go.

That's when I started. Told him what I had needed to tell all my life. Dellwood Barker, first person ever my body told the true story to, of myself. Dellwood Barker, first person ever there enough to listen.

Truth was, wasn't long before me and Dellwood Barker weren't even us enough to have stories, Dellwood hollering, me hollering, us laughing and making noises, kissing big, hugging.

When he was ready to come – you know how it is sometimes when you come – you just want to say the truest thing. When Dellwood Barker came, he yelled out loud: 'I'm scared to death of dying, son!' and started howling at the moon.

Then, when our fucking was over, Dellwood Barker didn't try to duck out of there, didn't try to hide. I figured that was why Sheriff Blumenfeld hated him so much. Those who got something they need to hide always hate most the ones who don't hide it.

Figured, too, that was what Dellwood meant when he said he was more who he was than most folks.

True stories, the best stories.

There was something else, though, something I always could never forget.

Truth was, the devil was going to know.

Truth was, sooner or later, I knew the devil was going to know.

*

Dellwood Barker's parents were murdered too – his mother *and* his father. Story goes, all three of them Barkers – mother, father, and Dellwood – were all traveling west from New York City on the Holiday Line when Dellwood was about my age – fourteen or fifteen. Just south of Fort Hall, along the Portneuf River, at a place they call Robber's Roost, Dellwood heard gunshots and no sooner had he heard them when his mother fell over dead with a bullet in her nose, then his father, dead bleeding in his vest.

Before the trip west, all Dellwood remembered about his father was that he taught English literature and loved poetry.

There was one time, though, with his father, that stuck out in Dellwood's mind – the time Dellwood hid in his father's study.

'I stood there for hours watching that guy, nose stuck in a book, only moving when he turned a page. I remember thinking, *My father is a stranger*. Then my father looked up at me, looked over his glasses at me, and stared, wondering who the hell I was, standing in his study. When he finally recognized me, my father said, 'My errant knight' – that's what he called me, and 'My little pip,' then 'My brave hero' as if I'd just up and jumped out one of his books.'

Dellwood's mother had what Dellwood called 'the second sight' on the piano, and what that was, Dellwood said, was his mother losing track of this world, and going into another while playing music your ears had never heard before, and wouldn't ever hear again anywhere else, the whole time sobbing and crying her eyes out.

'Buckets of tears just rolling down her cheeks,' Dellwood said, tears rolling down his cheeks. 'Never-ending tears.'

' "Grief inside me since the day I was born," my mother always said,' Dellwood said. 'Never knew what made her so sad. Maybe living with a stranger made her sad.'

Dellwood Barker got the second sight on the piano from his mother.

'Every time I hear a piano, I still cry my eyes out,' Dellwood said. 'Then I head straight for the piano and start making a hell of a racket.'

By the time the robbers were done robbing, everybody on the stage had been killed, including the driver and the shotgun, except for Dellwood Barker and an old man named Bush who claimed to be a Mormon prophet.

'The robbers left me and old Bush to bury the dead. We buried my mother first, then my father, then the rest of them. When we got done burying them, old Bush sat down and said he was having a revelation. What the revelation was, was that he was going to die. As soon as old Bush said he was going to die, he croaked right there and fell over dead. Then I had to bury him too.

'In the middle of nowhere and shit scared,' Dellwood said, 'I set off walking, following the river back to Fort Hall, with no gun, no nothing. Three days later, I had buzzards following me and a pack of coyotes. Ended up crawling up a tree in hopes of finding a safe place to sleep. The last thing I remember was falling out of that tree. Seemed I was never going to hit bottom,' Dellwood said. 'Maybe I never did.'

When Dellwood woke up, he was strapped to a stretcher being dragged behind a horse.

'Started yelling like a stuck pig,' Dellwood said. 'Pretty soon the horse stopped and an Injun woman came around and looked at me. Never seen such an ugly woman in all my days. She was big as a bear with part of her head shaved. Feathers were sticking every which way out of where she had hair. One eye, her right eye, shot off cockeyed, looking behind her. Her left eye was a steady roll. She had one tooth in her mouth, and bracelets wrist to armpit. Thought I was cannibalized, thought I was dead for sure. 'My name is Foolish Woman,' she said in Injun English.

'I didn't know then, but was soon to find out, that Foolish Woman was not a woman at all. She was a he. He was a man. Foolish Woman being a Berdache.'

Foolish Woman hauled Dellwood Barker up to Buffalo Head, Dellwood out of his mind – somewhere else, only bones, sweating waterfalls.

'No idea how long I was up here,' Dellwood said. 'Couple weeks I figure. Foolish Woman was about dead too, him trying to heal me, when all of a sudden one night the fever broke and I sat up.

'Knowledge became understanding,' Dellwood said. 'Was ecstasy. Everything was clear.'

Foolish Woman kissed Dellwood on the forehead and then pointed.

From a hole in the sky – silver with moon – just beyond the edge over the side, all the way to the horizon, came the buffalo, the special breed of buffalo – thousands of them – millions. Clouds rolling, they ran, fierce and proud, across the sky.

The Man Who Fell in Love with the Moon

'Me and Foolish Woman sat on the ledge and watched the buffalo run all night,' Dellwood said. 'At the same time, though, I was running with the buffalo, and Foolish Woman was running too.'

*

Up on Buffalo Head, after our fucking was done, I went to pull out of Dellwood, but he asked me to stay inside him. Said he wanted to hang on to me for a while longer. Said he always had to be the one who did the putting in and it was good to have a change. Said he loved me.

So we laid that way, me and Dellwood, holding on to each other, talking – that is, mostly him talking, me listening.

That night laying with the man who said he loved me, then laying with him the days and nights to come, me and Dellwood Barker up on Buffalo Head, I learned many things. Things Dellwood Barker had learned himself by living his own life and things he had learned from Foolish Woman. Things you can say out loud; things you can't. Some of what I learned, if you want to say out loud, there's words for, some not. Most of what I learned, though, I'm still thinking about – probably always will.

Berdache I think about.

The Wild Moon Man another.

Moves Moves is another.

What I understood Dellwood Barker to say about Berdache was this: men fucking men and women fucking women is the same act, no matter what you call it, no matter what language you speak, no matter what words you use. The words you use for men fucking and for women fucking in Indian, though, mean something different than the words you use for men fucking and for women fucking in tybo.

'You make things how they are by the way you think of them,' Dellwood said.

'Tybos think it's a sin,' Dellwood said, '– that fucking is a sin, whether men do it, or women do it, or men and women do it. Only time you can fuck is to have a child, and then it's something you want to be over with fast.

'Most Indians love to fuck,' Dellwood said, 'like they love to eat, and breathe, and take a good shit – ain't no sin or hell damnation or fire – it's just another part of the Great Mystery.'

The fuck part.

'In Indian,' Dellwood said, 'in most tribes, if you were Berdache, folks figured that, since you weren't like most men, and you weren't like most women, that you were something different altogether, meaning somebody special, not bad. Berdache were looked up to as spiritual leaders and healers. Even though they usually lived alone, they weren't outcasts. Berdache took care of children, made bread, gathered berries, went hunting, tanned hides; in short, did everything the men did, did everything the women did too, and sometimes even became a second wife to a man if the Berdache thought the man was worth it.

'Depended on what kind of person you were, what kind of Berdache you were – if you wanted to dress up as a woman and stay with the children, then that's how you were and that's what you did. If you lived alone, your tipi set off from the others, and were a powerful Berdache enough to call a different man to your bed each night, then that's how you were and that's what you did. Some Berdache were feared warriors because their medicine was so strong.

'One of the first things the Christian missionaries did to the Indian people,' Dellwood said, 'once they got here, was kill the Berdache in the name of their god because the missionaries knew that if they got rid of the Berdache, they could get rid of a lot of what was Indian.

'Damned near succeeded,' Dellwood said.

Besides Berdache, what I learned up on Buffalo Head, from Dellwood Barker, and something I always think about, is the Wild Moon Man.

Story goes that the Wild Moon Man lives at the bottom of a lake down south. Nights when the moon is full, he can up and grab you and pull you down into the lake with him.

Not many people have seen the Wild Moon Man, but those who have say he's covered with hair and rusty mud.

Wild Moon Man doesn't like people much – Indians he don't like much and tybos he plain hates. But he's always looking for young men, special young men, him trying to get them to sit by the lake at night or come in skinny-dipping.

When he pulls you down, story goes he takes you to the bottom of the lake to his home, and teaches you how to breathe water instead of air. If you don't trust him and do what he says – you drown and they find you floating the next morning. But if you do trust him and do as he says, story goes, when you start breathing water, that muddy old hairy goat turns into a beautiful, strong warrior and he teaches you many secrets about the true power of being a man.

We were sitting by the fire, moonlight on the darkness all around us. Dellwood Barker told me, 'When the Wild Moon Man takes you underwater, to the hairy rusty mud, he's taking you to your asshole.' Dellwood said, 'To the place that's as female as a man can get. You find your natural male power through your asshole, not your dick. You find your prostate. Fire down there under all that mud and hair and water. You find in yourself what most men love women for: their ecstasy, their hole into the other world. By receiving a man into you, by receiving a man like a woman, by being as female as a man can get, what you find – if you don't drown – is the beautiful warrior in yourself who knows both sides.

'Men like us are lucky,' Dellwood said. 'We've learned to breathe water.

'It ain't been easy, though – it never is.

'Even when you're accepted by your people – like with the Injuns – when the Wild Moon Man gets done with you, you're different, and when you're different you're different, that's all – and you and everybody else knows it.

'But don't get me wrong, with Injuns it was a great honor for a father to give his son to the teachings of a Berdache, and a greater honor to be chosen by the Wild Moon Man.

'But I don't care what you say – Injun, tybo, or whatever – a father wants his son to be like *him*. Simple as that.

'In most cases, though, the young men were different even before the Wild Moon Man swallowed them up. Why else were they sitting alone by the lake at night? Probably writing poetry or some damn thing.

'One thing's for sure – you'll never find a Berdache who's worth his salt with a dried-up prostate, I promise you that.'

Free from woman's hole.

'P . . R . . O . . S . . T . . A . . T . . E,' Dellwood spelled. 'Means to put in front. To cause to stand.'

Then he showed me where prostate was.

Wasn't long and I was breathing water.

'E . . C . . S . . T . . A . . S . . Y,' Dellwood spelled. 'To derange,' he said. 'To cause to stand,' he said. 'Being beyond reason and self-control.'

You never could tell what Dellwood Barker was going to come up with next. That's why I stuck around him so long – just to see what was going to happen. One minute he was talking about some old rusty man who lived at the bottom of a lake and then all of a sudden he was talking asshole and prostate and knowledge and understanding and being beyond reason and self-control.

Then there was Moves Moves. Moves Moves is the way you'd say it in tybo. Don't know the Indian word for it. What Moves Moves is, is sperm retention — that is, having orgasm without ejaculating.

'R . . E . . T . . E . . N . . T . . I . . O . . N,' Dellwood spelled, 'means saving sperm.'

'E . . J . . A . . C . . U . . L . . A . . T . . I . . N . . G,' Dellwood spelled, 'means shooting sperm out.'

I already knew how to spell *sperm* and what it was.

Why Indians call it Moves Moves is because, as Dellwood Barker explained it to me, the way Foolish Woman explained it to him, *Moves*, in Indian, means 'life.' Anything that has life moves. There isn't anything that isn't alive. So everything moves. Even things like rocks are alive, and dirt. Even boards and tin roofs are alive although they are harder to see move. But they move. Just got to know how to see them move.

So, that's the Moves part.

Moves Moves is what makes moves move. One move is a heartbeat. Moves Moves is what it is that's beating the heart — your heart and my heart and everybody else's.

Your ejaculation, your sperm, is the move that makes moves move, or at least what you can see of Moves Moves in the man.

The Wild Moon Man makes Moves Moves down in his lake.

If you don't ejaculate your sperm and save your sperm, then you and Moves Moves and the Wild Moon Man can get to be one and the same thing, which is mighty powerful, which is how most Berdache are.

When Dellwood Barker told me about Moves Moves it was right after when he'd told me about the Wild Moon Man. We were still laying on the ledge of Buffalo Head, the sound of the waterfall splashing. The little tipi of kindling was then a fire burning low. Metaphor was laying by the fire, a dog rug. The moon was big and on top of the rocks, sitting on the one buffalo arm coming out of the buffalo head. Moon on top of rocks, moon another rock, rolled smooth by someone big's big hand, rolled smooth by the big river sky, moon that color, just so.

Dellwood reached his hand down between us and wiped some ejaculation sperm off my belly. He smelled the sperm and showed the sperm to me.

'Good strong stuff that's come out of you,' he said.

'Not all of that has come out of me,' I said.

'All of it has come out of you,' he said.

'That's not possible,' I said. 'Not *all* of it.'

'*All* of it,' he said. 'Most certainly has, and you'd better start learning quick how to come not come before you give away all your Moves Moves.'

'You've been coming right along with me, every time, time for time,' I said.

'I've been coming, alright,' Dellwood said. 'But not ejaculating.'

'How the hell do you do that?' I asked.

Since we were in a place where you had to tell the truth, Dellwood Barker told me.

What you have to do, Dellwood Barker said, is make a line with your breath from your mouth down all the way to your balls. When you get the breath in your balls, you pull the breath back behind your balls and in front of your asshole where the Wild Moon Man lives. Then you take the breath through the crack in your ass and up to the base of your back. Then up your back to the base of your skull. Then up to the top of your head.

When you get the line of breath going good from your mouth down to under your balls, across the crack in your ass, up to your back, then up your back to the base of your neck and then to the top of your head, you're ready to get your dick hard.

Just when you're ready to ejaculate, you quick take a breath and make the line to your balls. Then you take all that sperm that the Wild Moon Man has made hot for you down in the prostate that hasn't come out yet and you pull the sperm across the crack in your ass to the lower part of the back, up to the base of the neck, then to the top of your head. You got to clench your fists, too, screw up your face, make your feet like they were claws, and tighten up your asshole.

'That's when you're really living,' Dellwood said. 'Died and gone to heaven you're living so well. You're coming but not ejaculating. You're getting a taste of knowledge becoming understanding. You're being put in front, caused to stand, being deranged, beyond reason and self-control,' he said. 'Ecstasy,' he said.

You never knew what Dellwood Barker was going to say next. I was waiting for those rocks on Buffalo Head to come tumbling down on top of us, because, not only did Moves Moves not sound like the truth in that truthful place, but it sounded like the biggest load of bullshit I had ever heard.

The rocks didn't fall.

The next time me and Dellwood had our hard-to-hard, I put my head down close to Dellwood's cock and stayed close to make sure I saw everything that was going on. Wasn't long and Dellwood was clenching his fists, making his feet like claws, screwing up his face, and there was no way even my little finger could've fit up his asshole. Pretty soon, Dellwood Barker was beyond reason, excruciating, out of control, deranged, moaning ecstasy loud and calling my name out and screaming something like you would've expected from Alma Hatch.

Wasn't a drop.

Not a damn drop of Moves Moves.

After that, his dick went down. Dellwood was panting and laughing and kissing me all over like you do.

I decided right then I needed to start believing in something. So I started believing in Dellwood Barker.

Then it was my turn. I got to breathing like he had said to. Got the breath to my balls, then under, then across and up my back to my neck, then up top my head. When the breath was flowing pretty good, Dellwood started sucking on me and giving me directions at the same time.

When it got time, I clenched my fists, curled my feet like claws, screwed my face up, and tightened my asshole. Dellwood was yelling, 'Make it your single intention! Breathe deep! You've got it! That's right! Careful! Suck in your asshole! The back's the hardest part! Now the head!'

What I felt was killdeer in my head – so much that it made me want to fall over. Then I fell over. Then all my Moves Moves was going down Dellwood Barker's throat.

'Takes practice,' Dellwood said, smiling and wiping off his mustache. 'Took me years.'

*

Me and Dellwood Barker stayed up on Buffalo Head until the horses ate up the hay. Our food was gone about the third day and we stayed at least two days longer.

Our last night together, we both knew it. Dellwood's arm was under my head and my face was in his armpit. Just after sunset, without a piano in sight, Dellwood up and started crying. Sobs so big going through him made me want to cry too.

Told myself I was not going to cry, and I didn't; that is, not until he reached over and took my hand – right hand to right hand – the way tybo men usually only touch each other – men shaking hands, offering friendship.

My father's sobs were mine too. Couldn't tell whose was whose, was his was mine, was his father's too, was every man's.

Was Metaphor's – howling up a storm.

The next morning, at the crossroads, where he went that way and I went this one, Dellwood scratched me out a map on the sand. Showed me where the mountains started, where to hook back up with Kally's River the quickest. Gave me his .22 automatic rifle. Told me about the trading post in Bliss Station, Idaho, where I could get some decent clothes, and not to let anybody see how much money I had when I paid for them. Told me how to get to the Sage Hill Ranch if I changed my mind.

'Full moon's in the thighs next month,' he said. 'Sure would like to be there with you.'

I looked down at Metaphor. He was giving me that dog look like it was going to break his heart if I didn't come along.

I couldn't talk, so I just reined Princess due west. Dellwood Barker waved at me until he was just a little spot that I only guessed was waving.

Princess didn't like parting any more than me, him acting up the whole time, stepping sideways – downright ornery – snorting air through his nose.

Took me til afternoon to realize that all of me was sore – not so much from the sheriff's beating, but sore in my heart, sore in the crying place behind my eyes, and especially sore where me and the horse blanket came together.

The sun was big and the wind wanted to pick you up and carry you off with it. Me and Princess just kept going. I told Princess all my names out loud, told him about my mother, how she died, and Billy Blizzard. Told him about Ida Richilieu and Alma Hatch. Told him the truth. Told him what I had told Dellwood Barker with my body but never spoke.

Which was everything.

The devil wasn't going to hear anything out loud from me – that is, except in front of my horse. Only person in the world you can say true things out loud in front of is your horse.

Dellwood Barker had done just about everything to get my story out of me. I just told him that if I opened my mouth I'd have to tell the truth, and to trust me – that if I spoke the truth, we'd both be in trouble, so the best thing for me was stay shut up.

I let Dellwood know the important things, though. Let him know how my heart was. Let him look in my left eye as deep as he wanted to look. Let my body be so there was nothing in between in the way. Let him know how my eyes were seeing him, how my fingers felt on his skin. Language to language I told him everything, I told him all.

Was more than one time where I stopped Princess and turned him around, Princess raring to go back – but I kept telling myself I needed to find the buffalo, needed to find what my name meant, Duivichi-un-Dua – even though my name – what it meant – wasn't as important now that I had found Dellwood Barker.

That's how the killdeer bird is: I found the tybo side of me when I was looking for the Indian.

For the moment, though, lost was what I was. Me and Princess lost in a flat world, not going anywhere but away from Dellwood Barker.

Figured if I could find my father in a jail cell in a land as flat as that, I could find anything. Felt good, though, just being what I was, even if it was lost.

The first night alone, I built a big fire and slept with my back against a rock – Princess not two feet away. Sleeping isn't what I did, though. I just sat cross-legged with Dellwood's .22 rifle across my lap.

Next day was the same as the first. Princess put one foot in front of the other. The land was as flat, less rocky, more sagebrush. I could have been anywhere, though. In the thousands and millions of places in the world, I was only in the place that missed him, Dellwood Barker.

How could I have fucked my father?

How could I have left him?

'Do you fuck women?' I had asked Dellwood on our last night.

'Yup,' he said.

'Do you like it more than with men?' I asked.

'Usually not, but it depends on the woman,' he said.

'Do you do Moves Moves with women too?' I asked.

'Especially with women,' Dellwood said, 'unless you want to father a child. Otherwise, women's the worst ones to give your Moves Moves to, because they're already twice as powerful as a man, let alone be the place where he stores his Moves Moves. Pretty soon what was his is hers.'

'Is it the same with a man?' I asked. 'I mean can a man make another man's Moves Moves his?'

'Yup,' Dellwood said, 'that stuff's gold to any Berdache who's worth his salt.'

'Ever been in love?' I asked.

'Am right now,' he said.

'. . . I mean before,' I said.

'Yup, once,' he said.

'Was it with a woman?' I asked.

'Yup,' he said.

'Did you ejaculate in her?' I asked.

'Yup,' he said.

'Was it the same woman as the one in the photograph in the book in your bedroll?' I asked.

'Yup,' he said.

'What was her name?' I asked.

'Buffalo Sweets,' he said.

'Did she have a child?' I asked.

'Twins,' he said. 'A boy and a girl.'

'Twins!' I said.

'Twins,' he said. 'A boy and a girl. I saw them after they were first born – for eleven days,' he said.

'What happened?' I asked.

'We was living near Fort Lincoln. It was late fall. Winter wasn't far away and I wanted some more deer meat to smoke up. I went hunting up around Pocatello, Idaho, and one of the biggest storms that has ever hit this part of the country hit. Took me two weeks to get back to home. Buffalo Sweets and the twins were gone. Folks said she had gone to find me. Never saw her or the kids again.'

Dellwood Barker was quiet for a long time after that. Then he said, 'Now that I have told you every damn thing about me, how about telling me something about you?'

'Are they dead?' I asked.

'Story goes they were winter froze,' he said. 'All of them.'

'Do you ever think about the twins?' I asked.

'Never stop,' he said.

'And you loved her, the woman, Buffalo Sweets?' I asked.

'More than anything,' he said.

Out on the plains alone, me and Princess wandering through the wind, no single intention, what I thought about was *twins*. What I thought about was *more than anything*.

By the fourth day, the lava rock had left the valleys and stood in slabs along the hills, armies of Indian warriors, tired and beaten, still proud. The lava slabs stared ambush down at me and Princess as we made our tiny way over the sand that rolled across the valley floor.

At Bliss Station, I stopped and bought clothes: a hat, a pair of socks, some boots, pants, and a red shirt. At first, the trading post owner wouldn't even let me in his store – him being tybo, me being Indian and being in all that open space for such a time, me half-naked, and I figure crazy-looking from practice on my Moves Moves.

When I waved a twenty-dollar bill at him, though, he changed his mind. All of a sudden Indian wasn't so bad, and with a change of clothes I'd look twenty dollars better.

The town – if you could call Bliss Station a town – was two buildings. One building was both a trading post and a bar, and the other building a stables. Only reason Bliss Station was a town at all was because the stagecoach needed somewhere to stop.

There were cowboys standing around everywhere you looked, smiling that mean Indian-killer look at me. Almost decided to stay. Could have made a fortune out in the shed.

On the fifth day, we crossed the Portneuf River and got into some marshy bottoms. Me and Princess stopped midday by a stream full of trout because we were bone-tired and bored crazy with just going ahead. We made camp by some scrub trees and a big batch of willows growing right next to the water. That evening, after I'd caught a big cutthroat and had a swim, after I'd cooked up the trout and ate, I sat in the clearing, grass neck high to me sitting, and looked across the miles. All there was to see was marsh grass blowing with Idaho wind that never knows when to stop.

I stared at the world. Listened to the wind blowing the high grass. Not one damn buffalo in sight.

Was easy to see how a man could go crazy living out with staring and listening at things; especially after a smoke of locoweed crazy.

The sun setting for you – beauty bigger than you'd ever hope to be or think or dream of – comes right up to your eyeballs and skin, goes right through you – through your eyes – pushing colors into your head, onto the back of the inside of your head, through your head to no end behind and all around you. Then the marsh grass starts showing off gold and pink and red, fancy with wind.

Hot ball going down. Cool ball coming up in the blue and the black, in the blue dress like Ida's; taffeta stars.

All around me cool-ball light. The damned howling-at moon. Marsh grass silver with dark breathing and heart beating. Campfire so low only red under black – now and then a spit.

Man could go crazy sitting – Dellwood Barker crazy sitting, looking at how things are, at the shadows, the light, looking at the beauty, trying to know, going crazy trying to understand.

Next morning, I was still looking. Couldn't remember if I'd ever stopped. Figured I could've dreamed I was looking. But if I had dreamed, I'd have had to sleep. If I had slept, I'd have had to wake up.

There had been no waking up. There had been only looking: the cool ball going down, the hot ball coming back up again.

At sunrise, hot-ball shadows were long – a man's shadow and a horse's shadow, one shadow moving over the marsh grass, marsh grass waving with wind.

When the sun was the hottest ball, when shadows went inside of things, me and Princess came to a place where all around the ground went up steep and flattened out again. When we made our way to the top, things were different.

Indians, my mother's people – the me part of not me – and the buffalo – weren't far away.

Part Two

Owlfeather

The first thing about Fort Lincoln was the trees. Big old tall trees standing in line one right next to the other same way as the lampposts in Owyhee City. The trees went up both sides of a road, the road went up to a two-story brick building, and the building was a school. Me and Princess went up the road down the middle through the trees, the wind making poplar leaves talk something how aspen trees talk up in Excellent. But there was something wrong. I stopped Princess and looked around and listened. Princess heard it too.

The trees sounded scared.

They were standing together in the middle of a flat nowhere. No tree in its right mind would ever think of growing in a place like that – unless they were forced to – and I figured, being forced to, they'd all clumped together making the best of things like a family would, standing proud and tall, bringing shade to a desert that didn't have any. Lampposts standing in a row one two three four five one after the other wasn't a problem, but when *trees* started acting that way, there had to be something wrong.

When I looked up at the building, I got scared too. Looked more like a castle than a school – bars on the windows and an iron gate on the front door. Above the door, the words in the stone read: *Saint Anthony's Academy*.

Around back of the school there were more trees in rows. When I came around the corner, my eyes saw something they didn't know what to tell me it was. They were people – women, I think – dressed up in black with white stiff pillows on their heads.

There were three of the Pillow Women. Could have been devils if they weren't so funny-looking. One of them was standing in the doorway. The other two were closer to me, each one with a group of children.

The more my eyes looked the more I saw things besides the Pillow Women. The one Pillow Woman was with Indian girls and the other Pillow Women was with Indian boys.

When I saw the Indian girls and Indian boys, the afraid in my heart stopped and my heart started pounding another way. Then it was hard for my eyes to see because what I was seeing was my first real Indians - seeing for the first time my mother's people.

The three Pillow Women just stood in place. If they saw me, they never acted like it. The one with the girls looked at the girls. The one with the boys looked at the boys. The one in the doorway looked at everybody.

The Indian girls stood on both sides of something that was stretched between them and they bounced a ball back and forth, never letting the ball touch the ground.

The Indian boys stood in a line, waiting to be the one who kicked a ball that another Indian boy rolled on the ground to him. What it looked like was you kicked the ball and ran. Other boys tried to catch the ball, or hit the running boy with the ball.

Before I was older, I had a ball once. It was smaller than the balls of the Indian girls and Indian boys. My ball was red, white, and blue. One morning I woke up and it was gone. Figured one of my customers had taken it.

Took a while for my eyes to see what was missing. The Indian girls were standing in place like the Pillow Women were standing. The Indian boys were standing in line. Hitting the ball, kicking the ball.

What was missing was what my ears weren't hearing.

They were all dressed up the same too. Girls all looking the same. Boys all looking the same. Kids who were photographs of kids. All of them the same girl or same boy kid. They weren't running around, no kids wiggling and yelling, no kids laughing.

Me and Princess stood and stared. The trees were in rows and the redbrick building had bars on the windows and the Indian girls stood in place and the Indian boys stood in line and the one Pillow Woman watched the girls and the other the boys, and then, the Pillow Woman in the doorway who was watching it all raised a bell that was in her hand and rang it twenty times. I wasn't the only one counting because on the fifteenth, every Indian girl, every Indian boy, turned toward the door and walked, girls on the right, boys on the left, into the Saint Anthony's Academy.

Me and Princess rode out of there, past a castle church that was even bigger than the castle school, with a high tower and a big cross on the tower, trees lined up scared all around. Wasn't long before we were standing at the top of a slope that went down.

There it was: Fort Lincoln. I knew it was Fort Lincoln because it was just the way Dellwood Barker had said it was: 'Five buildings facing every which way searching for a town.'

Wasn't a tree down there, or a river, or anything. Just the five buildings, their shadows, the railroad tracks, a big cloud of dust, and the Idaho wind.

Princess didn't want to go any closer. I didn't either, really, but after we had a little talk, we ended up going forward again. Princess's heart was going fast as mine. The closer we got to the five buildings, the more there was a smell in the air that my nose didn't know a thing about. There was a sound, too – every once in a while – that was somebody with a high voice, or maybe a child, screaming. I told my nose just to keep on smelling and my ears to keep on listening until they got it right, and when they did, to let me know.

The dust was coming from wagons and horses and people gathered behind a big wood building with a tin roof. I tied Princess up to a hitching post in front of a log cabin with two windows and a door in between that was painted white with one long porch that you had to step high to get on to. The sign above the door said, *Licensed Government Traders.*

I laid my head against Princess's shoulder and had another talk with him – told him I'd be back soon and not to worry about me. I slung Dellwood Barker's .22 automatic rifle in the leather scabbard over my shoulder, then walked toward the dust, toward the crowd.

Must have been hundreds of people – Indian people – standing in the street in the dust, in the sun. No shade to stand in. They were all facing one way – toward the big wood building with the tin roof, facing the sign on the building that read: *United States Government Commodity Outlet.* Under that sign was another sign: *Loading Dock.*

Same as with the children up at the castle school, my ears told me that the sound of the crowd of people standing in a hot street wasn't how a crowd of people sound. Only fear sounds like that. Then there were the screams coming from I didn't know where.

Wondered who had died. Smelled as if everything had died.

Sitting on horses, at the edges of the crowd, were soldiers in blue uniforms. There were soldiers, too, standing on the loading dock. They were looking me over real good – me and the .22. Whenever tybos look at you that way, there's one of two things going on: either his sex story is going wild out of control on him, or it's the other one going wild. Wasn't so much that they wanted to fuck you as kill you. With tybo men there isn't much difference between fucking and killing.

The more I looked around, the more my eyes began to see why the soldiers were paying so much attention to me. I was in my new clothes – my new boots, new hat that I'd bought at Bliss Station. I was a head taller than the tallest in the crowd, me all fancy cowboy, me looking like I ate food. Me not a whipped dog. Me still with my balls and brains enough to keep myself in one piece. Looking like a human being who's not tybo – something tybos hate looking at.

The Indian men of my mother's people were mostly dressed in tybo clothes that didn't fit. The women were wrapped in cloth, covered – only their eyes you could see staring out. Then too there were women all uncovered – head bare – dresses ripped, tits hanging out, drunk – vomit all down the front of them. Men laying in the dirt of the street made mud by what was coming out of them. Them covered with flies.

There was a big open door in the side of the United States Government Commodity Outlet. Indians were going in the door, some with packhorses, a couple with wagons – most folks just carrying baskets. Not even the babies were crying. The babies stared out at the clouds of dust from their cradleboards on their mothers' backs, or, from their mothers' arms, stared up into mother the way mother was staring at the United States Government Commodity Outlet.

I made my way through the crowd to the door. Two guards in blue uniforms stood blocking the way. They wouldn't let me in any further.

'Not til your name's called,' the one said, 'and you show us your ration ticket.'

Ration ticket: Sheriff Blumenfeld back in Owyhee City had

asked me for my ration ticket the night he had marched me to jail.

I moved to the side and stood next to the door. I could see inside the building.

There was a road that went between two loading docks all the way through the building to an open door on the other side. The loading docks were about waist high. A tybo man, not in uniform, was up on the one loading dock shouting out orders at two Indian men who carried sacks and boxes and cans to the Indian people waiting on the road.

One of the soldiers at the door called out a name. The wagon of the family whose name was called went inside the building, onto the road. It was usually the oldest woman who would pull out the beaded pouch and, with trembling hand, show the tybo the ration ticket. Then they would get a sack of something, a box of something, smoked meat, and cans of things. The family would go out the back door, and the next name would be called.

I stepped away from the door and walked back through the crowd, through my mother's people. I put my body in among them, smelled their firewater beer sweat and buckskin, put my skin next to their skins, let my hands brush against theirs.

My eyes into their left eyes, no one looked back.

They couldn't see me. I looked at my body. It had not disappeared.

'Commodity Day,' I heard someone say. I turned and saw a man. He was bare-chested, barefoot, the bottom half of a pair of long johns tied onto him with a piece of twine. His hair was pulled out of his face by a red bandanna. His face looked old but his body still moved young. He was holding a paper bag with a bottle he'd drink out of. He wasn't looking at me. I didn't know if he was talking to me or not. Then he handed me the bag, still not looking. The wine was sweet and smelled like his breath.

'Charles Smith,' he said.

'What?' I said.

'Charles Smith,' he said again, and stuck out his hand for the bottle.

'Some people call me Shed,' I said, 'and some others don't.' I took a drink, then handed back the bottle.

Charles Smith took a long drink, wine coming out the sides of his mouth. He wiped his mouth off with his forearm and burped. The white parts of his eyes weren't white. He stumbled back some, then caught his balance.

'Once a month like women,' he said. 'Commodity Day.'

'Commodity Day?' I asked. 'What kind of day is that?'

Charles Smith lowered the bottle and looked a hawk eye at me, then laughed. 'Day us Injuns get fed,' he said.

'What do you mean? Who feeds you?' I asked.

'America,' Charles Smith said. He held the bottle out to me. 'Another drink?'

I took the bag and drank the last of the wine.

'I'm looking for the buffalo,' I said.

'Buffalo?' Charles Smith said.

'Or what's left of them,' I said.

'We can get more wine,' Charles Smith said. 'Costs a dollar. Got a dollar?' he asked.

'Dollar's a lot for a bottle of wine,' I said.

'What kind of Injun are you?' Charles Smith asked, and stepped back, looking red-eyed at me full up and down. 'This is the reservation. Bottle of wine's a dollar, sometimes more than a dollar. Sometimes two dollars. What kind of Injun don't know Commodity Day? What kind of Injun is looking for the buffalo?'

I didn't know how to answer Charles Smith about what kind of Indian I was, so I just said, 'I got a dollar.'

He kept looking at me. His left eye hated me. Then: 'Follow me,' he said. I followed him.

We walked through the crowd again, through them waiting

for their bell to ring twenty times, passing their bottles, waiting, holding on to their beaded pouches.

'Sam True Shot!' the tybo yelled. 'Annie-In-The-Woods! Benjamin Henry! Moses Face Dog!'

We walked north and east, me and Charles Smith, along a road with other Indian people walking, their baskets full for the month, leading their packhorses, riding in wagons pulled by half-dead mules. At first, I thought that everyone was as drunk as Charles Smith because they were walking that way: as if there was only that one step.

But they weren't just drunk, though. They were tired, walking one step at a time, as if there might not be another step. My mother's people had come to this: to this dusty road with nothing left but the step they were taking. Then one more step. One more.

The screams were getting louder and the smell stronger the closer we came to a stone building. Charles Smith told me it was the slaughterhouse.

'Meat for the white man,' he said.

We cut across a field of dead June grass and empty wine bottles, crawled over a wooden gate and jumped down. We were in an alleyway that was surrounded by corrals with cattle all smashed together in them. All the cows looked at me, wanting to talk, wanting to find a human being to talk to, waiting. One cow had her horn caught under a railing, nose to the ground, blowing air and snot out, eyes on fire, wondering why. Other cows pushed up against her. Someone was cracking a whip. A chute door slammed shut. Runny green shit coming out of those animals, penned up, bawling, going to slaughter, no hope at all of getting out.

There were other animals locked up in the pens, too. I looked into one of the pens, and as soon as I saw the pigs, my nose and ears finally knew. What I had been smelling was blood. What I'd been hearing were these animals dying.

Charles Smith opened a metal door into the slaughterhouse and walked in. My body told me not to, but I followed him inside.

Soon as I walked in the door, I remembered the time I had shot a deer. When I ran up to the deer and saw the deer laying warm and dead, I cried to my mother, 'Surely it is wrong to kill!'

'All of us,' my mother had said, '– the four-leggeds, the winged ones, the fish, the animals who crawl, the two-leggeds – what we really are, are spirits trapped inside our bodies, begging to be set free.'

Inside the slaughterhouse, 'Free' was the word my lips spoke out loud, but *free* was not the word in my heart.

Up to that time in my life, I'd heard about the devil – how he was, how you never told him your name, how your eyes saw him one way and your heart saw him another – but up to that time, even with my mother getting murdered and me getting my ass pounded from Billy Blizzard, I had never been so close to the smell, to the scream, so close to the deranged that was how the devil was.

Charles Smith told me to stay at the door – to not come any farther in. He walked through the red screaming room to a door and then was gone. I stood in the slaughterhouse – all of me standing there – my eyes, my ears, my nose, skin trying to crawl away, feet wanting to run, breath pumping in and out of me, my heart!

Indian men in breechcloths, eyes dead as a dead pig's, stood in a chute barefoot in pig shit, tying a rope around the hind legs of a pig, pulling it up, the pig squealing the scream I had heard half a mile away – pig trying to make things right side up again, helpless legs too stumpy without respect climbing air. Another Indian man was above on a platform holding a knife. Human being eye to pig eye, stuck his knife a flash of light deep into the pig's throat – the red, the smell of red, the blood death splashing down over him, over pig, down into the gutter, into the blood gutter. When the blood stopped gushing, when the blood was only dripping, the pig was pulled across, head back throat cut open – a mouth stretched with scream too wide for any heart – to a table where more Indian men sliced and cut and gutted, pig feet going down one chute, pig head down another, pig guts down another.

Then a door opened and another pig was shoved in squealing, pulled up, the flash of knife going deep into the throat, into the scream in the throat, the blood.

It wasn't me who could stand in that place any longer. My stomach was trying to go up and out my mouth, and my mouth was trying to make my stomach stay down where it belonged. Before I knew it, my feet were in the next room where Charles Smith had gone. He was standing next to another Indian man whose naked body was covered with blood. I heard a shot and my body thought it was dead. I started to reach for the .22 strapped to my back, but I saw then that it was a cow that was dead, not me. I turned just in time to see the cow, standing in the light from the window above, slump over from the bullet, falling a beautiful dance to the floor. Dead on the floor, the cow was just a pile of stuff.

Free.

Without Moves Moves we're nothing.

In the corner there were more men pulling ropes. Cows rolled by on a moving table, their legs stuck up the four of them in the air, belly pointing up to sky. Cows' heads on all wrong – turned away crooked from death, eyes open.

'Eyes,' I said to my eyes, 'don't look into those eyes.'

I was out the back door, running. Took my body and threw it down on the earth, put my face into the dirt, picked up dirt with my hands, held dirt against my heart, ate dirt.

What was in my stomach came out my mouth. I rolled over and laid on the ground looking up at sky, on the dusty brown in the dry gold looking up at blue. I prayed to fly away from this dream, the devil's dream.

There was no flying away. Only laying and looking.

Charles Smith walked out the back door searching for me. He couldn't see me where I was. He walked through the corrals and around to the front of the building.

I didn't know if my body would let me get that close to the slaughterhouse again, but I got up anyway, picked up the gun, and started walking back.

When I walked around the corner of the slaughterhouse, I saw that there were Indian women standing around a hole in the side of the building. When I looked over at them, a big pile of guts came out of the hole and fell into a bloody trough on the street. The women bent over the guts and quickly picked them up with their bare hands, bare arms – the sound their hands and arms made. They put the guts into wood boxes, into sacks, into cans. They carried them to the wagons and dumped them in. You could hear the flies. There were guts hanging out from holes in the wagon sides, guts dangling down onto the wheels, guts on the axles.

Charles Smith was talking to one of the women. When she started talking, she motioned with a bloody arm back to where the *United States Government Commodity House* was. I watched her mouth speak. I couldn't understand a word. Then she said: 'Owlfeather.'

When Charles Smith saw me standing behind him, he walked over to me. He told me we were looking for Owlfeather. A man named Owlfeather.

*

When Charles Smith saw Princess tied to the hitching post in front of the Licensed Government Traders, he smiled big – smiling probably just how I smiled first time I saw Princess.

Then, when I walked up to Princess, and Charles Smith saw that Princess was my horse, Charles Smith's smile turned to something else.

'Where'd you steal the horse?' he asked.

'Didn't steal him,' I said. 'Bought him.'

'Bullshit,' Charles Smith said. 'Indians ain't got that kind of money. Government gave him to you, didn't they? What'd you have to do?'

'Didn't have to do anything for the government,' I said. Then I said, 'My father got him for me.'

'And that outfit of yours too?' Charles Smith said. 'Them boots, that hat, that Winchester – he got those for you too?'

What Charles Smith was asking me was no business of his at all. I was about to tell him just that, too, but when I laid my left eye on him, my mouth just couldn't say the words it wanted to say, because staring back at me through Charles Smith's eyes was my mother, and my mother's people.

I just said, 'Yes.'

'He's a white man, ain't he?' Charles Smith said. '. . . Your father.'

Most all of me right then wanted Charles Smith to shut up. My ears were ringing with twenty bells and my eyes were looking for what I could stuff into his cussed mouth.

'You look like an Indian but you ain't one,' Charles Smith said. 'You ain't crazy enough. Too much white daddy money and no Indian balls,' he said.

Charles Smith was smiling when he said 'Indian balls.'

Wasn't a joke.

I smiled back at him the way he was smiling, a joke not a joke.

'Where's this guy Owlfeather?' I said, lashing the .22 scabbard onto the saddle, making my eyes look at my hands, making my hands steady so I could tie the knot.

Charles Smith walked up to Princess with his hand out. Princess wouldn't have anything to do with him and danced sideways. I climbed into the saddle. Princess rared up.

What I saw laying in the dust of the street was Billy Blizzard's dead horse, bleeding from his left eye.

I reached my hand down, Charles Smith took my hand, got his foot into the stirrup, and swung himself up behind me.

Princess took off running. I could barely stay on, let alone Charles Smith hanging on to me from behind.

'At the blacksmith's!' Charles Smith shouted in my ear. 'Let's try there!'

He was laughing then, hugging himself to me. I reined Princess in the direction where he was pointing – toward the railroad tracks. Charles Smith reached down and cupped my balls for a second, laughing at the joke. White man's balls no Indian balls a joke.

The road went down some as we got closer to the tracks. Just ahead of us was a tin building set into the hill with smoke coming out its chimney. When we rode around to the front of the building, pieces of iron lay in twisted clumps in the sagebrush and weeds same way as around Thord Hurdlika's shop in Excellent. More iron things: railroad tracks, piles of cans, wagon parts, all over the place.

The way the sun hit the tin building, it was hard for your eyes to see. You had to look away the hot ball was so hot. Then when you could look, the inside of the building was darker than night gets. Black inside, hooks and chains hanging. Too bright outside, too dark inside.

There was a wagon in the yard jacked up in front of the tin building. My ears heard iron hitting iron.

Under a big clump of sagebrush, Indian men were sitting hunkered down the way my mother used to sit. Charles Smith's grip tightened around me. One of the Indian men wore a bowler hat, two others wore wide-brimmed hats. I could see that Bowler Hat had hair short the way tybos had hair.

Princess was still spooked, but was walking – high-stepping, tail up.

A couple of the Indian men were wearing white shirts and ties. Bowler Hat with the short hair was wearing a white man's suit and vest and wearing shoes. The rest of them wore blankets. I stopped Princess right in front of them.

Charles Smith spoke some kind of Indian language to the men, and as they talked back and forth, bright things – bracelets, earring dangles, necklaces, beaded bags, silver conches – flashed out from the dusty grey brown red black of them, splashes of light and water in a dust storm.

Their eyes looked at me without looking at me.

Then a gun went off and buckshot was landing all around. Princess rared and Charles Smith slid off the back onto the ground. Princess was trying not to step on him, Princess not knowing which the hell way to go. I couldn't stay on any longer either and landed smack on my butt hard, me still holding on to the reins. More shots and more buckshot. Charles Smith was running more jackrabbit than human being into the sagebrush.

I had landed right next to the Indian men. I let go of the reins and rolled to where they were hunkered down, then jumped in the middle of them, covering my head and keeping my ass low.

When I was me enough again to think, I looked up and what my eyes saw was a big bald tybo man with a black beard in a white undershirt that was black with black on his hands and face, black from his waist down to his black boots, just white pretty much around his eyes and under his arms when he raised them up.

What my ears heard after the gunshots was the Indian men laughing. Rolling around on the ground, laughing. Then my ears heard the white man who was mostly black, cussing or reciting the Bible – couldn't tell which.

'Lord Jesus, damned thieving Injun Charles Smith, you keep your thieving Pharisee Injun ass out of here!'

Charles Smith was still running, jumping sagebrush and running. Indians still laughing. The black white man put another shell in his shotgun and snapped it shut. He turned around to me and started walking closer. The Indian men piled out of his way fast, leaving me alone. Every step he got closer.

Devil again.

Out of the corner of my eye I saw Princess, and seeing Princess made me feel better. What my ears heard was me yelling the loudest I'd heard my mouth yell out so far – something that wasn't tybo, wasn't Indian. Was pigs screaming – mouth stretched out wide – no hope left. Killdeer sitting on her nest, no tricks left, wings ready to fly into the face of it.

The black white man raised the gun and pointed the gun at my forehead. My feet took me closer to the gun.

'Stop it!' I yelled.

'Stop killing us.'

The black white man put the gun down. The Indian men weren't laughing anymore and the gunshots had gone into sky. Only breathing and heart beating, and the black white man's boots on the hard dirt walking up to me, close. Him looking me in the left eye.

'I don't like the killing neither,' the black white man said. 'Been too much of it. "Thou shalt not kill," the Bible says.'

'Name's Zacharias Ward, son,' he said, offering me his hand. 'And that Charles Smith *is* one thieving Pharisee bastard. Been stealing ten years from me. I wouldn't lie to you.'

I shook his hand. 'Some call me Shed,' I said. 'Some others

don't. I'm looking for a man named Owlfeather. He's supposed to know where I can find the buffalo and buy a bottle of whiskey.'

'Whiskey ain't good for you, son,' Zacharias Ward said. 'Especially for you Injuns. It's against the Lord's commandments to partake of strong drink.'

'Do you know this man Owlfeather?' I asked.

'Did you hear what I just said?' Zacharias Ward said.

'I heard you,' I said.

'Well?' Zacharias Ward said. 'Don't you know the word of God when you hear it?'

'Do you know this man Owlfeather?' I asked.

'Smart-ass know-it-all Injuns,' Zacharias Ward said. 'All of you cut from the same cloth.'

'Owlfeather,' I said.

'Yup, I know him,' Zacharias Ward said. 'Don't know where he is, though. Was supposed to show up here this afternoon, but he hasn't yet. Maybe these Injuns can tell you where he is.'

Zacharias Ward pointed the shotgun over at the sagebrush.

Was one of the longest walks I'd ever taken, from where I was standing to where the Indian men were sitting. I looked at my new boots walking on the hard dirt of the blacksmith's yard. Looked at my shadow not going any farther than right under me. My body was trying to get big, trying to disappear at the same time. Then I was standing in front of my mother's people, not knowing what to say, so my mouth just went ahead.

'Any of you know a man named Owlfeather?' I asked.

I had never seen men like them before. Two of them were about my age. There was Bowler Hat with the short hair, wearing a tybo's black suit, black shoes, no socks, a white shirt gone brown red from living next to dirt, and a black tie. The other young one had his hair pulled back and braided in one long braid down the back, the hair on top of his head sticking up like a porcupine. He was wearing a big shirt and buckskin pants and moccasins.

Besides these two men, there were three men Dellwood Barker's age. They wore wide-brimmed hats, their long hair coming down straight and shiny and black – or curly from out of a wet braid like my mother used to do. One of them had an animal hide wrapped around his waist and circles of necklaces hanging down his chest. I looked at the beads on the necklace real close. Tiny beads all sewn together in a pattern like the American flag – red, white, and blue.

'Where'd you steal the horse?' American Flag said.

'Didn't steal him,' I said.

'Then it was the government,' he said. 'What'd you have to do?'

'Become a Christian?' Porcupine asked.

'No,' I said.

'Go away to school?'

'No,' I said.

'Get adopted by a Mormon family?'

'No,' I said.

'Cut your hair?'

'No,' I said.

'Buffalo Bill's Wild West Show?'

'No,' I said.

'Sign your land over to the reservation supervisor?'

'No,' I said. 'My father got him for me.'

'Who's your father?'

'Teddy Roosevelt,' I said.

'Ignorant Injuns,' Zacharias Ward said, shaking his head when he heard me say Teddy Roosevelt. Then he walked over to the wagon he had jacked up and went back to work on the axle. Soon as Zacharias Ward left, the Indian men started laughing.

'Who's your mother?' Porcupine asked. 'Queen Victoria?'
Indians laughing again.

'No,' I said, 'my mother was the Princess. She was Bannock. Her name was Buffalo Sweets. You know her or heard of her?'

The Indians didn't answer me, just looked ahead. I sat down under the sagebrush with them. Waited for more talking, more laughing. It didn't come. All we did was sit and look ahead and listen to the wind going through the sagebrush.

'Owlfeather going to be here pretty soon?' I asked.

'Are you really Indians?' I asked.

'Did there really used to be a million buffalo?' I asked.

Either they had forgotten how to speak tybo all of a sudden, or my mouth wasn't working again, or I had disappeared, because none of the Indians answered me or even looked as if they'd heard me talking.

Then Porcupine said, 'Owlfeather will be here.'

Then American Flag said, 'We're Bannocks – full bloods.'

Then Bowler Hat said, 'More buffalo than was numbers to count them.'

Then Bowler Hat said, 'Your horse.'

'What about him?' I said.

'Better go get him. Some Injun'll snap him up,' Bowler Hat said.

'What you call that black stallion?' American Flag asked.

'Princess,' I said.

Their fool heads off, them Indians laughing.

I walked over to where Princess was on the other side of the railroad tracks.

'Told you not to worry,' I said to Princess, then looked around. Charles Smith was long gone.

When the wagon was ready to go, Zacharias Ward called over to the Indian men. Porcupine ran behind the shop and over the rise toward town. Bowler Hat got up and walked to the wagon, followed by the others. Bowler Hat grabbed the wheel and shook the wheel.

'It'll hold!' Zacharias Ward said.

Bowler Hat said something in Indian to the other men. One by one they shook the wheel. They talked some more. Bowler Hat took a beaded wallet from out of his coat pocket. He carefully placed a silver dollar into Zacharias Ward's big greasy hand. Zacharias Ward picked up the silver dollar and turned it over, looking at the dollar close.

Porcupine came barreling around the corner on a horse and leading another.

Something made me scrutinize the horses. The something was that they were a matched team, big boned and healthy. So far they were the first things I'd seen in Fort Lincoln that didn't look like they were begged, borrowed, stolen, or about ready to die. I scrutinized the wagon then. The wagon was brand new too – painted red.

When I turned around from scrutinizing the wagon, there was an old man standing next to me.

He had the faces of the other men all wrapped up in his. His forehead, his wrinkles, cheekbones, chin, were all the same flat rolling dusty earth that I had been traveling through ever since I had left Excellent, Idaho. His skin draped itself over a skull that was round as moon. His eyes weren't eyes, they were holes in his head that let the light in him out. Moonlight. Sun's light reflected. The eyes of a child: nothing between to stop me from falling headlong into.

'I am Owlfeather,' he said, and coughed. 'You are looking for me.'

Scared sparrows came over the ridgepole of the tin shed. My mind forgot who I was, so I just stood looking.

'I need a bottle of whiskey,' my mouth said.

'Whiskey?' Owlfeather said. 'Thought you were looking for buffalo?'

'Yes, buffalo,' my mouth said.

'You want to look for the buffalo drunk on whiskey?' Owlfeather asked.

'No,' my mouth said.

'You want to find them first and then get drunk on whiskey?' Owlfeather asked.

'Yes,' my mouth said.

'You always do this when you look for buffalo?' he asked.

'Never seen buffalo,' my mouth said.

'Then you'll be needing some whiskey,' Owlfeather said. 'You'll need to come with me.'

'Get this young man some whiskey,' Owlfeather said to Porcupine. 'Got two dollars?'

I reached in my pouch, pulled out two dollars – making sure nobody saw how much money I had – and gave the two dollars to Owlfeather. Owlfeather gave the two dollars to Porcupine, and Porcupine ran off over the hill again.

'Where'd you steal the horse?' Owlfeather asked.

The Indians harnessed the team of horses and hitched them up to the wagon. They made a special place for Owlfeather with their blankets, then lifted him onto the wagon. When Owlfeather was situated, they sat themselves around him. I unsaddled Princess, put his saddle so Owlfeather could lean against it. Porcupine came running with the whiskey just as we were starting off. I tied Princess onto the back of the wagon.

Zacharias Ward came out of his dark shed with a big book just as we started rolling. He was reading from the big book about sin everlasting damnation and fire.

I watched Zacharias Ward and his bright tin shop get smaller and smaller. I looked down my dangling legs and feet off the back of the wagon at the dusty red brown dirt going by under me. Dirt going by underneath and the wagon moving slow over land you could see horizon all around, making you feel alone and small with just your breath, your heartbeat.

Then I felt a hand on me. It was Owlfeather's hand. It was Dellwood Barker's hand. It was the human-being hand reaching out the touch that feels so good you hurt for all the times you never felt it.

'You like Bannock Wolf's new wagon?' Owlfeather asked. He didn't wait for me to answer. 'He's the one driving this rig. The one in the bowler hat. Bannock Wolf's his name. Got the wagon the day before yesterday from the American government for cutting his hair and putting those new clothes on. Just had it two days and it broke down. Injuns ain't got no luck with white-man things. Last week Bannock Wolf was baptized Mormon. Says he wants to make something of himself. United States government's going to give him a house – one of those square houses with only half a window – for some reason, that's all the window the United States government will put in a house for an Indian is half a window. Going to change his name to white man's name next. Says he's thinking about Brigham. Brigham Hall Smith Jones, Brigham Wayne, Brigham O'Connor – one of those Brighams.

'Bannock Wolf is going to make something of himself. All you got to do is change your clothes, cut your hair, change your name, get baptized, and start farming. It's that easy to make something of yourself. Just ask Charles Smith – he'll tell you how easy it is. His name used to be Red Hawk before he got his wagon and team of horses.'

Owlfeather started coughing then, his whole body was coughing.

'Usually can't talk that much in one stretch,' he said between breaths he was taking.

'I told you my name, what's yours?' he said after he settled down.

'Duivichi-un-Dua,' I said. 'That's the Indian name my mother gave me. Her name was Buffalo Sweets. She was Bannock. My father I don't know for sure. He was one of my mother's customers. They call me Shed – that's short for Out-In-The-Shed because it's my job out there in the shed,' I said.

'Do you know what that name means, Duivichi-un-Dua?' I asked.

I went back to watching my legs dangle over the side and the brown red dirt going by slow underneath. That dust had been the taste in my mouth since I'd left Dellwood Barker. Fort Lincoln was out of sight and so were its smell and the screams. The road was making its way between clumps of sagebrush. Lava rocks were starting up, poking up out of the earth to look at me again. Princess walked behind, reins hanging loose. I looked at Princess and loved him so much right then.

'Duivichi-un-Dua,' Owlfeather said. 'It's not my language. These men and me, we are Bannock. This name is not in our language. This name is in the Shoshone language. Are you sure your mother was Bannock?' Owlfeather asked.

'I thought she was Bannock,' I said.

'On the reservation here there are many bands of Indians – Shoshone, Northern Shoshone, Bannock, some Nez Perce.' Owlfeather said, 'We all came together here because there was no place left, so it was here that we came where America told us to come. They put a square line around us like the square houses they build for us and we look out of our half window onto the world that was our mother that is now a place where we live. Now we stay in one place fenced in when we used to walk around.'

Then Porcupine said: 'We fished the salmon up north in the fall. We hunted buffalo, elk, moose, and antelope. In the spring we gathered seeds, berries, camas roots, and hunted smaller game. Then there were the pine nuts.'

'Up on Bear River,' American Flag said, 'up there was winter camp for the Shoshone.'

Bowler Hat said, 'The Shoshone took their dried meat there and berries, their seeds and lived a good life with our mother in their tipis there. We Bannocks sometimes went there and played winter sports with them – horse races, hockey, and dancing.'

Owlfeather started coughing again, his legs jumping around and his arms all over the place coughing. Porcupine and American Flag had to hold him down so he wouldn't fly off the wagon.

'Then General O'Connor came,' Porcupine said, 'and it was all downhill after that. He and his troops killed the Shoshone, killed the Indian people, killed us all at the Bear River Massacre – men, women, and children – killed us all. Two hundred and fifty bodies laying around dead. Cut women's throats while they were fucking them. The snow was bloody red. The waters of the Bear River were red.'

'They killed Chief Bear Hunter,' Owlfeather said. 'An American soldier put his bayonet in the fire til it was red-hot and then he stuck the red-hot bayonet in the ear of Chief Bear Hunter and ran it through his head til it came out the other ear.'

'Shoshone have never been the same,' American Flag said.

'They still got that hot bayonet in their heads,' Owlfeather said. 'We all do.'

Then: 'The enemy is within us now and we kill ourselves,' Owlfeather said.

'Duivichi-un-Dua,' Owlfeather said. 'It is a Shoshone name. From what I know, the name means something like "a boy's boy," ' he said.

'A boy's boy,' I said.

'Yes, I think that's it,' he said. 'A boy's boy – does this name make sense to you?' he asked.

'It makes sense,' I said. 'I am Berdache. I reached for the basket and the gourd.'

For the feathered boa!

Owlfeather's eyes opened wide. Bowler Hat just about fell off the wagon. The men who hadn't been looking at me, looked at me.

'Yes,' Owlfeather said. 'It makes sense, then – the name,' he said.

*

Owlfeather's house with a half window was a square of shadow in the moon. The moon, low on the horizon, a half window too, a sleepy eye looking down at us trying to see.

Down at us was children and dogs and cats running every which way, everybody trying to get next to Owlfeather.

When we helped him out of the wagon, when both his feet were standing on the ground, every human being – every child, every dog and cat – found some way to get Owlfeather to touch them. He touched them with his open hand, him smiling and talking, greeting each one of them, looking into their eyes.

When all the touching and greeting was done, Porcupine and American Flag picked up Owlfeather, carried him around back of the house, and sat him down on a tree stump under a couple of scrub elms.

Bowler Hat picked up Princess's saddle, threw the saddle over his shoulder, and handed me the blanket.

'Follow me,' Bowler Hat said.

I followed him to a barn just over a rise.

'American government's barn,' Bowler Hat said. 'But they'll never know about it,' he said, 'so you can keep your Princess stallion in the American government's barn for the night.'

Barn was red and had a barbed wire fence around it. There

was a sign: *Property of the United States Government*. Another sign said: *Keep Out*. Bowler Hat led me and Princess through a cut wire place in the fence. The barn door slid right open.

'Just like we owned the place,' Bowler Hat said.

I tied Princess in a stall and combed him down, talking to him, while Bowler Hat brought fresh water and hay – the American government's hay.

Bowler Hat looked in Princess's mouth and checked his teeth.

'Teddy Roosevelt,' was all Bowler Hat said.

I put the scabbard and the .22 in the stanchion next to Princess, then me and Bowler Hat walked back to the square house together, him not talking, me either. Croaking frogs were so loud that's all you could hear.

The sky was more deep blue than black. Stars – sweat beads shook off of someone big's big hand. The bonfire behind the square house was bright licking high into the deep blue. Next to the house, a tipi – a real tipi – and people sitting around the fire.

The closer we got to the fire the better we could hear them laughing. Somebody'd talk Indian and then they'd laugh. More Indian talk and then more laughter. Besides the talking and laughing and the fire, and the frogs, there was my boots and Bowler Hat's new shoes hitting the ground, dogs barking, a cat yelling at another cat, and the children.

Owlfeather was sitting in a rocking chair with a blanket over his legs, next to the stump where they'd first sat him. When he saw me, Owlfeather motioned that I should sit on the stump.

'We can eat tonight,' he said. 'Everybody's happy when they can eat. Injuns love food.'

There was a kerosene lamp in the square house. Big shadows of women were in the house and women talking Indian fast, chopping things up, and fat frying. Wasn't long before it smelled onions and meat. When the smell was everywhere, the children stopped running and tearing around. They sat down quietly near the stoop of the square house. In the firelight in their eyes what I saw was I had never been hungry.

Old men around the fire. One man now and then left and came back with wood. The old men smoked and looked into the flames. They spoke soft words and sat close to each other.

Young men around the fire, more in the shadows, wild in their eyes, did not speak, listened to the old men talk.

Owlfeather watched the young men. Smoked and watched us. The air was on you warm without a breeze. So quiet, pine-tar fire snaps made you jump. In all the whole round world, and even more, I with my name, with my mother's people, sat by a tipi around fire.

When the women brought out the kettle of stew, they set it on river rocks on the ground and put the plates and bowls and glasses next to the kettle. Then out came a big pile of fry bread and water in a big glass pitcher.

The women sat down, covering their legs with their skirts. Owlfeather stood up. Wasn't easy for him to stand up. He looked at the sky and opened his arms to the sky, facing east, north, west, south – his prayer in Indian how it sounds when you cry alone.

Everything in the night listening.

When Owlfeather lowered his arms and sat back down, everybody said the same thing out loud all at once, and then started in on the stew – children first, then the old men, the young men, then the women.

Best food I ever ate. Chunks of meat and potatoes and carrots and celery, dipping the stew up with the fry bread. In no time my bowl was empty. 'Go ahead, get a second,' Owlfeather told me.

My stomach agreed with Owlfeather, and my feet were on the way to the kettle of stew, when my eyes saw the child leaning over her bowl.

Month was a long time to wait for food.

I lit up one of Porcupine's cigarettes instead.

The dogs were all lined up silent and serious, the cats stretching, ribs sticking out, so skinny you could see their lungs work.

Owlfeather said something to the girl leaning over her bowl. The girl smiled big and left her bowl and went running into the square house. She came back out with the bones. The girl gave each dog a bone, each cat.

When it came time to wash things up there wasn't much to wash because everything was licked clean. I got up to help with the dishes. Owlfeather said something and all the Indians laughed.

'You can help us later,' a hefty woman said to me. The Indians laughed again.

That same woman brought a big chocolate cake out of the square house and a big bowl of some kind of berry pudding and set the cake and the bowl of berry pudding onto the stump where I'd been sitting. She laid a bowie knife down next to the cake. Owlfeather cut the cake, served the cake up into the same bowl you had for stew, and then handed the bowl of cake to the woman who put berry pudding on top of your piece of cake. He served the children first, him licking his fingers every chance he'd get. While he was serving the cake, Owlfeather started talking to me loud so everybody could hear.

'My wife Hazel here says you can help her later,' Owlfeather said. 'She's very happy to have a Berdache around here again. Been thirty years since any Injun's owned up to that. Doubt even if my sons know what that is. Maybe they know. Hard not to know about Berdache even if nobody ever talks about Berdache.

'We quit talking about our old ways and Berdache. Were afraid that America'd take our food away, or take our land away, or make us cut our hair, or make us stop believing in our religion. But they've gone and done that anyway, even though we kept quiet about Berdache to them. My own sons now might even laugh at you. My son Charles Smith would laugh at you. I know that's a fact. And I think of all my sons, he is the Berdache. Years ago that was a blessing, you know, being Berdache. Now just look at him. Look at my son used to be Red Hawk now Charles Smith now a drunken laughingstock. I should've helped him better.'

Owlfeather went into a coughing fit. Hazel took the plate of cake from him and waited. When Owlfeather finished coughing, he started up again on the chocolate cake and berry pudding.

'So my wife Hazel could use some help with the dishes, but really what she needs help with is for me to fuck you tonight so I'll quit bothering her.'

Even the dogs started laughing. Loud long hard laughing. Their fool heads off.

Hazel said something in Indian and everybody laughed again – even harder, if that's possible, especially the women laughing.

'Hazel says she hopes that you're man enough to bother me half as much as I claim to bother her,' Owlfeather said.

Me and the women did up the dishes. In the square house with half a window, the women and the smell of them, the arms of them in soapy water, was Ida Richilieu, was the whores I was raised with, was my mother, was Alma Hatch.

When I sat back down at the fire the men were drinking beers and passing a bottle of whiskey. The women sat down with the beer too. Some of them took sips on the whiskey.

When the bottle came to Bowler Hat, Bowler Hat passed the bottle on without drinking. When the bottle came to Owl-feather, Owlfeather looked at the bottle and said, 'I don't drink because my heart tells me not to. Bannock Wolf doesn't drink because the Mormon Church tells him not to.'

Owlfeather handed the bottle of whiskey to me. 'And you,' he said. 'You'd better drink up a good one,' he said. 'You're about to see your first buffalo.'

That bottle went around and then another one. I passed around the locoweed. The old men brought out drums and started singing songs and beating on the drums. The drums were moon language, my heartbeat, my breath.

Owlfeather leaned over and touched me again. 'I asked around,' he said. 'None of these folks remember a woman by the name of Buffalo Sweets. Are you sure your mother was a Bannock and not a Shoshone?' Owlfeather asked. 'The name she gave you, Duivichi-un-Dua, is Shoshone. Figures if she gave you a Shoshone name she was herself Shoshone. Or maybe she was Nez Perce, or another tribe – Cree.'

'I don't know,' I said, thinking about what I remembered about her.

'Don't be too disappointed if you never find out about your mother,' Owlfeather said. 'What happened to the Indian people is the same as if a giant wind had come along and threw us around for years and years. Killed almost everybody, this giant wind, then left the rest for dead. When the living, like your mother, went back to their homes, they couldn't find their homes, or the hills or the valleys where their homes used to be. Indian people got thrown around so much, got so used to misery and dying, that they started to forget things like why they were living. "Why do we live?" "Why do we live?" they went around asking each other. But nobody could remember. That hot bayonet was stuck through their brains ear to ear and they couldn't remember. There's only so much pain you can feel before you start forgetting. Pretty soon pain is your mother. Lost is your mother. Pain and lost is your home. You got to know who you are and why you live before you can find your way home.'

My mother's people sat around the fire, the men beating on drums, the men and women and children singing the coyote wolf howl. Outside the light of the fire, in the darkness beyond, all around them was only flat, only sagebrush and wind. Fences all around them, reservation – and beyond, in the darkness within the darkness, all around them was *Keep Out,* all around them was *Property of the United States Government,* all around them, surrounding my mother's people, was America.

Fire in front of my eyes, I took another swig off the bottle of whiskey.

Who I was, was Duivichi-un-Dua – boy's boy.

Why I lived was to find out who I was, and to find the buffalo.

I stood up.

'I want to see the buffalo,' I said.

'Behind America's barn,' Owlfeather said. 'Where you tied up your Princess stallion.'

My feet walked outside the light of fire, into the frogs croaking and the stars. I walked, Indian songs laying on the night, darkness all around me, to the darkness of America's barn.

The moon was bright behind the roof of the barn. I walked through the cut wire place in the fence, and opened the barn door. I didn't stop to lay my hand on Princess. Just kept walking through the barn, to behind the barn, to the buffalo. I walked out the back door where the moon was. Where the square pen was. Where the barbed wire was.

In the moonlight, out behind America's barn, in the pen, I found the buffalo. One old solitary buffalo. Breath rasping, ragged fur, head bent, she raised her tail and let go runny shit. In the square pen behind America's barn, the buffalo, my mother's people, standing at the fence looking out, trying to find where home was, why we were living, trying to remember how things used to be when we walked around free.

My feet walked right up to the buffalo. I stood, my eyes looking into the buffalo's blind eyes, and laid my hands on the buffalo's head. The buffalo snorted, bucked her head, and limped away.

I heard Princess. Heard something wrong. I walked to the

back door of the barn and opened the door slowly. There was a shot and my ear heard the .22 bullet go into the wood it was that close. I threw myself on the floor and rolled. More shots. Princess was kicking the stall and yelling horse yells. Then I heard: 'Fucking rich white daddy no Injun balls son of a bitch.'

'Princess!' I shouted.

The barn door opened and Princess was a shadow and Charles Smith was a shadow. The shadow jumped onto Princess. The .22 in his hand was a shadow. I was out the door and up against Princess and Charles Smith's leg. I was on top of Princess behind Charles Smith, me getting him hard by his Indian balls, me with my other hand pulling Charles Smith's head back so far his neck was a hair from snap. Princess crashed through the fence and ran toward the fire.

Then, there were men and women all around us and me and Charles Smith were laying on the ground, me still at his head and balls, him no longer a shadow crying out for the pain in his head and balls.

Owlfeather touched me again. 'We must not kill our own, Duivichi-un-Dua! Let go!' Owlfeather said.

My name. I let go. I stood up.

Owlfeather took the .22 from Charles Smith, from his son. Owlfeather laid the gun on the ground. Charles Smith put his hands between his legs and cried. Cried the way I'd always wanted to, for shame, for no name and my lost home. The frogs were silent. The fire was the light. The fire was the sound. Charles Smith crying was the sound.

My eyes looked over and the buffalo was standing behind Charles Smith – the light of the fire, the light in the buffalo's eyes. We all stood silent as the buffalo walked, favoring her bad leg, away from Charles Smith, past Princess, toward the square house with half a window, then stopped, turned, and walked toward the fire, horns and hump a shadow. The buffalo stopped, shook her head, backed up, pawed the earth, turned again, then walked out of the circle of light, back into the darkness.

'Back into her pen,' Owlfeather said.

The scream: at first my ears thought my mouth had gone wild again. But the scream wasn't mine, wasn't the buffalo's. The scream was Charles Smith's. He was standing up, his eyes gone clean out of his head looking at somewhere else. Owlfeather was on the ground. The .22 was in Charles Smith's hands. He raised the gun and shot Princess in the left eye, Princess falling graceful slow all the way down.

Without Moves Moves we're nothing.

I looked straight up the barrel of the .22 as Charles Smith shot. The bullet went into me, into my heart. I looked down at my blood on my chest. Looked back up. Charles Smith's gone eyes the devil's eyes. His smile the slit pig's throat smile, the flash of red-hot bayonet blade deep into his brain, slicing through, ear to ear.

Charles Smith turned the gun on himself. Put the barrel in his mouth. He shot and his brains flew into the air.

Then it was my breath, my heart.

Then it wasn't.

Charles Smith had killed me.

No light only dark.

Book Three

There was a Time: Homecoming

It was late spring, almost June, when I got back up on the stage and left Fort Lincoln. This time, I was riding up top because I wanted to.

At Robber's Roost, just out of Fort Hall, where the Portneuf River curves through a narrow valley, I scrutinized the land where Dellwood Barker's mother and father had been murdered. All my eyes could see was sun, flat, sagebrush, and an owl sailing through the blue.

The morning I got to Owyhee City, I walked to the Syringa, didn't stop at the porch to look in, pushed open the doors, walked into the saloon, stood myself under the chandelier from Salt Lake City, and ordered a whiskey. I looked the bartender with the mustache square in the eye and drank the whiskey down. About then, Sheriff Blumenfeld walked into the Syringa. Put his big belly up to the bar and ordered a sarsaparilla. Stood right next to me. Didn't recognize me, him having eyes for me that were only eyes for a shit-stained, shit-smelling Indian kid he had once cornered like an animal. Almost asked Blumenfeld if he'd seen Dellwood Barker around. Instead, I asked the bartender where I could find Ellen Finton and Gracie Hammer.

Sheriff Blumenfeld turned and looked his fat face at me. I looked him right back.

'Old friends of mine,' I said.

'Up in Excellent and Gold Bar last I heard,' the bartender said. 'The both of them.'

Back on top of the stage, back on the road, I watched the flat start breaking up into pieces – the pieces moving around – mostly ending up on the top of mountains they call mesas. The trees started in late afternoon – families of them clumped together by the river – poplars first and Russian olives, then higher up it was pines, spruce, juniper. The sky went back to where it belonged – on top of tall trees – and the air got cool the way it's supposed to be in early June in the evening. The stagecoach leaned through the switchbacks. Forever was straight down on each side of me, me smiling away because the wind was all around me, because I was being snagged by the spirit of Not-Really-A-Mountain, because I was headed home.

*

After Charles Smith shot me, looking for where I was was where I was.

Sometimes, I was outside my body. Sometimes, I was inside.

When I was outside my body, it wasn't so hard figuring out where I was, who I was – not hard to tell that I wasn't Porcupine, or Owlfeather's wife, Hazel, or Bowler Hat, wasn't the square house with half a window, wasn't American Flag, or the tipi, or the Indian kids, or the dogs, wasn't the rocking chair.

Inside my body, it was harder. There wasn't a place where I could point to and say, *There I am, that's me.* No matter how hard I tried, the me who had this body just wasn't to be found.

Even when it was me who was doing the looking.

What I could find was the moves but not who was making the moves.

So, I promised myself that when I was done laying down from

this bullet, that when I got back up, I was going to be especially grateful for my name – and be very careful telling my name out, because, as it seemed to me, there was no me except that I had a name that said I was the me who was named that.

I floated around outside my body only at first – right after the bullet had gone into my heart – looking at Princess, at the buffalo, at Owlfeather and Charles Smith.

They were not me. Who I was was the guy with the hole in his heart, holding on to his chest, staring up at the moon.

It wasn't long though, and I wasn't outside at all and I was only inside.

Inside, the longer I stayed, the harder it got not to be everything.

Inside, I went to fever, to where I went when Billy Blizzard had pounded my ass down. Went to forever. My head was Buffalo Head and my arms were lava rock buffalo arms. Someone big had piled me up, just so. The rest of me was different parts of the world. My ass was Minneapolis, Minnesota. My feet were over the horizon, stuck up in Rome, Italy, out of the earth, out of Ida's husband's little dick ashes. My left eye was lunar lunacy, my right eye too afraid to look. My dick was a hole full of snakes.

All around me, what I heard were Indians, my mother's people, singing and crying and singing. Next to my head was a fire and the round white river rocks in the fire were singing to me too.

I was with Owlfeather and we were riding on Princess – riding around free, no reservation, no fences, no square house with a half window. Just us, riding over hills with June grass that was always green and blowing nice with wind. Buffalo everywhere. Owlfeather was talking – always talking, telling me important things, telling me the truth, telling me jokes, showing me how my mother's people looked at the world, the round Big Mother world – us digging camas root, hunting the four-leggeds, gathering pine nuts, spearing salmon in white clear fresh cold water.

I was sweating, laying in a dark cold place sweating, fire by my head and Indians singing their coyote wolf howling songs, killdeer songs. *Go here*, they seemed to be saying, *turn here, go that way*.

I was flying with owl above everything, flying into the sun that was always setting, trying to get to the edge where the horizon was.

I was in a tipi and there was a snowbank drifted against the tipi that had cracked the pole by my head and split another. There was a fire inside the tipi and people huddling around the fire. They were covered with blankets and hides. It was cold – out-in-the-shed cold, only more. Commodity Day was nowhere in sight.

There was a baby crying. Seemed like forever that baby was crying. Then the baby stopped.

Story goes when I woke up the next spring, I was spelling words, was talking about a mountain not being a mountain, and singing a song about the moon.

First thing I did was try to get up. I started walking but my feet didn't agree. They were still in Rome, Italy, and not used to doing what they were told.

What I remember was Porcupine pouring cool water on my face. I opened my left eye and looked into his human eye. Took me days to open my right eye. When I opened my right eye I looked down to the hole in my chest. Looked as if someone big had poked his finger there.

The next time I tried walking, Porcupine helped me out of the tipi. I had to keep a hold of Porcupine and walk slow. When I got outside, a bunch of people that I didn't know gathered around me. Then I recognized a couple of them – American Flag and Bowler Hat and Owlfeather's wife, Hazel. Each one of them came up to me and touched me – even the children came up and touched me. They were smiling and some of them had tears in their eyes.

'Welcome back,' they said. 'Welcome back.'

Porcupine took me to where they'd made Owlfeather's fire bed – on the side of one of those hills with lava rock Indian warriors standing in slabs. The morning was sunny, and the Idaho wind almost picked me up and took me with it. The June grass was just coming up that new green color, moving fancy.

All that was left of Owlfeather was a burnt spot on the ground. I stood and looked at the burnt spot, thinking about the other burnt spot in my life. Little did I know then about the big burnt spot that was yet to come.

'Tell me the story,' I said to Porcupine, having to yell because the wind was so strong.

Porcupine sat down cross-legged, facing the burnt spot, wind blowing his hair the way the wind was blowing the grass. He started talking but I couldn't hear him, so I went over to him and sat down right next to him, so close I could smell the buckskin and sweat of him and what he'd eaten for breakfast. When I did that, he got big tears in his eyes and he laid his head on my chest and sobbed. I put my arm around him, lifting the blanket up I'd tied around me, and me and him sat that way. When he could talk, when he quit crying, Porcupine told me this story.

'After Charles Smith shot you, before I knew it, Owlfeather was on your heart sucking the bullet out of you. And he got it out, too. I saw the bullet sticking out between his teeth,' Porcupine said, talking like he had a bullet between his teeth.

Porcupine waited for a while, thinking about what he was going to say next. Then he said, 'What happened after that shouldn't have happened at all.' Porcupine got up, and as he told the story, he moved his body through it, as if the story was really happening.

'Owlfeather turned to Charles Smith,' Porcupine turned. 'He tried to spit that bullet out, but it was just too much for him. He was already sick from too much healing – him taking on just about every ache and pain in the Bannock nation – Shoshone too. Plus, there he was – Charles Smith – Owlfeather's own son flopping around like a chicken with his head cut off.' Porcupine shook his arms and legs. 'Then I saw the bullet go into Owlfeather and I knew it was the end. I ran over there and put my mouth to his, sucking with all my might, but I'm no medicine man – no Berdache like you – I couldn't make that damned bullet inside him budge. I asked him to please tell me what to do. He told me to tell the truth. All I could say was, 'I love you and don't want you to go.' Owlfeather smiled at me and told me that if I really loved him I'd kiss him like that again.

'I jumped up to get some help from somebody, but everybody was just standing around not doing anything just staring. When I looked down again, I saw Owlfeather blow his dying breath into you – was like a big puff of smoke that came out of his mouth and then went into yours. When I walked over to Owlfeather he was dead. You were breathing again.'

Some stories are harder to listen to than others. Porcupine's story was one of those. All the while he was telling it, I was looking at the burnt spot. I had always known the devil was close to me, but right then, the devil seemed as if he *was* me. Anybody with the luck of getting too close to me had always suffered.

'Why did he do it?' I asked.

Porcupine thought for a while and then shrugged his shoulders. 'Because it was there to do,' he said. 'Owlfeather always said a medicine man never had to go looking for a fight. Said a medicine man's everyday life was his battleground – no different from the rest of us – it's just that the medicine man has the knowledge his life is his battleground, and never forgets it.

'That's how Medicine men do it, you know – healing – they take on the sickness themselves.' Porcupine touched his heart. 'Then they heal themselves of the sickness – or don't. Only way you can help them is to tell the truth while they're healing – but you know all about that,' Porcupine said.

'About what?' I asked.

'About medicine,' he said.

'Me?' I said.

'You,' he said.

'How so?' I asked.

'You're here. You're alive. Any other man'd be dirt by now.'

'Owlfeather was the one,' I said, 'not me.'

'You did it, alright,' Porcupine said. 'And you know it. You're Berdache, ain't you?'

'But you said yourself that Owlfeather blew his spirit like a big puff of smoke into me,' I said.

'He crawled over to you, alright, but you were helping him,' Porcupine said. 'Owlfeather couldn't have done that alone – but don't get me wrong – I'm not saying you forced him to do something he didn't want to do. It's simple – you asked him for his breath and he agreed so he gave his breath to you.'

My heart was beating so hard I thought my heart would bust again, but I just kept sitting by the burnt spot. The longer I sat, the harder it got listening to Porcupine's story. I pulled the blanket over my ears. I wanted to keep the wind out of them so I could hear myself think. That's when it dawned on me.

'Porcupine,' I said, 'those people back at the tipi. Why were they so nice to me? They hardly know me.'

'Just friendly I guess – friendly Injuns,' he said.

'Porcupine,' I said, 'tell me the truth. Do those folks think I'm Owlfeather?' I asked.

'The truth?' Porcupine asked.

'The truth,' I said.

'They think you're Owlfeather,' he said.

*

The hotel was still pink and pink was the color of sunset when my eyes first looked up and saw.

I crawled down off the stage. Attended to my luggage. First thing I heard was her singing the man-in-the-moon song, her voice deep and sounding like something about to break. I watched my feet walk up the seven wood steps, my ears listening to the sound the steps had always made. I looked in the window. Ida Richilieu was wearing the blue dress.

She didn't see me, least she didn't let me know she saw. I walked around the side of the building, the windows open, her song going with me. There were no sheets on the line. The ground wasn't pink anymore. When I got to the shed I stopped. There was a padlock on the in door. Around back there was padlock on the out door. I pressed my face against the window. The window Ellen Finton had been the last to see my mother alive through. There was my bed, my Hudson Bay on my bed. The deer hide. The petticoat that was a curtain still hanging down from the curtain rod that was an old broom handle. The braided rug on the floor. The kerosene lamp on the stand, burnt matches next to it. The same matchsticks. Just the way I had left them.

Up the back stairs of Ida's Place, my eyes carried me up more than my feet. I seemed to be hanging from my eyes, just floating along, looking at all those special things, really not special at all except that my eyes were looking at them again, looking at the then and the now: the slick on the banister, the soap stuck in the corners of the steps, wainscoting I used to pretend were doors for thin little people, the window at the landing where I'd always rest the bucket of hot water and look out. No matter how many times she washed the doily curtain it always smelled of dust.

In the upstairs hallway it was part of the dream I'd had when I was dying while Owlfeather sucked the bullet out of my heart, me running down the hallway, bare feet on the flowers of the carpet, searching for Ida.

I walked to the banister. The bar was full of tybos drinking, getting hungry for their sex story. Business looked good. Below me was the piano, Ida Richilieu's blue taffeta back, her pile of hair and combs, her feathered boa, pearls *from the ocean*, her skinny arms sticking out like sticks, her fingers long piano keys themselves – ivory smooth against ivory, she played the song about the man in the moon.

The door to Ida's room was open, the color from the room coming out into the hallway one big patch of rose. The smell of her on everything.

When I looked in, Alma Hatch was on the bed.

'Two dollars,' she said, smoking, not looking around at me. 'Meet you in room 11 down the hall. I'll be there in five minutes.'

I laid my two dollars on the end table so she could hear their silver one two. In room 11 I laid down naked in the feather mattress on the bed. Clean stiff white sheets in the dark.

Alma Hatch walked into room 11 and locked the door behind her. The darkness filled with her smell of rosewater. I listened as she took off her dress. When Alma Hatch touched me, she fluttered her hand down the front of me, she threw her hair back and laid her cheek against my chest, she reached down under and cradled my leg and ass cheek, she trailed her hair down, feathers against my skin so soft drawing blood, pulling heart blood down to balls, her soft hair on my balls, her mouth around the crown of me, Alma's tongue circling, her sucking.

Downstairs Ida Richilieu was singing.

Upstairs, Alma Hatch had me pinned, stretched out, another

specimen of hard dick, like her father's brains in bottles. Alma put me inside her woman's hole, her shuddering, a frail bird, eagles in me, hawks. Ida's song was as sweet as Alma's sugar.

Woman's hole, dick into darkness. Every sorry man's reach for ecstasy. Head up Ida's cunt – up my mother's – my dick in Alma's, I scrutinized. Looking for where I was, where I was.

My hand reached around a hunk of Alma's hair, and pulled her hair down to the white sheets of the feather mattress. Sparrow whimpers in Alma, I shifted her woman's hole, her language beneath me. My fists were bracelets, hobbles, around Alma's ankles. I spread her legs wide as my arms are wide. Pulled my dick out of her. Scrutinized down at my hard-on bouncing, pink-sugar wet, pointing at where I wanted back into. Penetration.

'P . . ,' dick head my face, piss slit lips a smile, nosing in.

'E . . ,' resting against Alma, against woman's hole.

'N . . ,' the easy smooth slide.

'E . . ,' slow all the way in up to balls.

'T . . ,' Alma resistance, chintzy gratification.

'R . . ,' man's hole, woman's hole – a hole is a hole – what is the difference?

'A . . ,' the slide back and out, dick crown of me surrounded by her inside flesh, Alma's brown dark pubic hair.

'T . . ,' I put Alma's legs on my shoulders. I took my hand and pushed each ball up into her. They were my eyes. I was surrounded.

'I . . ,' looking for the inner contents of, the meaning of, my eyeballs scrutinizing inside dark for where I was, for who, for home.

'O . . ,' I said. 'Oh!'

Alma said, 'Oh!'

'N . . ,' I said, back to spelling, in and out, P and E and N and E and T and R and A and T and I and O and N – penetrating

Alma's woman's hole off the bed, onto the floor, into a ball in a corner, under me.

'Shed!' Alma screamed.

She slapped me when I lit the lamp.

I slapped her back, harder.

Then Alma Hatch jumped at me the way women do turning mountain lion on you. I was ready for claws down my back and my ear to get bit off, but instead what I got was her embracing me, Alma Hatch embracing me.

'God, Shed,' Alma Hatch said. 'I'm so sorry.'

I pulled Alma Hatch from the ear I thought she was going to bite off. I watched the language come out of her mouth: *I'm sorry*. It took that ear and the other one too a while to hear all the rest of what she was saying.

'Ida's damn near dead from missing you,' is what my ears heard.

Alma jumped up, wrapped the sheet around her, and ran out the door. She leaned over the railing and yelled down, 'Idee! Idee! Get your ass up here quick quick!'

'We'll learn to love each other, too,' Alma Hatch said to me. 'You'll see.'

Wasn't no time at all that Ida Richilieu was standing in the doorway of room 11, me bare-assed bent over looking for my pants, breathing the air there wasn't enough of, my heart beating fast, me and not me all over the room.

Naked and didn't want to be naked but was. Tried to cover myself up with something like a shirt, but then I knew how dumb I looked, me trying to cover my dick up for Ida Richilieu.

Out the window of that room, the first thing I ever remember remembering was moving the geranium over on the sill, looking down into the dusty street and seeing the devil Billy Blizzard kill his horse.

The times I had made that bed. The times I had brought

whiskey to men in that bed, men fucking Gracie Hammer and Ellen Finton, fucking all the rest of them who had passed through the doors of Ida's Place, fucking Ida, fucking Alma, fucking the Princess.

The times I had taken men out of that bed down out back out in the shed, men fucking me out in the shed.

The three of us – Ida Richilieu, Alma Hatch, and me. I took a deep breath and stood straight up, dropping the shirt. I made myself big, not big the way men get big – puffing up their chests and hard outside – but big the way women get. Me a man big like women – solid, supple, strong enough to fall down and get back up again. Me, a man, big – free from woman's hole.

The blue dress. Ida walked over to me. I'd forgotten the how dark of her eyes. Skinny damn dame, tiny white, white person. I touched her hair, the combs in her hair. She put the feathered blue boa around my neck. Looked at me the way she always could – in the left eye. There was nothing between us. No Ida Richilieu, no me or not me, just us, us being one not two. For a while I thought I was her looking at me. Then she reached out and put the palm of her left hand on my heart, onto the hole in my chest where Charles Smith had shot his devil's bullet. She laid her other hand on her own heart.

'Oh! The humanity,' Ida Richilieu said.

We went to Ida's room and locked the door, me and Alma and Ida on the bed. We started drinking whiskey and smoking hemp, and smoking opium, all of us on Ida's sheets, three human beings.

Wasn't long and there was a knock on the door and then Gracie Hammer was on the bed too, and Ellen Finton.

Those two females screamed like stuck pigs when they saw me.

Right off they had to tell the story about breaking me and Dellwood Barker out of jail.

Human beings just got to tell stories.

Sitting on Ida's bed, Ellen Finton told the story the way she remembered it. Then Gracie Hammer told the story the way she remembered it.

Ida Richilieu and Alma Hatch listened to Ellen's story, Gracie's story — stories that Ida and Alma had probably heard a dozen times.

Me with the girls on the bed, though, the feathered boa around my neck, what I was listening to was a different story altogether — the story Ida Richilieu always told about me, a baby laying on my stomach on that very bed, surrounded by women, me not reaching for the feather or the bow but the feathered boa.

Later on, when the bar was closed, when Ida and me went down to the bar in the dark to get another bottle and to make us up some food — in the kitchen just after she lit the lamp, Ida grabbed my arms and pulled me to her. I looked in her left eye and saw that she didn't know what she was going to do next. Ida leaned hard on me as if I was the something she craved and feared was running out of.

'You are my son,' she said, 'and I love you. Please don't ever leave Ida's Place again. I would die. This is your home. After I'm gone, it's yours.' My ears weren't sure if they were hearing right. Some things were best left unsaid, and there was Ida Richilieu saying them. Saying *son*, and *love*, saying *home*.

Then some big dynamite passed through Ida's bones, and she was hanging on to me, a scared cat, her claws in my shoulders and my knees, us in the kitchen, us not the two of us, the one again all blue feathers and the beads.

Back upstairs, Ida acted as if nothing had happened down in the kitchen, Alma knowing something had happened down in the kitchen. We spread the food out on Ida's bed — cold chicken and apples, and cheese Ida'd got in Boise, and more beer. Ida with a new bottle of whiskey, we really started into telling stories, me more than them.

Told them the story of Dellwood Barker and me; our escape, told them about the Franciscans. Told them how me and Dellwood Barker had fucked on a mountaintop – those two whores giggling schoolgirls when I told them. Alma Hatch hooting owl hoots. Told them that next to them I loved Dellwood Barker most.

Told them about Dellwood Barker coming-not-coming, which made Alma Hatch fall off the bed laughing.

Ida Richilieu slapped her knee and said right out, 'That's a damned lie, son. That's an impossibility – it ain't human,' she said, 'for a man. I'll believe it when I see it with my own eyes and not until.'

I didn't tell them any more about Moves Moves except for that. Didn't tell them about my mother's photograph. Didn't tell them about the twins that Dellwood Barker said my mother had; that is, not til the next day did I ask Ida about the twins. Didn't tell them that I thought he was my father.

Alma Hatch's stories were all about love. She talked about how her heart was full of love for me and Ida now that I was back home. She talked about the hot springs and opium and fucking. She told us about the blue jay nest she had found and that in her neck of the woods folks call swallows 'flycatchers.'

'Did you see how fat the robins are this year?' Alma Hatch said. 'Did you see the finches in the lilac bush next to the barbershop this morning?'

Alma Hatch also talked about her hair, and by the time we were on the second opium cigarette, she was screaming turkey buzzards. You never could tell when that woman would just start in.

Ida talked about these mountains. 'For two years in a row

now, Devil's Pass hasn't gotten snowed in until after Christmas,' she said. 'Both years thawed out by April.'

Toward the end of the evening, Ida got around to talking about some big old cowboy hearts she'd broken; how hers had been broken a couple of times too. Talked about some big dicks she had run into, some little ones too. Ida talked about opium, and locoweed and fucking.

Mostly, though, what Ida talked about was Mormons and how they were moving *in droves* into Excellent. According to Ida, the *Mormon movement* was due primarily to one thing, rather one person, whose name was William B. Merrillee.

'One of the twelve apostles of the Church of Jesus Christ of Latter-day Saints,' Ida said. 'Claims to have had a vision that his people had to have a gold mine and a mill up here in Excellent. He's the one responsible for the new church over by the school, too. Got *two* of those dang things in this town now. Painted it *green* for God's sakes. A white one and a green one. Makes me want to build another saloon. Paint it *purple*.

'You should see this town come Sunday morning! It's a regular parade! Saturday night most those men are in here drinking and fucking, and come Sunday morning, there they are with those Relief Society women – those two-by-fours that call themselves women, that is – relief no where in sight of them, going to church,' Ida said.

'But I shouldn't complain, I guess,' she said. 'At least they're here on Saturday nights. Trouble starts when it's all Sunday morning and no Saturday night. Takes a devil to make a decent angel.'

*

Sparrows woke me up in the morning. Ida Richilieu's body, Alma Hatch's body, and my body were all so mixed up with each other I had to ask my arms and legs which ones they were.

I finally got those two crabby girls out of bed with a pot of coffee – Ida cussing, Alma whining – got them somewhat dressed and started off to the hot springs. We were just down the stairs and out the front door of Ida's Place, when right off we met a bunch of folks I'd never laid eyes on before – all-dressed-up men and women and children – tybo men all looking like the same tybo man, the women the same woman, the girl children the same girl child, same thing with the boy children.

It was Sunday morning. These were the Mormons Ida had been talking about.

I looked over to Alma Hatch. All she was wearing was her corset and the slip over it and a skirt. Ida was even worse. She was wearing my pants and shirt and hat, smoking a cigarette the way she does with the cigarette hanging out her mouth. Me, I was the worst – in my underwear and Ida's shiny red robe hanging open across my shoulders.

Alma Hatch winked at one of the men and smiled. She lifted her arms, showing her armpits, and started piling her hair up in the back.

The Mormon women started herding their children out of there as quickly as possible, the children all staring up at us as if they'd never set eyes on human beings that weren't Mormon before. The man Alma had winked at took off too, and so did other men, but mostly the men stayed and stood and stared at us, but not the way the children had stared. The men stared with hatred, stared the way only Christians can hate, especially Mormons. One of the men standing there was Josiah Helm – the Reverend Brother Josiah Helm, that is. Didn't know it then, but I'd soon know his name and a whole lot of other things about him too. The Reverend Brother Josiah Helm was not a big man but held himself as if he was – chest sticking out, chin out, wearing a tall hat. He held up his Bible or Book of Mormon – whichever one of the two it was – I don't know – it was a big book. Then he cursed us, me and Alma Hatch and Ida Richilieu, cursed us to everlasting damnation and fire.

Same as with Billy Blizzard, I should've killed Helm right then and saved the world from a whole lot of misery.

Ida Richilieu, who wasn't walking very straight that morning, walked down the steps, walked not very straight right up to that Reverend Helm, took the cigarette out of her mouth, and spit right in his face. Then I couldn't believe my ears when Ida said what she said:

'I hate your little dick even more than you do!'

Wasn't much the reverend could do, after his mouth closed back up, but huff and puff, and quote somebody else's words out of the book he was holding. Nothing he could do but hightail it out of there – him and the rest of the Mormon bucks.

Ida turned around and said, 'Best damn thing in the world for a hangover is the hot springs.' Then she almost fell over, but Alma Hatch caught her in time. We walked that way – me and Alma Hatch holding up Ida Richilieu – down Pine Street out of town to the hot springs.

The official day for whores at the hot springs had always been on Wednesday. Nobody had ever paid much attention to what day it was, though. That day, as we had just found out, was Sunday. Me and Alma and Ida discussed whether or not we should go up to the hot springs on a Sunday, and we decided to go ahead, because it was early in the morning, because we were already halfway to the hot springs, because we were just three human beings needing a bath, and as Ida put it: 'To hell with 'em!'

Then I said, 'They can't throw the mayor out of the hot springs even if she is a whore.'

Then Alma said, 'Ida ain't the mayor no more.'

Then Ida took a deep breath the way she always did when there was something hard to do and she said: 'Nope, that

Mormon bishop's the mayor of Excellent now. The Reverend Brother Josiah Helm is the mayor now.'

As soon as my ears heard Ida say the Reverend Helm was the mayor, trouble started laying itself on things. Before – the trees, the fog, the ground under my feet, what you could see of the sky, the rocks – were just things you usually saw and were how they were. After hearing Ida wasn't the mayor, though, things weren't just things anymore, weren't how they were – things were trouble.

Any minute, I figured, a herd of wild Mormons would come running out of the fog, brandishing big books, looking their fearful right eyes at us – their left eyes completely blind, cursing us to everlasting damnation in hell.

Fire is what I felt. The fire inside things. Billy Blizzard fire inside people, whose hearts have been cut in bloom, folded onto themselves, and pressed flat, smoldering between the pages of their big Christian book.

Trouble: each step we took that morning, each step we took after that morning, every step we took from then on, brought Ida Richilieu, Alma Hatch, and me closer to it.

When we got to the hot springs, me and Alma crawled down the bank to the pool. Ida didn't want any help. She made her body into that dead-limb kind of way and stiff-legged her way down, bringing an avalanche of rocks with her.

My underwear and Ida's robe were off in no time and I jumped in the hot pool, splashing big, making lots of noise, my noise echoing. I stayed under the water, down under with the Wild Moon Man, trying to breathe water, trying to get the awful knowing off me – the fire and the trouble off me.

When I came back up, my whole body was only a head bobbing in a pool of steaming water. From above, water fell from the rocks onto my head. Just spitting distance away, the cold river flowed by full white. The water falling, the river, wind in the trees, and my head floating was what my ears could hear.

Alma was sitting naked on a rock beside the pool, her legs crossed, one foot in the water. Ida was standing next to her, unwrapping ropes and ropes of Alma's dirt brown hair. The patch of hair in Alma's lap, the nest in the branches of her, was darker. Skin pinker than ever.

Ida was naked too, frog-belly white, her glowing with a light of her own. Next to Alma, she looked like the pictures of angels with little wings on their feet, floating around holy saints, attending.

When Ida was finished with Alma's hair, Ida took the combs out of her own hair, her arms back, the hair in her armpits. Their smell always slapped at my heart. Ida's nipples were big dark circles of being sucked on. Her hair was a bushel of black alfalfa spilling out, down off her head. The hair of her woman's hole was black. Black hair that fanned out onto her legs. As the hair moved down her legs, the hair got lighter and lighter to her ankles – that was when Ida still had ankles.

Ida and Alma laid out all their soaps and feminine toiletries along the rocks. Alma circled the water, looking for the right spot. Ida just held her nose and jumped.

I stood up out of the water, and crawled up the side of the bank, big slick green moss hanging on the rocks, hot water over my hands and feet, morning wind on my naked wet skin. The waterfall on Buffalo Head had that same kind of moss. I sat down where I had sat a thousand times, the water splashing down onto me. Leaned back into the waterfall. My ears heard water the way rocks heard water.

Below, Alma's hair was floating around her in the pool. Ida was picking up rocks from the bottom of the pool and looking at them in her hands under the water. A deer stuck its head out of the fog, and we all looked at the deer the way the deer was looking at us.

When the sun was full up, the fog got to be a petticoat curtain over the window of things. You could see the trees and the river and patches of sky, but they were hazy the way the rose-colored light was in Ida's room.

I looked up and there it was, Not-Really-A-Mountain. Made you want to fall over backwards. Gave you a hard-on that mountain – the mountain that had powered us all here, snagged us up and was making us think that what we were doing was what we were doing.

Ida started up the bank to where I was, her crawling like a spider, hanging more on to her web than anything else. She was all gooseflesh and blue by the time she reached the top and had sat down next to me.

Ida smiled at me big.

Woman's hole: spent my life trying to get as much of that smile as I could.

'I met a man who knew my mother,' I said.

'Lots of men knew your mother, Shed,' Ida said.

'He had a photograph of her,' I said. 'Same one as mine. Said he loved her more than anything. Said she was his wife and the mother of his children,' I said. 'Twins,' I said. 'A boy and a girl.'

Ida didn't have a cigarette. If she had, though, Ida would have put the cigarette in her mouth then, hanging down, and she'd have struck a match against something hard and lit the cigarette, then inhaled deep. The smoke would stay in her for a long time, then two thin trails out her nose.

'Do I have a twin sister?' I asked.

'No,' Ida said.

'Did I ever?' I asked, looking her in the left eye.

'You had a sister, alright,' Ida said, 'but she died.'

'How?' I asked.

'She was a baby. Crib death,' Ida said.

'What was her name?' I asked.

'Don't remember,' Ida said. 'Was a long time ago.'

'What's this cowboy's name?' Ida asked.

'Dellwood Barker,' I said.

'The one you fucked on the mountain? The one who claims to have orgasms without ejaculating?' she asked.

'That's him,' I said.

'He's just full of surprises,' she said. 'You think he's your father, don't you?'

'I do,' I said.

Ida got up to leave.

'Promise me, Ida,' I said. 'Promise me you'll never tell a soul about him being my father.'

Ida took a deep breath that made her ribs stick out even more.

Keep your promises, keep clean, keep going.

'I promise,' Ida said.

'How much does Alma know about Princess and me?' I asked.

'Hell, I don't know,' Ida said. 'Just hearsay, I'd guess, but don't you worry about Alma Hatch. I'll take care of her.'

Ida looked both her eyes into my eyes. She was sober.

I always believed Ida – whatever she did or said – but I believed her more when she was sober. Was more there to believe. When she was drinking – which was most of the time – Ida didn't know how to listen to you, that is, she listened to herself more than to you. What was going on in her head she thought was going on in yours too. Even though it wasn't. So, you could have a conversation with Ida and not even know what you were talking about. *She* knew what she was talking about, though, and that was all that mattered. That's just the way she was.

I always believed Ida, but I always could tell when she was lying.

And she was lying – about my twin sister, Ida Richilieu was lying.

Ida crawled back down the bank and slipped into the water. She floated under the water, then came up into Alma's floating hair.

Not-Really-A-Mountain above me, those two women in the water below, I tried hard to think what it was I was doing that I thought I was doing.

What it was that was making Ida Richilieu lie.

The next day, I hiked up Not-Really-A-Mountain, to my place, to the meadow.

I crawled down the granite rocks and walked through the meadow straight to the edge. The purple flowers were blooming, and the Indian paintbrush, and the yellow ones. On the edge, on the rock that stuck out the farthest, a gust of wind hit me. I stood myself into the circle I had drawn on the rock where I had promised, so long ago, to free myself from woman's hole.

I looked over the edge. You could see everything – Excellent down there, the river, the hot springs, Ida's Place, the new Mormon church and the hole in the side of the mountain where William B. Merrillee was building his gold mill.

Everything. The mountains up and down, jagged, rolling, to the horizon. Snow on some even in August. You could see Gold Hill, and Gold Bar – not the town itself but the valley of it. Devil's Pass. Where the Boise Valley started up. The road to Owyhee City. People traveling on the road.

And more. Sometimes, at night, when there was no moon, you could see the forest fires. You were sitting on the edge of the world, the language silent in you, the world silent, and beyond the edge was darkness and fire.

And more. Dellwood Barker out there. Buffalo Head too, and the waterfall. Out there, a photograph of my mother pressed in the pages of a book about the moon, that book in a bedroll tied to a saddle on a horse named Abraham Lincoln. Owyhee City, Sheriff Blumenfeld, Fort Lincoln out there. The slaughterhouse, the devil Pillow Women, American Flag, Bowler Hat, Porcupine.

Everything. Everything had been so real. And more.

But now it was a dream; something I did while I slept – somewhere else – where I went when I'd gone inside after Charles Smith's bullet.

But I had lived to tell the story.

Standing on the rock, looking out, I understood what the story was.

Here's the story: life is a dream.

It's all a story we're telling ourselves. Things are dreams, just dreams, when they're not in front of your eyes. What is in front of your eyes now, what you can reach out and touch, now, will become a dream.

The only thing that keeps us from floating off with the wind is our stories. They give us a name and put us in a place, allow us to keep on touching.

Standing in my place, in the circle on the rock in the meadow on Not-Really-A-Mountain, I yelled this out:

'This is my place. Me, Duivichi-un-Dua, Boy's Boy. This is my story. This meadow is where I will die. Where my mother died. Where knowledge will become understanding.'

As soon as I spoke my words, my words were gone. A shadow passed between me and the sun. I shaded my eyes and looked up. An owl was circling in the sky.

My body jumped. Owlfeather was standing next to me. He was telling me important things. He was telling me a joke.

Knowledge becoming understanding: all that was left in front of me was me looking at what was in front of me. All I could do was laugh.

That night, I went to Dr. Ah Fong's and knocked on his door. Through the window, I watched the flame of his candle move toward me. Dr. Ah Fong put the candle up to the glass. I put my face so he could see. He slid the bolt and opened the door.

Dr. Ah Fong bowed deeply.

'So pleased to see you again, Mr. Shed. It has been long time.'

Then, 'Opium?' he said. 'For Ida?'

I bowed, stepped toward him, and took his hands. 'No,' I said. 'Not for Ida, for me – opium for me.'

'Opium for Mr. Shed,' Dr. Ah Fong said. 'Wait here.'

How many times had I stood in Dr. Ah Fong's office in the candlelight waiting for opium for Ida's cold, for Ida's sore back, for Ida's headache? Shelves of books behind glass. Bottles and tins, papers with Chinese writing on them. Things shiny red and dark green and blue. The chart with the human body with lines to the different parts. Chinese language: words, not our words, people making those sounds and understanding them. Written down the words more like little trees, shadows of kerosene lamps against a wall, or dreams that you understand until you wake up.

'Oh,' Dr. Ah Fong said, 'opium for Mr. Shed.' He bowed and I bowed. I gave him the money.

Killdeer down in Chinatown was big. Gunnysacks stretched across the sky, fish bones in the street, and that music. I walked down the main street, turned to the right, left, then down the stairs. Rented the bed with the red sheets where Ida had told me the story of Big Foot. I fixed my cigarettes with the opium, took my boots off, took my clothes off, got under the covers, lit the first one, and smoked it. Smoked a second.

Dr. Ah Fong had ice cream on Sundays. My favorite was cherry. My mother's too. Killdeer running all over this town, looking in on things, scrutinizing.

Homecoming

The best feeling I could remember was watching Ida in her circle of light, writing in her diaries, writing secrets I needed to know about, stories I had to hear.

Now I was back home in Ida's Place in Excellent, Idaho. Everything different. Everything still the same. Me, down the stairs in Chinatown, laying on the red sheets, smoking stardust again, me still playing killdeer, still looking to solve the mystery: who I was, why I lived, where was home.

Above me, above Excellent, Idaho, that mountain, Not-Really-A-Mountain, snagging my spirit back to Excellent, making me think that what I was doing was what I was doing.

What I was doing was lighting another cigarette. It's a story about crazy people told by a crazy.

Should only make you wonder.

*

This is what the poster tacked to the front door of Ida's Place said: *There are those among us who are evil and purnishus.*

That sentence was written in big fancy curly letters. The next sentence was written in bigger black letters: *Citizens of Excellent, Idaho, Beware! Prostitutes and False Men Walk Our Streets.*

In the middle of the page was a picture of a hand pointing at this: *Fornicators! Evil Doers! Devils! The Anti-Christ!*

Then in smaller letters:

We, the law-abiding citizens of Excellent, Idaho, are gravely concerned about the evil prostitutes, alcoholics, and drug addicts here in our fair city and their shameless flaunting of sins too forbidden to mention here.

A meeting will be held this next Sunday at 3:00 in the afternoon at the First Ward Chapel at the south end of Pine Street. All are invited to attend.

I counted ten of these posters around town. Tore them all down and hung them up in a row on the porch of Ida's Place.

Ida made up her own poster: *Ten-dollar reward for the man, woman or child who first comes up with the correct spelling of Purnishus.*

When I started to spell *pernicious* for Ida, she said, 'That goes for everybody except you, Shed, and if you can't spell it, I don't want to know about it.'

In Ida's Place, and all over town, folks tried their damnedest to spell that word. Heard so many ways to spell *pernicious* that I'd have to go back and spell it to myself now and then just to make sure I had it right.

The contest went on for weeks, and for weeks *pernicious* was all you heard.

Even Gracie Hammer and Ellen Finton got in on it, and they couldn't read, let alone spell.

When somebody asked Alma Hatch how you spelled *pernicious*, she was so tired of that word by then, she spelled it: 'E . . A . . T . . S . . H . . I . . T.'

One day, at the post office, when I was picking up Ida's mail, out of the blue, Fern Hurdlika said, 'P . . R . . E . . N . . I . . T . . I . . O . . U . . S.'

'Nope,' I said.

Then Fern said, 'That Ida Richilieu's filled up with more get-up-and-go than ever since you've been back. How long was you gone?'

'More than a year,' I said.

'Lordy, was it that long? Let me look at you!' Fern said, looking at me.

'I say,' Fern said. 'You're turning out to be a fine figure of a man. When you going to quit growing?'

'Six and a half feet tall,' I said.

'At least,' Fern said. 'But you know, I can't quite figure who you look like,' Fern said. 'It's somebody I know but it ain't your mother. You don't look like an Indian, but then, you don't look like a white man, neither.'

'Look like myself,' I said.

'Best way to look,' Fern Hurdlika said. Then: 'P . . U . . R . . N . . I . . T . . I . . O . . U . . S,' she spelled.

'Wrong,' I said.

Thord Hurdlika was banging away on a piece of iron in his shop, his lips moving like a horse eating hay. I sat down next to the bellows. Took him a while to see me, but when he did, he threw down his hammer, took off his gloves, yelled out, 'Shed!' and gave me a big bear hug. After we were done hugging, Thord Hurdlika didn't know what to say, and he just turned red. We were standing smiling at each other, me not knowing what to say either, and finally Thord said, 'P . . A . . R . . N . . I . . C . . I . . O . . S.'

'Nope,' I said.

'You back for good?' he said.

'Yup,' I said.

'You growed up,' he said.

'I growed up,' I said.

'Are you still, ah . . . ?'

'Out in the shed?' I said.

'Yah,' he said. 'Out in the shed.'

'Sure am,' I said.

'Maybe, some morning, if it's alright, I'll come over early,' he said.

'Anytime,' I said.

'P . . O . . R . . N . . I . . C . . I . . O . . S?' he said.

'Nope,' I said.

'Sure good to see you, Shed,' he said. 'Glad to have you back. I'll bet Ida's glad too.'

'Yup,' I said.

'You're like a son to her,' he said. 'Heard her say that more than once.'

About my third day in town, walking down Pine Street, just before the bend in the road, I ran into Damn Dave and Damn Dog. They were looking more like each other every day. Damn Dave started jumping up and down, making sounds, and Damn Dog started barking. First off, I thought Damn Dave was drunk again, but when I got closer to him, you could tell he wasn't drunk, just glad to see me. I did have to settle him down though. Thought maybe he was going to have a heart attack the way he was carrying on. I held his hands the way Ida used to do, and breathed deep with him until his eyes quit crossing. Pretty soon Damn Dog quit barking. You could tell Damn Dave was alright when his dog quit barking.

Damn Dave wouldn't let go of my hands. He wanted to lead me somewhere so I followed him. He slid open the big door of the stables and closed the door behind me and Damn Dog. The smell of horse shit and fresh straw, horses, and leather. In there too the smell of applewood and smoked hams. Damn Dave led me around his wagon to the southeast corner of the stables, to the end stall.

The stall was the place where he lived. I'd never seen anything like it. There was a mattress on the shiny wooden floor and the bed linens were clean and neatly folded. Ida's pillow I had given him years ago lay on the bed as if it was his most important thing. The walls were covered with torn pieces of paper – mostly old envelopes – with drawings on them. One wall had an old post office thing of letter boxes that had numbers on each box and doors with keys where people could pick up their mail. I opened one box and there was a little doll's head. Opened another box and there was a shotgun shell. Opened another and there was an old watch. Each post office box had a treasure in it. Then, Damn

Dave showed me a map he had of Excellent and Gold Bar. He pointed to a number he had written on the map – 102 – then pointed to the post office box numbered 102. He had found the doll's head at that spot and recorded it. The exact spot. The map was covered in numbers.

The drawings on the wall were Damn Dave's. They were the way children draw trees and houses. Stick figures with faces that have two dots for eyes and a line for a mouth. The drawings were more than children's drawings, though. They were just plumb crazy: things like horses growing out of the ground, houses with faces, and trees with arms and legs.

I had to look hard at them, and for a long time, before what I was seeing was Damn Dave's story of how he saw the world. What I was seeing too was that, same as with Ida Richilieu, Damn Dave had been keeping his own history of Excellent, Idaho.

Took me quite a while, but the first thing I started to figure out, after an even longer while looking, was who the different people that Damn Dave was drawing *were*. Then, after more looking, I figured out what it was those people were doing.

Here's just some of the drawings on Damn Dave's wall: Ida's husband and his little dick jumping off Not-Really-A-Mountain. Billy Blizzard beating his horse to death. People smoking opium down in Chinatown. Billy Blizzard holding a gun to my head and humping my ass. Ida Richilieu scrubbing the back stairs. Me hauling water up to Ida's bath. My mother driving off after Billy Blizzard in Ida's wagon. Me standing at Ida's window looking in at her circle of light. A drawing of Alma Hatch in that hat she wore the first day. Me getting on the stagecoach. Me coming back on the stagecoach.

There were a lot more drawings and I wanted to look at them, but I didn't; that is, not that day, because Damn Dave, seeing how much I liked the drawings, took me by the hands again and led me to a door next to his stall. He opened the door and I followed him in.

I stood in the dark while he lit the lamp. When I could see, I saw a room, a lean-to shed on the back of the stable that in all my born days in Excellent, Idaho, I had never noticed. The walls were covered in more post office boxes, a treasure in each box: nuts and bolts and pieces of glass, photographs, pieces of cloth, an old fork, an empty morphine bottle, rocks, doorknobs, gold nuggets, hinges, nails, a ball of string.

There were more drawings, too – thousands of them – and like the treasures, the drawings were all mixed in together: the William B. Merrillee Mining Company Inc., Ida and my mother fighting in the mud, the new Mormon church, Mormon women and children going to church, Dr. Ah Fong, the Dry House, Thord Hurdlika marrying Fern. Men waiting for me out in the shed. The American flag. Devil's Pass. Me finding my dead mother and Billy Blizzard's red boots. Doc Heyburn standing drunk at the bar. People soaking in the hot springs.

Me sitting in my circle on the rock in my place up on Not-Really-A-Mountain.

A drawing of Owlfeather.

I pointed to his drawing of me on the rock in my place. Damn Dave smiled and pointed up at Not-Really-A-Mountain.

I pointed to his drawing of Owlfeather and made a sign to him that I didn't understand who it was.

Damn Dave pointed to me.

'Me?' I asked, tapping my chest.

Yes, Damn Dave nodded. *You*, he moved his lips.

Then Damn Dave handed me a piece of paper. At first I couldn't make out what the drawing was. Then I saw it. It was a drawing of the word *pernicious*. Damn Dave had drawn the word misspelled.

The next day, Doc Heyburn was standing where he always stood at the bar. Drunk as ever. When he saw me, he spoke the first words ever to me. 'You back?' he said.

'I'm back,' I said.

He ordered another glass of whiskey.

'P . . E . . R . . N . . A . . I . . C . . I . . O . . U . . S,' he spelled aloud, so that everybody in the place could hear.

'Nope,' Ida Richilieu said.

'Just give me a little while,' Doc said. 'It won't be long here and I'll tell you how to spell it.'

Nobody ever did get it right.

Pernicious was the word that me and Ida and Alma used most after that poster. We called each other that: pernicious – pernicious whore, pernicious alcoholic, pernicious flaunter of forbidden sin, pernicious false man. It was: Pernicious Ida, Pernicious Alma, Pernicious Shed. Pernicious Ida's Place. All the other whores there too: Pernicious Ellen Finton, Pernicious Gracie Hammer, Pernicious each one of them. Ida even made up a song about pernicious and played it on the piano: Ain't it delicious, / being so pernicious. / Fuck these Mormon sons o'bishes.

It was funny for a while. Pernicious was funny. But then, with Ida getting the way she was getting, pernicious wasn't so funny.

After the pernicious poster, Ida was never the same. Ida never the same, nothing the same. Everything was different.

Was war. Ida Richilieu declared war on the Reverend Brother Josiah Helm and the Church of Jesus Christ of Latter-day Saints.

'The fact that some dumb Mormon,' Ida said, 'in writing,' Ida said, 'in my town could say that about me and my hotel and my friends means war.'

That next Sunday, Ida organized her own town meeting. Free

drinks and entertainment starting at three in the afternoon. The bar was packed. Every pernicious character in the county was there. Ida played the piano for them. You could hear 'Drink to Me Only with Thine Eyes' and 'Tavern in the Town' all the way over to Gold Bar. 'Rock of Ages' at the First Ward was nothing to compare. Then they made a parade of her. Ida on the shoulders of two big miners – the whole bar marching behind – down the steps of Ida's Place and up Pine Street, singing loud, especially in front of the First Ward, especially her song in front of the First Ward: Ain't it delicious, / being so pernicious. / Fuck these Mormon sons o'bishes.

It was war, alright. It was trouble.

After that, each day, I swear – even though it sounds impossible – Ida Richilieu got thinner, bonier, whiter, drank more, smoked more, fucked more, and cleaned the hotel more. The sheets on the line in the sun were white as her bones poking through. In the mornings she'd put on her petticoats and good dress with the clean apron over it, put her lipstick on, and go to work on something – scrubbing the stairs, wiping the bar glasses, sweeping, mopping, ironing, always something, always running around telling people what to do. *Hey you, come over here, boy.* I just got out of her way.

Got so that's all people talked about was the new mayor, the Reverend Brother Josiah Helm, and the old mayor, Ida Richilieu, and their war. Their religious war. Mormons called it the forces of good against the forces of evil. Ida called it a cockfight.

Me, mostly I walked around at night, that summer, a yearning big for I don't know what. Wasn't anything that would satisfy. Was something I was missing, that I was pining for, that I had no idea what it was. For love. For Dellwood Barker. For Owlfeather. But it was more than that. I was pining for some part of myself that was missing.

Mostly, I'd end up at Dr. Ah Fong's.

Sometimes, I'd just start running the way I did when I was a kid looking for killdeer. See how fast I could run in the night. I'd close my eyes and pretend I was blind and I'd run, close my eyes and run. Then I'd put that thing that was me, that was missing about me, in front of me and I'd run to it. When I'd open my eyes there was always nothing there. I'd wake up at night, the terrible sound of my heart beating in me, my breath in and out. The only thing that would soothe me was Ida – going to Ida's window, standing outside, looking in, her at her desk in her circle of light, writing in her diary.

Sometimes I wondered if there really was a secret to know, or if watching Ida through the window writing all those years had just made it seem as if there was a secret.

Maybe she wasn't writing about mysteries at all, maybe she was just writing down recipes. Maybe she wasn't writing philosophy, just writing about Mormons and her war. Writing about big dicks, or little dicks.

I kept on watching Ida, though, through her window at night – never did stop – because, I figured, the secret, the mystery – what had always pulled me back to her window at night – was how watching Ida write made me feel.

Made me feel like there was a secret, a mystery.

Sometimes, at night, that summer, I'd walk down to where the William B. Merrillee Company was building the mill, down where the river doglegged just north of Excellent, to the big gash out of the side of the mountain they had made. Moonlight on that granite scar made their excavations look like the moon. Big trees lay in piles curing out. Already some of those trees were stuck back into the ground as posts.

I watched as that building got big. Watched Mormon men build a rock foundation. Watched as huge iron things came up the road from Owyhee City – twenty-mule teams hauling some of that iron up. Big iron pots and girders and bars and pipes. Watched them haul in the tin for the roof. Hardest part to watch was them cutting up through the forest all the way to the mine two miles away. Watched them roll out the cable, two miles of cable – one up, one down – cables carrying the buckets filled with ore down the two miles to the William B. Merrillee mill, those buckets going back up empty for more, and more, up and down, more and more forever. Watched as more and more families moved up to Excellent – Mormon families. Mormons finished that gold mill one year later in the summer of 1904, or maybe it was 1905.

Story goes that when William B. Merrillee had his vision of gold, what he saw was the members of his flock all living together in harmony in the mountains of Idaho, far away from anybody not like them, living off the gold mine and the mill, eating the food they grew, living in the houses they built, not depending on anybody else not like them, for anything.

Story goes that anything or anybody who stood in the way of this vision was the devil.

Story goes too that what happened to us, to Ida Richilieu, to Alma Hatch, to Dellwood Barker, and to me, was punishment from God for standing in the way.

Least, that's how the Mormons told it.

*

I moved back out in the shed. Started taking on customers even though Ida didn't want me to. She said I didn't need to whore no more. Said I had a home and plenty of money. But I went ahead with it. Mostly out of just being bored. We had to be more careful though, with the Mormons and all, them thinking about sodomy the way they do. Ida and Alma and the rest of the girls scrutinized their customers more than ever. So I wasn't as busy.

Homecoming

Plus I wasn't no kid anymore. I was grown up, somewhere around twenty years old, and wasn't no cute-butted kid anymore. I was a man, big and dark, with a dark place in me that scared most men away no matter how soft I tried to be.

Me and Alma grew to love each other like she had promised we would. In fact, me and Alma and Ida got to be some kind of family; mother being Ida, me and Alma mothering her more and more. Sister being Alma when she wasn't mothering or lovering Ida. Ida mothering me more than ever. Got to be difficult, how Ida started mothering me – mothering and teaching me about the English language and English literature. Me being her child, her student more and more, me packing her up to bed, me keeping her thoughts away from the war with the Mormons as much as I could, me doing the heavier chores and stuff like that.

Then too, the three of us we were just good friends. Money was good. Business was good. There were Mormons to fight. Stayed drunk a lot of the time. Got to be so that it was normal being drunk and smoking down in Chinatown. I still got everything done like I was supposed to do. So did Ida. So did Alma. Sheets were cleaned. Stairs were scrubbed, bar glasses wiped, whiskey ordered, beer kept cool as possible, fucked our customers. Every now and then I'd get away to the hot springs. Would go up regular to Not-Really-A-Mountain. Sometimes stayed up there for days. Then there were the drawings to look at, and the treasures at Damn Dave's.

Truth was, though, something was missing.

The secret. The mystery. I couldn't figure out what it was and I tried every day. I'd look at my hands, fingers touching one another from each side, and I'd say to myself: 'This here's me – I'm the one telling the story – I'm the one who knows what the secret is – I'm the one who knows what's missing – so go ahead, tell me what it is!'

Never worked though.

What went around in my head, when I had smoked enough, drunk enough, down in Chinatown, what kept sliding into my head hot bayonet ear to ear was Owlfeather, was me laying for months somewhere dead and then waking up again. Was the death of my mother, was my twin sister, was Ida lying about my twin sister, was the photograph of my mother in Dellwood Barker's bedroll, was how I'd fucked my father and how much I'd enjoyed it, was Moves Moves, the Wild Moon Man and Berdache, was Commodity Day, was the buffalo.

It was autumn then it was winter. Devil's Pass didn't get snowed in til past Christmas again. Thawed out early in April again. Then it was summer again.

Our honorable mayor, the Reverend Brother Josiah Helm, appointed himself an assistant. The mayor chose an old friend of mine: Sheriff Blumenfeld from Owyhee City.

Sheriff Blumenfeld was Excellent's new assistant mayor.

Story goes Blumenfeld had lost his last election for sheriff in Owyhee City. Story goes he'd been caught doing unnatural acts with one of his prisoners. At least, that's the story Gracie Hammer and Ellen Finton had heard.

Everybody else – the Mormons, that is – had heard a much different story about Blumenfeld – one of their brethren. Stories of an honest, God-fearing, law-abiding sheriff who had fallen victim to a corrupt political system.

Trouble.

Then one morning I woke up.

That day, two years to the day, was the day I saw Dellwood Barker again.

Wasn't long after that and I uncovered the secret. Solved the mystery.

Found out what real trouble was.

*

According to Ida Richilieu, Ida saw him first. She was just out of her bath and had stepped into the corridor to scrutinize the crowd in the bar when Dellwood Barker walked in.

'I went right back in my room,' Ida said, 'and put the blue dress on.'

According to Alma Hatch, Alma saw him first. She was pouring whiskey at the bar. When she heard him order a whiskey, Alma looked up, and went eye to eye with Dellwood Barker's green eyes scrutinizing.

'I put some rosewater behind my ears,' Alma said, 'shook my hair loose, pushed my tits up, and poured the man a whiskey.'

Alma Hatch fucked him first because she was the closest to him. Dellwood Barker was on one side of the bar and she was on the other.

'I got rid of the bar in between,' Alma said, 'and just about everything else – including his clothes and mine – and was fucking him up in room 11 before Ida Richilieu even had her blue dress buttoned up.'

Story goes, when Dellwood Barker started coming, he came like no other man Alma had ever met, him squirming around and hollering and praising the Lord the way only women do, namely Alma Hatch.

Of course, Dellwood was coming-not-coming, saving his Moves Moves, but Alma Hatch got so interested in what Dellwood Barker was going through that she didn't realize that what he was doing, or not doing, was not ejaculating.

Ida Richilieu snagged him with the piano. Ida in her blue dress coming down the staircase, that white skin of hers white as her pearls, combs in her hair, blue feathered boa, Ida walking down the stairs to the piano, sitting down at the piano and playing her favorite song about the man in the moon – snagged him. 'Buckets of tears just rolling down his cheeks,' Ida said. 'Ever since my late husband, never seen a man cry like that.'

Ida figured Dellwood was crying because he had a little dick. But before she had the chance to find out, before she finished the song, before she could invite this man up to her room for some comfort, consolation, and closer inspection, Dellwood Barker lunged toward the piano and started playing.

'God-awful shit he started in on,' Ida said. 'Some sort of piano racket like your ears never wanted to hear,' Ida said. 'Like a soul possessed – eyes wide like he'd just seen the devil, crying like an infant child.'

Ida got two men to subdue Dellwood Barker, and they hauled him up the stairs to Ida's room, where Ida gave him a powder. Then they fucked.

'I'm so glad he didn't have a big dick,' Ida said later. 'Would've ruint everything. There he was a nice parlor size and gentle, him crying sweet as can be.'

Ida hadn't ever seen a man come the way Dellwood Barker was coming either. Like Alma, Ida said Dellwood came like women come, coming with your whole body not just a thing hanging off it.

But when Dellwood was done, wasn't a drop for Ida.

Ida Richilieu looked him in the left eye and then looked him in the dick, then looked him in the left eye again.

'You're Dellwood Barker, ain't you?' Ida said.

I was out in the shed, alone.

He wasn't there. Then, he knocked on the door. He stepped inside. There he was, Dellwood Barker. Everything was different.

The first time I saw Dellwood Barker, back in Owyhee City, I thought he was somebody I dreamed up. I closed my eyes, wished for a special person, for him, opened my eyes, and from darkness, he stepped out of a piece of light the size of a door.

After seeing him beaten by Blumenfeld and his deputy, and then me being beaten the same way, that night, in the jail cell when he stuck his hand into the square of moon, I got to thinking that I hadn't dreamed up Dellwood Barker at all, but that I actually was him.

Then, later on when he was Dellwood again, and I was me, whenever Dellwood started in on how we are who we are because of the story we're telling ourselves who we are, the line between him and me would start to get thin again.

Then the photograph of my mother, his wife, and Dellwood Barker, my father.

Then there was me and Dellwood fucking how we did, for as long as we did, the fun we had fucking, the Moves Moves and the Wild Moon Man.

Even before, though, before Dellwood Barker came along, there had been me and not me and the two of them fighting over which one I was.

So that day, when Dellwood Barker knocked on the door, stepped in the shed, and there he was, my body didn't know what to do except what my body had always done, and that's go every which way. Feet trying to run, heart beating, breath in and out, arms reaching out to touch, hands fists, dick hard, head trying to figure out the dynamics of the situation.

Looking for who I was was who I was. Me trying to be somebody enough to hold myself together in one place. Be somebody enough that this could happen to, that Dellwood Barker could happen to.

Ida had cleaned him up. She knew I thought he was my father, but the old whore cleaned him up anyway and pointed him at the shed.

He was wearing a white shirt, clean pants, shiny boots. His hair was slicked back, still wet, smelling barbershop. Fern Hurdlika had shaved him, had strapped her razor and shaved the white skin of Dellwood's cheekbone up to the line of hair, black at the sideburns, silver at the temples.

'Full moon tonight,' Dellwood Barker said, green eyes shining, scrutinizing my left eye. 'Full in the heart. And not only is the moon full in the heart, but there's also an eclipse of the moon. Says so right in my book. "Lunar eclipse," it says.'

'Eclipse?' my ears heard my mouth say.

'E . . C . . L . . I . . P . . S . . E,' Dellwood spelled, 'means that's when the earth gets between the sun and the moon, and the moon goes dark.'

'Always something coming in between,' I said.

'Not tonight, Shed,' Dellwood said, and stepped the smell of him and barbershop up closer.

'Full in the heart,' Dellwood said, putting his arms around me, leaning hard on me. 'Best moon of the year for being with who you love.'

I looked around at things – the Hudson Bay on my bed, the deer hide, the stove, the pile of wood, the braided rug, the curtain that was really a petticoat, the window my mother was last seen alive through, the mirror, the kerosene lamp – they all looked different. All of them suddenly glowing with a light all their own. Thought maybe it was the sunset making things fancy, but it wasn't the sunset. It was Dellwood Barker.

'Love?' I said.

'Eclipse only happens once in a coon's age, and here it is happening tonight – to you and me,' Dellwood said. Then he said all this at once:

'I've always said that first you make the story happen in your head and then sooner or later the world will tag along. You being in my arms has been the story I've been telling myself since Buffalo Head. So, I guess I shouldn't be surprised at all that here you are standing with me now – but I tell you, son, I can't stop thinking what a dang miracle it is that I found you again. My sore heart is so happy to see you. Can't tell you how happy.'

Dellwood took his hand and put his hand on his heart when he said that about his sore heart, then he put his hand on my heart, on the hole in my heart.

'Ida said you was shot,' Dellwood said. 'You alright?'

'I'm alive,' I said. 'And with my family. Now you're here.'

'Who shot you?' Dellwood asked.

'Charles Smith shot me,' I said. 'He's dead now,' I said. 'If you stay long enough, I'll tell you the story,' I said.

'We got all the time' Dellwood said. 'Tonight will cinch it for good.'

'Cinch it?' I asked.

'You and me and full moon in the heart and the eclipse,' Dellwood said. 'I can't believe you don't know about eclipse.'

'What's there to know?' I asked.

'All sorts of tales about eclipse,' Dellwood said, pulling off his shirt, me pulling off mine. 'Story goes that when the moon is dark – for those minutes when the moon is completely dark – men can become women and women, men. Heard too that lovers fucking can cross over the boundary and become each other.'

Dellwood Barker stood himself in front of me, laying his head against the hole in my chest.

'Berdache Indians from the old days say that knowledge can become understanding during the dark of the moon – that you can come face to face with who you are and who you think you are,' Dellwood said. 'And most people can't take seeing that who they are is who they think they are, and they end up going plumb crazy.'

Dellwood Barker's mouth at my ear, him in my arms again.

'Heard tell too you can talk to your shadow, and your shadow will talk back,' Dellwood said, '. . . that's what it is, you know, the dark of the moon is a shadow – you see, the earth comes between the sun and the moon, and what darkens the moon is the shadow of the earth. So, like my book says, the sun – being the source of light – gets blocked by the earth – earth being the

place where we all think we are who we are – and the thinking
we are who we are, the earth shadow – gets cast onto the moon –
moon being our secret selves – secret being the fact that we're
not who we think we are at all.'

My face was in the crook of Dellwood's neck. Against his skin,
my ear listening to language in him coming up.

'Anyway, the upshot of the whole thing is,' Dellwood said,
'during the dark of the moon everything goes the way it normally
don't.'

The moon was a patch of window on the sheets, and on
Dellwood's back. My hands in the patch of moon on his back, no
dark touching.

'You got a place we can go that's a clear view of the sky?'
Dellwood asked.

I raised myself up on my elbow. 'Follow me!' I said.

Soon as we got outside, Metaphor came running for me and
jumped up in my arms, smiling, tongue hanging out. Abraham
Lincoln made a horse sound with her lips and nodded when I
touched her neck.

'Where's Princess?' Dellwood asked.

'Charles Smith,' I said.

'We got all the time,' Dellwood said.

The night was big. We waded across the river, water ankle
deep and shining with full moon in the heart. We started
climbing.

When we got to the granite outcropping, I started running.
Ran up and looked down into the meadow. The moon was as big
as I'd ever seen it, red-orange with August fire.

'This is my place,' I said. 'Where knowledge will become
understanding,' I said. 'Tybos call it Indian Head but its real name
is Not-Really-A-Mountain.'

Dellwood put his arm around me and I put my arm around

him and we stood, me in my place with Dellwood Barker, him not saying a word for a long while, him scrutinizing.

'Who died here?' Dellwood asked.

'Died?' I said.

'Somebody you know died here,' Dellwood said.

'A man named Big Foot died here,' I said.

'Did you know him?' Dellwood asked.

'Knew of him,' I said. Then: 'My mother died here.'

'Your mother?' Dellwood asked. 'Charles Smith kill her too?'

'We got all the time,' I said.

'And tonight we'll cinch it for good,' Dellwood said.

'Cinch it?' I asked.

'In the dark of the moon,' Dellwood said. 'Tonight, we'll become one another.'

I climbed down the rocks and Dellwood followed. We walked through the meadow straight to the edge. On the rock, in the circle that I had drawn there, we sat on the edge of the world, and dangled our legs over. Moon was a perfect red-orange ball in a blue night sky.

'That's another thing about eclipse,' Dellwood said. 'Dead can come alive and walk around.'

I looked around.

'We better go,' I said.

'Too late,' Dellwood said. 'Look!'

The red-orange full moon in the heart had an earth shadow bite out of it.

'Tonight there's no coming in between,' Dellwood said. 'It's me and you and Moves Moves and the full moon in the heart being eclipsed.'

'And the dead walking around,' I said. 'My mother walking around,' I said.

'And men becoming women and women, men,' Dellwood said. 'And lovers becoming each other,' he said.

'Anything you're hiding will come out,' I said.

'And you'll be face to face with who you are,' Dellwood said.

'And you'll be face to face with who I am,' I said.

'Your shadow talking to you,' Dellwood said. 'Knowledge becoming understanding.'

We took our boots off before we started kissing, us laying in the circle I had drawn. Moves Moves coming up big, big as the shadow biting at the red-orange round big moon floating in the sky far away. My hands on his red-orange white back, on his hips in the moon, at his neck.

Entering by overcoming resistance.

My hole the woman's hole, Dellwood's dick in me, Wild Moon Man, man becoming woman, me becoming woman, me Alma Hatch, Ida Richilieu, Gracie Hammer, Ellen Finton, those females.

Outside the circle, the dead walking around the circle. My mother, the Princess, Dellwood's wife, walking around the circle, her bare feet, her leather skirt and red blouse.

'Eyes,' I said to my eyes, 'don't look in your mother's eyes.'

Dellwood's dick poking into my insides bringing up forever, bringing up pain. Penetration – I'll tell you this – big dick or little, you got to let yourself open or it hurts.

Secret of woman's hole is open so it don't hurt.

Secret is when you're open, when you're moon reflecting light, the sun is yours, everything's yours.

Truth is, most men don't know that. Every sorry man needs to know he is alive, and truth is, the only way he knows he is alive is that he penetrates, he overcomes resistance, he leans hard onto.

Proof: you enter darkness, you are alive.

Truth is, he's just hungry for his mother's tit.

Woman's hole is mother's hole.

Every sorry unweaned man – head up his mother, dick up you.

Truth is, every sorry man don't ever look down at his own two nipples. Don't know he's sitting on his own dark secret – the undiscovered, unpenetrated moon hole in him he's been packing around all along – the contents of or meaning of – he hasn't the slightest idea.

Truth was, the moon, dark, next to Dellwood's head, was a head. On the ground, in the circle next to us, was our humping-up shadows.

'Your father, your mother,' the shadows said. 'The man, the woman,' they said, 'the light.'

Beyond the shadows, beyond the circle, my mother's eyes were great glowing stars too big to look at, but I looked, scrutinized my left eye into hers.

'Mother,' I said to Buffalo Sweets. 'You are dead,' I said. 'There is no room for you in me, no room in Dellwood, and him and me are going alone.'

'Shed,' Dellwood said, bringing his face close up to mine. 'Look me in the left eye,' he said.

Green eyes even in the dark.

'Screw up your face. Make your hands fists. Your feet claws. Bring the Moves Moves up from your balls, across your ass, up your back, to the top of your head. Don't ejaculate.'

Light shooting through my body, I ejaculated.

'Is it me?' I said, becoming him. 'Is it me?'

Knowledge, understanding: devil has no light. Devil is only a shadow – our own shadow we call the devil, that darkens.

*

Ida said she had a big dinner waiting up in her room for me and Dellwood. As far back as I could remember, Ida'd never had dinner in her room before – for more than two people, that is – namely for her and, while she was ovulating, the one she was wearing the blue dress for.

Ida wasn't even wearing the blue dress, was wearing the white dress. Alma Hatch was wearing her white dress, too. The tablecloth was white. There were candles on the table in the candlestick holders Ida called her 'chandelabras.' The room was the rosiest I'd ever seen it.

Ida sat Dellwood Barker across the table from her, and Alma Hatch across the table from me.

'Dinner is steak and whiskey and bread,' Ida said.

Since there was no steak and bread on the table, we started with the whiskey.

Ida poured the four shot glasses on the white tablecloth up to the brim. Ida took her glass first, raised it to Dellwood Barker, and said, 'Hello, stranger.'

We threw back the whiskey, nobody saying anything, and then Ida poured us another round.

I looked around the table. Alma Hatch, with the color of the room on her white dress and on her skin, looked the most beautiful I'd ever seen her. So was Ida beautiful. In her white dress, hair pulled up off her neck, and the rhinestones in her hair. And Dellwood, beautiful, his white skin, his line of sideburn, his green eyes, hair slicked back, wearing his white shirt and collar.

Ida always poured the first two rounds of drinks, and after that it was up to you. I went for the third drink first – Ida Richilieu, Alma Hatch, and Dellwood Barker in the same room together – figured could drive anyone to drink.

Wasn't long before Ida told the feathered-boa story, slapping her knee when she said: 'He didn't reach for the bow and the feather. He reached for the *feathered boa*.'

Ida started with that story and then went through her version of all the stories. The running-away-with-twenty-whores-chasing-me story. Painting the hotel pink. The fucking-Alma-Hatch story, Ida always making things more than what they actually were, all the while claiming it was the God's truth – God's truth with Ida never being that far from her own.

While Ida was talking, Dellwood got up to pour himself another drink. Alma Hatch got up then, too, and held her glass out as Dellwood poured her glass full, Dellwood smiling, Alma batting her eyelashes.

Alma Hatch had that look in her eye – the kind of look Ida'd get when she wore the blue dress. Only it wasn't Ida.

'You're such a gentleman, Dellwood,' Alma said. 'Do you like birds?'

'Moon's waning now til the sixteenth of September,' Dellwood said back to Alma. 'If you got any potatoes in the ground, better wait til the sixteenth.'

'Ain't it delicious, being so pernicious. Fuck these Mormon sons o'bishes,' Ida was humming.

We all had another drink.

It was sometime after I'd quit counting which drink I was on when I remembered that we still hadn't had dinner. Then, all of a sudden Ida Richilieu set her drink to the side, cleared the empty plate, the knife, the fork, the spoon, and the napkin away from in front of her, put her elbows on the table, made her hands into fists, banged the table with her fists, and yelled out:

'Tell me, Mr. Big-Shot Man-In-Love-With-The-Moon Dellwood Barker, just what the hell is your ass doing here in Excellent, Idaho?'

When I looked over to Ida, what I saw was Ida scared. Scared of Dellwood Barker, my father, scared of the lie she'd told about me and my twin sister.

Most men would have had the sense to get up and get out while they still could. Being in Ida's hotel, in Ida's room in her hotel, at Ida's table, drinking Ida's whiskey was no place for a sorry man if Ida Richilieu was going to go mountain lion on you.

But Dellwood Barker was no sorry man. He looked Ida

Richilieu, scrutinizing, in her left eye, Ida's eyes twitching – only other times I'd seen that twitch was with my mother, Buffalo Sweets, and the day Alma Hatch walked into the saloon.

'I came here for one reason, and for one reason only,' Dellwood Barker said.

'You came here for Shed,' Ida said.

'No,' Dellwood said, 'I didn't know Shed was here.'

'You came for me, didn't you?' Alma said.

'Nope,' Dellwood said. 'Came for one thing and one thing only,' he said.

'P . . E . . R . . N . . I . . C . . I . . O . . U . . S,' he said.

'Oh! The humanity!' Ida Richilieu said, slapping her knee. Then she said, 'Glorious!'

'Glorious! Glorious!' she said.

We poured ourselves another drink.

After that, Ida Richilieu asked Dellwood Barker everything a person could ask another person. Where he was born, who was his parents, where he was educated, how he'd learned to play the piano that way, where he'd got his education, where he lived, how much money he had, and who he liked to fuck most, men or women.

Dellwood Barker answered every one of Ida Richilieu's questions. Didn't hold a thing back of his human-being story: how his parents died at Robber's Roost, Foolish Woman the Berdache, why pianos made him crazy. Told them about that book of his, *Secrets of the Moon*, and about the specific times when the moon was right to eat certain things, when not to eat them, when to clean your ears and have sexual intercourse. He even told them about Moves Moves and the Wild Moon Man. Said it depended on the person, not the sex of the person, who he liked to fuck most. Said he liked fucking me the most.

'Shed?' Alma said.

'Why's that?' Ida asked.

'Because I love him,' Dellwood said.

Alma Hatch had been lustfully quiet most of the evening, except for laughing at pernicious and a birdcall now and then, her casting those sideways glances at Dellwood every time she got the chance. When Dellwood said that about loving me, though, a change came over Alma Hatch, as if a slow fuse inside her was being lit.

'Ever been married, Mr. Barker?' Alma asked.

I looked at Ida. Ida looked at me, then at Alma. Alma looked back.

'Yup,' Dellwood said. 'Years ago. To an Indian woman named Buffalo Sweets. Lost her and the twins, though, a boy and a girl. Winter froze.'

'She was an *Indian*?' Alma asked.

'Bannock,' Dellwood said.

'Your mother was Bannock, wasn't she, Shed?' Alma asked.

Dellwood looked both eyes into my left eye.

'Shoshone.' I gulped down my whiskey, poured another. Stared at Ida. Ida stared at Alma. Alma stared back.

'What was her name?' Dellwood asked me.

'Princess,' I said.

'Princess?' Dellwood said.

'She was called something else around here, though, wasn't she?' Alma asked.

'Called her a two-bit whore,' Ida said, looking at Alma.

'Excuse me,' my ears heard my mouth say. 'Got to piss.'

I got up, watched my feet walk out of Ida's room, into the corridor, then out the back door of the second-story landing. Watched myself piss over the side.

When I turned and looked into Ida's window, me looking in this time, instead of seeing Ida Richilieu writing down human-being stories in her diary, I heard a human-being story being told; namely mine.

The Man Who Fell in Love with the Moon

Ida Richilieu was telling the story, and Alma Hatch and Dellwood Barker were listening to it. This is what I heard:

'I never saw a kid love his mother so much as Shed did. Spent most of his days waiting for some kind of acknowledgment from her. Attended to her like a suitor. Kept her room clean, made sure she ate, ran errands for her, slept with her every chance he got, carried water up from the horse trough for her bath – four buckets up the back stairs every day. Even took her thunder mug out in the morning. Princess was not a happy woman, and she was selfish, and she treated Shed like a servant. Made no bones about it.

'But don't get me wrong, Shed wasn't no fool. When he wasn't attending to his mother, Shed was quite a different breed of cat. That kid could take off for weeks when he was just a little tyke and live out in the wilds like an animal. Never saw anything like him. Could run like a deer. Disappear in a second. Half the time, you didn't know he was around. Before he was five years old, there were already hundreds of stories about that kid. Once, when Billy Blizzard killed his horse out front here, Shed went into a frenzy – he started dancing and yelling around like a deranged person, foaming at the mouth. Cried for two days straight.

'Then there was Billy Blizzard, bless my heart – and his. He raped that kid in front of our very eyes. Held a gun up to Shed's head and fucked him right out back here, me watching, his mother – the whole damn place watching. We thought Billy'd killed the kid. I ran down and Billy hit me hard and then kicked me. Put me out of commission for nearly three months. Billy Blizzard got on a horse and hightailed it out of here, the Princess after him in the wagon driving the mules in hot pursuit. Wasn't til the following spring she was found. Shed found her body up on Indian Head. Shed found Billy Blizzard's red boots, too – which some people take as evidence of his death, but I don't. That ring of Billy Blizzard's wasn't on his hand, and I won't believe he's dead until there's better evidence than just a pair of boots and some pieces of old clothes.

'By spring, Shed was on his feet again, but he wasn't right. He did speak his first words of English – that I'd ever heard, anyway – *She was my spirit of things*, he said. Damned near broke my heart.

'His mother used to point to him and say, "Shed!" – meaning "Go out to the shed!" That's how he got his name.'

'Now, I'm telling you this, Mr. Dellwood Barker, and you, Mrs. Alma Hatch, because this is the God's truth – this is the truth of what happened. If you hear anything else, it's a human distortion. I'm telling you this because you got to understand the excruciating pain that kid has had to deal with in his life, and it's *never* anything to joke about, or to fool with. It is simply too painful.

'*That's* why we don't talk about his mother,' Ida said.

'Do you understand me, Alma Hatch?

'Dellwood Barker?'

I had never heard Ida Richilieu's version of my story before. As she told it, what my eyes saw was me reflected in the window looking in. Saw Damn Dave's stick figures, drawings of me on torn pieces of paper doing what Ida said I'd done – along with horses growing out of the ground, houses with faces, trees with arms and legs. Full moon and a bloody knife stuck through it, ear to ear.

The truth according to Ida Richilieu.

Truth was, though, Ida was lying. Ida's story about me – according to me – wasn't the story about me and my mother at all. Was really the story of me and Ida Richilieu.

Story of a crazy, told by a crazy.

Should only make you wonder.

I was still standing at the window when Dellwood Barker came out onto the porch. He pissed over the side too, and lit a cigarette.

'That's quite a story you've got,' Dellwood said.

I didn't look over to Dellwood, kept looking in the window. Ida Richilieu hauled off and slapped Alma Hatch so hard it sent Alma to the floor. Alma covered her head with her hands. 'I'm sorry, Idee, I'm sorry,' Alma was saying. 'I don't know what got into me. I won't do it again. I promise!'

'Not the best topic of conversation around here, your mother,' Dellwood said.

'Nope,' I said.

'He killed her and raped you, huh?' Dellwood said. '. . . Billy Blizzard?'

'Yup,' I said.

'Shed?' Dellwood said. 'Why didn't you tell me? About your mother.'

'She died and I lived,' I said.

'But why didn't you tell me?' Dellwood asked.

'Didn't know where to start,' I said. 'And besides,' I said, 'so far, you been too busy talking about the moon.'

When me and Dellwood walked back into Ida's room, finally it was dinner: steak and bread was on the table. Everybody had a fresh glass of whiskey. Ida and Alma were back sitting at the table, Ida in her place, Alma in hers, both of them smiling and talking as if nothing was out of the ordinary.

With Dellwood Barker, me and Ida and Alma's family of three became a family of four without a problem; that is, except for Alma Hatch. Alma thinking she was in love with Dellwood Barker being the problem.

Alma Hatch thought it was love. But it wasn't love. Wasn't locoweed, either. Was just how Alma Hatch was.

Here's how Alma's story always went: Alma would see a man and fall in love with him out of the blue same way as she did her birdcalls. Soon as she saw him and right after she fell in love with him, Alma Hatch started to hate him. Falling in love was something Alma had to do, and since she had to do it, she hated it. Hated him because she was in love with him. Hated him because now she loved him he was going to penetrate her which she hated which she loved.

All this took place in one instant, before Alma had even talked to the man. The man was just another sorry man at the bar having a drink. Alma Hatch would walk up to the man at the bar and within five minutes they'd be up in room 11, doing what Alma loved and hated most. The affair usually only lasted two weeks. Alma would feel everything there was to feel. She'd feel orgasms like never before. She'd feel used and unappreciated. She'd feel beautiful and fulfilled. She'd feel like nothing but a pussy and an asshole and a mouth walking around. She'd feel that she finally knew the meaning of love. She'd feel that she was losing herself. She'd write poetry and sometimes, right in the middle of fucking, she'd climb off and, clutching a sheet to her, would go out to the banister and recite one of her poems for the whole damned saloon to hear.

All the while, the sorry man she'd fallen in love with had no idea about what was going on. To hear him tell the story, he was having a drink one evening and this long-haired beauty wanted him, so he leaned hard on her.

Alma Hatch was the worst ever with Dellwood Barker. Worst ever, I figure, because she really did, I think, love him. Worst ever because Dellwood Barker loved her too – the way I figure we all loved each other.

In that family of ours – when the family was three – what we were missing was a father. When the three of us got to be four, the fourth of us being Dellwood, a father was something we weren't missing anymore.

Father to me, flesh and blood – that only me and Ida knew about. Father to Ida the way she was mother and Dellwood being so much like her ex-husband. But as far as Alma Hatch was concerned, Dellwood Barker wasn't so much father as he was *daddy*.

'Same as with you and your mother,' Dellwood said to me once. 'Alma just never got the loving from her father she needed, so now that's the story she keeps telling herself with damn near every man she meets. You told me once that you're trying to free yourself from woman's hole, but what about Alma? She doesn't even know she needs to make herself free, let alone what from.'

Alma Hatch was the worst ever with Dellwood Barker, though, because Dellwood Barker wasn't just another sorry man, because Dellwood Barker was a lunatic, especially when it came to people's stories and how people tell their stories to themselves. With Alma Hatch, Dellwood Barker found a story, more clearly and simply told than any you'd regularly find. So Dellwood fit himself right in, filling in the places of Alma's story that needed filling in. Dellwood playing along, playing the devil, fueling the fire, so Alma could feel all she had to feel – more glorious, more excruciating than ever.

Dellwood Barker did the same thing with Ida Richilieu. He filled in the spaces of her story that needed filling in. Dellwood sat back and let Ida be Ida. He became her biggest admirer. Hated Mormons with her. Talked about dicks with her. Always took her side. Treated her like a queen, the authority, the one in charge. Fueled her fire, too, the way Ida's fire needed fueling; namely, by agreeing with everything she said except for philosophy. Dellwood Barker disagreed with Ida Richilieu point for point whenever it came to philosophy. They had both read a lot of English literature, too, so they talked about literature, but mostly what they did was disagree about literature because, as Dellwood put it, 'You can't talk about English literature and not talk philosophy too.'

Dellwood argued with Ida because, he said, he knew Ida

needed to argue. Needed somebody smart as her to argue with. So he supplied her.

Guess Dellwood Barker fueled my fire the same way, although he said he didn't – couldn't, and that's why he loved me so much.

'Most folks are damned fools,' Dellwood said, 'and have no idea they're making themselves up. But you're different, Shed. You live with the knowledge and understanding that who you are is a story you've made up to keep the moon away,' Dellwood said. 'And since you know what it's like to live without a story, you've made yourself an expert on stories and what stories do.

'What's a human being without a story?' Dellwood said. 'It's a half-breed pervert of a kid chasing a killdeer bird, looking in windows, at people inside, looking at who they think they are, how their story goes – and how they get away with it.'

I thought for a long time about what Dellwood Barker said about me. I came up with this: there's one story I believed in, still do: we were a family. Ida Richilieu, Alma Hatch, Dellwood Barker, and me were a family.

Some of the best times of being a family was after Ida taught Dellwood how to play the piano. Wasn't long at all and Dellwood could control his crying. Then it wasn't long at all and Dellwood was playing real pretty music. I loved to sit and listen to him play. Ida liked his music, too. Of course, Alma Hatch thought Dellwood's music was the finest music ever in the whole world. Said it made her feel like she was flying. She'd make bird noises you can't imagine. Ida called his music *classical*. Dellwood had to disagree with her. He said it wasn't *classical*, it was *romantic*. They argued about that one until the very end.

When Ida and Dellwood were both at the piano, playing duets, they were the same person, the male and female of each other, one person with the music they were making. That was some fun to have, those two playing and me and Alma Hatch dancing the way tybos dance – that is, when Alma wasn't pouting or threatening to kill herself – polkas we'd dance and waltzes, dances like Ida's Jewish tribe, dances like Ida's ex-husband's people, the Italians, danced. Glorious dancing, Ida called it.

Ida and Dellwood sometimes slept together but didn't fuck. At least, I don't think so. Ida never did place much importance on fucking, and with me being there and Ida knowing how I felt about Dellwood, and her remembering the mistake she had made falling in with Alma Hatch and losing me over it – and then with Alma Hatch after Dellwood like a mare in heat – Ida probably figured Dellwood's hands were already full of the human-being sex story. Besides, Ida said – or was it Dellwood who said? – 'The sex story is only one of the ways that human beings can touch each other.'

Dellwood Barker did spend a lot of time with Alma Hatch. More than I ever got used to. There was a couple of times when I meant to rip out every one of the strands of Alma Hatch's hair, her pulling some of those stunts she did – trying to make Dellwood jealous with other men, buying pies from the Relief Society and telling Dellwood Barker she'd baked them, always finding one thing or another in her room that need to be moved or repaired, telling Dellwood Barker she wanted his child and begging him to give her his Moves Moves.

But I didn't raise a hand to Alma Hatch. Reason was because of what Dellwood had said about Alma Hatch and her father, and also because of what Dellwood kept on saying to me over and over about love being big.

'When you got love,' he said, 'it makes you bigger, makes you want to share it more and more.'

When it came right down to it, though, I knew I had the ace in the hole, so to speak. All this talk about love and being big with love and the sex story not the only way to express love made sense alright. Thing was, though, and what I always kept in mind

– the truth was – that Dellwood Barker liked me to fuck him. He had said many times that he'd spent his whole life mostly putting it in, while all along he'd been hankering for it the other way around, and now that he'd found a reliable other way around, and since it was me, Shed, somebody he loved, that he was doing the other way around with, and since neither Ida nor Alma were equipped to do the other way around with to him, as far as I was concerned, it was perfect, was pernicious.

One day up on Not-Really-A-Mountain, I sat myself down with my legs dangling over the edge. I thought about knowledge becoming understanding while I looked down at the world – at the mountain ranges, at Ida's Place, at the window of Alma's room, where Dellwood Barker and Alma Hatch were probably fucking – and I started to understand. I'd been getting pretty good at saving my Moves Moves and, the more I saved, the more knowledge, the more understanding, the more love I seemed to have.

Understanding: Dellwood and Alma were me, and Ida was me, too. The four of us were the whole world – every story that was ever told we were – fucking and fighting and playing the piano, us a family, the human-being family story.

'Sticking together,' as Ida put it.

'Through thick and thin,' Dellwood said.

'No matter what,' they said.

'A family,' I said.

'Better than any Mormon family,' Ida said.

*

It all fell apart, or all came together, one Saturday night in the middle of September. Alma Hatch was at her worst, which was her best, hating Dellwood Barker because she loved him. They had been for a walk up at the cemetery. Dellwood had just penetrated her and she'd had an orgasm like never before and was feeling everything there was to feel – beautiful, fulfilled, and just a pussy, an asshole, and a mouth walking around. Alma Hatch was yelling at Dellwood Barker, telling him and the whole county that he was as crazy a cowboy ever was, a titched-in-the-head, not-all-there, half-baked, harebrained, foolhardy, moon-struck drunk of a man.

That's about the time I ran into them on the front steps of Ida's Place. As soon as Alma Hatch saw me, she started in. Said just about the same things to me she'd been saying to Dellwood. When she was done whooping and hollering and cussing a blue streak, she stormed up the front steps.

Me and Dellwood looked up. Alma Hatch's dress had got caught in her belt or corset or whatever, and there it was – Alma Hatch's bare butt – staring us in our faces.

Me and Dellwood laughed our fool heads off.

Alma pulled her dress down, ran inside Ida's Place, stormed up the stairs and into her room. Later on, when me and Dellwood were standing at the bar, having a whiskey, Alma Hatch came out to the banister and started reciting one of her poems – something awful about her bare butt being the moon and the object of everyone's desire.

About an hour later, she came over to Dellwood and told him, 'You're sleeping with me tonight!'

'No, I ain't,' Dellwood said. 'I'm sleeping with Shed tonight.'

Then Alma Hatch said, 'I'm going to kill you two.'

Me and Dellwood were real quiet getting out of bed the next morning, but not quiet enough for old Hawkeye Alma Hatch. When she realized that me and Dellwood were taking off alone together, 'I got so dang mad I couldn't see straight,' she told Ida later. Alma did see straight enough, though, to grab Ida's shotgun from beside Ida's bed and, as the story goes, run out of Ida's Place after us that morning, hair flying and half-dressed.

Homecoming

When me and Dellwood walked out the back door of Ida's Place, the sun wasn't up yet, and the moon was shining down. Not-Really-A-Mountain was black and starless against the navy blue sky. Things were pink, though, as Ida's Place, and gold by the time we'd crossed the river and started up the mountain. Metaphor had to come along too. That dog was half mountain goat.

About midmorning, we rested at the timberline. I spoke the first words.

'That night up here, during the eclipse,' I said, 'did you really become me?'

'I did,' Dellwood said.

'What did it feel like, being me?' I asked.

'Felt big,' Dellwood said. 'Felt like laughing.'

'That's all?' I asked. 'Wasn't there anything else?'

'Felt your mother, and Big Foot,' Dellwood said.

'Did you see my mother?' I asked.

'Didn't see her, no, but I felt her,' Dellwood said.

'What did my mother feel like?' I asked.

'She loved you very much,' Dellwood said.

'That's all?' I asked.

'Is there supposed to be more?' Dellwood asked.

'No,' I said. 'Just curious.

'No Billy Blizzard?' I asked.

'No Billy Blizzard,' Dellwood said. 'Just your mother and Big Foot.

'And what about you?' Dellwood asked. 'What did it feel like being me?'

'Felt like I was on the moon,' I said.

'That's all?' Dellwood asked.

'That's enough,' I said.

In the meadow, walking to the edge, the wind blew our hair the way the wind was blowing the grass. The grass was dry and

251

brown and gold except for where there was underground water. The Indian paintbrush were dried up and so were the purple flowers and the yellow ones.

Dellwood reached over and put his arm around me. I never did get used to getting touched by him. Hurt the way a bad tooth wants more hurting.

'Let's jump,' I said.

'Surefire way to learn to fly,' Dellwood said.

That's when Alma Hatch opened fire on us.

With all that buckshot landing around, me and Dellwood and Metaphor flat on the rock, asses low, what I thought was: Billy Blizzard still alive.

Here's Alma's story: after she unloaded both barrels of Ida's shotgun on us, Alma reloaded and shot again, reloaded and shot again, then threw the gun down, ran down the mountain a madwoman, crossed the river, ran into Excellent screaming bloody murder, into Ida's Place, up to Ida's room where she confessed to Ida Richilieu that she had murdered both me and Dellwood Barker in cold blood and now was going to kill herself.

Ida Richilieu took Alma Hatch into her arms and they collapsed into a wailing heap on the floor. The two of them stayed that way most of the day, Ida not leaving Alma for fear that she'd do herself in, too. Then, that afternoon, me and Dellwood Barker walked into the bar and opened a bottle of whiskey.

Ellen Finton looked at me and Dellwood as if we were ghosts, and then ran upstairs into Ida's room. When Ida came out her door and saw me and Dellwood in her saloon drinking and alive, she turned on her heel. When Ida came back out, I was just getting ready to tell her that Billy Blizzard was alive and back and had tried hard to kill us with her shotgun, and would have, too, if he wasn't such a damned poor shot, when the next thing I knew, Ida Richilieu had Alma Hatch by the long hair and was swinging her almost like a lariat above her head. When Ida let go of Alma, Alma went flying and made a one-point landing on her head halfway down the stairs, then rolled the rest of the way down, landing right smack at Dellwood's feet.

Alma Hatch sitting on the saloon floor, hair undone and hanging all over, looked at us as if she wasn't Alma Hatch no more and we weren't me and Dellwood Barker.

Ida Richilieu came down the stairs, a bat out of hell, took her shotgun from my hands, popped two more shells in the barrels, went over to Alma Hatch, grabbed her by the hair again, pulled Alma's head back, stuck the shotgun barrels against Alma's neck, and said all this in one screaming breath:

'Let's get this clear right now. You, Alma Hatch, are going to grow up. You're going to let go of this man here Dellwood Barker and let him in peace. But first, you're going to stand up and offer your hand in apology to these two men for all the spiteful malevolent female bullshit crap you've been pulling on them and everybody else around here for the past two or three weeks. Your exaggerated histrionics are boring and stupid and have gone just too far. Now, stand up and act like the strong woman you are and say you're sorry or I'll blow your head off!'

Alma Hatch stood up, pulled her hair back from her face, weaved around, her body not quite situated on her legs yet, and her legs not quite on her feet. She looked at me and then at Ida and then at Dellwood. It took a while for her mouth to move the language coming out from inside her, but finally, she spoke:

'I didn't kill you, thank God!' she said even though she didn't believe in God. Alma pulled a strand of hair from her mouth.

'I won't bother you anymore, Dellwood,' she said. 'I promise,' she said. 'I'm sorry. I can't tell you why I do this. Will you forgive me? Dellwood?'

'I forgive you, Alma,' Dellwood said.

'Shed?' Alma said.

Forgive was a word I knew how to spell. Knew what it meant, too. But I'd never done it before, or ever thought about doing it.

'I forgive you, Alma,' I said the way Dellwood had said, the words coming out of me, sounding strange to my ears — words saying I'd do something that I never before knew I knew how to do, but when it came down to it, I did.

'I forgive you,' I said again, mostly just to hear myself say it.

*

Glorious was Ida's new word. She said 'glorious' as much as she said 'pernicious,' 'Oh! The humanity,' and how much she hated Mormons.

'G . . L . . O . . R . . I . . O . . U . . S,' Ida spelled. 'Means better than anything that's come along.'

Glorious was Ida's word for the four of us — Ida Richilieu, Alma Hatch, Dellwood Barker, and me. And *the glorious days*, according to Ida, were the days the four of us spent together, before the trouble came in between.

The way Ida put it, the day Alma Hatch asked for forgiveness was the day that Alma Hatch grew up, and with Alma growing up, we all grew up.

'Started into being a family,' Dellwood said.

'Better than any Mormon family,' Ida said.

Ida poured whiskey all around. She held her glass up before she drank. We held out glasses up too.

'As long as we all shall live,' Ida said, 'may nothing ever come between the four of us again!'

We all raised our glasses high and clinked our glasses together.

'May nothing ever come between us again,' we all said together, 'for as long as we live.'

Alma Hatch kept her promise, and we had two hundred of

them – glorious days. Pernicious days, together. Nothing coming in between.

Then everything came in between.

Then there wasn't anything left at all except for what had come between.

There was this one special day, though, just one in the two hundred of them, that I remember, that sometimes I wish I'd forget.

It was a Sunday, late September. The nights were already getting cold and the mornings, too. Wasn't until high noon you felt warm. We were all wearing the clothes that Ida had sent away for from the Sears and Roebuck catalog. They were white. Every stitch of clothing was white.

Me and Dellwood opened our package from Sears and Roebuck out in the shed. I'd never seen clothes like that before in real life – only the drawings of them in the catalog. The clothes were all folded up nice in thin paper that crackled: white shirts with collars, white trousers, white suspenders, white jackets, white socks – even white shoes made of thin leather that only came to your ankle with white shoelaces tying up the front. I even had a white tie that Dellwood had to show me how to make the knot. The hats – Dellwood's was a bowler like Bowler Hat's in Fort Lincoln only white. My hat was straw with a red band.

And those two women: both Alma and Ida threw away their old white dresses when they got their new ones. Both of them had parasols and were wearing big white hats. Most of Alma's tits showing up above the scoop of lace that made her neck and shoulders into a waxing moon, those two moons of Alma's almost exposed to the pink nipple. Ida looking as if somebody had spilt sugar on her, lace up to her neck that you could sort of see through, the dress tight on her, not wearing petticoats like Alma, her black diamond of hair down there, her big bruised nipples poking through the white, her lips so red that afternoon, I will never forget. Both Alma and Ida in white silk stockings, wearing Sears and Roebuck underwear. Underneath Alma's dress, so many petticoats that were all different colors – pink and blue and yellow. The sound of them when she walked.

We walked that Sunday through town, past the new green Mormon church just as William B. Merrillee's people were getting out of service – Ida Richilieu, Alma Hatch, Dellwood Barker, and me – walking down Pine Street through town, past Damn Dave's stables, Stein's Mercantile, and North's Grocery, all of us in white.

When we passed by the barbershop, the men sitting on the bench stopped talking. Just then, the Reverend Brother Josiah Helm and Excellent's new assistant to the mayor, Blumenfeld, stepped out of the post office and into the street. They were right under the American flag when they saw us. They stopped in their tracks.

It was the first time we'd seen Blumenfeld in town. Ida Richilieu and Alma Hatch kept walking and didn't say anything. I didn't say anything either. But Dellwood Barker did. He tipped his white bowler hat:

'Good afternoon, Sheriff!' Dellwood called out to Blumenfeld. 'But it's no longer "Sheriff," is it? What a pity!' Dellwood said, making his language sound as if he was somebody who'd always worn white clothes. 'We could use some law and order in this pernicious town.'

Me and Ida and Alma all laughed when Dellwood said 'pernicious.'

'Hear tell, though, you're still in public service,' Dellwood said.

Blumenfeld's eyes went into slits in his face.

'But nobody seems to know just what *kind* of service that it *is* that you're doing to the public, Sheriff. Would you kindly care to elucidate?' Dellwood said, leaning onto his cane.

Blumenfeld didn't move, didn't speak.

'Well, now, Sheriff, whatever that service is,' Dellwood said, sliding his cane along the inside of his thigh, 'please don't hesitate to ask if you need a hand.'

Ida Richilieu really loved Dellwood Barker right then. You could see the love in her eyes, her eyes just inside the shade of her white parasol. Loved him for speaking up on his own, for fighting the war, for making her war his war too.

We had all stopped walking and were standing on Pine Street, not far from the spot where Billy Blizzard had killed his horse, not far from the spot where Damn Dave had the humps going through him that night Billy Blizzard got him drunk – that spot under the flag where so much had happened.

Blumenfeld stepped off the boardwalk and walked slowly toward us. Seemed forever him walking. He wasn't wearing a gun anymore. The men by the bench – couldn't see a gun over there either. Dellwood didn't move an inch, just stood, leaning against his cane, smiling-not-smiling. I wished I could change my clothes.

Ida Richilieu didn't move – surprised the hell out of me, but she didn't say a word. Neither did Alma Hatch.

Blumenfeld stopped right in front of Dellwood. He was twice Dellwood's size.

'Dellwood Barker,' Blumenfeld finally said. 'Fancy meeting you again!'

Dellwood was looking his eyes into Blumenfeld's left eye.

'And the Bible salesman,' Blumenfeld said, hitching up his pants, looking at me. 'Aloisius Hatch, isn't it?'

Then Alma: 'Surely you're mistaken, Mr. Assistant Mayor. Aloisius Hatch was my own dear husband!'

'Pardon me, ma'am, but I never forget a face,' Blumenfeld said.

'Last time, though,' Blumenfeld said, 'as I recall, Aloisius Hatch wasn't so gussied up; in fact, he smelled like Injun shit.'

The Reverend Brother Josiah Helm smiled when Blumenfeld said that, and a couple of the other men too. Seeing them smile did something to me, and all of a sudden, before I knew it, my body started going every which way, and my leg jerked up and kicked Blumenfeld square in the balls. Could feel his balls through the thin white leather of my shoes. A little farther south and I'd have buried my foot up his ass.

Blumenfeld doubled over and started vomiting something terrible. Sounded as if he was yelling at his boots.

We stood in the street watching him, Ida Richilieu, Alma Hatch, Dellwood Barker, and me. The Reverend Brother Josiah Helm stood there too, and the men in front of the barbershop, watching. Up in Ida's Place, Gracie Hammer and Ellen Finton pulled the curtain back from the window of room 11. No one moved.

After a while, the four of us started walking again. We were just past Ida's Place when Blumenfeld found his voice. 'I'm going to get you two!' he yelled. 'I may not be sheriff anymore, but I'm going to get you. You mark my words. The two of you are dead men!'

Then the Reverend Brother Josiah Helm started cursing us to everlasting damnation in hell.

Then it seemed like the whole town was yelling.

'Ain't it delicious, being so pernicious. Fuck these Mormon sons o'bishes,' Ida started singing, then Alma started singing, then Dellwood, then me.

When we got done singing, though, none of us spoke a word.

We walked through Chinatown, through the cemetery, past

the hot springs, along a path by the river, Ida and Alma arm in arm under their parasols, me and Dellwood behind them, to the place that Ida had it all set up – the table with a checkered red and white tablecloth on it and four chairs around the table in the shade where the river looked green and was its widest. Sitting down at the table, we drank Italian wine and ate food Ida said they eat over there in Europe – black fish eggs, chicken livers, smoked salmon and duck, cheese that smelled bad, a Jewish kind of bread, and some fruit. Spent the whole day sitting at the table by the river eating those European things, drinking Italian wine from real wineglasses she'd got from Sears and Roebuck too; the afternoon growing hot for one of the last times, the river going by over the rocks putting that sound in your ears, the sun gold the way the sun gets in the fall, gold shining down on things that are gold and brown and dry; yellow jackets landing on the fruit, grasshoppers making the sound that you can't copy no matter how you lay your tongue.

That's the day I'm not forgetting, that afternoon when the four of us sat around the table wearing white in the shade by the green river.

It had been Ida's idea. Said she was tired of *barbarism*.

'Tired of fucking cowboys and miners and fighting Mormons,' Ida had said. 'What I need,' she said, 'is some grace and beauty in my life.' Was about time, she said.

So she ordered all the clothes from the Sears and Roebuck catalog, and when they got to Excellent, and when they didn't fit, Ida and Alma altered them – Ida and Alma almost totally remaking the dresses – cutting the neckline low for Alma, making the dress tight, no petticoats for Ida. My jacket was too tight and so were the pants.

'That boy'll never quit growing,' Ida said.

Ida was going to send my white suit back, but she said she

couldn't wait that long. I don't know how she did it, but the next time I put the jacket and the pants on, they fit.

Ida had sent for the food and the wine, too, from an old whore friend of hers in Portland, Oregon. The food was in tins. Took the food four months to get here. The day it arrived, Ida screamed so loud I thought we had trouble, but what it was was the food and wine she'd sent for.

That afternoon, we were mostly quiet, mostly just sat watching and listening, enjoying the view from where we were. The white clothes we were wearing made us feel like we were somebody else. Made us feel shy. Alma Hatch brought a mirror along. Most of the time, she just sat looking into the mirror. Dellwood all in white was something my eyes couldn't get enough of. That white skin of his, and the shadow of his beard poking through smooth. Ida looked like a bright spot in the day, a place so sunny you had to squint to look. Alma told me I looked like some foreign prince come to America wearing American clothes.

Ida told a story she'd never told before about a volcano in Italy where her husband's people lived. 'There's a saint there, forget his name,' she said. 'In a Catholic church, they've got some of his blood in a bottle. Every year everybody in the town prays to the saint so the volcano won't erupt. If they pray hard enough the blood turns liquid and they know they'll be safe. If it don't, they know they're going to burn.'

Ida's hand held the stem of her wineglass as she told the story. When she finished the story, Dellwood poured more red wine into her glass. On the table, next to her glass, were slices of bread cut from the loaf. There were bread crumbs on the checkered tablecloth.

Dellwood told us how once he'd run into a little animal one night that hopped on two legs and had big ears that spoke English and told him secrets.

'The moon is God's left eye,' Dellwood said the little animal had said. 'Told me too that I would die in the arms of my own true son in my own true place.'

Alma Hatch translated what the birds were saying around us. 'The birds are saying that their hearts are full of love,' Alma said, 'because the four people in white at this table right now – the hearts of these four people – are full of love in a way that most people never know.'

I didn't say much. When the four of us got together, I never did. Unless we were drinking and smoking. In that case I talked a lot. Out-Of-His-Mind, Dellwood would call me. Then I'd never remember a thing I said. That day I felt like talking, but didn't know what to say. I mean I knew what I wanted to say, but didn't know how to say it.

If I was to say now what I wanted to say then, I'd still find it hard, even though it's simple enough:

'Thank you, Owlfeather, for breathing your breath of life into me, so I could live to be here in this day.'

I'd have said: 'Thank you, Great Mystery, for letting me be around people who talk to animals and the animals talk back to them.'

I'd have said: 'Thank you for this Italian wine and how my feet look in these shoes, them on this golden grass in this golden sun.'

I'd have said: 'Thank you for Damn Dave drawing this picture of us down on an envelope somewhere.'

I'd have said: 'Thank you for Dellwood Barker, thank you for Alma Hatch, thank you for Ida Richilieu, thank you for me.'

'May nothing ever come between us,' I'd have said. 'Between me and Ida and Alma and Dellwood ever again.'

'May nothing ever come again between me and me.'

What made all this hard to say, and the reason why I didn't say anything that day, was because I was afraid if I said all this out loud, that all this would go away. You never spoke your name out loud in front of the devil. Same way you never said what you felt right out for the fear he'd hear and would take everything away – and something *would* come in between. But something came in between anyway. So I might as well have spoken.

Book Four

There was a Time: Devil

Part One

The Wisdom Brothers

The day that everything started coming in between was the day that Ida Richilieu found out that William B. Merrillee was coming to town.

That was also the day of the three posters: the Mormon poster, the Wisdom Brothers' poster, and then Ida's poster.

It was me who saw the Mormon poster first; that is, I was the first person who wasn't a Mormon to see it. Any person who wasn't a Mormon who saw that poster would have done exactly the same thing I did right off: bring it to Ida – and nobody had brought it to her yet.

The poster was printed on white paper in straight black letters and was tacked to the green Mormon church door. I didn't have to read far to know what it was saying. It was saying *trouble*.

Ida was standing behind the bar in a patch of sunlight in her good dress and apron, wiping glasses. It was just Doc Heyburn in the bar, and her. I closed the door behind me. Thord Hurdlika's stove had things warmed up good. I handed the poster over to Ida. She unrolled it, and read out loud:

'Official opening of the William B. Merrillee mill,' Ida read. 'William B. Merrillee himself,' Ida read, 'the marching band from Mountain Home – box social,' Ida read, 'a picnic at the church –

at *both* churches – the white one *and* the green one,' Ida read, 'and fireworks – to be held on the Fourth of July.'

I'd stood myself over by the stove, partly to get warm, but mostly to give Ida some room. But what I was giving her room for wasn't what she started doing. Ida Richilieu started dancing, holding the poster next to her like a partner, dancing and twirling all around the saloon. Me and the Doc just looked at each other. When Ida stopped, she was out of breath. Then Ida gave the poster a big kiss.

'Whoop-te-doo!' Ida said. 'The one and only! We finally get the opportunity to set eyes on the prophet of God – William B. Merrillee! Himself in the dang flesh here in Excellent! Oh! The humanity!' Ida said. 'Glorious! Glorious! Finally, the devil gets his due.'

Ida ended up dancing with the second poster too. *Providence*, she called the second poster.

'P . . R . . O . . V . . I . . D . . E . . N . . C . . E,' Ida spelled, 'means how things are going to be.'

Ida saw that one before me. It was tacked to the back of that morning's stagecoach. As soon as Ida Richilieu laid eyes on that poster, she ripped it off the back of the stage – just like I'd ripped the first one off the green Mormon church door – and then ran over to Ida's Place and started dancing with it. There were more folks in the bar by then, not just Doc Heyburn. Ida didn't care though. She just started dancing and singing and saying 'providence' over and over.

Then she glued the poster to the mirror behind the bar. First time Ida'd ever glued a thing to that mirror. Gold curlicued letters trimmed in red: *The Wisdom Brothers: Ulysses, Homer, Virgil, and Blind Jude – Authentic Colored Jubilee Minstrels Playing Pure Plantation Melodies and Songs of the Sunny South.*

Authentic Negroes. Not tybos with burnt cork on their faces making their faces black, but *colored* people.

As Alma Hatch put it, *real nigs*.

As soon as my eyes got done reading the poster, I knew what Ida Richilieu was planning. She was going to win her war with the Mormons by winning the battle of the Fourth of July.

Ida spent all night up in her room in her circle of light making the third poster. The next day it was hanging in all different colors and ways of writing on the porch by the front door to Ida's Place:

Fourth of July Celebration at the Indian Head Hotel! All drinks half price in honor of our grand nation's INDEPENDENCE! Piano music and dancing and singing!

Special Entertainment: The Wisdom Brothers! Former Slaves All the Way from Their Louisiana Plantation! Authentic Colored Jubilee Minstrels Here in Excellent for Your Enjoyment and Edification!

It took about three months for providence to get to Excellent, Idaho. While we were waiting for providence, me and Dellwood Barker, Alma Hatch and Ida Richilieu did pretty much the same things we always did. Family things: tended to business, did the spring cleaning, kept our customers happy, sold a fair amount of whiskey, drank whiskey ourselves, spent time in Chinatown.

Ida played the piano and Dellwood played the piano. Me and Alma danced.

We sat around the kitchen table the way any family would and talked about business, about our customers, talked about big dicks and little dicks. We talked about philosophy, Dellwood and Ida disagreeing.

The biggest argument they'd had so far was over a tree falling in the forest. Dellwood said if there wasn't anybody there to hear it, the falling tree wouldn't make a sound.

Ida said that was horseshit, and that anything that fell made a sound, whether someone was there to hear it or not.

Dellwood said, in fact, there weren't even trees, or forests, if you weren't a person who was telling yourself the story of trees and forests.

Ida said if you fell down and broke your arm, your arm'd still be broke even if nobody saw you fall down and break it.

Those two could go on arguing forever. Especially over that tree falling. Dellwood said, though, that what he and Ida were arguing over wasn't the tree – was philosophy. What they were arguing about was what was real. Got to be their only argument after a while: real and what real was.

Myself, I figured what real was, was what killdeer was, so arguing about it could only be a waste of time.

Besides talking about what was real, Ida talked about Mormons, and William B. Merrillee's visit to Excellent. Dellwood Barker talked about the moon. Alma talked about the spring birds and her hair.

Something, though, that was new that we talked about was the Wisdom Brothers, and because we were talking about the Wisdom Brothers, we talked about Abraham Lincoln, too – not the horse, the president – and the Emancipation Proclamation, and the Civil War, and slavery, and colored people in general.

Only thing I knew about colored people was that Big Foot was part Negro and what I'd heard about the Buffalo Soldiers. None of my mother's people liked *tutybos* (black white people) much, because tutybos were the Buffalo Soldiers, and the Buffalo Soldiers had killed so many Indians.

Dellwood Barker knew a lot more about tutybos. He said that he had lived cheek to jowl with colored people as a boy in New York City. He said they were just folks telling themselves stories the way any other folks do.

Alma Hatch said she had only seen a couple of Negroes who had worked as maids and cooks in her neighborhood when she was growing up in Minneapolis, Minnesota. Then, when she was selling Bibles with her husband, Aloisius Hatch, Alma said that her best customers were colored people. She had known a dwarf Negro when she was in the circus whose name was Pickaninny Pete, no taller than up to her crotch. Alma said Pickaninny Pete was polite and funny, but had a real mean drunk in him that you had to watch out for. Other than that, Alma said she had just seen Negroes in minstrel shows. She said they all loved to dance and sing and praise the Lord and they looked like monkeys and had big lips that always made her laugh.

'And that's not the only thing big on them,' Alma Hatch said.

Ida Richilieu had seen a number of Negro dicks in her time. She agreed with Alma that they were the biggest in the world, but said you had to be careful what stories you believed about colored people because most of the stories you heard about colored people were told by white people, and most white people when it came to colored people were a little bit to a whole lot crazy, and stories about crazy niggers told by crazy white folks should only make you wonder.

Negroes were something else that Dellwood Barker and Ida Richilieu agreed on – the philosophy of them, that is. I mean the philosophy that people were just human beings no matter how they parted their hair or how big their lips were, or what tribe they came from.

'Just some folks got more asshole on them than others,' is how Ida put it. 'No matter if they're black, white, red or green.'

Dellwood put it this way: 'Each one of us puts our pants on one leg at a time. The pants change and the legs change, but what it comes down to is how well you do the putting on.'

Dellwood and Ida were similar that way. Both of them believed that all human beings were created equal – like it says in the Constitution of the United States of America – that is, except for Mormons. Ida Richilieu believed that Mormons weren't human beings – along with most Catholics, and some of her own people, the Jews, and maybe some Baptists because, as Ida put it, most religious people had given up their right to being human beings by claiming they had the God's truth and nobody else had any truth.

'A person without her or his own truth ain't a person at all,' Ida said. 'Anybody who tells you different – is a jackass, and no longer deserves to be called human being.

'That's what this country stands for – people being who they are and letting other people be. That's what *I* call freedom,' Ida said. 'So, Mormons, most Catholics, some Jews, and Baptists aren't just not human beings, they aren't Americans either.' Ida held these beliefs because, as she would tell you, that's just the way she was.

'Don't ask me to change,' Ida said.

Dellwood Barker held these beliefs too, because he always agreed with Ida Richilieu when they weren't arguing philosophy and what was real.

*

William B. Merrillee's celebration was on Sunday. Sunday, July 4. Ida's celebration, though, started the Friday before, on the second of July.

Providence was a sound. I don't know how long I'd been hearing it – the sound of change coming, the sound of trouble. Maybe I'd been hearing that sound all my life and for some reason that morning just noticed it.

It was almost noon. I was in room 11 changing the sheets on the bed. There was a ruckus, not a usual sound – like Dellwood Barker at the piano before Ida'd taught him how to play – a noise, a second-sight noise that made the hairs on your neck stand up. Made your balls climb back up into you.

The sound started faint and got louder. When the sound got so loud my ears could no longer not hear it, I went to the window, looked out the window of room 11. Moved the geranium out of the way, and looked down into the street.

Where once I'd seen Billy Blizzard beating his horse to death.

Where once I'd seen Damn Dave by the ponderosa pine, under the American flag with his dick out, the humps going through him, Damn Dave laughing his fool head off and Damn Dog howling.

The same spot where I first had seen Sheriff Blumenfeld again.

And once again, that morning, looking out the window of room 11, what my eyes saw they couldn't believe what they saw.

Providence.

Authentic Negroes.

Four black human beings sitting next to each other on the seat of a wagon. Pots and pans and hanging things making a ruckus like Chinese music. The wagon was something I'd never seen before – painted every color of the rainbow, being pulled by a rough-looking, ornery, loud-mouthed braying mule.

I ran down the back stairs and out the door, tripping over my feet as if I was a kid again, ran along the side through the lines of wet white bed sheets hanging – into the street in front of Ida's Place – into that same spot on Pine Street by the ponderosa, under the flag.

Never was a wagon like that wagon.

The wagon was painted yellow and red and green. Each one of the spokes on each wheel was painted a different color – not just yellow and red and green, but black and blue and colors I didn't even know the names of. A couple of the spokes were painted a pink that was even pinker than I'd painted Ida's Place. On each side of the wagon there was a big picture painted of authentic Negroes singing and dancing, one of them playing a long-necked four-string banjo, everybody smiling big smiles. Across the top of this picture, on both sides, in big red and yellow curlicue letters, was: *The Wisdom Brothers — Ulysses, Virgil, Homer, and Blind Jude. Authentic Freed Negro Slaves!*

Then under the painting of the Negroes dancing and singing was this: *Singing Songs of Jubilee, Pure Plantation Melodies, and Songs of the Sunny South.*

I walked around to the back of the wagon. A Union Jack flag was sewn onto the back flap. The word *Freedom* was scratched onto the canvas under the flag with an ink pen.

I raised the flap and looked into the wagon. All I could see was dark. What I smelled was leather, liquor, ripe fruit, barley flour, and a manly sweat so powerful I got dizzy.

The mule was wearing a straw hat with a red carnation in it — and I swear it's true too — that mule was wearing red lipstick on its big mule lips. When that animal started braying, showing its teeth, and contorting its red lips, it made you laugh a way you didn't know you could.

The Wisdom Brothers were running around, trying to stop the mule from making so much noise, but the more they tried, the more that mule acted up — kicking, farting, and trying to bite a hole in the nearest body. I walked over to Dellwood, who was standing with Metaphor and Damn Dave and his Damn Dog in front of the post office. Damn Dave was laughing so hard, you'd think he had a hard-on, and of course then there was that dog of his barking and carrying on as bad as the mule. Metaphor was yearning, too, to jump into the fray. Dellwood was holding his dog close, and doing what he always did with anything new: scrutinizing.

'It's an act,' Dellwood Barker said. 'You scrutinize close enough and you'll see,' Dellwood said. 'This is how the Wisdom Brothers make a living.'

About that time, the mule kicked one of the Negroes — had to have been the blind one because he walked right into the mule – kicked the blind one so hard that he rolled clean all the way to the other side of Pine Street.

Each one of the Negroes was yelling, too – yelling at each other, and at the mule, in some kind of damn language that only now and then sounded anything like English.

By that time there was a crowd of folks standing around taking it all in – folks from inside the bar, some Mormon folks, too – gawking, wondering what in the hell their eyes were seeing. Thord Hurdlika came running, lips quivering, Fern Hurdlika following right after him. Doc Heyburn stumbled out of the bar. The men who'd been sitting in front of the barbershop all stood up to get a better look-see. Ellen Finton and Gracie Hammer were hanging out one of the hotel windows.

Wasn't long and people got to laughing just because they didn't know what else to do – myself included. Ida Richilieu was out on the porch by then. She was holding her stomach laughing. Only time I ever saw Ida laugh like that sober.

'Mule needs water,' is what I finally figured out the Negroes were saying. I ran into Ida's Place, got a bucket from off the back porch, and gave the bucket to the one guy. I showed him the red spigot by the horse trough, in front of the barbershop, across the street. He ran over to the spigot, filled the bucket, and ran back over to the mule – just as another one of them Negroes came barreling around from behind the wagon, knocking the bucket out of the one guy's hand and all over the back of the mule. Mule hunched its back and started bucking. Another one of them grabbed the bucket again, ran over to the spigot, filled the bucket up again, ran back, tripped, and threw water all over the mule again. Mule hunched his back and started bucking.

By the time those guys were done trying to get that mule some water, every one of them Negroes was soaked to the bone, and the street – from spigot to wagon – was one big puddle of mud that each one of those guys had fallen down in at least twenty times. Finally, the one guy – the biggest of them – got the bucket up to the mule's big red lips. The mule took a long drink of water – the guy smiling and looking at the crowd all pleased with himself. Then, all of a sudden, that mule rared his head back and spit that whole damn bucket of water back into the Negro's face.

First time I'd ever seen Mormons laugh.

That's when the four of them lined up along the side of the wagon – 'Homer Wisdom!' the biggest guy said. 'Ulysses Wisdom!' the next guy said. 'Virgil Wisdom!' the next guy said. 'Blind Jude Wisdom!' the blind one said. Then they all bowed deeply to their audience.

I looked across Pine Street. There must have been forty people standing, clapping, cheering. Never seen Pine Street that way. Never have again, either.

'First round's on the house!' Alma Hatch yelled out. 'Come on, boys!'

Most everybody – even the Mormons – followed Alma Hatch into Ida's Place. Who was left was us standing on Pine Street: the Reverend Helm, Blumenfeld, Ida Richilieu, Dellwood Barker, Damn Dave and his Damn Dog, me, the Wisdom Brothers, and their mule.

It started to rain then even though the sun was shining. Rain over Pine Street and sun just about everywhere else. 'Devil's beating his wife,' Ida would always say whenever it was raining and sunning at the same, and that's what she said then. Ida Richilieu standing on the porch said, 'Devil's beating his wife.'

One of the Wisdom Brothers – the one I would come to know as Ulysses – stepped forward and spoke to Ida Richilieu. I couldn't understand him even though he spoke slowly. What he said was something like this:

'We'll just stay out here with our wagon and our mule, ma'am.'

Ida Richilieu had to ask Ulysses to kindly repeat what he had said. All of us, Ida and Alma and Dellwood and me – for the day and the night the Wisdom Brothers spent with us – that's mostly what we said to them: either 'Excuse me,' or 'Pardon me,' or 'Could you repeat that please?'

'We'll be fine out here with the wagon and the mule, ma'am,' Ulysses said.

'Nonsense,' Ida Richilieu said. 'You're stepping lively right in here into my bar and you're having a drink with me,' Ida said.

'Don't mean no trouble, ma'am. Wagon's fine,' Ulysses said.

'Fine wagon! Fine wagon! – name's Homer, ma'am,' Homer said, stepping up next to Ulysses. 'The wagon's a fine wagon, ma'am!'

The one they called Virgil shook his body and bent over and scratched his knee and stood up straight again. 'Wagon's our home,' Virgil said. 'Best not to leave the wagon.'

The blind Wisdom Brother, Blind Jude, didn't step forward, just stood smiling, same way he'd been smiling all along.

'Follow me, gentlemen!' Ida Richilieu said, the way she always said things to men, to her customers, the way a teacher or a mother would, not a whore.

Ulysses looked at Homer and Virgil, and Homer and Virgil looked back at Ulysses, then at each other, then all of them looked at Blind Jude.

'Madam Full Charge,' is what Homer said quiet to his brothers, shrugging his shoulders. 'She Miss Ann! Praise the Lord! We never done this before, but if she say go, we better go!'

Ida pulled her skirts around, and walked into the saloon. Ulysses followed Ida into Ida's Place first, then Homer, Blind Jude, and Virgil; then Dellwood and me. When we were all inside, I turned around and looked. The Reverend Helm and Blumenfeld walked up onto the porch and stood at the open door.

Alma Hatch was behind the bar pouring drinks for the men crowding up. The Mormons all stood along the opposite wall, some of them drinking sarsaparilla and looking around at a real bar. Most of them, though, stood up close to the window, as far away from whiskey as they could get. Ida motioned to a place on the floor where she wanted Ulysses and the rest of us to stand. Ida walked up the stairs then, stood in the corridor where she always stood at the railing, scrutinized the crowd, and then walked into her room.

The Wisdom Brothers, Damn Dave and Damn Dog, Dellwood, and me stood where Ida'd told us to, between the Mormons and the men drinking. Dellwood got each of us a whiskey – even got a whiskey for Damn Dave.

Ida took as long as she usually took choosing a dress, then came back out and stood at the railing again. She was wearing the blue dress.

Dellwood Barker looked over to me the look of his that says he knows what's going to happen next. I looked up at Ida then and knew it too.

Ida's speech: 'Gentlemen, and ladies, you all know me. My name is Ida Richilieu. I am the proprietress of this hotel and saloon. I am also your friend and neighbor, and in many cases, your business partner.'

When Ida started talking, the bar was loud, and she had to raise her voice to make herself heard. By the time she got to 'business partner,' though, the bar was quiet.

'What I am about to say, I say as the proprietress, as your neighbor, your friend, and your business partner.

'Our country fought a bloody civil war, brother against brother, for the cause of freedom. Abraham Lincoln, our greatest president, was murdered because of his stand against slavery. We fought a bloody war, brother against brother, and we won. The Emancipation Proclamation has ended slavery in this country.

Negroes are free people, just like us white folks are free. Free to pursue life, liberty, and happiness.

'As proprietress, friend, neighbor, and business partner, I, Ida Richilieu, in the spirit of our great president Abraham Lincoln, will not tolerate any actions of an unfree and enslaving spirit against any human being, including these men here: the Wisdom Brothers. If any of you disagree with me, then leave this bar and never return. You are not welcome in my house. I will not tolerate harm against something I cherish so dearly: the inimitable sacredness of the human spirit.

'There's free whiskey if you stay. But you can't touch a damn drop of it if you don't welcome these men.'

Ida was in heaven. Every man's, every woman's eye was on her. She walked the length of the corridor, down the steps, holding the skirt of the blue dress up, exposing her ankles and calves. At the bar, she grabbed a bottle of whiskey, poured herself a glass, walked up to Ulysses and filled his glass, then filled Homer's, and Virgil's, and Blind Jude's.

'I propose a toast!' Ida said, raising her glass. 'Wisdom Brothers! Welcome to Excellent, Idaho! Consider my saloon your home! Your rooms upstairs are ready, and your whiskey's free!'

Everybody started cheering and clapping – even some Mormons were clapping – Mormon women and children, that is. Then, all of a sudden, it was only me and Dellwood, Ellen and Gracie, Alma and Damn Dave and Thord Hurdlika who were cheering and clapping.

I looked around. The Reverend Helm had walked in off the porch, along with Blumenfeld, and the both of them were standing inside Ida's Place.

'They should stay in their wagon!' Blumenfeld said. 'Where they belong!'

'They're used to sleeping in their wagon!' the Reverend Helm said. 'These are white men's beds!'

'Ain't no place for them kind in here!' a man at the bar yelled.

'This is white man's whiskey!' another yelled.

'Book of Mormon tells us all about these people,' the Reverend Helm said. 'Now, kindly, I ask all Latter-day Saints who are faithful to leave this saloon.'

Damn Dave started in crying loud whoops and wails and his dog too. Wasn't any other sound in the saloon, except for the rain, except for the people walking out. Mormons left first, then the men at the bar. Doc Heyburn ordered another whiskey, belted the whiskey down, then left too.

Thord Hurdlika stayed. Ellen Finton and Gracie Hammer stayed. Damn Dave and his Damn Dog, Alma Hatch, Dellwood Barker, the Wisdom Brothers, and me stayed.

Ida didn't bat an eye.

'Now I raise my glass to the Wisdom Brothers, our brothers of another color, our brothers of the same human spirit. Welcome to our town.'

We all drank.

Alma poured another round. We drank that.

Outside, the devil was still beating his wife, sun coming in one window, rain in the other.

Homer hesitated, but went ahead, eyes sweating, and poured his glass full the third time around.

'Much obliged for the hospitality,' Ulysses said, but I don't think anybody understood what he said, but nobody wanted to say 'Excuse me,' or 'Pardon me,' or 'Could you please repeat that?' just then. Instead, we all nodded like we'd understood him and had another drink.

Ida took them upstairs and showed them room 11 and room 12. Blind Jude and Homer in room 11. Virgil and Ulysses in room 12.

'Before you sit down on those beds,' Ida Richilieu said, 'just like everybody else who stays in my hotel – you all got to take a bath. Bathhouse is on the side here, next to the creek. It'll be ready for you in half an hour. You can set up your wagon in the back. I already sent you half your money. You'll get the other half Sunday. Any questions?'

Out in the shed, me and Dellwood watched out the window. When the Wisdom Brothers walked into the bathhouse – each one with a clean towel, washrag, and piece of soap – Ida Richilieu walked in after them. Ida talking to them in a loud voice – so loud that most of Excellent could hear.

'If you close the door tight, and seal the windows, you get the effect of a steam bath in here,' Ida said. 'Or leave them open if you want. You can fill the tub up with that bucket by the door. Only thing I ask is that you leave the place as clean as you found it. Towels're yours for two days at a time, so Sunday if you need another towel, just see me about it. Any questions?'

As soon as Ida Richilieu went back into the hotel, me and Dellwood ran over next to the bathhouse.

Wasn't long before a brown arm poked out each one of the windows and pulled the windows shut. The glass steamed up. Dellwood stood by the one window and me by the other. At first, I couldn't understand a word they were saying. They could have been speaking French or Greek for all I knew. Then, after a while, my ears got used to hearing how those guys talked.

Later on, out in the shed, me and Dellwood compared what I'd heard with what he'd heard. This is what we figured they said:

Madam Full Charge is what they called Ida. They called her Miss Ann, too.

One of them said, 'Hallelujah, we dead men. This town's g'wan to be lynching them some niggers for sure! How the hell we getting out of this one?'

Then another one said, 'Let's clear out of here right now, while we still can.'

'And get ambushed on that road tonight, no sir!'

Then, I think it was Ulysses who said, 'Already too late. We just got to play it as it lays.'

'We dead for sure.'

'We lynched.'

'We bear food.'

Then they didn't say anything for a long time. Then I recognized Homer's laugh. 'Lordy, Lordy,' he said, 'can you believe this shit? Here we are the Wisdom Brothers staying in a white man's hotel, using white man's towels and soap, sitting in white man's bathtub. Lordy, shit damn, hell of a damn deal.'

'And did you see those white women looking at us?' – it was Virgil – 'Ain't no white woman ever come right out and looked at me that way!'

'Jesus Christ Lord have mercy!' Homer said. 'I saw them. Saw them two white men looking too just like we was in New Orleans! Must be cabin fever. Shit damn! Here in Idaho, praise the almighty Lord.'

'Maybe we get us some white fucking while we're here!' one of them said.

'Shh! Hold it down,' another one said. 'Never know who's listening in.'

I pressed myself up against the bathhouse wall as a hand wiped the steam off the window glass.

'You never know.'

They didn't talk after that for a long while, and all I could hear was water getting poured into the tub, and them laughing – once them laughing so hard, I started laughing too even though I had no idea what was funny.

Dellwood said he heard them make a pact to always stick together, that is, except for the possibility of a piece of ass.

I heard one of them say that Ulysses should carry the gun.

The Wisdom Brothers

The next morning, early, I woke up to music. I looked out the window, out back, and then I looked again. Everything had changed. Where the Wisdom Brothers' wagon had been was now a stage. Around the stage was hung a purple velvet curtain draped over crossbars supported by four poles. On the velvet curtain it said in gold glittery letters: *Funny Comedians*, and *Opera Vocalists, Genuine Negro Jubilee Minstrels*, and *Ethiopian Melodies*. In front of the stage on the side closest to the shed was a wooden box that said *Main Ticket Office* on it. Chairs from inside Ida's Place were sitting all around.

I got my pants on quick, and boots, and ran out to take a look. The Wisdom Brothers and Dellwood Barker were hard at work, Wisdom Brothers singing the whole time, Blind Jude playing on Ida's piano.

'How'd they get the piano out here?' I asked Dellwood.

'Me and Homer and the mule,' Dellwood said.

'More coffee for anyone who wants it!' Ida yelled out the back door.

'And anything else you might need!' yelled Alma.

In the kitchen, Ida and Alma were cooking breakfast. I'd seen Ida cook breakfast before – once or twice – but my two eyes had never seen Alma cooking. Ida was wearing one of her good dresses and had her hair tied up in a scarf. Alma had a good dress on too, hair pulled back in a bun.

Everything had changed.

Plain as day: it was love.

Alma Hatch in love. Ida Richilieu in love.

Ovulating, the both of them.

'You'll make some lucky men fine wives,' I said to Ida, to Alma.

Neither one of them heard what I said; that is, acted like they heard. They just kept on cooking.

I poured me a cup of coffee and went back outside. Ulysses, Virgil, Homer, and Dellwood were pulling something out the back of the wagon I thought was a rolled-up carpet. Ulysses and Virgil carried the one end while Dellwood and Homer carried the other, Dellwood putting his body as close to Homer's body as he could.

Plain as day.

Dellwood Barker ovulating too.

I sat myself down with my coffee in a piece of sun on the steps of the back porch and scrutinized.

What I saw was one big happy family. Ulysses and Virgil and Homer and Dellwood were carrying the rolled-up carpet onto the wooden platform, rolling the carpet out that wasn't a carpet at all, but a big picture. The backdrop, they called it. Dellwood and Homer pulled the one end up while Ulysses and Virgil pulled the other end up, and before my very eyes, there it was: a huge beautiful painting of a big white house with pillars and the kind of trees Homer said were down south. Blind Jude was playing a catchy Ethiopian melody that just made you want to dance.

They were dancing, Ulysses, Virgil, Homer, and Dellwood on the stage dancing.

'Soup's on!' Ida Richilieu said, and her and Alma carried out plates of eggs and big slices of Damn Dave's cured ham and sourdough bread and spuds. I went in and got the cups and another pot of coffee and we all sat down, cross-legged on the stage in front of the big white house with the pillars and the trees. Ida asked Homer to pray, and Homer prayed, his voice singing and talking at the same time to the Lord and then we all dived in.

While I was eating I was scrutinizing.

When the Wisdom Brothers first arrived, they had all looked alike – like the same Negro to me. They were all black, with black nappy hair, dressed in old clothes. Big smiling lips the color I wondered if any other place on their bodies was that color. Blind

Jude had been the only one who had looked different – eyeballs in his head, lost smooth black river stones rolling through white. But that morning, me sitting in the sun watching them work, and sing and talk and laugh and cuss, then me sitting and praying and eating with them, suddenly they all looked different. Looked each one of them like any other person looks: like how they are.

Ulysses was the oldest, although he could have been thirty or sixty. He was the father, the boss, the rest of them doing pretty much what Ulysses said; that is, except for the mule. Ulysses had a gold tooth in front and was wearing a diamond ring on the little finger of his left hand. After he was done eating breakfast, Ulysses lit a corncob pipe. Was something to watch, Ulysses lighting his pipe. Made smoking a pipe look so good I promised myself I was going to buy me one.

'The man's intelligent,' Ida Richilieu said. 'And he's got a streak of sacred in him,' she said. 'Any man with long fingers like that, taking that kind of care to light a damned pipe as if it was some kind of holy ritual – has got to be intelligent and have a feeling for the sacred.'

Professor Wisdom, Ida called him, and she took to Professor Ulysses Wisdom right off.

Homer ate more eggs and ham and spuds than even me. He was the tallest and the biggest of the brothers. Biggest in all ways, as Dellwood Barker was about to find out. When Homer stood, he stooped his shoulders, I figured so he wouldn't be so big around tybos. Homer was also the one who was always laughing. Figured he was the one who was most afraid. There were always beads of sweat around his eyes. He would say something and laugh, say something and laugh, and then pull the handkerchief out of his pocket and wipe around his eyes.

Homer was also the preacher. He was always referring to the Bible when he talked, saying 'Praise the Lord' all the time instead of cussing.

Dellwood Barker just couldn't resist sticking his nose into Homer's story. Can't say as I blame him. Homer was a bunch of things that didn't go together – laughing when he wasn't laughing, praising the Lord when he wanted to cuss Him, studying the Bible sitting on that dick, making himself the fool all the while him scrutinizing, scrutinizing.

Virgil moved more tree squirrel than human being. Picked at his eggs and gave Homer his ham. While we were sitting and eating, Virgil must have jumped up and down a dozen times. His walking wasn't the way most people walked – wasn't taking steps. His walking was more floating on top of the ground.

Alma Hatch called him 'my little hummingbird.'

Figure Virgil never did get over Alma Hatch. Of course, he didn't have much time to. Started on a Friday. Ended Saturday. Seemed forever we knew those guys.

With Virgil, I don't know if it was fucking a white woman or fucking that particular white woman – hard to say – whatever, as it turned out, Alma Hatch was just too much for Virgil Wisdom.

Then, as I look back, we were all too much for them. Ida Richilieu, Alma Hatch, Dellwood Barker, and me – we were all too much for them – for Ulysses, Homer, Virgil, and Blind Jude Wisdom.

They were too much for us.

None of us were ever the same.

As Ida put it, though, 'Nothing's too much!'

And Dellwood, 'Ain't nothing that can happen to you that you aren't ready for.'

Including death.

Something else, too. They weren't black. Those Negroes weren't black. They were brown, different shades of brown – it's the same with tybos; for example, Ida Richilieu and Alma Hatch – both of them were tybo, but Ida was white white with dark nipples and black hair, while Alma was mostly pink with pink nipples and brown hair that went blond. Same as with the Wisdom Brothers – parts of them were black, but mostly they were the color of wet pine bark, or loamy soil. Smelled as good, too, especially Homer.

Blind Jude. I scrutinized Blind Jude all through breakfast, all through the whole day.

Blind Jude was the shortest of the brothers. On top of his head there wasn't any hair, and where there was hair, the hair was like chunks of crabgrass on a ditch bank. He had a beard because he said his brothers got tired of shaving him – trimmed up neat the way Fern Hurdlika liked. He was the color of wet buckskin. His hands were as beautiful as his feet.

That's how Blind Jude looked, but scrutinizing, I couldn't figure out one thing about his human-being story. Then it happened – I was walking down the corridor, past Ida's room. I looked into Ida's room, and on her bed, looking out the window, was Blind Jude. I walked over to him and looked out the window at what he was looking at. Outside, Dellwood Barker, Alma Hatch, Ida Richilieu, Homer, Ulysses, and Virgil were putting the finishing touches on the stage.

This is what Blind Jude said:

'You think you're some kind of bird, don't you? – a bird with a broken wing. And you think no one can see you.'

Blind Jude looked his gone eyes into my left eye and right then I knew that no one had really ever looked at me before.

'The other one – the old Indian man,' Blind Jude said, '– he's the one people can't see. But *you*, Shed, you they can see.'

Then I looked up, and standing beside Blind Jude was Owlfeather. Owlfeather was leaning over and whispering in Blind Jude's ear, telling him a joke, telling him the truth.

Damn Dave and his Damn Dog walked in Ida's room then, natural as can be, and there we were: one who couldn't talk, another who couldn't see, the other who was dead, and me.

For all of us, it was the same: we all knew who we were and why we lived. Knew that we were home.

The afternoon sun was full onto Ida's windows, the windows open at the bottom. Through the open windows, outside, you could hear the voices of Ida and Alma, of Ulysses and Virgil, Dellwood and Homer talking, somebody hammering, Ida telling everybody what to do, then Alma a bird sound, Homer laughing and praising the Lord, Dellwood laughing too.

Damn Dave sat down at Ida's desk and started doodling on paper. As far as I could tell, he was drawing a picture of himself sitting at Ida's desk drawing a picture of himself.

Owlfeather sat down on the bed with me and Blind Jude. Blind Jude reached over and touched the hem of Ida's blue dress hanging in the closet. Then, all of a sudden, Blind Jude just up and took his shirt off and his pants off. I had to ask my eyes what they were seeing when they saw Blind Jude stripped down to his white underwear. Then Blind Jude took the blue dress, stepped into it, put it on, and then wrapped the feathered boa over his shoulders. He stood in front of Ida's mirror as if he could look in the mirror and he said:

'Oh! The humanity! Shed, help me with the buttons!'

The language coming out of Blind Jude sounded exactly like Ida Richilieu language. First thing I did was grab my heart, me thinking Ida Richilieu was inside Blind Jude's mouth talking. Then I started buttoning up the buttons – those I could button – it was Ida's voice, but not Ida's skinny body in that blue dress.

'And my pearls,' Blind Jude said the way Ida Richilieu'd say. 'Help me with my pearls.'

Blind Jude wrapped the feathered boa around his neck. I put Ida's hat on him, the one Alma Hatch had given her, with the peacock feathers. He stood himself exactly as Ida stood herself.

'Gentlemen, and ladies,' Blind Jude said, 'you all know me. My name is Ida Richilieu and I am the proprietress of this hotel and saloon. I am also your friend and neighbor, and in many cases, your business partner.'

Ida Richilieu had turned into a black man.

'The Emancipation Proclamation has ended slavery in this country. Negroes are free people, just like white folks are free. Free to pursue life, liberty, and happiness.'

Damn Dave started taking his clothes off. Wasn't long before he had Ida's white dress on – at least as much as he could get it on. He was standing the way Blind Jude was standing being Ida Richilieu. Damn Dave was being Ida Richilieu too, walking like Ida, making his face like hers.

Owlfeather worked himself into the red dress. Fit him good, him being a ghost. The slit way up to his thighs, his long Indian hair piled up like Ida's – putting Ida's combs in his hair, sitting at the dressing table, looking in the mirror at himself the way Ida looked at herself. He lit a cigarette.

'Pernicious!' Owlfeather said into the mirror. 'P . . E . . R . . N . . I . . C . . I . . O . . U . . S,' he said. 'Ain't it delicious, being so pernicious. Fuck these Mormon sons o'bishes.'

'Consider the source,' Blind Jude said. 'A story about a crazy man, told by crazy people, should only make you wonder.'

'The deck's stacked against you – might as well figure on that,' Owlfeather said.

The sun coming in the back windows made the room bright, no rose color, and the room smelled of men and sun against window glass in the summer.

Outside you could look through the windows down and see the real Ida helping Ulysses straighten out a tent pole.

Real.

'Come take a trip in my airship and we'll visit the man in the moon,' Owlfeather sang.

'You ought to see the dick on that one,' Blind Jude said. 'Those Negroes got the biggest dicks in the world.'

I put on one of Ida's good dresses. The dress didn't fit me at all. Put red lipstick on my lips. Knelt down on the floor with the bucket from the hall closet and started scrubbing the floor.

'Hey you!' I said. 'Come over here, boy!'

'Oh! The humanity! That's just the way I am,' I said. 'Don't ask me to change!

'Keep your promises, keep clean, and keep going,' I said.

'A woman's got her pride,' I said.

'How do you spell *emancipation*?' I asked. 'How do you spell *proclamation*?' I asked.

'How do you spell *inimitable sacredness*?' I asked.

'How do you spell *mother*?' Owlfeather asked.

'I..D..A..R..I..C..H..I..L..I..E..U!' I spelled.

By the time I was done spelling *mother*, I wasn't laughing no more.

I just laid down on the floor.

Woman's hole: if you took Ida Richilieu out of my life, there would be no life.

Emancipation Proclamation, I thought, *free*.

Owlfeather sat down by me and took my head in his hands. Pretty soon, Damn Dave was laying next to me, holding me, and so was Blind Jude laying next to me. Four men laying on the floor dressed up like women. They didn't try to stop me crying. They put their arms around me.

Just before the sun went down, Virgil ran into Ida's room buttoning up his pants. Alma Hatch wasn't far behind him.

That's when we heard the shots.

Providence.

'Posse! Posse!' Virgil was yelling. 'They g'wan lynch us for sure!'

Me and Damn Dave got Ida's dresses off of us in no time. Blind

Jude just sat down on the bed. Owlfeather wasn't around anymore. I had my shirt on and my pants pulled up by the time I got to the window.

There were about a dozen men on horses riding in circles around the shed and the Wisdom Brothers' wagon. You could hardly see because of the dust. They were shooting off their guns into the air and whooping and hollering the way men do herding cows. Two of the men held signs.

Nigger, Read and Run.

The words were printed in red.

Ulysses Wisdom and Ida Richilieu were standing in the middle of it all, Ida cussing and kicking and swinging her arms, Ulysses backed up against the stage.

'We're leaving now, boss, don't hurt my brothers!' Virgil was yelling, darting his head in and out of the window.

Alma Hatch opened another window and shouted out, 'Who the hell you boys think you are! You're on private property!'

In the room over, Ellen Finton and Gracie Hammer started yelling out the window too.

Down in the shed, I could see Dellwood pulling back the petticoat curtain.

I went for Ida's shotgun, the one she always kept by her bed, but it was gone.

I ran out in the hall and started down the back staircase. At the landing, I looked out the window again, and my eyes saw Blind Jude, still in Ida's blue dress, walking through the running horses, the commotion, the men and the dust, with Ida's shotgun over his shoulder the way a soldier would.

I ran down the rest of the stairs and out the back door. By that time, the horses had stopped running, and it was scary quiet. The men were all looking at Blind Jude as if he was some kind of apparition.

Dellwood and Homer poked two rifles out the shed window.

Virgil and Alma were in Ida's window, each one of them with a gun. Ellen Finton and Gracie Hammer were standing in the window of room 12. They both had guns. Damn Dave had a gun too. He was at the kitchen door. Never seen so many guns all together in one place. Thord Hurdlika came running around the corner of the hotel. He was carrying a gun too. Blind Jude was walking the way Ida walks and singing the man-in-the-moon song. By the look on her face, Ida Richilieu didn't know whether to slap him, run, or praise the glorious Lord for what was coming toward her in her blue dress.

Blind Jude walked right up to Ida Richilieu and handed her the shotgun.

'Madam Full Charge! Miss Ann! Mrs. Ida Richilieu! Your shotgun!' Blind Jude said in Ida Richilieu's voice.

Ida took the gun, pointed the barrel at the sky and shot, and then shot again. The horses shied and rared.

One man on a horse aimed his gun right at Blind Jude. There was a shot and his gun went flying out of his hand.

'Nigger shot me! Nigger shot me!' the guy yelled.

'Wasn't no nigger, asshole, it was me,' Dellwood Barker said, and shot again before anybody had the chance to make a move.

'Now you sorry bunch of cowards, make tracks out of here,' Dellwood yelled, 'or I'll turn Madam Full Charge Ida Richilieu loose on the bunch of you.'

I scrutinized the crowd. The men were all looking at each other. Wasn't one face I recognized.

'Go on!' Ellen Finton yelled. 'You heard him! Get!'

'Get!' I yelled.

'Make tracks!' Alma Hatch yelled.

'Move 'em out!' Gracie Hammer yelled.

Thord Hurdlika's lips were moving faster than I'd ever seen them.

'Get them skinny white asses of yours out of my town!' Blind

Jude yelled with Ida Richilieu's voice, and smiled up to where Virgil was, then over to where Ulysses was, then to Homer.

Then Ida Richilieu said it. 'That's right! Get them skinny white asses of yours out of my town!' she yelled.

Those tybos were looking scared. Were looking around at the guns pointed at them. Were looking for the fastest way out of Excellent. One man spurred his horse and took off, then a couple more followed him. Wasn't long before the whole posse was making dust down Pine Street and out of town.

We were all smiling glorious – especially Ida Richilieu.

She'd won the battle of the Fourth of July. 'Oh! The humanity!' Ida said, and then let off two more rounds of shotgun. 'Get them skinny white asses of yours out of my town!'

Ida poured the first two rounds of drinks, and after that, we poured our own.

Couldn't drink enough whiskey, all of us, couldn't smoke enough locoweed either, each and every one of us glorious, celebrating fools.

Ida, Alma, Dellwood, Thord Hurdlika, Damn Dave, Ellen Finton, Gracie Hammer, and me – we were celebrating because Ida had won the battle of the Fourth of July.

Ulysses, Homer, Virgil, and Blind Jude, however, were celebrating something else: they were still alive.

'We alive now but won't be for long,' Virgil said.

'Surprised we done made it this far, praise the Lord in heaven,' Homer said.

'We dead for sure,' Virgil said. 'No way we g'wan to get out of here alive.'

'Nonsense!' Ida Richilieu said. 'You're safe here in Ida's Place.'

Ulysses, Virgil, Homer, and Blind Jude just looked at the floor.

'Trust in the Lord, He will find a way,' Homer said.

'This is the twentieth century!' Ida said. 'Don't worry about them ne'er-do-wells!' Ida said. 'It's all over. You saw them horses hightailing it down Pine Street. We won! We won!'

'That sure was a fine sight indeed, I *must* say!' Ulysses said, smiling at Ida.

'Fine sight! Fine sight! Never was so happy to see horses' asses!' Homer said.

'Never felt like that before,' Virgil said. 'Never seen white men running away before. Yes sir, did my heart good.'

None of us were saying 'Excuse me,' or 'Pardon me,' or 'Could you please say that again?' to the Wisdom Brothers. Wasn't any of us speaking English by then. We were speaking whiskey.

Ulysses followed me when I went out to piss. Before he stepped out the door, he asked me, 'Is the coast clear?'

I didn't know what he meant. 'Excuse me?' I said.

'Nobody out there g'wan shoot me, is they?' he asked.

'No!' I said. 'We're safe here.'

Ulysses looked all around him as he walked out. He stood himself next to me and started pissing. Then Virgil and Homer came out, looking every which way. Coming up next to Ulysses, they started pissing too. 'My brothers,' Ulysses asked, looking down at himself pissing, 'I would just like to ask one solitary thing: just *how* did we get ourselves into this predicament?'

'Ain't never done the things we been doing before, and way out here in *Idaho*, for God's sake!' Virgil said.

'We must be some crazy niggers,' Ulysses said.

'G'wan die fucking,' Virgil said.

'G'wan die in heaven,' Homer said.

'G'wan to Glidden!' Homer said. 'G'wan to Calcutta!'

*

Damn Dave brought the poster to Ida. He drew a picture of where he'd found it: on the post office door.

Unfortunately, due to pernicious elements, the long-awaited visit of the Right Reverend William B. Merrillee has been postponed until a more suitable time.

'At least they spelled it right this time,' Ida said.

Nobody showed up for the Wisdom Brothers that night; that is, except for us – Ida Richilieu, Alma Hatch, Ellen Finton, Gracie Hammer, Thord Hurdlika, Damn Dave and his dog, Dellwood Barker, and me.

We all kept looking around to see if anybody else would show up, but nobody did.

Figured it was just as well.

Ida was wearing the blue dress. Alma wore her dress with birds on it. Dellwood had his hair slicked back and was wearing his white shirt.

Made my heart jump when I saw Dellwood. Made Homer's heart jump too. I scrutinized it.

Thord Hurdlika was in no condition to go home to his wife, Fern, so I put him in a shirt and pants of mine after he washed up.

Me, I was all in Sears and Roebuck white like the day me and Ida and Alma and Dellwood had the picnic by the river. The straw hat with the red band.

Even Damn Dave looked good. Me and Dellwood had taken a scrub brush to him in the bathhouse.

'So clean he squeaks,' Ida said.

When the curtain opened up, it was way after sunset but the sky was still fancy. The valley was dark. What you saw when the curtains opened up was a lighted stage and the beautiful backdrop painting of a big white house with pillars and the kind of trees that were down south.

First thing I noticed, after I noticed the Wisdom Brothers were all still standing, was that their faces were black. I mean really black and so I asked Ida why their faces were so black, and she said it was burnt cork and that was just how minstrels did things – they wore makeup like that. Dellwood said, though, that it had only been recently that Negro people had their own minstrel companies, that usually it was tybos in blackface, pretending to be Negroes, that were the minstrels, and that when Negroes finally started doing themselves what the white man had been copying the Negro do, the Negro copied the white man copying the Negro.

Crazy stories, crazy people.

Ulysses was playing the banjo, which Dellwood said was a gourd covered with coonskin. Virgil was playing the fiddle, Homer played the tambourine and was what they called the interlocutor. Blind Jude played the harmonica and the jawbone.

The first song they played was called 'Far from the Old Folks at Home' that Ulysses sang in a deep sad voice. In the middle of the song, he quit singing and just started filling up his corncob pipe. He started talking about when he was a kid in Alabama and about the friends he had played with, how he'd eaten possum, and how the sun looked on the cotton fields in the hot time of day. Ulysses talked about his mother and father and how sad he was on the days that they had died.

'Ain't a dry eye in the place,' Ida Richilieu said.

Then Blind Jude sang a real pretty song called 'Carry me Back to Old Virginny;' him smiling the way that always made you think he knew something you didn't.

'Ladies and gentlemen,' Blind Jude said, 'my brothers, Ulysses, Virgil, and Homer, and myself would like to dedicate this next song to Ida Richilieu.'

The Wisdom Brothers started up playing a song that made your heart feel good. It went something like this:

'Sing the jubilee; everybody free. / Welcome, welcome, 'mancipation.'

We all got to singing with the Wisdom Brothers on that song and we sang it over and over.

Still hear that song in my head from time to time: 'Sing the jubilee; everybody free. / Welcome, welcome, 'mancipation!'

Then the band started playing jigs. 'Sliding Jenny Jig,' 'Pea Patch Jig,' 'Genuine Negro Jig.'

Above us, the moon pressed bright against the tent sway, pressed each one of us against each other into shadow, all us dancing. Ida was dancing jigs with her Professor Wisdom, Alma Hatch with her little hummingbird, Virgil, Thord Hurdlika with Ellen Finton, Gracie Hammer and Damn Dave, Damn Dog and Metaphor walking around through the people dancing. Dellwood was sitting in a circle of light on the piano bench next to Homer, wick turned low, Dellwood with the piano-music look on his face.

Blind Jude came from back of the stage holding a tin. He opened the tin with his fingernail, dipped his finger into the tin, and started spreading burnt cork onto my face.

'Now you're a genuine Negro too!' Blind Jude said.

Ida Richilieu saw Blind Jude making my face black and wanted burnt cork on her face too. Then so did Dellwood Barker, Alma Hatch, Gracie Hammer, Ellen Finton, Thord Hurdlika, and Damn Dave.

Wasn't long before all of us looked the same, all of us black, the same color black, looking like white people trying to look like Negroes, and Negroes trying to look how white people thought Negroes looked.

Started out that we were all laughing, fooling around with our black faces, but truth was, we were scared – scared all of us, all of a sudden, in a way we hadn't expected.

Burnt cork made us all the same.

Although we already were all the same, we all knew we weren't.

Burnt cork on our faces changed that.

Burnt cork was a mask on our faces, and what was underneath wasn't black, wasn't white, was human being.

'Walk about! Walk about!' Virgil shouted, and started in on his fiddle. Ulysses picked up his banjo, Homer his tambourine. Blind Jude started playing on the harmonica.

As Homer interlocuted to us, the *walk-about* was a dance where folks stood around in a semicircle. Somebody would sing a stanza while everybody listened to that person singing, and when the singing was done, the walking started and everybody sang the chorus loud and all together as they walked around, moving your body the way your body wanted to move. Then one person would *advance to the center* of the semicircle and stand alone and dance, dance the human-being story, however that story was, however that story felt and however you wanted to dance it, while everybody else watched.

Homer started out singing while we all stood in the semicircle:

'The nigger trader think me nice. / The white folk sell me for half price. / I'll fetch a thousand dollars down. / Underway, underway, ho! / We are on the way to Georgia.'

Then Homer advanced to the center, his tambourine banging that butt of his, him dancing, moving his body the way no human body'd ever been moved before, shaking his shoulders, swaying his hips, tapping his feet, humping his butt up and back, and cupping his free hand over his big self in front.

Next time around, Virgil sang:

'Ida Richilieu got a place, / A hotel that's been our saving grace. / That's if we don't get blown outa here. / Underway, underway, ho! / We are on our way to Glidden.'

Virgil dancing as if he wasn't touching the ground, dancing Alma's little hummingbird, darting around, twirling, feet moving so fast you could barely see them.

Ulysses singing:

'W. C. Handy had a troupe. / Got the smallpox – put 'em in a coop. / Snuck out in darkness like we'll do. / Underway, underway, ho! / We are on our way to Owyhee City.'

Ulysses dancing his gold-toothed diamond-ring story, heavy shouldered carrying the weight, facing Ida, showing her his kindness, his respect. Ida blushing like a schoolgirl.

Ida had to go next:

'Will'em B. Merrillee thinks we're sick. / The truth is though he's got no dick. / Fuck that Mormon son of a hick. / Underway, underway, ho! / We are on our way to Hades!'

Ida dancing her showgirl, kicking her legs in the air, pulling her blue dress up showing us her behind.

Blind Jude pushed me and I advanced to the center. My body didn't know what to do. Even when I was normal I couldn't talk, let alone rhyme, let alone rhyme while folks was watching me, and there I was drunk. So what my body did next surprised me as much as anybody else.

I stripped. Took my Sears and Roebuck clothes off, dancing in time to the music, my white soft leather shoes, my white jacket, my white pants, my white shirt and tie, my straw hat, my white underwear.

Blind Jude brought his tin over to me and proceeded to rub burnt cork on my body – on all the rest of my body.

Was quite a sight. Story goes, even Homer was impressed.

Wasn't long after my dance that each couple found their bed. Then it was just Blind Jude and me, him at the piano in the circle of light, me laying, a genuine Negro, on the stage.

'Was a colored man who had no eyes,' Blind Jude sang. 'White man poked them out with his lies. / What hurts most is what else they took. / Underway, underway, ho! / We are on our way to oblivion!'

I sat down next to Blind Jude. Watched his hands on the piano keys. What I wanted to ask, I didn't have words to ask, so:

'Is Oblivion same place as Glidden?' I asked.

'Could be,' Blind Jude said.

'Where is it?' I asked.

'Glidden's in heaven,' Blind Jude said. 'Oblivion's everywhere else.'

'Dellwood says heaven's in your head,' I said. 'Ida says heaven could be a real place, but then it might not – so you're best off figuring there ain't no heaven, so when you die, if there is one, you'll be surprised.'

'Sounds just like Ida Richilieu,' Blind Jude said. 'Sounds like Dellwood Barker, too.' Then: 'White folks here in Ida's Place sure ain't regular white folks,' Blind Jude said.

'How they different?' I asked.

'Blind Jude's fingers started playing out the man-in-the-moon song.

'Well, they different and they the same,' Blind Jude said. 'For example, Ida Richilieu gives us a bed to sleep in in her hotel, and we use the same toilet the white folks use, and the bathhouse – white folks sit at the same table with us, we share the whiskey and we share the smoke – and that's all different – and that's good, and that's new to me and my brothers.

'What's the same is the white man – what he love most – is being the boss. What she love most is being Madam Full Charge – and that's no different from anywhere else.

'And something else too,' Blind Jude said. 'Here in Ida's Place, it's no different from anywhere else – just easier to see. My brothers and me – we ain't each of us a person – we just a load of black bulls come up here to breed. So far here, nobody's seen past we just something peculiar to fuck.'

I put my hands on Blind Jude's hands so he'd stop playing. Looked at him the way the first time he had looked at me. Put my lips onto his lips, holding him close, all that night, held Blind Jude close. Never held a human being so close to me, bodies together, face to face, arms within arms, legs wrapped, my dick and balls up against where his used to be, us one breath in out, one heart beating.

When I woke up, first thing I did was grab for my crotch. Everything was still there.

Me and Blind Jude were wet. I thought it was rain, but it was us. I looked around in the dark but couldn't figure out where we were. Then, by the smell of things, I knew we were in the wagon. I pretended I was blind. Moved my hand around, found a box of matches, struck one against an iron pot, and lit a candle. My eyes looked at the flame. Was glad I had eyes that could see.

Inside the wagon there was everything – bottles, cans, boxes, books. There was a smoked ham, and clothes hanging on a rack. There was a bridle and a saddle. Me and Blind Jude were laying on a blanket that was spread over a bale of hay and a sack of oats. A chest of drawers. Cups and dishes and more pots and pans. Behind me was a stuffed horned owl with glass eyes.

Then, I remembered the dream: Owlfeather and I had been fucking. When I started to come he stopped me. He told me something very important. He told me to listen carefully and to remember.

But I did not remember.

When Blind Jude woke up, we both knew it was time. We let go of each other, got up, and I started looking for my clothes. I wanted to say something to Blind Jude about him and me sleeping together, about how I felt that he was me and that, if I could, I'd give him my dick and balls, every once in a while, but my mouth didn't know how to say the words out loud.

Ulysses was in Ida's bed with her. When I touched his back, he damned near jumped out of his skin. He didn't wake Ida, though, thank God.

Virgil was fucking Alma Hatch in room 11. I watched their black white in the moon shadow for a while, and then called out to him in a whisper.

'Ulysses wants to see you,' I said.

Virgil started coming, Alma started moaning.

Thord Hurdlika and Gracie Hammer were on the floor of room 12. Ellen Finton was fast asleep in the outhouse. No telling where Damn Dave was.

Out in the shed, Dellwood Barker was a white butt and Homer Wisdom was a black butt in the sheets of the bed. Both of them were snoring bull moose. Before I woke them up, I scrutinized Homer's dick – just curious.

We met in the tent, on the Wisdom Brothers' raised wooden stage, in front of the painting of the white house and the kind of trees in the south. We all still had burnt cork on our faces.

The night before burnt cork had made us all the same. That morning burnt cork made us all different.

'Heard you howling last night,' I said to Dellwood.

Dellwood smiled. Homer looked back at me and his brothers when we looked over at him.

'Praise the Lord,' Homer said.

The way we figured it, the best plan was to leave the wagon and mule behind. We'd follow the fire road to where the William B. Merrillee Company had cut the swath of timber down for the cables going up to Gold Hill. We'd follow the cable, cut south of Gold Bar, then down into the valley and Owyhee City.

I drew a map on the ground with a stick and showed them the lay of the valley, and our route out of it, just in case we were separated.

Ulysses asked if there was any water along the way. I told him I'd fill a canteen.

Virgil asked if there were any bears.

'Shit! Lord almighty!' Homer said. 'Bears the least of our worries.'

'Still want to know,' Virgil said.

'There's bear up there alright, but they'll leave you alone,' Dellwood said. 'You got a gun, don't you?'

'We got a gun,' Homer said.

I had Dellwood's .22. Dellwood had his Colt and another rifle.

We made good time despite the darkness, some steep climbing, our hangovers, and helping Blind Jude along. We only stopped once when we came upon two elk, a doe and a bull, standing so still only Blind Jude saw them.

The sun was just about ready to top out from over the side of Not-Really-A-Mountain, when we came to the William B. Merrillee Company's clearing, and the cables.

I walked out into the clearing, stopped, and looked down into the valley. Blind Jude followed me. After a while, Ulysses and Virgil, Homer and Dellwood walked out into the clearing too.

Providence.

Blind Jude reached over and grabbed my hand. When I looked over at Blind Jude, I remembered the dream.

Remember! Owlfeather had said. *Keep your heart open in hell*.

The sun poked over the top of Not-Really-A-Mountain. Below, in the dark valley of Excellent, Idaho, there was a burst of flame. It was Ida's Place.

That's when we heard the first shot. Virgil grabbed his bloody face and fell. The second shot had Ulysses down.

Blind Jude let go of my hand, raised both arms to the sun, hands out, palms up. The bullet forced him back.

Dellwood threw Homer his rifle. We were all down on one knee, guns pointing every which way.

'All my people!' Homer screamed.

Seemed as if bullets were coming from every direction. Then

Dellwood pointed west. 'From over there,' he said. 'The gun smoke.'

Homer dived for the six-shooter in Ulysses's back pocket. The bullet got Homer in the stomach. He grabbed his middle, blood spurting out from under his hand. Homer looked at the blood, looked up at me and Dellwood, and then started running west.

'Fuck you, fucking white bastards!' Homer was screaming, shooting. 'Fuck you, fucking white bastards!'

'Get your ass down, Homer!' Dellwood yelled.

The second bullet took off most Homer's head.

Dellwood and I pressed against each other, shooting at whatever we could see. All we could see was trees and rocks and dirt.

When we stopped to reload, the sun was full up.

The shooting had stopped.

Dellwood let out a whoop and headed west across the clearing, running and shooting, me following. We got farther than Homer did. At the stand of trees, all that was left of the ambush was footprints and empty shells.

The morning was silent.

Smoke rose up into the morning sky between the earth and the sun.

Running back down to Excellent, me and Dellwood turned ourselves into deer, into eagles flying, us taking big leaps over the side of the mountain, sliding down inclines, losing our footing, rolling over logs. Trees were flying by, and the only sound was breath, heartbeat, and boots pounding the ground.

When we got to the cemetery, we stopped. A big lick of fire was sitting on Ida's Place like one of Alma's hats. Black smoke in the sky halfway to the moon.

We heard two shots.

'Look!' Dellwood said.

A man was running with a torch in his hand. The man doused the torch in Hot Creek, and then started running straight toward us. His hand was bandaged. The day before Dellwood had shot a gun out of that man's hand – the gun that was pointed at Blind Jude.

We waited, Dellwood behind a tree, me behind another. The man ran right between us.

Was this man's turn to be a trapped animal. Dellwood raised his rifle and cocked it, pointing at the man's head.

'Nigger-loving pederasts!' the man screamed at us. 'Sodomist devils!'

My body jumped. I lifted the man up in the air and then threw him to the ground, him making a sound of losing air. I grabbed him by the bandaged hand then and started dragging him. Dragged him to Hot Creek, through Hot Creek, to the back of Ida's Place – all the while him yelling, 'Reverend Helm! Reverend Helm!'

I dragged him so close to the burning heat of Ida's Place, I thought my head was going to burst.

'Did you do this?' I asked the man. 'Did Helm pay you to do this?'

'He didn't pay me,' the man said. 'It was the Will of the Lord! Sinners shall be cast into everlasting damnation and fire.'

When my ears heard *everlasting damnation and fire*, I looked around and I was standing in the same spot where years ago Billy Blizzard had pushed himself up my ass.

I put my hand on the man's forehead. I pushed his head back. The sound of his neck breaking.

The man's body went limp, but he was still breathing and looking at me. I pulled his face close to mine.

'Everlasting damnation in hell,' I said, picked him up, and threw his body into the back door of Ida's Place, into the kitchen, into the fire.

'You killed him, Shed,' Dellwood said. 'You killed him.'

When we got around to the front of the building, Ida was screaming at a naked Alma Hatch who had just run into the flames of Ida's Place. Dellwood grabbed Damn Dave and kept him from running in after Alma, and then Dellwood ran into the wall of flame after Alma Hatch himself. Was forever those two inside the flames, finally Dellwood carrying Alma out, him cooked meat, Alma's hair smoking.

Dellwood dumped Alma into the horse trough, next to what was left of Ellen Finton in the horse trough, Alma sputtering and howling.

'My book!' Alma was screaming. 'My *Ornithological Studies in the Pacific Northwest*!'

Alma stepped out of the trough and then proceeded to run right back into the flames. Dellwood caught up with her, doubled his fist, and punched Alma Hatch in the jaw the way tybo men punch other men. Alma's body folded, and she fell to the dust of Pine Street. Then I remembered Ida's diaries.

Next thing I knew my body was inside Ida's Place on fire. The stairway was going fast. I shinnied up one of the posts and pulled myself up to the banister and into the corridor. Killdeer everywhere.

Ida's room was that rose color – bright. Nothing was burnt yet, but there was fire on the other side of the windows and the wallpaper was bubbling. I grabbed for the drawer where she kept her diaries, held my shirt up like an apron and collected her diaries. I saw Ida's blue dress on the bed and I reached for it. Just then the floor collapsed all around me. I jumped onto Ida's bed as the bed fell with everything else to the first floor into fire.

Keep your heart open in hell, I said to myself, and headed for the door, for where I thought was the door.

Next thing I knew my body was standing next to Dellwood Barker on Pine Street.

'What do I have to do, knock you out, too?' Dellwood yelled in my face, and then threw his arms around me. Ida's diaries fell out of my shirt, onto the dust of Pine Street.

Ida Richilieu, Dellwood Barker, and me – we looked down at burnt Gracie Hammer on the street, at Ellen Finton floating in the horse trough, at Alma Hatch sitting dazed, naked, cross-legged, hair burnt off, next to Gracie Hammer's body, and at the black leather-bound gold-leafed diaries in the dust at Gracie's feet.

'Look at them! Mormons standing all around,' Ida said. 'Not one of them trying to help. For a while there, the Reverend Helm was standing under the flag in his nightshirt and his big book under his arm, smug as you can be – him talking fire and brimstone and hell and punishment and the Lord.'

Alma pointed her arm and said, 'There she goes!' We heard a crash, and as we looked, the sign, *Indian Head Hotel*, the words bubbled up with heat, fell off its hinges.

Ida's Place fell into itself, folded into itself the way Alma's body folded when Dellwood had hit her, collapsing, a fainting tybo lady, logs shifting as the fire went down.

Set free.

Without Moves Moves we're nothing.

Only the back chimney was left standing.

The look on Ida's face was a look I'd never seen on any human being before.

The ponderosa pine – the pine tree that Pine Street was named after – had gone in flames like one of Virgil Wisdom's matches.

Damn Dave crying, Damn Dog howling.

By noon, all that was left of Ida's Place that wasn't ashes was Ida's white dress, Ida's diaries, Ida's shotgun, the piano out back on the Wisdom Brothers' stage, some chairs, the shed, a blanket, a case of whiskey, Alma Hatch, Dellwood Barker, Ida Richilieu, and me.

Next morning, me and Dellwood headed up Gold Hill, me and the mule following Dellwood and Abraham Lincoln, my heart pounding, my breath in and out.

At the clearing, when I got off the mule, my knees were shaking so hard, my legs couldn't stand. So when my feet hit the ground, the rest of my body hit the ground too.

When I got back up, I just let my feet and my legs go. They took me out into the clearing and stood me in the pile of bodies: Virgil, Ulysses, Homer, and Blind Jude.

Turkey buzzards hungry in the trees.

Flies in a slaughterhouse.

Heard the story once that if a deer gets scared enough, its heart will burst.

Fear is not what bursts the human heart.

Dellwood still had his scrutinizing on, so we got to work, laying Virgil, Ulysses, and Blind Jude across the mule. We laid Homer across Abraham Lincoln.

Ulysses's little finger with the diamond ring had been cut off. His face was busted in and his gold teeth yanked out.

On the way down the hill, I didn't say one word. Dellwood Barker talked all the way.

'All your life, you've been chastising yourself for letting the devil get to your mother,' Dellwood said. 'Same way as with Owlfeather – you thinking he died so you could live. Now it's the Wisdom Brothers. If you want to keep telling yourself that same old tired devil story, then that's your business, but as far as I'm concerned, it's a crock of shit and I don't believe a word of it.'

Sun was setting by the time we made it back to town. We laid the Wisdom Brothers right next to each other, between the shed and the wagon. Then we put Ellen Finton into a potato sack, and Gracie Hammer into a potato sack, and laid the two of them next to the Wisdom Brothers.

I borrowed two of Damn Dave's shovels and up in the

cemetery, me and Dellwood dug the holes, him shoveling like a lunatic until bedrock and me trying to keep up. We weren't digging in the main part of the cemetery – that is, the Christian part – but some distance over, in the part Ida called her part, where murderers and prostitutes and ne'er-do-wells go buried.

Six holes and six bodies, and later, Thord Hurdlika's hands.

All that was left of Thord Hurdlika was his big hands burnt leather soft. It wasn't til things cooled down that we found his hands in a pile of ashes that was Ida's Place – three days later. Dellwood folded Thord's hands together in the box that the red Italian wine had been sent to Ida in. We buried the box next to Gracie Hammer.

There were two funerals – same day – two funerals. One was the Reverend Helm's funeral for a man named Lawrence Satterfield – *a brave, God-serving, law-abiding Mormon citizen of Excellent, Idaho, who had been killed fighting the fire of a local hotel.*

I had killed a man named Lawrence Satterfield.

Story goes they found his body where the back porch had been. There was just enough of Lawrence Satterfield left for folks to tell.

The other funeral was our funeral. For Virgil, Ulysses, Homer, and Blind Jude Wisdom. For Ellen Finton, and Gracie Hammer.

The whole town attended Helm's funeral for Lawrence Satterfield.

We attended ours.

Helm's funeral was held in the Mormon church. The new green one. There was a big coffin and flowers and you could hear the organ and people singing the songs they do when tybos die. Music when you hear it makes you want to die too.

Ida, Alma, Dellwood, and me, we held our funeral between the shed and the Wisdom Brothers' wagon. Ida played the piano. 'Carry Me Back to Old Virginny' like I'd asked her. She didn't know the song too well but she played it through. Didn't sound anything like when the Wisdom Brothers had played it. At our funeral, there weren't any coffins – no money to buy coffins, no time to build them.

We'd cleaned them all up as best we could – all of them gone to Glidden, gone to Calcutta.

Ulysses with his corncob pipe.

Homer with a Bible and his tambourine.

Virgil with his fiddle.

Blind Jude with nickles on his eyes and a silver dollar in his pocket.

Gracie Hammer and Ellen Finton in potato sacks. I tore my Hudson Bay in two and covered Gracie Hammer with half, and Ellen Finton with half.

Alma picked wild flowers. Sprinkled flowers on top of each one: Indian paintbrush, the purple ones, and the yellow.

We were a sad sight burying the Wisdom Brothers and Ellen Finton and Gracie Hammer. Ida Richilieu was burnt white the way the posts sticking up out of the ashes of Ida's Place were burnt. Alma Hatch's hair was sticking up all porcupine around her head. Part of her face was peeling off and her eyes were all red from crying about everything, mostly her hair. She was wearing a pair of Dellwood's pants tied up with string and his white Sears and Roebuck shirt. Ida was wearing the white dress. Dellwood was flash-burnt and had a gash on his head that wouldn't stop bleeding.

Dellwood, Ida, Alma, and me lifted the six bodies up into the Wisdom Brothers' wagon. Made something die in you, picking up dead bodies, picking up their dead bodies – Moves Moves gone out of them, only meat left.

We unloaded the bodies at the cemetery and put each body into a hole.

When they were all laid out, the holes, from east to west,

went: Ulysses, Homer, Virgil, and Blind Jude, Ellen Finton, Gracie Hammer. Three days later, we buried Thord Hurdlika's hands next to Gracie Hammer.

Dellwood started singing Indian songs high in the throat. Damn Dave too. Ida started singing her Jewish tribe songs – Jewish, I figured, because I hadn't ever heard the likes of that singing before. Alma went into some of her large bird-death ecstasy sounds – sounds the earth would make if she was feeling awful as us.

With the four of them groaning, crying, and wailing away, I figured I might as well too. I closed my eyes, pretended my eyes were Blind Jude's. I let the sound that was inside me out.

Made that mule start bucking.

The sound I was making got louder.

'Made that other funeral stop singing,' Dellwood said.

'Surprised you haven't raised the dead,' Ida said. 'Sounds like hell.'

Made Alma start kicking her feet and flapping her arms.

Dellwood finally tapped me on the shoulder because he thought I might be going out of my mind.

I looked around then, to the other funeral, just north a piece, in the Christian section of the cemetery. Folks over there were standing in the sunlight. They were so clean, so sure they were right.

Truth was, I wanted to go over to them and ask them how to do it – be clean and sure the way they were. How to love God or Joseph Smith or whoever it was you had to love to make the sun shine on you that way. You with your mother, your father, your brothers and sisters – you with your own child, clean and confident – your whole family with you living in a house with more than half a window, with lots of rooms that you called home.

Truth was, I wanted to be white, be tybo. I wanted to be a
Mormon. Have Mormon rules. Read the book. Have a wife and
children. Have a big coffin and things clean and orderly when I
died.

The more I wanted to be tybo and Mormon, the louder I sang.
Kept singing long after everybody else had quit – us and the
Mormons. What my ears started hearing was what Homer had
said:

Fuck you, fucking white bastards.

Ida finally got me stopped. Kicked me in the butt and told me
to shut up.

We took turns shoveling. We filled up the holes. Each
shovelful of earth was a shovelful of Ida, of Alma, of Dellwood, of
Damn Dave, of me getting thrown in on them.

*

Sheriff Archibald Rooney, from the county seat in Sawtooth,
came to make his investigation about a week later. Sheriff
Rooney spent the day talking to the Reverend Helm and
Blumenfeld. By late afternoon – being that there wasn't any
whiskey to buy in town, and no longer a place to get himself a
piece of ass – Sheriff Archibald Rooney got on his horse and rode
out of Excellent.

Ida Richilieu, Dellwood Barker, Alma Hatch, and me were
waiting for him around the first bend.

'Aren't you forgetting something?' Dellwood Barker asked.

'Aren't you forgetting the Wisdom Brothers?' Alma Hatch
asked.

'The Wisdom Brothers?' Sheriff Rooney said.

'Ulysses, Virgil, Homer, and Blind Jude,' I said.

'Oh, them!' the sheriff said. 'The nigger band – case is closed.'

'Then how do you explain their deaths?' Alma asked.

'Simple,' the sheriff said. 'Open season,' he said.

*

After Sheriff Rooney left, Ida went down to Chinatown.

She had lost the battle of the Fourth of July, lost the whole war, and Ida took it bad – not fighting-back bad, but whipped.

I kept expecting, any minute, for her to go for her shotgun, Ida walking down Pine Street with her shotgun, Ida blowing a new hole into the Reverend Helm and into Blumenfeld. But Ida never went for her shotgun. Her place burned down, the Wisdom Brothers dead – those weren't so bad as, how Ida put it – 'The lack of intelligent justice in the land.'

There was something else, too. Ida would never admit it, but she was lost in a world with no Ida's Place. Ida was the Madam Full Charge – the kind of person who needed to be the one who told everybody else what to do. It was always Ida's Place, her whiskey, her girls, her music, her food. Ida'd give it away or sell it to you cheap, but you always knew that she was the one who was doing it for you.

Out in the shed, down in Chinatown, Ida in the dirty white dress, skinny arms and legs, Ida, no saloon, no blue dress, no mirror to watch herself sip whiskey and smoke stardust in, no bath, Ida was taking it bad.

Stayed drunk and smoking, both her and Alma. Alma with hardly any hair and no ornithological bird book, not much better off than Ida.

Stayed nasty drunk, both of those women, crying and drinking and feeling sorry for themselves, then fighting with each other, Alma telling Ida that she'd warned her about taking Negroes into her hotel.

'But you wouldn't listen,' Alma saying.

Ida getting on her high horse again about what she called human values and how some people were just born leaders and felt a duty in their heart to lead the masses out of the darkness and stupidity of their little lives.

Alma saying, 'Bullshit.'

Ida saying, 'Chicken shit.'

Those two screaming and going at it again and again, and then after a while they'd be hugging each other, crying.

Truth is, though, I liked it when those two were going at it with each other, because when they were at it with each other, they weren't going at it with you.

As Dellwood put it, 'Ain't nothing worse than fallen royalty turning their spiteful wrath onto you.'

With all four of us living out in the shed, it was more times than not, those first couple months, that Ida and Alma did that – turned their spiteful wrath onto us – so me and Dellwood got to spending more and more time up on Not-Really-A-Mountain, camping in the meadow, in my place, getting on top of things, so to speak, looking down, *getting perspective*, as Dellwood put it.

Those times when I was sitting up on the mountain looking down, it was hard to believe that Ida's Place was no longer – that all there was was a square of black. I'd close my eyes and I just knew that when I opened them back up, Ida's Place would be pink wood again, and that the burning down had just been a bad dream I could wake up from – the way you do when you don't like the way a story ends and you decide to end it better.

When I opened my eyes, though, Ida's Place always wasn't there.

The Wisdom Brothers, the fire, Ellen Finton, Gracie Hammer, and the lack of intelligent justice in the land brought me and Dellwood Barker closer together; that is, brought me closer to Dellwood.

Even though Dellwood Barker got farther away. Farther away,

Dellwood Barker trying to heal us. The gash in his head, his sore heart and our sore hearts, taking him farther away.

Everything coming in between.

I shaved Dellwood's head so he could keep the gash in it clean. Then he decided to shave all the rest of his body hair off. Shaved his mustache, shaved off the hair on his chest and stomach and balls and ass.

When I asked him, he said Indians cut their hair when someone they love has died.

Dellwood bought another horse and called it Killdeer. Kept the horse in the stable next to Abraham Lincoln. Outfitted Killdeer with a bridle and blanket and saddle.

Dellwood started buying himself extra winter clothes. Clothes that didn't fit him – clothes that were too big.

Started talking about dying, about Buffalo Head. Started talking about living as if it was yesterday and something he used to do.

Got Dr. Ah Fong to tattoo him. The tattoo was a red heart on top of his own heart with the names Shed, Alma, Ida, Virgil, Ulysses, Blind Jude, Homer, Princess, Willow, and Moon Bear.

When I asked him who Willow and Moon Bear were, Dellwood said those were the names of his children who had died.

Willow and Moon Bear, the twins who had died.

Dellwood bought him a special rifle.

'The kind they used in the Civil War,' he said.

The rifle had a bayonet attachment.

*

Then there was the day that it was payday in Gold Bar and we were all still in Excellent. The day that Dellwood and Ida started arguing again about the tree falling and what was real. Then what followed was the contest — to see who could have the most fun — men or women. Truth was, though, the contest didn't have anything to do with having fun, or men or women. Truth was, the contest was between Ida Richilieu and Dellwood Barker — who was right and who was wrong. What was real.

Then there's the legend about that night.

How much we drank.

How much we smoked.

Who had the most fun.

Who won the contest.

Who was right and who was wrong.

Dellwood started it. Actually, Ida started it because of what Alma did. What Alma did was steal a bottle of whiskey I'd stashed in the rafters of the shed. We only had eight bottles left, so I took what I thought was my share and hid it.

I caught Alma stealing the bottle red-handed. When I told her to put it back, Alma Hatch acted as if all of a sudden she couldn't understand plain English. Then Ida walked in, and when she found out what Alma was up to, Ida took my side and ended up slapping Alma aside the head. Alma wasn't going to take that from Ida anymore, so she lit into Ida, and right then and there was the biggest catfight that Excellent, Idaho, had ever seen since the muddy day with the bright sheets and the sun that my mother, the Princess, took on Ida Richilieu over fifteen years ago.

Ida Richilieu and Alma Hatch, both of them women turned mountain lions — screaming and punching, pulling hair, kicking, yelling, and cussing.

That's when Dellwood Barker walked in. At first, he looked at us as if we were strangers. For a while, I wondered if he even saw us at all.

Then: 'Why are they fighting this time?' he asked.

I told him.

Dellwood sat down heavy on the bed. I sat next to him. We watched Ida and Alma go at it until they ran out of steam, Alma laying on the floor, Ida on the bed, them panting and sweating, Ida bleeding from her nose.

Outside, I could hear crows. Inside it was quiet except for Ida and Alma breathing hard. The sun was just starting to come in the window and make a patch on the floor. Dellwood got up, walked around the room, pulling whiskey bottles out from under the bed, from beside the stove, from in the woodpile, and some places I didn't even know about. He put the bottles in the center of the room, walked outside, and then pretty soon came back with two more bottles. He stood the bottles in a row. Twelve of them.

'Bring out all the rest,' he said.

We all looked at each other. At first nobody moved. Then Dellwood threw out a handful of rolled cigarettes and then a leather bag. I threw out all the locoweed and stardust cigarettes I had. Alma reached in her pants, pulled out a hemp-filled hanky and then her stardust. Ida reached into her skirt and pulled out a tobacco tin and threw it in the pile.

'Anybody holding out?' Dellwood asked.

Ida left and came back with three more bottles of whiskey and a pint of peppermint schnapps.

'Anybody else?' Dellwood asked.

We all looked at Alma.

Alma unbuttoned her pants and threw out another hankyful. Then pulled two cigarettes out from under the towel she had wrapped around her hair. Then a pouch from between her tits.

'That's all,' she said.

We kept looking.

Alma got up and stomped out the door. She came back with a pint of Russian vodka and a bottle of the red Italian wine we had that day we all wore white.

'That's it, I tell you,' Alma said. 'Ain't nothing else!'

Dellwood sat four glasses on the floor – one in front of each of us.

Alma was sitting curled into herself on the floor, her arms around her knees. Ida was back on the bed, her facing the wall. The air was cool and we hadn't made a fire because we'd had enough of fire. No snow yet. The past two years it hadn't snowed until late – Christmas and even later. Ida had said it would be the same way this year – late.

Ida said that winters and such came in threes, said it the way she said things – like there was no way in hell she could be wrong.

The way the sky looked that day – clear blue and full of sun – made it look like Ida was right again.

The sun through the window moved on top of the bottles. Sun on the bottles making little circles of light around the room, sun on the whiskey in the bottles – the color of sunlight in the late fall. Sun on the vodka making rainbows onto Dellwood's face.

Dellwood touched the vodka bottle with the tip of his boot, moving the rainbow just enough.

Looking at Dellwood Barker right then, I thought of the times when me and him had moved rainbows between us.

Ida rolled over and stared. We all stared at the sun on the bottles.

Dellwood reached down and picked up the nearest bottle to him and poured us each a shot. When he started talking, his voice was like the patch of sun. Sounded like his old self.

'Sticking together!' Dellwood raised his glass and toasted.

Nobody moved.

'A family,' Dellwood toasted.

'Real as any Mormon family!' I said, and toasted.

'Because we got each other!' Alma said.

Then Ida said, 'As long as we live, may nothing ever come between us again.'

We raised our glasses high.

'May nothing ever come between us again,' we all said together.

Alma lit one of her cigarettes and passed it to Ida.

The next time I looked the patch of sun had gone away, and so had the pint of vodka, and one of the bottles of whiskey. Ida and Alma were sitting next to each other on the floor. Me and Dellwood were sitting on the bed.

Ida heaved a big sigh, and looking out the window, at where Ida's Place used to be, she said, 'The deck's stacked against you – might as well figure on that. Keep your promises, keep clean, and keep going – that's all you can do.'

Usually, when Ida said something she always said in the way she said things – like the deck's stacked against you – Alma Hatch, Dellwood Barker, and me would just be quiet, or nod our heads.

That day, though, after Dellwood Barker had tried to be the peacekeeper, he couldn't help but say this:

'I am so tired of hearing that same old shit from you, Ida,' Dellwood said. 'Poor old Ida Richilieu – deck stacked against her but she keeps on going – ain't life a grizzly bear and ain't Ida Richilieu a brave tough old girl,' Dellwood said. 'I tell you I'm tired of hearing it. There ain't nothing that happens to a person that ain't that person. The world out there only does what you tell it to do. The world is happening to you the way it is happening because you're telling yourself the story that way. If you want to change the world so damn bad, Ida, then where you got to start is how it is you're looking at it.'

Real.

Ida reached for the bottle Dellwood had opened, and poured another round.

'So, what you're telling me, Dellwood Barker,' Ida said, 'is that my hotel burned down because of how I am?'

'That's right,' Dellwood said. 'You're the one who declared the war.'

'The war needed declaring,' Ida said. 'If I didn't do it, nobody else would have. I was forced into the situation.'

'Who forced you?' Dellwood asked.

'The Mormons. The lack of intelligent justice in the land.'

'You hating Mormons because they don't act the way you want them to act has nothing to do with it, right?' Dellwood said.

'Mormons need hating,' Ida said. 'Anybody who thinks she or he's a saint, latter-day or otherwise, needs hating, needs to be fought. That's just the way it is, and that's just the way I am. Don't ask me to change.'

I poured another round of drinks.

'Yeh hell, we've heard that one before, too,' Dellwood said. 'Don't you see, Ida, you keep your ass covered that way? If you think life is a deck of cards stacked against you – if you think that you got nothing to say about what happens to you – if you think that all you can do is suffer opprobrium, then the world is going to do exactly as it's told and be the way you say it's going to be. But just let someone hold a mirror up to you – just let someone dare and try to point out to Ida Richilieu that she just might have something to do with how the events of her life are unfolding – and the first thing Ida Richilieu does is hide behind that worn-out, sorry damn story – that she's just the way she is and everybody had better just accept that because Ida Richilieu is not about to change.

'From my way of looking at things,' Dellwood Barker said, 'I'd say that was pretty goddamned dogmatic, and a coward's way of living your life because everything you don't like about your life turns out to be everybody else's fault.'

'What about the Wisdom Brothers, then?' Ida said. 'You think they was ambushed, shot to death like dogs, because they wanted to be? If my place burnt down because of how I am, then they died – like your sorry tired damn story – because of what they was telling themselves. I don't believe it and I never will. Those men – those Negroes didn't choose to be born into a world that hates them. The deck of cards was stacked against them, and all they could do is all that the rest of us can do – and that's grab life before it grabs you, take one step at a time, be the best person you can be – and keep going,' Ida said.

'And if that's bearing opprobrium, then that's what I do alright, along with every other mother's son and daughter on God's green earth.'

'O . . P . . P . . R . . O . . B . . R . . I . . U . . M,' Dellwood spelled. 'Means suffering disgrace for something you done wrong; namely, being born.'

Dellwood poured us all another round of drinks.

'And you be careful, Dellwood Barker,' Ida said. 'Ain't nobody calls Ida Richilieu a coward.'

'That's right, Ida, when you're cornered – throw out the threats,' Dellwood said. 'Why not declare war on me? It'd give you a reason to go on living.'

Ida picked up a whiskey bottle and threw it at Dellwood. Dellwood ducked and the bottle broke against the wall. The bottle was an empty one.

Dellwood jumped across to Ida, grabbed her by the collar, and put her face next to his.

'What are you so afraid of, woman?' Dellwood said, his teeth set together, moving only his lips. 'Why can't you stop just once and take a look at yourself?'

'There is a world out there, Dellwood Barker,' Ida said, teeth set the way Dellwood's teeth were set. 'I can see it and taste and feel it. It ain't just something I'm making up. And that damn tree that falls in the damn forest is going to make a damn noise because there's a world out there – not just some idea some moony cowboy thinks he's making up – and in that world when a tree falls it makes noise, whether or not I'm there or you're there to hear it.'

'That's just the way it is then, right, Ida?' Dellwood said. 'You have spoken?'

'That's just the way it is,' Ida said. 'I have spoken.'

'And it's never going to change?' Dellwood said.

'And it's never going to change,' Ida said.

Providence. Ida jumped.

'What's the day today?' she asked.

Dellwood looked at Ida, then Alma, then at me.

Nobody knew, but I knew because it was Halloween.

'It's Halloween, October thirty-first,' I said.

'Payday!' Ida let out a whoop. 'Oh! The humanity, how could I forget that date? It's payday in Gold Bar!' Ida said. 'Now just who am I that this is happening to me?' Ida asked, looking over at Dellwood.

'You're a dang stubborn mean woman,' Dellwood said.

'Not as stubborn and mean as most of the men I have known, including you, Dellwood Barker,' Ida said.

'Ain't no whores in Gold Bar! What are we doing here?' Alma said.

'Let's hitch up that mule to the Wisdom Brother's wagon and make us a delivery,' Ida said.

'First of all, let's have a drink,' Alma said, and poured us all another round.

'To trees falling in the forest,' Ida toasted.

'And to being there to hear them,' Dellwood said.

After that round, we poured ourselves another round, threw our drinks back, and poured another round. Alma lit another locoweed cigarette.

Sometime around in there, Ida said something to the fact that women were stronger than men. Dellwood said he agreed – thought it was true that women were more powerful than men, but men, he said, always knew how to have more fun.

'It's a physical impossibility for a man to have more fun than a woman!' Ida said.

Then I said, 'All most women are trying to do is grow a dick.'

'That's all most you men are trying to do too,' Alma said.

And that's how it started, and finally, what it led to was the contest.

Ida Richilieu and Alma Hatch claimed that they could have more fun than me and Dellwood Barker.

Me and Dellwood Barker claimed that we could have more fun than Ida Richilieu and Alma Hatch.

More fun turning out to be who could drink and who could smoke the most, and laugh the hardest.

When we started, there were fourteen bottles of whiskey, a bottle of Italian wine, a pint of schnapps, seven hemp cigarettes, and a pile of stardust that fit in the palm of my big hand.

'May the best man win,' Dellwood toasted.

'May the best woman win,' Ida toasted.

What I remember about the contest is that the contest started late afternoon and that the contest started with fucking. Not fucking but talking about fucking. Ida Richilieu said her best had been with Billy Blizzard. Alma Hatch said hers was Virgil Wisdom. Dellwood Barker said he hadn't had his yet. I remember trying to say who was best for me but couldn't find the language. What I would have said, though, if I could have, was this: best fuck was Charles Smith's bullet.

That's when Dellwood Barker called me the name: Out-Of-His-Fucking-Mind. I remember all of us laughing about Out-Of-

His-Fucking-Mind, us sitting around the kerosene lamp in the rose-colored light, the family of us – Alma's face, Ida's face, Dellwood's face – darkness not far beyond our light.

What happened next was we were all outside in the moon. It was the hunter's moon, full. We were in the ashes of Ida's Place. Dellwood sat a chair down where the piano stool had been in front of the piano. Alma was behind the bar, by the door, where she had always stood, so she could get to whoever was coming in first. Ida, in her white dress, still on both her legs, was dancing in the moonlight on the bar, in all that black, Ida in her white dress, dancing on what was left of the bar.

'Come take a trip in my airship and we'll visit the man in the moon,' she sang – not a whore in a saloon, but Ida dancing with her man, waltzing with a man that she loved, maybe her husband, maybe a young man who'd come in, really just a boy.

I was standing where I had always stood – in the doorway to the kitchen, looking in, watching them, my family.

The next thing I remember it was morning. I woke up cold, covered in black, alone, out in the shed. Everyone was gone. Ida Richilieu and Alma Hatch and Dellwood Barker were gone.

When I looked out the window I saw the snow cloud up on Devil's Pass. The cloud was beautiful – a slow-floating bag of goose down hanging in a blue October sky. I watched the cloud for some time. Thought about how it looked: a bird, a hand reaching, a woman running.

I thought about snow – snow on Devil's Pass – thought about Ida Richilieu being wrong about the snow this year.

I thought: payday in Gold Bar and Gold Bar on the other side of that snow.

I jumped up quick, my legs and feet doing as they were told, and ran over to where Ida had left the Wisdom Brothers' wagon. Sure enough, the wagon was gone. Mule was gone too.

'Like a bat out of hell,' Doc Heyburn said is how that wagon'd left town the night before. 'Just after sunset,' he said, 'that Negro wagon flying out of here like a bat out of hell.'

I ran down Pine Street. Ran up Pine Street. Ran over to Chinatown. Ran back.

At the barbershop, I stopped running and stood in front of where Ida's Place used to be.

'Like bats out of hell!' the Reverend Helm said. He was standing on the porch in front of the barbershop. Blumenfeld was standing next to him.

'Like sinning black-magic voodoo!' he said. 'Drunker than skunks!'

'Skunk whores!' Blumenfeld said. 'To the devil with them!'

I could have killed both those men, right there in the street. But I didn't. Figured that getting to where Ida and Alma and Dellwood were was more important.

I ran over to Damn Dave's and slid back the stable door. Inside, Abraham Lincoln looked over at me, and so did Killdeer, and Dellwood Barker.

Scared me how happy I was to see Dellwood Barker. I wanted to run to him and touch his face and feel him breathing, and I started running to him – but I stopped because there was something wrong.

Dellwood was cussing and in a hurry and Dellwood Barker was never in a hurry. He was saddling up Abraham Lincoln, walking around fast, knocking things over – lariat in one hand, water canteen in the other, trying to lash them to the saddle.

'They're up on Devil's Pass,' Dellwood said, 'and they're in trouble, Shed, I know it. Ida and Alma are caught up in that cloud up on Devil's Pass, and you and me got to go help them.'

Dellwood threw me the new winter clothes of his that were too big for him, and I lashed them to Killdeer's saddle. We rode out of town, full gallop, *like bats out of hell, hell-bent for leather.*

Dellwood ahead of me on Abraham Lincoln, me on Killdeer, us heading up the road to Devil's Pass, to the cloud covering Devil's Pass.

Abraham Lincoln was half Morgan and half quarter horse, level-headed, but slower than Killdeer, who I figured was mostly Arabian. Still, Killdeer was slow for what I wanted him for. Fastest horse in the world wouldn't have been fast enough.

Foam was working up on Killdeer's neck, on Abraham Lincoln's neck too. Us fast through the darkness of trees, fast through shadows and light, heart beating, horses' hearts beating, hard breath all around, horses' hooves; me thinking *opprobrium, hell, keeping my heart open in hell*, thinking *devil*. At the third bend in the road, where the road goes into the **S** curve, we pulled the horses up and stopped.

There was the cloud.

In the clear blue sky, sitting on Devil's Pass the way fire had sat on Ida's Place, a floating white mountain sitting on a mountain, glowing from the inside.

Me and Dellwood looked at each other. The horses didn't like the cloud either. We got off and walked the horses the rest of the way up. Walked right up to that cloud. Was sunny and blue right up to the cloud. Then we were inside the cloud and it was cold, layers of cloud all around us the way fog is in layers on the river in the mornings. I unlashed the winter clothes from the saddle and pulled the woolen pants on, the coat, and the scarf. I didn't think about it then, but all those clothes fit.

Farther in, when the fog cleared, what we saw was snow. Big snowflakes were falling, some of them as big as your fist, falling-down-jewels, slow and silent.

Couldn't get enough of looking at snow coming down, snowflakes landing on my face and arms, landing on the horses' ears and manes. Made you want to get off and run around and play.

Abraham Lincoln and Killdeer got all stomping and farting – frisky, even though neither one of them were showy horses.

No trace of wagon tracks.

We rode into the cloud until the snowflakes weren't pretty anymore, and it was dark and cold. At the last switchback before the top, we stopped. Dellwood yelled over to me that Devil's Pass wasn't more than a quarter mile away. Snow had drifted over the road, and we couldn't see much past the horses' ears. There were gusts of wind that liked to blow you right over.

We kept on for a ways longer, leading the horses, kicking around in the drifting snow, but it wasn't any use. We were getting froze ourselves, to the bone. We were about to turn back, when Dellwood kicked up a whiskey bottle. Still could smell the whiskey. I walked over to the edge, where the road switched left almost back onto itself. On the raw edge where the snow was drifting off, I saw the rocks scraped and overturned. Down below it was dark forever.

'Ida! Alma!' My ears could barely hear what it was my mouth was yelling.

I yelled their names again, and a gust of wind hit me in the face, smelling of roses and Alma Hatch.

It was then I knew.

Just then a big burst of sun came onto the world. Sun so bright we had to cover our eyes. Me and Dellwood watched the cloud float off Devil's Pass due north.

From where we were standing, below us was straight down to a big rock that was jutting up a fist out of the snow. Beyond the rock, all you could see was more straight down to forever. There were pine trees on the one side of the rock. On the other side were smaller rocks, and some scrub pines.

Just then, a turkey buzzard landed in the trees just to the left of the rock, big wings flapping down slow, coming to rest next to the other buzzards in the trees – must have been twenty or so.

'Thank you very much,' Dellwood Barker said to that buzzard, and took off running to a place on the side of the road, just up from where we were standing, where the earth sloped down instead of going off sheer. Dellwood led Abraham Lincoln down the slope and I followed with Killdeer. The ground was blown dry for a ways, but then there was snow, deep snow, and, with the ledge being so close, you couldn't tell if where you were stepping was on snow with ground underneath it or not. Took us all morning to plow through to the rock, snow in places drifted to above our heads.

All the time the sun on us, bright as God. The buzzards circling, landing, making their noise. It got so bright that even Blind Jude could've seen. I put Dellwood's new scarf over my face, and poked two holes in it no bigger than my little finger to look through. Light coming in those holes was sharp as knives. My nose and the roof of my mouth were burning. All Dellwood had for a hat was his Stetson. The gash in his head had started bleeding again. The brim of the Stetson stopped the sun from above but didn't help him with the glare from the snow. Dellwood kept burying his face in his arm and just walking ahead.

It was bad for the horses, too. They were getting spooked. I was going to tie some blanket or something around their heads to protect their eyes, but it could've just made things worse. We were in no place for a horse to go wild with that forever going down next to us on one side, so I figured I'd better not chance it.

There were a couple of times I knew I was a goner, knew I was going to have to learn how to fly, that edge got so close.

When we finally got to the rock, we stood in the shade of it, not even trying to open our eyes. Then, when we tried, seeing felt like bleeding.

First things my eyes saw, besides the bright shine of God, was those turkey buzzards flocked around Alma Hatch. She was standing, leaning up against a tree. There were hundreds of them birds around her, but not one of them was eating on her, not yet, although they wanted to.

I ran into those birds, cussing them, calling them every name I'd ever heard in tybo or Indian. The sound of their wings was all over in my ears, was all I could hear except for me screaming.

Along the rock it was clear of snow. I ran up the ridge to where the trees started. Between the rock and the trees was an open space where the wind was coming up through strong. There, back up the slope toward the road, I saw the red and yellow and green sign and the painted picture of the Wisdom Brothers. The painting of Ulysses, Virgil, Homer, and Blind Jude was in the snow, and they were all smiling at me. Next to the sign was the half-eaten dead mule, and a wagon wheel, but no Ida.

I ran to the tree, into the shade, up to Alma. I was just about to her when I saw that her feet weren't touching the ground. Saw that there was a branch sticking out of her – between her legs, a branch sticking out, poking up her skirt, out of woman's hole, a tree branch.

Trying to grow me a dick here while I was waiting for you guys, I could just hear her say, laughing after she'd said that.

Alma Hatch. Her eyes were open. No buzzard would ever dare to eat those eyes – so beautiful that they were how flying was to them. She was looking straight ahead, like she thought it was nice there. Her arms weren't on her body anymore. They were up higher in the tree, wings, waiting for the rest of her to catch up.

Dellwood came up behind me and put his arm across my shoulder and we looked up at Alma Hatch.

Then we heard somebody laughing. Me and Dellwood looked at each other to see if the other one was crazy yet.

It was Ida Richilieu laughing.

At first I thought Ida was playing hide-and-seek with us, and couldn't keep from laughing any longer because me and Dellwood were so close.

We dug her out of the snowdrift. Ida Richilieu was a sack of bones. Most of them broken. Her legs were the worst. Bloody, puffed-up frozen meat. Must have landed feetfirst.

Ida laughed that way again, a couple of times, as if somebody was telling her jokes. Dellwood said it was the Great Mystery she was talking to.

I knew different. Ida only laughed like that at her own jokes.

We wrapped Ida up in blankets and laid her in the sun while we got Alma off the tree. I climbed up and got her arms. Dellwood lashed Alma to Killdeer, then Alma's arms to Killdeer.

We fashioned a stretcher for Ida out of limbs and saplings, tied the stretcher behind Abraham Lincoln with Dellwood's lariat, then tied Ida onto the stretcher.

Took us another half day to get back to Excellent – into the night, and it had started snowing heavy.

Me and Dellwood unlashed Ida from the stretcher, carried her into the shed, and laid her on the bed. Then we carried Alma in, and laid her and her arms on the floor. Dellwood went for Doc Heyburn. I started a fire in the stove and got some water heating.

When it started to warm up in the shed, I took Ida's white dress off her and the rest. The skin on her legs looked as if it had been burnt and was red and blue and scaly. I unlaced her boots. You could hear the flesh growing right out of the boots. Never smelled anything like it.

So I left her boots on. Was afraid I'd pull her feet off.

I bathed her down, took a cloth and washed her forehead, her lips, her neck. Washed those skinny blue arms. Fingers that were icicles. The hair under her arms. Bathed her breasts, her nipples, her stomach. Washed her woman's hole. Picked her up on the bed so she was sitting up, her face against my shoulder. Washed her back, her butt, washed her legs down to her boots. Washed the boots. I combed Ida's hair out with my brush. Laid her back down. Black curly hair turning grey all around her head, Ida laying on the white pillowcase, an angel in a circle of light – rose-colored light. I covered her with the hide.

Ida Richilieu.

When Dellwood got back he said that Doc Heyburn was out drunk.

Dellwood pulled the covers off Ida. He took one look at Ida's legs. I could see it all over his face.

Dellwood left. When he came back he was carrying a saw.

When my eyes looked at the saw, my mouth told Dellwood to wait. My feet ran over to Dr. Ah Fong's, snow up to my knees, to just up below my knees, heavy wet snow blowing against me in the dark. I rang the bell on his door like I'd done since I could remember. Pretty soon there was a light. I rubbed the wet off the glass, and watched the flame move closer to the window. Dr. Ah Fong put the candle right up to the glass. I put my face so he could see it. He slid the bolt and opened the door.

'Opium,' I said, 'for Ida. She's hurt.'

'Ida hurt? How?' Dr. Ah Fong asked.

'Her legs,' I said. 'She's froze her legs.'

'Floze her regs,' Dr. Ah Fong said. 'Oh, too bad. Floze her regs.'

Dr. Ah Fong closed the door behind me. 'Wait here!' he said, like he'd always said. 'I get opium for Ida's regs.'

He lit the candle on his desk, nothing else on his desk, just the ledger closed, bowed to me, and walked down the hallway, his head a shadow, his feet shuffling. I looked up at the books on the shelves behind the glass, the bottles, the papers with Chinese written on them, things red and dark green, and that blue. There was the chart of the human body with lines to the different parts and in Chinese saying what those parts were.

How many times had I stood there for opium for Ida in the dark? For Ida's cold. For Ida's sore back. For Ida's headache. For Ida's frozen legs.

Dr. Ah Fong walked back through the hallway, the opium in a glass, the glass in a red paper sack folded in three folds.

'Oh,' he said. 'For Ida's flozen regs.'

I gave him the money. He bowed and I bowed. When I got back to the shed, Dellwood had filled every bucket and bowl I had with water. Had a pile of sheets and towels and pieces of cloth. The fire in the stove was hot – the whole shed hot as an oven. He had moved Ida to the table, her legs hanging over the edge. The lariat wrapped around Ida, lashing her to the table. Around both legs, above the knees, he'd tied a piece of cloth, *tourniquets*, he called them.

I snapped the top off the glass bottle and poured the opium onto the red paper. Fashioned the opium into lines with a knife. Rolled up a piece of that red paper and sucked up a line of opium and then blew it up one side of Ida's nose, sucked up some more and blew it into the other side. Took some with my finger and put it on her gums, under her tongue. Opened her mouth and poured some in her mouth. Put some up her ass, in her woman's hole – trying to think how best to get that stuff in her. Rolled some into a cigarette, smoked it myself, blew opium smoke into her mouth, my mouth on her mouth, deep into her. Gave the cigarette to Dellwood. Dellwood blew smoke into her, his mouth on hers.

Dellwood put a stick of kindling into Ida's mouth and told me to put the iron frying pan on the stove. I put the frying pan on the stove and put the washbasin on the floor under Ida's legs.

Dellwood told me to keep Ida's mouth closed over that stick no matter what.

Dellwood Barker stood in the circle of light, the saw in his hand. The hair on his head was just starting to grow back. The gash in his head was bleeding. He was sweating and his eyes weren't looking at anything. I could feel the opium coming on some, I think he could too.

Dellwood put the saw to Ida's left leg first, on the bone just below the knee. He pulled the saw up toward him across her leg, the saw making that sound. Dellwood pushed the saw back down, then stopped, took a breath, then started sawing again. The skin broke and the blood started, then the saw moved into the bone, making a different sound then, more like it was cutting wood. Ida tensed up and started moaning, trying to open her mouth to let the scream out, but I wouldn't let her. Held her chin tight. Blood was spurting up all over onto Dellwood's face, onto the table, onto Ida. You could hear it dripping into the washbasin below.

Good thing Ida was so damn skinny and had such thin bones. Halfway through the bone, the bone snapped and Ida's leg dropped down and was just hanging there by the flesh. Dellwood took his knife out and sliced through the flesh and cut the leg off. He didn't know what to do with the leg, so he laid it in the washbasin. Then he grabbed the frying pan, forgetting how hot it would be. I could smell his flesh burning from where I was. He let out a curse and started crying. I handed him over a piece of towel. He rolled it up, put it around his hand, and picked up the frying pan again. That towel started smoking. Dellwood brought the frying pan to where Ida's leg used to be connected to the rest of her and held it there. Frying meat. Ida bit right through the kindling. Dellwood was still crying, pressing the frying pan against her stump. Ida was thrashing around, screaming. I was afraid she was going to swallow the stick but I couldn't get my fingers into her mouth. She was snapping like a rabid dog. Sounds coming out of her weren't screams.

Dellwood put the frying pan back on the stove, puddles of blood on the stove bubbling up. He was still sobbing and crying hard. He started in on the second leg, but had to stop and vomit. Ida'd gone limp. I figured she was dead so there was no sense in cutting off the other leg. I told Dellwood to stop but my voice was a tiny thing in a very loud room with the frying and the screaming left over and the throwing up and my heart beating and all.

Second leg was harder to get through. Dellwood's hand was burned bad and there must be harder bones in the right leg – wouldn't snap like the first one. Dellwood had to hit the leg hard because he wasn't getting anywhere with the saw. When it snapped, Dellwood cut the skin again and put that leg with the other leg. Then put the towel around his hand again, picked up the frying pan. and smashed it up against her right leg. Ida didn't move. On the floor, the right leg hadn't hit the basin and was laying bleeding with the boot on it, right next to Alma Hatch's arms.

Dellwood took the tourniquets off, wrapped a sheet around each leg, and then put the tourniquets back on again. The sheets turned red. We unlashed Ida from the table and then we carried her to the bed and laid her down, put my hide around her again.

Dellwood went outside and was sick again. My stomach was trying to come out of my mouth too, but I wouldn't let it. I had too much work to do. I poured all the buckets of bloody water out, hauled in more snow for water, and scrubbed. Scrubbed the saw, scrubbed the table, scrubbed the floor, the places on the walls. Ended up just throwing buckets of snow into the shed. This hiss when the snow hit the stove. I didn't know what to do with Ida's legs. Thought about putting them outside where they'd freeze, but a bear or something would get them for sure. So I just left them in the basin.

When Dellwood came back in the shed, he started taking off his clothes. When he took off his shirt, I looked right at his tattoo. He told me to take off my clothes too – to stoke the fire good and take off my clothes.

Dellwood went to the bed and laid down next to Ida. He told me to lay down next to Ida too, on the other side.

Me on the bed, Dellwood on the bed, Ida in between facing Dellwood. Dellwood put his arms and legs around Ida. I did the same.

Ida fit between our necks and knees, just a little bag of bones between us. I could feel her blood on my legs. I pulled the hide over us.

Dellwood closed his eyes and started breathing deep. I closed my eyes too and made myself breathe with Dellwood, me opening up my eyes now and then to see what was going on. The lantern was right above us. The wick was low. Dellwood opened his eyes. His face was right next to mine. He kissed me, his tongue in my mouth, and put his hand on my neck.

'And now, my young Berdache,' he said, slowly humping against Ida, 'we're going to need all the Moves Moves we can get.'

'Ida's between us,' he said. 'We got to take all that we got for each other, all the love, all the love we have for her, and put it into her heart. Healing Ida must be our single intention. Whatever you do, don't ejaculate.'

Then he kissed me again. I kept thinking about sawing bones, and blood, and arms and legs not attached to bodies.

'You got to think straight, Shed, and clear, and only about one thing: healing Ida with your Moves Moves. Get the rest of the shit out of your head or she'll die.'

Then Dellwood kissed Ida deep on her mouth. Saw his tongue push out her cheeks, him still humping against her. I thought about Ida living with no legs and I figured that was better than Ida not living at all.

I pulled my dick up so it was against her, between her legs, next to Dellwood's dick, just below her woman's hole.

'Don't enter her,' he said. 'Put the Moves Moves around her heart.'

'How?' I asked.

'Just do it!' he said.

So I took my Moves Moves and put it around Ida's heart.

Ida shuddered.

'Now make the bleeding stop!' Dellwood told me.

'You too, Ida, make the bleeding stop!' Dellwood said to her.

We laid on the bed together, eyes closed, making Ida's bleeding stop, Dellwood Barker, Ida Richilieu, and me, sweat pouring off us, us with our breathing, with our beating hearts.

I could hear Ida's breath, her heart.

'Now tell the truth!' Dellwood told me.

'About what?' I asked.

'About everything. A story – anything. But you must speak only the truth. Keep your dick hard. Don't come. Put your Moves Moves around her heart. Don't think of anything but healing Ida.

'Tell the truth,' he said. 'I love you,' he said. 'We got all night. Tell it all.'

*

When somebody's waiting for you, things inside of you coming out can take a long time, especially when it's the truth.

Truth was I couldn't think of anything to say.

Through the cracks in the stove, I could see the fire. Snapping pine boughs, rose-colored fire in the stove, making places of fire onto the walls and ceiling.

Under the covers, bodies making fire. Dellwood's dick hard and rubbing smooth just below Ida's woman's hole, my dick beside his, sliding against his, sliding smooth against her wet. You could hear us moving up against each other, us breathing, me and Dellwood breathing.

Ida breathing.

My Moves Moves jumped up and wrapped itself strong around her heart, her beating heart, and held her heart close.

Then, I figured since Ida was breathing, since her heart was beating, Ida'd be listening too. So I opened up my mouth so words could come out. There was language inside me, language for Ida to hear. The truth down deep for her to hear, truth in me deep, truth coming from where everything is, where knowledge is and understanding. Truth in me, everybody's truth – the truth Porcupine had spoken to Owlfeather, when Owlfeather was dying.

'I don't want you to die,' I said to Ida. 'I love you. Ida, you don't have legs and Alma's dead, but I don't want you to die. Dellwood's here and I'm here and we'll always stay with you. We're a family,' I said. 'We stick together. Nothing comes in between. Real as any Mormon family.'

I felt something in Ida move.

A family – that day last September when we all dressed up in the white clothes from Sears and Roebuck, and we were sitting at the table with the red and white checkered tablecloth in the shade where the river looked green and was at its widest. We were on vacation from *barbarism*, from *fucking cowboys and miners and fighting Mormons*. We were putting grace and beauty into our lives with the Italian wine and the food they ate in Europe, and we had told stories.

Alma, Ida, Dellwood, me.

Truth was that day I hadn't told a story. Only thought about if I would, what I'd say. What I would have said, and what I did say out loud then, laying next to Ida Richilieu with no legs out in the shed, humping up my Moves Moves with Dellwood, me telling the truth, was this:

'Oh Great Mystery,' I said. 'If you're the devil, then it's not me telling this story. My name's Out-In-The-Shed. You might know me as Duivichi-un-Dua. You have the knowledge and the understanding of things and we don't. I don't know why we don't, but we don't. Don't know why you won't let us know why. But you won't. I'm not complaining.

'The way I figure it, though, if I keep working on my Moves Moves, I'll make knowledge become understanding up on Not-Really-A-Mountain and die happy. Meanwhile, while we're waiting here, I'd very much like to thank you for making me live. Thank you for me knowing Owlfeather, for him giving me a new life. Thank you for letting me be around loving people like Dellwood Barker and Alma Hatch who talk to animals and the animals talk back. Thank you for Ida Richilieu raising me after my mother died. Maybe it don't look that way, but she did a pretty good job.

'Wherever she is, please give Alma back her arms or give her wings instead.'

When I quit talking, what I heard was Dellwood Barker snoring and Ida Richilieu too – the both of them, snoring away. Thought for a while that it was me snoring, us being so close together in that bed, arms and legs all tangled together as if there was one of us and not three.

But it was not me snoring. You can't snore and think too, not at the same time, that is, so I figured it was them sleeping and snoring and me awake.

Then Dellwood yelled at me in a voice I didn't recognize as his: 'Keep going, Shed! Get your Moves Moves up. Healing Ida is the single intention. Don't ejaculate. Tell the truth.'

Truth was I didn't know how much longer I could keep it up – meaning the truth and being under the sweaty blankets, and humping, and staying hard without ejaculating.

Ida shuddered again – her shudder or mine, I'm not sure – me pressed up against her, hard-on next to her, Dellwood hard too, our balls rolling up against one another's just below Ida's woman's hole. The three of us, one, fucking ourself.

Truth was, I knew Ida had to wake up. She'd always said she couldn't sleep if there was a hard-on in the room.

'There's hard-ons in the room,' I said, and I thought I saw Ida smile, but the light was so low by then it was hard to tell. Was hard to tell what was what, hot and wet and hard to breathe. Hard to tell. Rose-colored fires and shadows in a dark room.

'The truth,' I said out loud – I guess it was out loud.

'Truth is, can you say the truth out loud?

'Ida, you're the one who brought Billy Blizzard here. He fucked me because he was after you. Killed my mother because he wanted to kill you.

'Truth is, I wish he would have killed you instead of my mother.

'You brought the Wisdom Brothers here, Ida. They were casualties of war – your war. Truth is, I wish the ambush had been for you.

'You and your dicks, Ida. You're as crazy with dicks as you say men are. When it came to my dick, truth is, Ida, you looked at my hard-on that first night and saw something you could sell.

'Truth is, for some reason, Ida, you're lying to me about my twin sister.'

Truth was, Moves Moves was coming up big and hot, sweaty, wet. I put my face close to Dellwood's face. He was gone, him and Ida gone on vacation from barbarism.

Those two gone, leaving me here with the truth, alone with saying the truth, the language of it. Out loud the language being more how Alma Hatch howled, more how you feel when you're coming.

'Keep your heart open in hell,' Owlfeather said. Owlfeather was laying next to me on the bed.

'Don't ejaculate,' he said.

'Don't stop!'

'Ida, your skinny bony body. Your sex on you like underthings you put on when it's time to get to work. Sex on you – underthings you take off and put on, wash out and hang up, white sheets without a stain, on the line.

'Truth is, Ida, your body is a business.

'Truth is, how you treat your body is how you treat the world.

'Truth is, Ida, you are Madam Full Charge. You think you're always right and that's just the way you are and you're never going to change. Even when you're wrong, you're right. Winters come in threes – follow the same pattern three years in a row, right, Ida? Well, then, if that's true, where's your legs, Ida?

'I'll tell you where – they're in the washbasin there, froze off from a winter you said wasn't going to happen.

'Truth is, you won't hear any story but your own.

'Truth is, there is no room for anybody else in a life like yours.

'Truth is, you're a latter-day saint. You're as bad as the Mormons you hate.'

Me humping up hard against Ida's bony butt, me wanting to make her see, fuck her til she understood.

'Ida Richilieu. You are woman's hole. Woman's hole is Madam Full Charge is you.

'Woman's hole gives you life. Madam Full Charge takes your life back, makes your life her own. Everything in Madam's life belongs to her.

'You even named me after one of your buildings.

'Truth is, my life is the story of getting my life back.'

Truth was, I was starting to come-not-come. Dellwood's eyes into my left eye, him starting too.

Truth.

Then I knew.

A bayonet through the head.

I had to tell the truth.

'My mother was Princess,' I said to Dellwood, the voice coming out of me, not me. 'Her Indian name was Buffalo Sweets.

'I have the same photograph as you. It's behind the mirror if you want to see.

'The photograph of my mother, your wife.'

Those words, *my mother, your wife*, humping up against my head as I was humping Ida, as Dellwood was humping.

'It is your son's body that you love so well, Dellwood.

'It is the truth,' I said. 'Couldn't you ever tell?'

Me the whole time talking, my eyes looking into Dellwood's left eye, then my eyes seeing the blood drip from the wound on his head, into the corner of Dellwood's mouth. The blood running down his chin. The fire in the stove red under black, that fire the same fire in Dellwood's eyes.

'Shed?' Dellwood said, and that's all, him looking at me, hearing the truth, knowing it.

'You are my father,' I said.

'I am your son.'

That's how most Berdache die, Dellwood said once. *They got their power, too much loving, not enough common sense, and they end up biting off more than they can chew.*

That's the way it had happened for Owlfeather.

That's the way it went for Dellwood Barker too. Not that he ever had any – common sense, that is. Always had plenty of loving, though – too much as it turned out.

Too much, the bite that Dellwood took out of Ida Richilieu that night.

Too much, the bite I took out of him.

I watched Dellwood take the bite. Watched him suck the sickness in Ida out and into him. Watched him swallow darkness.

'I am your son. You are my father,' I said.

'Shed?' Dellwood said.

Moves Moves, Dellwood and me at the same time, Ida in between.

Owl, flying low, gliding through the night sky. Dellwood sucking Ida's sickness into him. The bite too big. His mouth on her mouth, blowing his breath into her.

'You are my father. I am your son,' I said.

'Shed?' Dellwood said.

Part Two

The Diaries

The photograph wasn't behind the mirror. I stood, trying to make my eyes look at behind the mirror, at where her photograph used to be, my bare feet on the cold floor, me hugging my arms around me, breath coming out my nose. Outside, the wind was at the shed, gusting in big through the chinks and cracks.

Don't know how long it took me to get all of myself into one piece out in the shed – how long I stood standing shivering looking behind the mirror. Out the window, all my squinting eyes could see was bright. Could see no things out the window, just hurt on my eyes. Slowly, what my eyes started seeing was the snow.

The firewood was stacked on the floor the way Dellwood Barker did things. My clothes were laid out, too – the winter ones too big for Dellwood, clean and dry. There was coffee, bread, eggs, and smoked trout in the cabinet. My water barrel was full. On the bed, there was a new Hudson Bay and the hide. Not a stain. Not a sign of blood. Not even the smell.

The bright got pink and gold and things were shadows, then one big shadow, no moon at all that night. I ate. Slept like I was dead too. Was surprised that I woke up to another morning.

A bright, clear, cold Excellent day. My feet could walk so I made it over to the barbershop. Had to cover my eyes. When I opened the door, it took me too long to see who was in the barbershop.

'Keep those eyes covered or you're going to lose 'em.' It was Doc Heyburn.

'How's Ida? Where's Dellwood? Where'd they bury Alma?' I asked.

'– 'bout dead – gone – and next to the niggers,' Doc Heyburn said.

When I could see, I didn't see anybody. Just the Doc, drunk as ever.

'Where is everybody?' I asked.

Doc laid himself back in the barber chair. An empty whiskey bottle rolled down onto the floor. Doc looked at the whiskey bottle when he spoke.

'Some of them are burying their dead. The rest are a posse looking for the murderer.'

'Who's dead?' I asked.

'The Reverend Helm and Sheriff Blumenfeld. Found 'em myself, just two days ago, hanging from a tree next to Merrillee's mill down there. Both of them their brains pierced through ear to ear with a bayonet.'

'Dellwood Barker?' I asked.

'Afraid so! Finally went over the edge. Fell in love with the moon, that guy. Crazy as any one man can get. Loony. Outa his mind. Folks saw him late out in the cemetery, howling away, burying somebody. Closer inspection, they found it was Alma Hatch with an extra set of legs. When he was done there, he rode through town naked, freezing cold. Folks locked their doors. Helm and Blumenfeld went after him right off. Next morning I found those two down there hanging, ears bleeding. Dellwood Barker nowhere to be found. Posse was out after him the next morning.

'They almost strung you up, but you looked like you were already dead – or close to it. When they asked me, I told them you were good as dead. But I knew you weren't.'

'How long ago did the posse take off?' I asked.

'Two days ago now,' Doc said, 'about ten of them. They planned to split up – half of them down the main road, the other half over Gold Hill and down.'

Doc Heyburn was still talking when I was out the door. Could still hear him talking at the horse trough, at the dead ponderosa pine.

'Ida Richilieu's in the jailhouse if you want to see her – what's left of her. Wasn't any other place to put her. Wouldn't go anyplace where there was Mormons!

'And get you some of them colored glasses!' Doc Heyburn shouted out the door. 'Those eyes of yours are snow-blind bad. Going to lose them for sure if you don't take care!'

I rang the bell on Dr. Ah Fong's door. I rubbed the wet off the glass, put my face at the window so he could see it. Dr. Ah Fong slid the bolt and opened the door.

'Ida sick. Need opium,' Dr. Ah Fong said when I walked in.

'Yes,' I said.

'How Ida's regs?' he asked.

'Gone,' I said.

'Oh! Too bad,' he said.

'And I need colored glasses for my eyes,' I said.

'No colored grasses,' Dr. Ah Fong said. 'Only grasses for brind man,' he said.

'Give me those then,' I said.

Dr. Ah Fong walked down the hallway, his head a shadow, his feet shuffling. I stood under the chart of the human body. I looked at the human body's legs just below the knee. I looked at the human body's arms. Looked at the ears, between the ears. Looked at the brain. At the eyes.

Dr. Ah Fong walked back through the hallway, carrying the opium in the red paper folded in three folds, and the glasses for a blind man.

'For Ida no regs.' He pointed to the red paper. 'Grasses for brind man.'

I put the glasses on. Dr. Ah Fong's candle was only a smudge of light in the dark.

'You brind man?' Dr. Ah Fong asked. 'Oh! Too bad!'

I gave him the money. Dr. Ah Fong bowed and I bowed. Outside, through the glasses, the snowy world was dark yellow. I walked through the dark yellow to the jailhouse.

Ida was laying in a bed alone in the cell. No sheriff, no doctor, no nurse. Just Ida. She looked more Ida dead than Ida. I walked up real slow and stood at the end of the bed. Took the glasses off. Stood there long enough for the patch of sun through the window to move from the floor onto the side of the bed. Under her knees the covers went down. Her hair was flying out all over the place. I tried to smooth it down, wished for a brush so I could brush it through, so it could lay on the pillow around her head, black and grey curls.

When I touched her head, Ida opened her eyes. She saw that it was me. She smiled a way that made me know we both were going to live.

She began to speak, but I couldn't hear, so I leaned down, and when I did, she put her hand on the back of my neck and pulled me close.

'Shed,' she said, 'don't ever leave me again.'

I said I wouldn't, not ever.

From under the covers, she pulled an envelope. 'Dellwood,' she said, and then she closed her eyes. I put the folded red paper of opium in her hand. Curled her fingers over it.

At the window, I opened the envelope. My eyes could not see at first, but when they did, they saw two photographs of a woman. An Indian woman. The two photographs of my mother. Laid a photograph on each eye.

At Damn Dave's, Killdeer was looking lonely for Abraham Lincoln. Damn Dave helped me saddle Killdeer. Damn Dave wanted to come with me. I told him to stay and take care of Ida. He showed me his drawing of Alma dead. His drawing of Ida's legs. His drawing of Helm and Blumenfeld with the bayonet stuck through their ears. His drawing of Dellwood Barker falling in love with the moon.

I rode over to the shed, rolled up my Hudson Bay and my hide in my bedroll. Coffeepot and a pan, matches. Got all the food. Got the Winchester and all the bullets. Water in the canteen. Put on Dellwood's new winter clothes.

The clothes he had bought for me, so I could go after him.

At the cemetery, on Alma's grave, next to Thord Hurdlika's hands, there was a cross. I got down close. It said *Alma Hatch* on it, *May Nothing Ever Come Between*.

I looked around. At the Reverend Helm's funeral, Blumenfeld's funeral, in the main part of the cemetery, in the Christian part, Mormon folks stood in the sun, so clean, faithful, sure they were right. White people singing to God, burying their preacher and the assistant mayor.

I wondered how Dellwood had laid Ida's legs in Alma's grave. How he'd put Alma's arms in. Wondered how he'd sung and danced. Cried his sore heart out. When I got up on Killdeer, I reached inside my coat pocket. Touched the photographs. Gave Killdeer a nudge, and me and Killdeer started out on the road to Owyhee City – wouldn't be going to Owyhee City, though – just down off the mountains, I'd cut southeast along Kally's River. I figured two and a half days to the Saint Francis of Assisi, a day and a half more to Buffalo Head.

Where Dellwood Barker had gone to die.

*

Me and Killdeer started out on the main road, putting one foot in front of the other. I pulled my hat down and covered my face with the scarf I'd made two holes in, and wore the blind man's glasses. The day was sunny, and through the glasses the world looked the way it looks through a kerosene lamp's dirty chimney. A world of yellow snow.

The first night I stayed at the halfway house. The house was empty and so was the horse shed – the stagecoach not passing through again until spring. The posse had been there not long before me – the snowdrift in front of the door shoveled through, and footprints and horse prints everywhere.

In the horse barn, I unsaddled Killdeer, brushed him down, and tied him in a stall. There was still some hay, so Killdeer got his fill. I laid down in the stall next to Killdeer, but didn't sleep. Before sunrise, I doubled back up the road about a mile. If anybody was after me, they'd be on to me by then. Waited til the sun came up. As far as my sore eyes could tell, there hadn't been a soul on that road since I'd passed over it.

At Kally's River, me and Killdeer waited for the morning fog to lift. About thirty head of deer came out of the foothills. I let them drink their fill, then spurred Killdeer, and we ran into the middle of the deer, the deer scattering, running along the river, crossing the river, me and Killdeer – the tracks of Killdeer – lost in deer tracks, river rocks, and river.

Second day, the sun on the river was hard to take at times, even through the glasses. I could feel my heart beating in the sores in my nose and roof of my mouth. Me and Killdeer stayed right with the river, though, crossing back and forth through the water. The river was never deep, only up to your knees in places. Killdeer never complained. Knew where he was going without me telling him.

Me not for sure where I was going.

Trusting my heart that I knew how to get to Buffalo Head.

By late afternoon, the earth had flattened out, snow drifting against anything that cast a shadow. At a wide, lazy spot in the river, me and Killdeer crossed the river and cut due south. By evening the rolling ground was giving way to the hills with lava rock Indian warriors in them. We camped that night in the good shelter of one of the rocks.

Sagebrush smells like God, Dellwood Barker always said.

Big dark blue cover over you and all those stars. Looking up at the sky, I knew Dellwood was looking up at the sky too.

The third day, I could barely get in the saddle. Every part on my body was complaining from horse. Figured Killdeer felt the same way about me, so I sang all the songs I knew to Killdeer. He seemed to like them, especially Ida's song, the one about the man in the moon.

When we came to the river again, it was near the place where Dellwood and me had stopped after we'd broke out of jail in Owyhee City.

I led Killdeer through the stand of willows, to the deep spot in the river. Showed him where me and Dellwood had first rested.

Then I saw it: the shiny coin on the rock. Saw the sun shining onto the silver coin, pushing light into my left eye, through the blind man's glasses to my left eye.

Dellwood's shiny thank-you coin.

I got off Killdeer then, and asked Killdeer to dance, and we danced, me and the horse, at the side of the river, dancing tybo, dancing Indian, dancing the way horses dance – farting and kicking-up dance, me yelling and saying thank you to things, to everything – to river, to sky, to sun, to snow, to rocks in the river.

I kept my eyes closed most all of that afternoon, the angle of the sun on my closed eyes telling me which direction we were going. Me and Killdeer stayed right with the river most of the time, though, crossing back and forth, going for whole stretches right in the water; that is, unless Killdeer's legs got too cold. Kept thinking about the shine of Dellwood's dime, kept my eyes looking at that shine. Kept going.

When we got to the dogleg in the river, it was about an hour til sunset. I led Killdeer through the tulies to the hot springs. I knelt down, dug through the snow to the sand below the snow, broke the frozen sand, and sifted the sand between my fingers. I took my glasses off, reached over to the cold water of the river, and put the water onto my eyes. Put the good medicine cold water up my nose. Cold water rinsing my mouth. Good medicine cold water on my eyes.

The sky was a smooth red pink, and the snow was too. The hill was a mound of dark against the red pink. The river was inside the dark of the hill – one long shiny ribbon.

At the sandy place by the hot springs, where me and Dellwood had made camp, where we had made the fire – on the snow – was another shiny dime. I picked this dime up and held it. Wanted to open my skin and lay the dime inside, just under, on a place on my arm, or under the skin in the palm of my hand where I could always look down and see, or if eyes couldn't see, could reach to feel.

When the moon started over the hill, I took my clothes off – there were a lot of clothes to take off – and got into the hot springs. The moon was a Dellwood dime, pushing light down onto the ice hanging around the spring – on the tulies and the willows. Icicles on the grass, ice all around each little grass. Figured the moon was made of ice, cold down deep from inside it, cold from hanging up high in the wind.

Sleeping by the red-under-black campfire that night, I dreamed I was on Killdeer and Killdeer was an owl. Me and owl were flying fast just off the ground over valleys, over mountains, over snow, looking for Dellwood Barker.

We found Dellwood Barker camped out on the moon.

Me and Killdeer followed Abraham Lincoln's tracks, followed Metaphor's tracks southeast, past the Saint Francis of Assisi. By afternoon, we were riding into country that sloped up and down – big piles of lava rock sticking up through slopes of snow, only the very tops of mountains.

It started snowing. By the time we got to Dry Creek, we couldn't see Dry Creek because the creekbed was drifted over with snow. The blizzard was all about us, me and Killdeer just taking one step at a time. No tracks to follow. The crooked trail through the lava rocks wasn't a trail at all except that we were following it – in and out and over and down rocks, sometimes on a path no wider than Killdeer, my feet sticking out over the forever blizzard going down, me and Killdeer, one step at a time, closer to Dellwood's shiny coin.

Ida Richilieu told the story once of a cowboy and his horse lost in a blizzard. Neither one of them had any idea where they were when they froze to death. In the spring, when the posse found them, the cowboy and his horse were only ten feet from where they were trying to get.

That's what worried me: getting so close and still being so far away.

That's what kept me going: Dellwood Barker just ten feet away. That shiny dime of Dellwood Barker's only ten more feet. Ten more feet.

Endless white and snow and cold over the dark, snow-crested scab of the Craters of the Moon.

Dellwood Barker our single intention.

Flying.

Ten more feet.

One step at a time.

Killdeer stopped. I pulled the scarf from my face, took the glasses off and, looking up, my sore eyes saw the sky, clear and blue, getting darker blue, the white snow on the world the same blue too, the sun on the horizon one thin slice of orange.

Buffalo Head. Poking up out of the blue-world sky, big and dark, lava rocks piled up by someone big's big hand just so, a tombstone.

'Where he's come to die,' I said.

Killdeer struggled through the last big hill of a snowdrift, snow up to belly, and then we were standing in front of the opening that was the mouth into the inside of Buffalo Head. Me and Killdeer walked into the mouth, out of the snow, and the dark of the snow, inside into black.

Echoes inside all around following us through.

Killdeer snorted. Then next to us was the sound, and smell, the warm body of another horse. Abraham Lincoln.

My own breath and my heart beating. I got off Killdeer and unsaddled him, my fingers clumsy with froze, all the while Killdeer acting like a damn fool for Abraham Lincoln. Abraham Lincoln acting like a damn fool too. Those two just not able to get enough of each other, raring up and all, big whinnies and farts.

Abraham Lincoln was in heat.

They're going to fuck like crazy someday.

Travel cold and weary, Killdeer still rared up and mounted Abraham Lincoln. Abraham Lincoln kicked Killdeer a good one. I jumped out of the way then, figured it best to let those two alone. Poured some oats out for Killdeer.

Killdeer was going to need some oats.

Providence, a sound. I thought it was my breath at first until I listened closer.

The waterfall. Out of the side of the mountain, warm water flowing, just enough water for one man to stand under, him standing in the pool, warm water halfway up to his knees.

Something else too: fire. Through the opening in the cave to the ledge, my eyes saw they could still see – fire, the shiny dime of Dellwood Barker's campfire.

My feet walked me to the opening. Heartbeat. Echoes of heartbeat. I asked please my eyes to see everything clearly, and as soon as possible.

First thing my eyes saw was Metaphor laying by the fire next to Dellwood's bedroll. Thought Metaphor was dead, but he wasn't, was just laying, staring ahead. I bent down and put my hand on him. Metaphor raised his head, yawned and whined, looked over at the horse-fucking sounds from inside the cave, looked up at me, back over to the fire, then laid his head back down again.

My eyes saw Dellwood Barker's clothes in a pile. My eyes saw the full moon rising on the horizon.

My eyes saw Dellwood Barker in the pool, leaning against the rock, under the waterfall.

Full moon on Dellwood's white skin.

Full moon on water.

My ear against his chest. His heart – Dellwood Barker was still alive.

Dellwood's body was more like Ida Richilieu's body. Just bones on him. Skull pushing through his face.

I put my mouth on his, and blew my intention into him – muscles back onto his body, flesh onto his face, the clear green scrutinizing back into his eyes.

'Dellwood,' I said. 'It's me.'

Dellwood opened his eyes.

'You've come,' he whispered.

'Yes,' I said, 'I'm here now. You're going to be all right. I'm going to heal you,' I said.

'I've been waiting for you,' Dellwood said. 'Knowledge has become understanding and I've been waiting for you, so I can dance for you, and tell you the story of my life. When I'm finished, you can take me with you.'

'Dellwood, I am Shed. This is Shed,' I said.

'The buffalo are here. Everything is ready,' Dellwood said.

'Dellwood, listen to me!' I said. 'I am Shed!' I said.

'Moon's full in the eyes,' Dellwood said. 'Good time to go.'

'What can I do?' I said.

'I'm ready when you are,' Dellwood said. 'Where would you like to sit?'

'Dellwood?' I said.

Dellwood stood up, water dripping off him, and stepped his skinny legs out of the pool. Moon was on the back of him, moon on his ass, up his spine. He walked to the fire, fire at his front, and hunkered down. Along his nose, on his chin and cheekbone, his skin reflected the flame. Dellwood put his hand into the fire.

'God, Dellwood, be careful!' I cried.

Dellwood wrapped his fingers around the red embers of a burning log. He stoked the fire with the burning log. Pine-tar snaps, sparks up into darkness, rose-colored stars.

Dellwood Barker started dancing.

I was death and Dellwood Barker was dancing for me.

'Dellwood!' I said. 'I'm Shed,' I said. 'You're going to be all right. I've come here to heal you.'

'Dellwood Barker's human-being story,' Dellwood said, as if he was Homer Wisdom introducing the Wisdom Brothers show.

'I was born in New York City. My father was a teacher of English literature. My mother taught piano.'

Dellwood twirled and jumped and ran. Fire and moon and dark on him.

'I used to sneak into my father's study and watch him. He always had his nose stuck in a book. He only moved when he turned a page. My father called me his errant knight, his little pip, his brave hero.'

Fire on his calves, moon on his dick.

'I don't remember much more about him. I remember that he called me errant knight, little pip, brave hero. I remember that he was a stranger living with me and my mother. I remember promising that, when I had a son, I would never be a stranger to my son.'

Dark in the armpit of him to his thigh. Fire on his chest, Dellwood dancing.

'My mother played the piano and cooked dinner. She was not a stranger. I got what she had – *second sight* on the piano. Never-ending tears in that woman.

'*Grief inside me since the day I was born*, she always said. I remember.

'Whenever she gave me her tit, I'd suck it dry.

'Truth is, what gives birth to a life must sustain it.

'My mother and father were murdered at Robber's Roost. Saw the bullet go into my mother's nose. Saw my father's vest soak red.

'I've killed two men in my life: Sheriff Blumenfeld and the Reverend Josiah Helm – a sheriff, and a preacher. Pushed a bayonet through their heads – same way General O'Connor did to Chief Bear Hunter of the proud Bannock at the Bear River Massacre.

'Truth is, what gives birth to a life must end it.'

Dellwood dancing. Moon dancing on Dellwood, fire.

'Foolish Woman, the Berdache, saved my life from wolves. Put me on a stretcher and dragged me up to Buffalo Head, where he healed me, taught me about Moves Moves, how to heal with Moves Moves, taught me about the Wild Moon Man, taught me how to fuck.

'Taught me: to the extent that I didn't know myself, I didn't know the world. Taught me: the difference between things and the meaning of things. Taught me: I could not understand the meaning of things until I understood who it was that I was who was trying to understand the meaning of things. Taught me: who I was was the story I was telling myself. Taught me: how to scrutinize the story I was telling myself. Taught me: listen to your heart, trust your heart. Taught me: knowledge would become understanding at my death, and that death would have to sit and watch, while I danced and told my human-being story.

'Truth is, Foolish Woman gave me a new life.

'What gives birth to a life must sustain it.

'Truth was, I got myself in trouble. Trouble: started thinking that the world was only me thinking it up.'

Moon on the curve of his back, dark and moon and fire on his feet.

'I met and married Buffalo Sweets – the purest, happiest person I had ever met. She bore the twins, our Moon Bear and Willow. They were strong, beautiful children.

'Whenever I spoke of my wife and children, what I always said was this: I loved them – more than anything – I loved them.

'But that is not the truth. I did not love them. I did not know how to love then.

'They died winter froze in a blizzard – that's the story I heard, that I believed – that Buffalo Sweets had gone to find me, and that she had died, winter froze, with the children.

'Never-ending tears. Then one day I stopped crying. Stopped feeling. Had to.

'What death brings to life must be forgotten.

'I went to the Sage Hill Ranch in Montana. I rode fences, and lived on the plains. At night, my only companion was the moon. Learned moon language and talked to the moon.

'*What's moon language?* folks would ask.

'*Language from the heart*, I would answer.

'But it's not the truth, moon language is not the language from the heart. Moon language is mind language.'

Fire on his butt, moon at his head, Dellwood running to the edge and back, leaping over fire.

'After a couple of years riding the open range, moon language was my only language. Moon language told me it was a fact: the world was only, and nothing else but, how I was thinking it up.

'Moon language my only language, I turned the world into myself. Came in handy – since I was the creator of pain – then I could uncreate it. If everything was my idea, grief was my idea.

'Grief was not a good idea.

'The mind can kill a heart.

'Then once upon a time, one day a big, strapping Indian buck of a beautiful young man came along.

'Out-In-The-Shed, Duivichi-un-Dua, Out-Of-His-Mind, Way-Out-Of-His-Pants. He pulled my head out of my moony ass and put something much better in there. Ran his big hands onto my body and gave me back my body. Gave me his love. Gave me moments of seeing clearly, when seeing was not yet completely clear.

'I'm a stubborn bastard, though. Mostly resisted him. Mostly stayed with moon language. Stayed out of my heart – trusting my heart.

'*It's all a story we're telling ourselves*, I'd say.

'*The body is only solidified mind*, I'd say.

'*Truth is, the world is me*, I'd say. *Shed is me*, I'd say.

'Ida Richilieu, Alma Hatch, Ellen Finton, Damn Dave; Ulysses, Virgil, Blind Jude, Homer Wisdom; Sheriff Blumenfeld, the

Reverend Helm, William B. Merrillee: *They only exist because I do*, I'd say.

'Then, all at once, it happened – the Wisdom Brothers, Ida's Place, Alma Hatch.

'No matter how I scrutinized, wasn't any amount of moon language that could console, that could make me forget, that could bring them back. I couldn't change a thing, couldn't heal a hangnail.

'I no longer had my moon language to hide behind – I was face to face with my grief – my own sickness.'

Dellwood rolled, stretched, bobbed, jumped. Danced Jew, danced Italian, cowboy dancing, Indian.

'The truth,' Dellwood said, '– that's what I told Shed to do. *Tell the truth*, I said.

'You are my father, Shed said. *I am your son.*

'The truth.

'What a fool I've been.

'As soon as I heard those words, I was no longer the story I was telling myself. The world was no longer something I was thinking up.

'I was made flesh the moment that my son, my flesh and blood, announced himself.

'The father and the son. He was not me, he was of me.

'The world was not me, was of me. Was the wall we hang our mirrors on.

'Love cannot be if there's only you and you are only what you think.

'The idea made flesh creates the heart.

'The heart reaches out to the heart of the beloved.

'Knowledge reaches out to understanding.

'You become one.

'Incarnated.

'Love is the bridge.

'Truth is, I am Dellwood Barker. Not the story of him. I am here, fully alive.

'This is Dellwood Barker's human-being story: what I thought I was doing was not what I was doing. Broken-wing trick: what I did was chase after something I already was. What I did was live my life not living it. What I did was what my father did – I became something I promised I'd never be: a stranger to my son.

'What gives birth to a life must sustain it.

'Now, at last, knowledge has become understanding, and the truth is, the truth has broken my heart.'

Dellwood Barker, his back to the fire, fire a red rim all around his body, looked his eyes straight into my left eye.

'I can go now,' he said, then looked his eyes up straight into the left eye of God, the reflected light of the sun, at the moon full in the eyes, the shiny dime, at the cool ball hanging up in the sky, closed his eyes, and fell.

I picked the bones of Dellwood Barker up, the body of him I had known so well, in my arms – his neck, his shoulders, his burnt hand, the tattoo heart on his heart, the hair on his chest growing back, his stomach, his cock, his balls. I carried him to the fire and laid him on his bedroll. I stoked the fire, took my clothes off, Metaphor watching, the horses fucking, laid down next to Dellwood, pulled my bedroll on top of us. Put his head on my shoulder, put my ear against his ear, wrapped my arms around him, pressed my cock against his cock, my legs locked around his legs.

We laid, Dellwood Barker, my father, his heart and tattooed heart to my heart, my breath to his tiny breath, by the fire, in our circle of light, in the great rugged scab of darkness, the Craters of the Moon. The moon, above us, just over the ledge, full in the eyes, full of light, full in darkness filled with stars.

'Dellwood,' I spoke his name, humping my Moves Moves slowly up against him.

'You can see me, if you'll only look,' I said.

'I am not death, Dellwood. I am Shed,' I said.

'You can love your son and know it, know me. You can see me, now, if you'll only look,' I said.

'You can know who I am.'

Moves Moves humping up. Fire spit. Dellwood cradled into me. Killdeer fierce with horse fuck inside Abraham Lincoln, me and Dellwood rolling horseback in the bedroll on the rolling plain. Metaphor a low whine.

Dellwood Barker opened his eyes.

'Shed?' he whispered. 'Is it you? Moon Bear, is it you?'

'Dellwood!' I said. 'Father!'

'My God, you're here,' Dellwood said.

'Shed,' he said, 'knowledge has become understanding. Now I can die.'

'Dellwood, please listen to me,' I said. 'You're not dying. Get your Moves Moves up. Me and you are going to heal you. You got to tell the truth and help me.'

'Truth is, I'm dying,' Dellwood said.

'No,' I said, and I touched his face. 'You're not dying. You can't. We just now started living,' I said.

'Shed,' Dellwood said, the palm of his hand on the hole in my chest. 'Please forgive me,' he said. 'I've been such a fool.'

Forgive.

'But I'm the one,' I said. 'I'm the one who knew.'

Looking into Dellwood's eyes, my left eye into his, Dellwood looking back, was the first time ever Dellwood not just the story of Dellwood, not just the idea or dream of Dellwood. First time, me Shed not just the story of Shed, not just the idea or dream of Shed. Me and Dellwood, us each with our breath, the breath within breath, us each one attending to the moment, first time fully alive.

'I am your father,' Dellwood said.

'I am your son,' I said.

'Feel like a virgin,' Dellwood said.

'First time,' I said.

'How did a son of mine get such a big dick?' he said.

'Must have been the buffalo,' I said, and we laughed. Our fool heads off, us two men one laughing man.

'Shed, look!' Dellwood said, and pointed to the sky.

To the buffalo in the sky.

Buffalo thundering toward us, stampede dust out of the north, millions of buffalo, woolly clouds reflecting moon – proud, fierce, my mother's people before the tybo.

Fingers of light down onto the charging herd, the light of a cool ball all around us, moon and dust all around us, unto everything. Buffalo leaping over, around our circle of light. Horns and hooves, hot breath, eyes red embers under black.

'Special breed,' Dellwood said.

'Most of the time, they're hard to see,' he said.

Dellwood Barker's clear green eyes, a child's eyes – nothing to stop me from falling headlong into. Foreheads together, we looked down at our bodies: sweaty hard-to-hards, man to man, one man, humping up Moves Moves in a buffalo stampede, one laughing man, dancing man.

'My errant knight,' Dellwood said.

'My little pip,' Dellwood said.

'My brave hero.'

Dellwood Barker ejaculated.

Into my left eye, over his tattooed heart, onto his forehead, past his forehead, over the edge, into the night.

Dellwood Barker was quiet. There in my arms he was quiet.

The sound of my heart, my breath.

The buffalo gone, only the moon, the fire in darkness.

Set free.

Without Moves Moves we're nothing.

Story goes that whenever a brave warrior died, his enemy would cut out the warrior's heart and eat the heart.

Dellwood Barker was a brave warrior.

I was not his enemy.

I was his son. He was my father. We were not strangers. We loved each other.

I licked up his Moves Moves. Every drop.

Licked him dry.

Just as I had built a fire bed for my mother, I built a fire bed for my father. Used every stick of wood Dellwood had stacked in the cave. Made the fire bed by lashing the larger of the tree limbs together. What wood I didn't use for the fire bed, I stacked underneath.

Before I lifted Dellwood onto his fire bed, I bathed him in the pool. Water on every part of him. My single intention, my touch on every part of him.

I waited for sunrise. Watched as the dark sky turned navy blue. Watched the full-moon eye fade. Watched the morning get fancy and make things glow.

I turned to the four directions, my arms outstretched, and faced the world. Touched everything in the world before he left. Told everything in the world to attend that Dellwood Barker was leaving.

The flames of his fire bed were highest as the sun broke free of the horizon.

'Sing the jubilee; everybody free. / Welcome, welcome, 'mancipation!'

*

The morning I woke up, Metaphor was laying next to Dellwood's fire bed, frozen.

I saddled up Abraham Lincoln and Killdeer and started riding. No tracks to follow, I rode north and west. Rode with the firewater brandy, rode into the Craters of the Moon. Lava rock, snow and ice, slabs of Indian warriors, wind.

Rode in circles. Kept going. Going where I didn't know. Ten more feet. One step at a time.

I pulled my hat down and covered my face with the scarf I'd made two holes in, and wore the blind man's glasses. Yellow snow – a world of yellow snow.

Mountain peaks growing into other mountain peaks. The crooked trail not a trail at all except that we were following it, sometimes the path no wider than Killdeer and Abraham Lincoln, my feet sticking out over the forever blizzard going down.

Nights by the fire, red-under-black embers at my head, moon at my eyes. I did not close my eyes. Did not open them.

No single intention.

No Dellwood's shiny dime.

My errant knight.

My little pip.

My brave hero.

*

Ida Richilieu hollering was what me and Killdeer and Abraham Lincoln heard – half a mile outside of Excellent. The closer we got to town, the more there was of her cussing and hollering Madam Full Charge.

'This whole town is a damn Mormon disgrace!' Ida yelled. 'You'd think there wasn't a dick or a pussy in it!'

Ida had kept going.

At the stables, Damn Dave threw his arms around me – picked me off the ground, Damn Dog barking, howling, jumping up.

Damn Dave let go of me, though, when he saw Abraham Lincoln, saw no Dellwood Barker in the saddle, no Metaphor.

Damn Dave sat down right there in front of the stable door where we were standing. His body got too heavy for his knees. I sat down too. Damn Dave started crying and Damn Dog howling. I didn't know what to do, but let them cry and howl. Held Damn Dave with one arm and held Damn Dog with the other.

When the two of them finally settled down, Damn Dave blew his nose on his shirt, then took me by the hand into the stables, into his stall where he lived. From his post office boxes he pulled treasures that he'd found in the ashes of Ida's Place – four pearls, a burnt piece of scarf, a string of seven rhinestones, pieces of broken dish, broken glass from the green water bottle in the kitchen, bits of mirror, a gold coin.

Damn Dave took the pearls and the rhinestones, the mirror, and the gold coin, and cupped them into my hand. He showed me some drawings. Took my eyes all morning to make them out: Sheriff Blumenfeld and the Reverend Josiah Helm hanging from a tree, a bayonet stuck through their heads, ear to ear. Alma Hatch's arms. Ida Richilieu's legs in her boots. Thord Hurdlika's hands. Ulysses Wisdom's finger and his gold teeth. Ida Richilieu laying in bed in the jail cell. Me riding out of Excellent on Killdeer wearing the blind man's glasses.

There was another drawing, too – of another severed finger – with a ring on it – not Ulysses' ring, but another ring.

Billy Blizzard's ring.

When I asked Damn Dave how he'd come up with that drawing, he took his bowie knife out of his pocket and made as if he was in a fight, him cutting off the finger of who Damn Dave was fighting.

'Billy Blizzard?' I asked.

Damn Dave nodded his head.

'Where?' I asked. 'When?'

Damn Dave shrugged his shoulders and shook his head.

I wasn't out in the shed for more than an hour when Sheriff Archibald Rooney knocked on the door. When I opened the door, I told him I wasn't open for business but he came in anyway. I was naked wrapped up in Dellwood's blanket and was wearing the pearls and the rhinestones Damn Dave had given me.

Sheriff Rooney asked me all the questions about Dellwood Barker. Told him Dellwood Barker was dead, winter froze out on the Mountain Home desert. Asked me how I'd known where to find him. Told him I just knew. Asked me if I had a hand in killing Sheriff Blumenfeld or the Reverend Helm. Told him no I didn't but wished I did.

Sheriff Rooney told me to watch my ass because he could take me in for questioning, could take me in for pernicious conduct, could take me in for aiding and abetting, could take me in for just about anything he wanted to take me in for.

Intelligent justice in the land.

I asked Open Season Rooney if he knew how to spell *pernicious*.

Sheriff spit in my face. Called me one of those tybo words for men loving men.

I spit back.

Wasn't long after old Open Season left that Doc Heyburn was knocking on my door. I invited the Doc in. The only place to sit was on the bed or on the floor. Doc Heyburn sat on the bed.

'Want some whiskey?' I asked.

Doc shook his head no. 'Haven't had a drink since the last time you saw me – going on four months. I'm reformed. Found Jesus Christ and the Church of Jesus Christ of Latter-day Saints,' he said.

I poured myself a whiskey. The look on Doc's face was the look of someone who was dead and still walking around.

Promised myself right then I'd never quit drinking whiskey if I was going to look like Doc.

'You ain't going to try to save me, are you, Doc?' I asked.

'No, no!' Doc said, sitting on the bed staring at his hands.

'Came to check your eyes out,' Doc said. 'Was worried about your eyes.'

I knew how my eyes were. What they could see wasn't much, and when they did see, it was usually only what they wanted to see – me not ever having much say about what it was they wanted. Never was sure that what was out there was really out there, or just out there because my eyes wanted it that way.

Was in the dark I could see best.

'Sure, Doc,' I said. 'Take a look.'

Doc's hands shaking were big butterflies against my face. He looked in my right eye, then he looked in my left eye – couldn't stand looking in that one too long.

'You're blind,' he said.

'Blind as Blind Jude,' I said.

Then the Doc started making sounds as if he was laughing, but he wasn't laughing. He was crying from someplace deep inside.

'Shed, I'm so sorry,' Doc said. 'You and Dellwood and Ida and Alma – the four of you – have been like a family to me, have been what's of my life that was any good.

'You did the living and I did the watching, and drinking. I think you're a brave, kind, and beautiful man. I miss Alma Hatch terribly. The world without Dellwood Barker I can't imagine. Every day when Ida Richilieu starts screaming at these Mormons, it gives me such strength I can't tell you.'

'But you're a Mormon now,' I said.

'Nothing left to do. Either that or start living,' he said, and laughed.

'Then start living,' I said.

'Too late,' Doc said.

'Too late?' I said.

'Too late,' Doc said, shaking his head.

Doc Heyburn cried some more and when he came up for a breath I asked him, 'He still alive, Doc – Billy Blizzard?'

'Could be. Nobody really knows for sure,' he said. Then he said, 'Is Dellwood dead for sure?'

'Yup,' I said. 'Dead for sure.'

Doc blew his nose big and wiped and put his handkerchief back in his pocket.

It got quiet out in the shed. You could hear Doc breathing and me breathing. I laid my arm across Doc's shoulder. The Doc stood up and went for the door.

'Too late,' Doc said. 'Too late, too late, too late.'

*

'Oh, Mr. Shed,' Dr. Ah Fong said. 'Opium for Ida?'

'Yes,' I said. 'Opium for Ida.'

Dr. Ah Fong lit the candle and walked down the hallway. I stood alone in the room with the picture of the human body. The hands, the legs, the arms, the eyes, the dick, the fingers, the teeth, the woman's hole, the heart of the human body.

Dr. Ah Fong returned with the four small bottles wrapped in red paper.

'Oh! Opium for Ida,' Dr. Ah Fong said.

It was Sunday, so I bought a dish of ice cream – cherry.

Dr. Ah Fong bowed and took the money, gave me the change. I took the change and bowed.

Along with the opium, I brought Ida three bottles of whiskey that I'd bought in Owyhee City, and the new dresses – a white one, a red one, and a blue one. Also, the black diary books with gold-leaf edges that Ida liked to write in, some other gifts, and flowers – the purple flowers that stick up, and the yellow ones, and Indian paintbrush.

There was nobody in the jail, and the door to the jail cell was open.

I pushed on the door and walked into the cell. From what my eyes could tell of the room, Ida had made herself a home. There was a dressing table with mirrors all around, curtains on the window, and the piano.

Ida Richilieu was in the bed, snoring. She looked like something that had gone through the ringer, something the dog had drug in, looked like the devil. Her hair was sticking up all over the place, her two front teeth were missing, and her red lipstick was smeared. The white powder she had on her face, and the thick rouge on her cheeks, could not hide the bone poking through.

I sat down on the edge of the bed. Ida quit snoring, and I could tell she was looking at me, even though her eyes were closed.

'A family,' I said.

'Better than any Mormon family,' she said.

'Nothing ever coming in between,' I said.

'Nothing,' she said. 'Nothing ever again,' she said.

'It was cold this winter, Shed. You ain't going to leave me again, are you?' Ida asked.

'Never going to leave you again,' I said.

Ida took my hand, looked around to see if anyone could hear, and pulled me close to her.

'Shed, the Mormons are up to something,' Ida whispered. 'They're being too frisky for Mormons. Don't know what they're up to, but it's something.'

I gave Ida the opium and the bottles of whiskey. Set the flowers in a vase and put them on her dressing table. Ida put the opium on the tobacco of a cigarette, rolled the cigarette, and we smoked. She took a swig of whiskey and handed me the bottle.

Ida opened the dress boxes, and when she saw the blue dress, she had to put it on. She sat on the edge of the bed, the way you'd sit dangling your legs over if you had legs, and stripped off what she was wearing – what she called her *Mormon drawers*. I helped her into the blue dress that was shiny and slick, taffeta. Carried her over to the dressing table, and sat her on the dressing table chair. Ida rolled and lit another cigarette, and she smoked in front of the mirror, watching herself in the mirror sit next to the flowers, drinking whiskey from a glass.

I brushed her hair, and braided it in the back. Got some water from Hot Creek, washed her face, and Ida put her lips back on red and smooth.

I clasped the string of pearls around her neck. The rhinestone bracelet around her wrist. I laid the feathered boa across her shoulders.

'Oh! The humanity!' Ida said.

The yellow square of sunlight through Ida's window was what I could see best. I kept my eyes on the square as we drank the whiskey, as we smoked, as Ida talked, as I listened.

'That bed's the most uncomfortable rectangle of mattress in the entire western United States,' Ida said. 'And just how's a person supposed to get to the thunder mug with legs like these?'

Ida pulled up the blue dress and showed me her legs. Two fingers of someone big. On the ends of them, where Dellwood Barker had cut, the skin was purple and red.

'Look like fungus growing on a pine tree, don't it?' Ida said.

'All winter I laid here in my own stink,' Ida said. 'Damn Mormons were too damn scared to do anything but drop off food, and a few sticks of wood, and then run out of here.

'I caused such a racket that they finally sent me two old maids from the Relief Society, Sister Irma and Sister Ima.

'Irma and Ima – now just who in their right mind would name

their children Irma and Ima, I'd like to ask,' Ida said. 'No wonder they're old maids. Who's going to fuck somebody called Irma?

'And here I am, Shed, Ida Richilieu,' Ida said, 'eating Mormon food, wearing Mormon clothes, and in the company of old-maid sisters of the Relief Society.

'Nothing more disgusting than old-lady Mormon breath waking you up in the morning, talking about the Lord and His prophet Brigham Young, as they set down some damn awful mush shit in front of you and a piece of hard bread and a cup of hot water they call tea.

'Sister Irma and Sister Ima washing me once a week, wrinkling their lips like that and washing me, keeping the part they aren't washing covered, then leaving the washcloth for me to wash my pussy and asshole with after they leave the room.

'I rub my pussy wet, then rub that washcloth brown every time – then throw the washcloth back at them.

'Never fails – always sends the sisters screaming out of here.

'Lately, though,' Ida said, 'like I told you, there's something going on with those two – with all these Mormons – they're acting too frisky for Mormons. Something's up. I know there is. You mark my words.

'I wrote a letter to the state of Idaho – to the Surveyor's Office in Boise – need to find out the boundaries of my land. Wrote that letter over a month ago. Should be getting a reply soon.

'When we get that letter back, Shed, you and me's going to Boise and buy a chandelier, and we'll build us another Ida's Place – in the same exact spot – bigger and better, and pinker than ever.

'You'll help me, won't you, Shed?' Ida asked. 'Build a new Ida's Place?'

'I'll help you,' I said.

'Then we can get into having some fun again – fuck us some

cowboys, and fight us some Mormons. Put some grace and beauty into our lives. What do you say, Shed?'

When the square of sunlight moved out of the room, I lit the kerosene lamp – the rose-colored light, her dressing table, Ida's feminine things laying all over.

Ida kept on talking – she always could have a right interesting conversation with you, even though you never got to speak a word – her talking about how her hotel was going to be three stories high instead of two, and three porches, front and back. The sign – *Indian Head Hotel* – was going to be bigger, better. The windows, the front door, the chandelier – bigger, better. The ponderosa pine – taller, greener, still alive.

But there were some things Ida Richilieu didn't talk about, didn't say a word about. Didn't say a word about Alma Hatch. Didn't say a word about Dellwood Barker. Not a word about the Wisdom Brothers.

The next day, Ida was still complaining, still talking about what the Mormons were up to, still talking about the letter she was waiting for from the Idaho State Surveyor's Office – so I said to her, 'Let's go for a walk.'

Ida looked at me, then looked at her legs.

'How do you propose we do that?' Ida said. 'You're blind and I ain't got legs below the knee.'

I hadn't thought of that. Then I figured that since we were a family, we could help each other out. Ida could be the eyes and I'd be the legs.

So when me and Ida went walking, this is what we did. I set her on my shoulders, little bag of bones that she was, and she put on her long winter coat over the both of us, me just with my poor eyes poking out in between the buttons, her with her hat on and that red lipstick on her lips, me wearing my spring-thaw boots, and we walked that way, me and Ida, one big tall person down Pine Street across town, past both Mormon churches.

'People gawking their fool heads off,' Ida said, me and Ida laughing so hard sometimes she couldn't see straight and I'd run us into a ditch.

When we passed the Mormon school, a crowd of kids started following me and Ida around, running alongside of us, scared to death with that giant walking through their lives – still loving it though, screaming and laughing, trying to get close but not too close.

'The devil,' Ida said. 'We're the devil,' she said. 'They can't get along without us, Shed. Just look at how these Mormon kids love the devil. Can't help themselves they're so fascinated.'

Then me and Ida started pretending we were the devil. She put some branches in her hair and she painted her lips red extra wide. I started running around, up and down Pine Street acting the devil, Ida with her arms spread out, me and Ida making all the kinds of noises that we could think of.

Wasn't long and there wasn't a child left outside. Weren't any adults either.

'Parents more scared than their kids,' Ida said. 'God bless the devil,' Ida said. 'What would we do without her?' Ida said.

I ran up Pine Street, through Chinatown, then down to Merrillee's mine, where Ida told me to stop. I peeked out through the buttons of the coat. Below us, the men had stopped working and were staring up at us.

'Scared of their own shadow,' Ida said to me. 'Staring at us like death coming to get them.

'Won't be long now,' Ida yelled down to them, 'and I'll be getting my letter from the Idaho State Surveyor's Office, and I'll be building me a whorehouse where you bastards can fuck your little dicks raw. Now there's a society with some relief for you!'

Ida let out a whoop, and I turned on my heel and I ran like the devil out of there. Ran and ran, my feet just going.

Before I knew it, my feet were in the cemetery. Soon as Ida realized we were in the cemetery, what we were doing wasn't fun anymore and she wanted to go back to her jail cell.

Since I was the feet, though, and the feet wanted to go see those graves, that's what we did.

If Ida's eyes didn't want to see, I figured she could close her eyes.

Ulysses, Virgil, Homer, and Blind Jude all laying in a row together.

Ellen Finton and Gracie Hammer.

Thord Hurdlika's hands.

Alma Hatch, *Beloved Friend*, and Ida's legs in with Alma Hatch.

Ida's thighs around my neck. Thought they were going to squeeze my head off. Ida never did like losing control, and there she was with me, her legs, not doing as I was told.

Didn't know how much longer I was going to breathe. But I kept standing, kept pointing Ida at the graves to make her see, make her look at her dead.

I was about ready to go down onto my knees when Ida let up.

Ida started in then, first time I ever seen her cry since the night in the kitchen when I first got back from Fort Lincoln – her crying harder than I think anybody's ever cried, cried as hard as she could laugh or drink or fuck.

Ida climbed off my shoulders when she was done, and the both of us sat at the graves.

'Do you remember anything about coming back to the shed and me and Dellwood?' I asked.

'Nothing,' Ida said.

'You know what he did, don't you?' I asked.

'Dellwood?' she asked.

'Dellwood,' I said.

'Cut my legs off,' she said.

'More than that,' I said, and I started to tell her about the rest of the story, of how Dellwood took her fever into him and him not being able to throw it off.

Ida pushed me away from her.

'Don't want to hear it, Shed,' Ida said. 'There's just certain things that are best left unsaid. So don't say them. I just won't hear it.'

'But Dellwood –,' I said.

'Dellwood is dead,' Ida said. 'So is Alma and the rest of them. Ain't nothing going to bring them back. That's how the cards were dealt. We made some bad choices, we took the wrong turns. Now all we can do is keep our promises, keep clean, and keep going.'

'Ever think the wrong turn was the right turn, Ida?' I asked.

'Nope,' Ida said. 'And you can save me that Dellwood Barker crap. That's one good thing – don't have to listen to that lunatic anymore.'

'You can't mean that,' I said. 'You got to be lying – covering up – same way as you're lying about my twin sister,' I said.

'Yes, yes, like your twin sister,' she said, spitting her words out rattlesnake. 'Like how you asked me once never to mention your mother in front of Dellwood Barker. I never did do that. Kept Alma Hatch from doing it too. And that you have to thank me for, Shed. And you damn well better believe it.'

'You know he's dead, don't you – Dellwood Barker – dead from saving your life!' I said.

Ida Richilieu slapped me hard across the face. She always could pack a wallop.

'Shut up, you, shut up shut up!' Ida screamed. 'You owe me too much to talk to me that way. No way you'll ever know how much you owe me!'

I sat with that slap on my face for a good long while.

'You don't always have to be strong, Ida,' I said.

'Ain't no other way to be,' Ida said.

'What's over is over,' Ida said. 'What's done is done.

'Got to look toward the future now,' Ida said.

I didn't argue with Ida anymore after that, didn't try and make her see.

We never talked about Alma Hatch, Dellwood Barker, the Wisdom Brothers – never talked about the dead – again.

Ida Richilieu was all the family I had left.

And that's just the way she was.

*

What happened next was these two things – same day, right in a row:

Ida Richilieu received her letter from the Idaho State Surveyor's Office.

The Mormons nailed up their poster on the post office door.

Dear Miss Ida Richilieu,

According to our records, the property in question in Excellent, Idaho, where the Indian Head Hotel was formerly located before the fire of July 4, 1905 (Pine Street, Section 5, Lot Number 1, 200ft x 467ft) has never been deeded to a private individual. Said property has always been in the possession of the state of Idaho, until only recently.

The sale of said property to the Church of Jesus Christ of Latter-day Saints for the construction of a new church was finalized on the 25th day of April this year.

On further investigation, our records show that the only property deeded to a Richilieu, Ida, is Pine Street, Section 4a, Lot Number 2, 30ft x 50ft – the lot adjacent to the southern boundary of Section 5, Lot Number 1 and north of Hot Creek.

The Mormons owned Ida's land.

All Ida owned was the land around the shed.

'You got anything to prove you own that land?' I asked Ida.

'Title deed free and clear,' Ida said. 'Burned up with the rest of Ida's Place.'

The poster on the post office door was printed on white paper in straight black letters. That's all I could see.

But I knew what the poster said: more trouble coming in between.

I tore the poster from the door and watched my feet walk across Pine Street to Ida's jail cell.

'Official opening of the William B. Merrillee Refinery,' Ida read. 'William B. Merrillee himself,' Ida read. 'A parade – the marching band from Mountain Home – box social,' Ida read. 'A prayer meeting and picnic at the new church site,' Ida read. 'Sermon preached by William B. Merrillee himself,' Ida read, 'and fireworks – to be held on the Fourth of July.'

That next morning, Mormons began putting up a big orange tent where Ida's Place used to be. Mormons were running around everywhere, putting up signs, cleaning, painting, scrubbing, singing the praises of the Lord, smiling, saying, 'Good morning, Brother So-and-So,' 'Good evening, Sister.'

Strung a sign across Pine Street from the post office to the dead ponderosa pine – big enough for my eyes to read – in gold letters trimmed in green: *Welcome Reverend William B. Merrillee! God Bless our gold mine!*

'I told you them Mormons were up to something,' Ida said. 'Conniving bunch of cutthroat businessmen parading as a religion! No wonder they were so frisky. Only time a Mormon shows any signs of life is when he's buying more property or getting ten percent,' Ida said.

'Adding insult to injury,' Ida said. 'First they get you down and then they kick you!' Ida said. 'But you'll see. They ain't got me beat yet. There's still some tricks up the old girl's sleeve. You'll see,' she said, then, 'Orange!' is what she said, and that's all she kept on saying after that.

Orange!

Ida cussing about orange and never letting up, her sitting in her jail cell, her voice floating out all over Excellent all the while those Mormons putting up their orange tent.

'Ugliest color on God's green earth, orange. Ain't the color of anything natural.

'Should have a *gold* tent! William B. Merrillee didn't have a dream about *oranges*, had a dream about *gold*.'

Didn't matter, though, how much Ida cussed. Wasn't more than two days before that big orange tent was setting right in front of the door to the shed. Sun on it in the mornings and evenings made things look forest fire.

The day William B. Merrillee finally came to town was the same day that Ida Richilieu got to be Peg-Leg Ida. It was Saturday, July fourth, one year to the day that the Wisdom Brothers were killed and Ida's Place had burned to the ground.

Providence, a sound.

When I woke up, I heard music playing. I looked out the window of the shed. All I could see was orange, so I went outside, laid down on the ground, and pulled the orange canvas of the tent up. Inside the tent was the marching band from Mountain Home.

Mountain Home Marching Band in yellow letters on the backs of their shiny green shirts.

I washed my face off in Hot Creek, and by the time I got to Ida's cell, Doc Heyburn was already there with Ida's peg legs and her false teeth.

'Ordered 'em through a catalog,' Doc Heyburn said.

'Sears and Roebuck catalog?' I asked.

'Nope. Was a special medical catalog,' the Doc said. 'Just got back on the stage this morning from Boise. Had to make a special trip to pick them up.'

'What time's the parade start?' Ida asked.

'Supposed to start at eleven o'clock,' I said.

'Doc, can you have these peg legs and these false teeth attached to me by eleven o'clock?' Ida asked.

'Should do,' Doc said.

He was kneeling on the floor, the stubs of Ida Richilieu's legs eye level to him, Ida sitting on the bed in her Mormon drawers.

'I don't like this one bit, Ida,' the Doc said. 'Takes time and practice to walk on these things. Shouldn't do more than walk across the room first off – let alone walk across town like you're planning. Don't like it. These legs of yours are still tender.'

'William B. Merrillee's not the only cock on the walk,' Ida said. 'Ida Richilieu is here too, and she's walking,' Ida said.

'We could put you on Killdeer or Abraham Lincoln outside the jail here and you could ride down to the parade,' I said.

'I'm walking, Shed. Do you hear me? I'm walking through that crowd. I'm walking through my town,' Ida said. 'Now help me get these Mormon drawers off, get me the white dress and the petticoats and the straw hat with the silk ribbon, and when Doc gets done here, help me put them on.'

I braided Ida's hair as she sat at her dressing table, legs pointed out so Doc could attach the peg legs.

Was like saddling a horse. First, Doc shaved Ida's legs halfway up her thigh, then put a layer of soft fabric over the stubs. Pressed the peg legs to the stubs. I held each peg leg tight against Ida's stub, while the Doc tore a long piece of white tape off a roll and started winding the tape onto the peg leg, then onto Ida's leg.

Next came the leather straps attached to the peg legs that fit like a bridle onto Ida's legs. Doc slid the bridle on and tightened the piece at the top. During that part – the tightening-of-the-bridle part – Ida had to hold her legs up in the air, Ida not wearing any underwear.

Doc Heyburn was sweating.

Ida with her legs in the air and the Doc sweating over Ida got me to laughing, then got Ida laughing – then Ida farted because she was laughing and in that position. That got Doc to laughing, too.

'You two are crazy,' Doc said. 'Always have been. And I still don't see how you're going to walk on rocks and mud and dirt, and then there's the boardwalk in front of the post office with all the holes in it.'

'I got help,' Ida said. 'Got you on one side of me, Doc, and Shed on the other. Two big beautiful men like you – what more do I need?'

The false teeth were made of wood and the Doc had to file the teeth down some before they'd fit. Ida opened her mouth wide and the Doc straddled her and pushed the teeth in. Ida's gums bled for a while and you couldn't see what the teeth looked like for the blood.

When she finally stopped bleeding, Ida smiled for us.

She looked like she had two white pieces of board stuck between her teeth.

I helped Ida put the white dress on, and the pearls and the feathered boa and her brimmed straw hat with the silk ribbon.

Ida took a deep breath, pushed herself up off the bed, and for the first time, Ida stood up on her peg legs. She tottered around at first, but wouldn't accept a hand.

All decked out, Ida looked terrible, but there was something about her that just made you feel good.

'What time is it?' Ida asked.

'Ten-thirty,' the Doc said.

'You got the chairs set up by the steps?' Ida asked me.

'Yup,' I said.

'Well, then, let's start the show,' Ida said, and took a hold of my arm, and Doc Heyburn's arm, and the three of us walked out of the jail cell, into the sunny day, Ida walking stiff, just putting one peg leg in front of the other, one step at a time, holding her head high, one single intention.

Hardly recognized the town. Everybody was all dressed up and walking around lively and smiling. You could smell food cooking everywhere. Apple pies, pumpkin pies, rhubarb pies, turkey and stuffing, sweet potatoes and squash, potatoes and gravy. Elk roasts and you name it.

Ida cleared a path through the crowd.

Everywhere you looked, somebody was talking to somebody else about her. Gentlemen tipped their hats. Women averted their eyes, but sooner or later, they stared. Stopped dead in their tracks, and stared.

The sun was shining through Ida's straw hat. Could have been the condition of my eyes, but I think not. Ida the most beautiful ever. Rose-colored sun on the skin of her face, on the skin of her skinny arms, her neck. Ida all in white, a virgin, smooth and cool as a swimming hole in August.

The grace and the beauty in my life.

Glorious, Ida Richilieu – gone from a skinny old crippled dame, boards for teeth, to what I saw beside me.

A woman's got her pride.

We walked down Pine Street, walked past the post office, the American flag, past where Billy Blizzard had shot his horse, where Damn Dave stood with his dick out laughing, the humps going through him, past where the Wisdom Brothers had first drove their wagon and the mule into town, past the horse trough where Ellen Finton and Gracie Hammer had died, walked past Stein's Mercantile, North's Grocery.

Ida, the parade.

We walked to where Ida had told me to set the chairs – by the wooden steps in front of Ida's Place – three chairs, just under the dead ponderosa. Ida sat in the middle, me on one side, Doc Heyburn on the other, her peg legs folded in, under her dress.

One thin red line of blood flowing out from beneath Ida's skirts.

I handed the bottle to Ida. She took a long swig, wiped her mouth, kept on smiling.

When I offered the bottle to Doc Heyburn, he fell off his Mormon wagon and took a swig too. Then another.

Parade didn't start til twelve-thirty, and began at one end of Pine Street and ended at the other. Never seen so many people all together in Excellent, Idaho. Everybody scrubbed up like Sunday. Clean tybos everywhere.

Even old Open Season Rooney was in town. Ida told me he was looking my way, giving me the scrutinizing eye. I waved to where Ida said the sheriff was and blew him a big kiss from across Pine Street.

When the parade went by, first there was the marching band playing one of those American songs, then a wagon full of people waving.

'William B. Merrillee's in that wagon, I'll bet,' Ida said, looking her eyes at me, looking the other way. I squinted my eyes but couldn't see.

Then there were children walking together singing, and a couple cowboys on horses.

That was the parade. Since it didn't last that long they doubled back through Chinatown and then down to Pine Street again and went through town again.

After that, everybody went into the orange tent and stayed in the orange tent all day.

'You call that a parade?' Ida said. 'Seen better funerals.'

By the time me and Doc took Ida back to the jail cell, we were all drunk. Doc Heyburn fell in the creek, and I ran into a building I didn't see. Good thing we had Ida with us, or we never would have made it back.

When I woke up that afternoon, the Mormons were still in the orange tent singing. I was on Ida's bed with the Doc – the Doc still gone to the world.

Ida was sitting at her dressing table, still in her white dress and hat, and peg legs and teeth. She was looking in the mirror watching herself drink whiskey from a glass, watching herself smoke.

'I really thought you were beautiful this afternoon,' I said to her.

'Oh! The humanity, Shed,' Ida said. 'You need your eyes checked.'

I walked up the river, to the nest, jumped off the big rock, into the clear green blue. Nothing better for a hangover. Swam through the clear green blue. My eyes: underwater world not much different from above-water world. Light moving in darkness. Stood shivering in the sun.

When I came back into town, the Mormons were still in the orange tent. Wondered what this William B. Merrillee had to say about God, so I walked up to the orange tent, but I couldn't hear anything.

Walked in the orange tent.

Hotter than the hubs of hell in that orange. There was a man up on the stage talking.

'That William B. Merrillee?' I asked a man standing by the door.

He nodded his head yes and put his finger to his lips.

As far as my squinting eyes could tell, William B. Merrillee was a big man with a beard. He was wearing a suit and talking about I didn't know what – mumbling about prophets and priesthood. Soon as he said *sin, hell, everlasting damnation, and fire*, though, a chill went through my body – toenail to head hair – and before I knew it, my feet were walking out of the orange tent, and the rest of my body following.

It was after sunset that the singing stopped. The Mormon families moved outside of the orange tent and sat down at the tables, kerosene lamp on each table, food served up, smelling good all the way to Gold Bar.

I asked Ida if she wanted me to cook up something for supper, but Ida didn't want supper.

'Opium,' Ida said.

Just as I walked out the door, Ida called me through the window.

'You and me's going to Boise City tomorrow on the stage,' Ida said. 'We're going to talk to the governor himself about these Mormons stealing my land, and we ain't leaving his office until we see some intelligent justice, and I get my land back.'

I got the opium from Dr. Ah Fong, and was on my way back to Ida, when the food smell from the Mormon's picnic took hold of my nose.

The Mountain Home Marching Band in their gold and green shirts were putting their horns and drums away so they could eat. The sun was down and the moon was up, getting full.

Full in the balls in July.

The tables were set all around inside and outside the tent, bugs flying around the kerosene lamps, and families eating supper. The night was warm, and you could hear kids playing and people talking, hundreds of people sitting around, eating and talking.

Made me want to be Mormon again.

But then I heard Ida's piano and Ida singing her song, floating out over the evening – Mormon folks sitting together at tables –

no different from any other folks, human beings, scrubbed up Sunday best in their circles of light, with their wives, their husbands, their children, brothers and sisters, cousins, uncles, aunts, grandparents, mothers, fathers; their food, their family, their religion, in the twilight.

Come take a trip in my airship and we'll visit the man in the moon.

My eyes didn't need to see the look on their faces: Ida Richilieu wasn't just a whore to them. She was a woman alone, childless at the time of day when we're all alone the most, when we reach out to touch, to hold our someone else before the night.

Ida Richilieu wasn't just a whore.

She was their darkness.

Takes darkness to see light.

My feet walked away from town, down Pine Street, walking to where the moon got brighter, Ida's song my single intention.

I was somewhere around William B. Merrillee's mill, when my eyes saw trouble coming in between – a man walking toward me in the moonlight. First thing I thought was devil.

Then I saw the flash of knife.

I dived to the ground and rolled, got myself on my feet again, asking my eyes to see, my ears to hear.

The man lit a match and put the match up to his face. I scrutinized. Then Damn Dog came running up to me and jumped up.

'Damn Dave, what the hell you doing?' I asked.

Damn Dave lit another match. His face was bruised and there was blood on his shirt. His lips were moving wild. He struck another match and Damn Dave showed me his open hand.

In his hand was the finger of a human being. There was a ring on the finger. Damn Dave lit another match. He brought the finger and the ring up close to my eyes.

I had seen the ring before.

Damn Dave moved his mouth and actual words came out. What his words said was this: 'Billy Blizzard.'

I ran through moonlight, through moon getting full in the balls, through darkness, to the circles of kerosene lights on the tables, through the Mountain Home Marching Band playing polkas, women dancing with women, men with men.

Providence, a sound.

Fireworks exploding all around me.

I ran past the orange tent, past the shed, over Hot Creek, up to Ida's window.

Through the window what my eyes could see was his bandaged hand. Saw Ida's peg legs in the air, white dress rucked up, pulled back, him humping into her.

Next breath I was inside the jail cell. I knew as I grabbed him, he was ejaculating. Grabbed him by the hair. Pulled him back. Put my face up to his face, forehead to forehead. Put both my eyes into his left eye.

What I saw my eyes couldn't believe what they saw.

It was Billy Blizzard.

It was the devil.

Billy Blizzard was a big man, big as me. So when he hit me, my body went flying onto the piano, piano making Dellwood Barker music. Billy Blizzard threw the rose-colored light and hit me in the head. Breaking glass and kerosene. I waited for fire. He was back to humping into Ida.

'Sin, hell, everlasting damnation and fire,' Billy Blizzard was saying.

I went for him again, but stumbled over something. It was Doc Heyburn. Couldn't tell if he was dead or dead drunk.

I picked up Ida's dressing table chair, lifted it high, and brought the chair down hard as I knew how onto Billy Blizzard's head. Broke the chair.

Billy Blizzard turned and looked at me before he fell.

I ran over to Ida. Saw that her hands were lashed to the bedstead. I started to undo the rope around her hands, but saw that her mouth was stuffed with feathered boa. I pulled the feathers from her mouth. She started coughing. I undid the ropes and Ida slapped me hard and bit my hand, thinking I was him.

'Ida, it's me, Shed,' I was yelling at her, holding her down.

'It's me – Shed – Ida, Ida, don't you know who I am?'

Billy Blizzard stuck the knife in the back of my leg. I turned in time to see the blade flash again – rolled out of the way, and the blade stuck into one of Ida's peg legs. Billy Blizzard was at the knife, trying to pull blade out of wood. I hit him full force. He fell back into the mirror and broke the mirror. I jumped on Billy Blizzard, beating him with my fists. He brought his legs up from behind, and crossed his legs in front of my face and pulled me back. Billy Blizzard hit me then the way I'd been hitting him. Then he was kicking me. I grabbed his foot and twisted him down. We rolled around grunting, breath and heartbeat. Darkness, no light. I stood up, didn't know where I was. Then it was the Doc standing in front of me, holding the knife out to me. Billy Blizzard hit Doc from behind with a chair leg and Doc went down.

Billy Blizzard lunged at me. I dodged, came around from the back of him, swinging the knife. Billy Blizzard grabbed my hand, the knife only inches from his heart.

My chest against Billy Blizzard's back, my arms around him, my mouth at his ear, his sweat and mine, my loins pressed into his butt, my hand around the knife, Billy Blizzard's hand around my hand around the knife. My single intention, knife into his heart. His single intention, knife away from his heart, knife into mine.

A blast of light against Billy Blizzard, forcing him into me, feet off the floor both of us flying through the air, hard against the wall. Pain in the hand that held the knife to Billy Blizzard's heart.

Ida's shotgun.

I hit the floor, Billy Blizzard's body landing on top of me, sinking down onto me, blood-sopped and heavy dead. Only darkness and shotgun blast.

Set free.

Without Moves Moves we're nothing.

Slowly, what my ears heard was Ida crying and the Mountain Home Marching Band playing the American song you had to stand up for.

Once again, the smell of blood in a tiny room.

I lit a kerosene lamp from the other cell. Brought it up close to Ida. Her white dress was fanned out around her black triangle, her woman's hole open and wet, legs spread as if she was giving birth, drops of his Moves Moves, blood, sweat on her, the peg legs hanging cockeyed by straps of leather. Ida belly-sobbing, her hands clutching the shotgun to her. False teeth crooked in her mouth, snot rolling out her nose, Ida staring straight ahead, at the ceiling, at nothing.

I slowly took the shotgun from her hands. I put my heart onto Ida's heart, breath to her breath, oh the humanity in my arms. Leaned hard on her, put my cock into Ida Richilieu, into the emptiness Billy Blizzard had left. Put light into darkness, Moves Moves into Ida Richilieu, into her woman's hole.

*

Story goes, the next morning, Sunday morning, standing on the stage in the orange tent, Sheriff Open Season Rooney announced to the congregation that the night before, the Reverend William

B. Merrillee had been shotgunned to death by Ida Richilieu and her half-breed in the jailhouse.

Newspapers in Boise City and Pocatello and as far south as Salt Lake City were telling the story too: *Peg-Leg Ida Kills Mormon Leader. Peg-Leg Ida and Half-Breed Shotgun Mormon Prophet. Peg-Leg Ida Held in Custody. Peg-Leg Ida and Half-Breed's Trial Set for Spring.*

That's just how people are. They just got to talk. You can't stop people from talking. They talk and pretty soon you got a story.

Nobody listened to my story.

Damn Dave's either.

Ida wasn't talking, was still staring at the ceiling.

The Doc was too drunk. Wasn't until a week later that the Doc got around to speaking.

Ida Richilieu never went to trial, though.

Health problems, the Boise newspaper said.

Truth was, Ida Richilieu was pregnant.

Sheriff Open Season Archibald Rooney, him being the county sheriff and him having a bunch of irate Latter-day Saints after him, arrested me for the murder of William B. Merrillee, but there wasn't enough evidence against me. Doc Heyburn had seen it all, and once Doc Heyburn was sober enough to tell the story of seeing it all, the sheriff had to let me go.

I spit in his face.

Sheriff Rooney grabbed my bum hand and squeezed it and told me to watch my ass because sooner or later he was going to put my ass behind bars for good.

'For pernicious conduct,' he said. 'For obstruction of justice, for just about anything I want to take you in for,' he said.

That sheriff's still trying to get my ass behind bars.

Still hasn't done it.

Ida never did talk again until the day before she died. Everything else was the same, though, with me and Ida – we still drank whiskey together and smoked locoweed. I still got opium for her. Her appetite was good. Sometimes I'd carry her up to the hot springs, especially at night when the moon wouldn't let us sleep and all there was was breathing and heartbeat. Mostly what Ida did, though, was lay on her bed, stare at the ceiling, and let her belly get bigger and bigger.

I talked to her all the time. Never talked so much in my life as I did when Ida Richilieu was pregnant. Talked to her and the child in her.

My child. Billy Blizzard's child.

Didn't matter to me that she didn't talk back, although I missed her cussing and yelling and complaining all the time, but I figured Ida Richilieu had done enough talking in her life. Figured she was working out some problem she hadn't reckoned on, and needed to shut up to do it.

One night, looking through her window, watching Ida Richilieu in her circle of light staring at the blank page I'd set in front of her, all of a sudden I understood.

Ida Richilieu had fallen into the place inside her where everything is. Same place I was after Charles Smith's bullet. Wasn't one place she could point to and say, *There I am, that's me*.

Looking for where she was was where she was.

On April first, Ida Richilieu gave birth to twins: a boy and a girl.

Me and Damn Dave helped Doc help Ida with the delivery, us bringing life into the world – the smell of blood and life in a tiny room.

Ida in her circle of light, a baby on each nipple.

It was one of those perfect days in the Idaho mountains in summer when the air is so that you can't tell where your body stops and the world begins. It was morning and the sun was done making things fancy. Shadows were growing. Not-Really-A-Mountain was big and sandstone shiny up against a blue sky. A white bird way up, flying.

You could hear the river, it was that quiet. Things smelled of woodsmoke, pine forest, frying eggs, side meat, and coffee.

I was sitting in a patch of sun by the jailhouse door, drinking my coffee.

'Shed,' I heard. It was Ida.

I walked in the jail cell. The babies were nursing. My eyes knew Ida was looking at me the way she used to look at me before she'd fallen inside. I expected her to cuss me out, or tell me to get her some opium, or *Hey you, come over here, boy*.

'Shed, I want you to burn the diaries,' she said the way she said things, so I wouldn't argue.

Still, I argued.

'Burn 'em,' she said.

I made a bonfire just outside the window so she could see. I threw the books on the fire and Doc Heyburn, from under where Ida couldn't see, would pull the books from the bonfire.

Just about every human being in the state of Idaho, and parts of Montana and Utah, two women from Wyoming, and a reporter from San Francisco were at Ida's funeral.

A Jewish rabbi came from Boise City to bury her. Nobody would give him a place to stay, and since Excellent didn't have a hotel any longer, the rabbi stayed with me, out in the shed.

Folks looked at him like some kind of lunatic when he started in on that language at the grave. The grave being in Ida Richilieu's part of the cemetery, next to *Beloved Friend* Alma Hatch and Ida's legs.

Ida wore the blue dress, the feathered boa, the pearls, and the rhinestones. I braided her hair.

After me and Damn Dave finally got the babies to sleep, we started drinking. Damn Dave got a hard-on and started laughing, so Damn Dog started howling – the Doc laughing, and then I couldn't help it – was just too excruciating – me laughing, all of us, our fool heads off.

Doc was the one who picked up one of Ida's diaries from the pile and started reading out loud. It was the diary of Ida's first winter at Ida's Place. As Doc was reading, I could see Ida sitting in her rose-colored room in her circle of light writing.

Ida's lie. I had no idea. Oh! The humanity, just no idea:

December 23, 1885. This morning I found an Indian woman huddled under the front steps. She had two babies wrapped up in a scarf. I got her up to room 11. The children had froze to death. The woman was delirious with pain and grief for her beloved children! I gave her some whiskey and she rested. Later on that afternoon, I sat with her on the bed and we talked. She speaks good English. Raised and educated by Mormons. I rolled some opium into a cigarette and we smoked it. Soon she was asleep. I don't know what my next step will be with her. Perhaps she can work here for me.

December 24, 1885. Christmas Eve. I dressed up like Saint Nicholas tonight. Didn't need no pillows to make me fat! Ellen Finton made up an eggnog. The bar was merry. The Indian woman – she says her name is Buffalo Sweets – was greatly and understandably depressed by the deaths of her children. She held her hand on my belly and felt the child growing in me. She wept so hard it was hard to maintain my composure.

December 25, 1885. I am due very soon. The child has dropped and is riding low. I'm sure he is a boy. Merry Christmas, Happy Chanukah.

December 26, 1885. I told Buffalo Sweets the story of my child tonight. There are certain things one does not talk about with other people — certain things that are private — but tonight I felt so close and loving to this woman that I told her the truth. The father — I'm absolutely sure it's him — is only a boy, hardly fourteen, but such a rugged and beautiful male I've never seen. His name is Billy and I must say has a terrible reputation following him of being a scoundrel. One day this young man walked in here, I was wearing the blue dress, and I took one look at him and I do believe it was love. Tonight Buffalo Sweets — I've decided to call her Princess because she is such a royal young woman — tonight Princess gave me an Indian name for my child. She wrote it down for me. It's Duivichi-un-Dua, which she says means 'the boy child of a boy father.' I think it's a wonderful name.

December 31, 1885. I have given birth to a boy child.

January 4, 1886. Princess and I have decided. She will take the child. Billy, the father, has been here several times threatening to murder me and the child if I do not marry him. Marriage is out of the question.

Princess and I have decided on this story: My child was stillborn. Princess was found out in the cold with twins, one of whom — the girl — died, and the boy lived.

Princess has promised to stay with me until the boy is grown. I shall assist in the upbringing and education of the boy. But he is, to all the world, Princess's child.

I shall never speak of this again and Princess is also sworn to secrecy. We have made our solemn oaths. This is the only record, which shall be kept under lock and key and burned unread at my death.

Epilogue

I named the twins Moon Bear and Willow.

The three of us, Moon Bear, Willow, and me, stayed on in Excellent out in the shed through the winter. The Doc kept an eye out on the twins too, and so did Damn Dave. The Doc and Damn Dave were always fussing over those kids. Damn Dave bought a jersey cow and a nanny goat and put them in his stable and milked them morning and night and brought the milk over for Moon Bear and Willow, along with some kind of treasure. The Doc was always checking their temperature and weight and length – checking their eyes and ears, and bowel movements. I was always telling Damn Dave and the Doc they were spoiling those kids and to just let them be, but I wasn't any better.

What gives birth to a life must sustain it.

Wasn't long before stories of the twins got around the valley – I mean legends. Everybody said so, even the Mormons said so – that those two children were the sweetest, most beautiful children ever born in these parts.

Something mysterious about how beautiful and how sweet they were.

If I may say so myself.

The twins being half Ida and half something else – either Billy Blizzard or me.

Billy Blizzard being my father, Ida my mother, the twins my children, or my brother and sister, or one of each.

One night, me and the Doc and Damn Dave gave the twins the test.

First, we laid Willow down on the bed and put the feather and the bow on one side of her and the basket and the gourd on the other.

Willow laid on the bed for a while and reached for the feather and the bow.

Next, we laid Moon Bear on the bed and put the feather and the bow on one side of him and the basket and the gourd on the other.

Moon Bear laid on the bed for a while then reached for the basket and the gourd.

Both of them – Moon Bear and Willow – out in the shed. Basket-man. Bow-woman.

We left Excellent, though – had to – in the spring. Sheriff Open Season Rooney got a court order from Boise City to put Moon Bear and Willow into good Christian homes – good Mormon homes was more like it – or in one of those Catholic schools where the kids all stand in line waiting to kick the ball with the Pillow Women looking at them all the time.

The night before Sheriff Open Season Rooney got to town with his posse to take the twins away, I had a dream – guess it was a dream. Hard to tell these days.

Owlfeather was sitting on my bed, laughing at a dirty joke, and woke me up. Told me to get those twins and get my ass out of town fast.

Moon was full in the knees when we left. The Doc and Damn Dave cried their fool heads off. Could hear Damn Dog howling all the way down the mountain.

The Shoshone and the Bannock weren't my mother's people anymore, but I still went to Fort Lincoln.

The three of us – Moon Bear, Willow, and me – were all part Indian because of, story goes, our grandfather – or great-grandfather – Big Foot – but hard to say what part. We were still half tybo – the Jewish part – and part tutybo too, like the Wisdom Brothers.

Part everything.

Porcupine and Bowler Hat and American Flag and Hazel loved the twins every bit as much – even though we weren't as Indian as we once thought we were. Porcupine and Bowler Hat and American Flag and Hazel were always telling stories about the twins – how mysterious they were, how smart, how beautiful. Everybody on the reservation still says so.

One day, on the reservation, Sheriff Open Season Rooney surprised us all with his posse and a warrant for my arrest.

Kidnapping.

I grabbed Moon Bear and Willow and ran to inside the square house with half a window just because there wasn't any other place to run. Porcupine and Bowler Hat and American Flag and Hazel fought tooth and nail with the sheriff's posse, but as always, Indians were no match for the American army.

Sheriff Open Season Rooney walked in the square house with a half window all puffed up with victory, ready to throttle me and take the twins. I was going to die first.

The sheriff walked right up to me, as if I wasn't even there in front of his eyes. I hauled off and landed a fist right above his nose. Knocked him out cold. The rest of the posse came running in the house then and they couldn't see me, or the twins either. Walked around the square house, walked right next to us, as if they were blind. I hit a couple of them over the head just to see. Not one of them could tell from where they'd been hit.

Then I got smart and started goosing them, pulling their pants down. That got them out of there in no time – jumped on their horses, threw Open Season over the saddle of his horse, and took off running, all of them tybos hooting with Injun spooks.

Owlfeather was laughing his fool head off.

All those years of thinking I couldn't be seen – paid off in the end.

Now, we travel that way all the time – Moon Bear, Willow, and me – being seen or not being seen according to how we choose. Twins are even better at it than me.

Sometimes, I have to look all over this Mother Earth before I can find hide or hair of them. Then, all of a sudden, there they'll be sitting next to me in my meadow up on Not-Really-A-Mountain, or on the steps of the square house with half a window on the reservation, or on the ledge of Buffalo Head, or out in the shed in Excellent.

Sometimes, when we're out riding around free, no reservation, no fences, digging camas root, gathering pine nuts, hunting the four leggeds, or spearing salmon in clear fresh cold water – after looking for the twins all day – out of nowhere those two will come running up from behind me and give me a goose, or step out from the shadow of a tree, scaring the wits out of me, me clutching my heart, breath in and out, cussing them, yelling, *Hey you, come over here, boy. Hey you, girl, come over here.*

It's a game with them. The twins call it killdeer.

Suppertime's the worst, or when I'm after them to sit down in their circle of light and do their reading and writing, or when it's time to take a bath – soon as I go looking for them they disappear and I'm left standing, scratching my head, wondering if they're really gone or I'm just blind. Hard to tell these days which one is which.

Only way to get them back is to quit running after them.

*

Sometimes, though, at night, full moon, I sit by the campfire and watch Moon Bear and Willow sleep, or I tiptoe into the shed and bring the circle of rose-colored light next to them sleeping, my breath in and out, my heart beating, my eyes weeping again all the old tears.

Dellwood Barker, not my father, lost in his mind, the man I loved most ever, died, his heart broken from the shock of love when he saw the wall he'd hung his mirror on – the world out there – saw someone loving him in it.

Ida Richilieu, my mother, lost in her heart, the woman I loved most ever, died, her mind broken from keeping secret, keeping promises, keeping private, keeping herself together while she kept going, playing her hand out, the deck of cards stacked against her.

Dellwood dying because he thought he was the world, Ida dying because she thought she wasn't.

Truth is, the both of them – Dellwood Barker and Ida Richilieu – died because they were Madam Full Charge. Neither one of them could hear any story but their own.

Truth is, there's no room for anybody else in a life like that.

Same story with Buffalo Sweets, Princess – not my mother – most of the time there wasn't room enough in her to take me with her.

Then there was my father, Billy Blizzard, lost in his mind, lost in his heart, the man I hated most ever, died eternal damnation and fire, lost in hell.

Now that I know who I am, though – this mother's son, that father's son – having this name or that name – truth is, doesn't really matter anymore. If you run after that damn killdeer bird long enough, it always leads you back home.

All the years, me yearning big for I didn't know what – the mystery, the secret – that part of myself that had always been missing – isn't anymore.

Knowledge becoming understanding: what had been missing was my own loving company.

Since the day the twins were born, from that day on, I've never been alone again. I have those two children – but more important, I have myself – the loving company of myself.

What the loving company of yourself is, is forgiveness, is the Great Mystery, is God. Before God can forgive, you must forgive.

God, the moment my son, my daughter, my brother, my sister, my flesh and blood, announced themselves.

God, the twins birthing out of woman's hole, me birthing too. Free of woman's hole. No longer me and not me. Now, it's me and myself, and of myself, the twins.

Telling this story is what I'm doing – learning to tell the story. Me, the one who has lived – the brave hero. Being the hero, though, isn't just telling the story. Hero's the one who, by telling the story, forgives the story – forgives the devil – himself, herself – for the darkness it took to see light.

*

I put my blue dress on, put the feathered boa on, and the pearls and the rhinestone bracelet. Paint my lips on red. I walk down Pine Street to the Solo Lounge with the neon blue moon in the window. Solo Lounge right down the street from the big brick Third Ward Mormon Church, where Ida's Place used to be, the haunted church nobody sets foot in. I sit down on one of the high stools at the bar, cross my legs, and adjust the stockings – Ida and Alma would have loved these stockings – I order a round of drinks for the bar, whiskey for me. The men at the bar all look around. The women at the bar look around. If they're new to the bar, they'll whistle or say something about the faggot. Sooner or later, one of them will slip out, run to the telephone in the post office, and call up Sheriff Open Season Rooney and tell the sheriff that The Man Who Fell In Love With The Moon is back in town, expecting to get the one-hundred-dollar reward for my arrest.

That crotchety old bastard Open Season Rooney is still getting reelected. Republican. I swear some things never change. Still no intelligent law in the land. Getting worse.

That's what they call me: The Man Who Fell In Love With The Moon.

I'm not worried about old Open Season, though – still know how not to be seen when I don't want to be seen. Besides, the sheriff's pickup takes him half a day to get him here to Excellent.

After the first round of drinks, I order another round. I open the purse, bring out the piece of mirror that used to be part of Ida's mirror, and watch myself retouch the red on my lips.

'Tell us the story,' someone says. 'Tell us the story about the man who fell in love with the moon.'

I don't turn around. Don't look at them. I look into the piece of mirror and watch myself take a sip of whiskey.

A woman's got her pride.

'A crazy story told by a crazy old drag queen should only make you wonder,' I say.

I order another round. Light up some locoweed, pass it on.

'Come on, tell us the story,' another one says. 'Tell us the part about Alma Hatch's eyes.'

'Tell us the part about dancing the walk-about with the Wisdom Brothers.'

'Tell us the part about Billy Blizzard fucking Peg-Leg Ida, then you fucking Peg-Leg Ida.'

'Tell us about Ida Richilieu's legs walking around the hills trying to find the rest of her.'

'Tell us the part about your father.'

'Tell us the part about your mother.'

'Tell us the part about the twins being half Ida and half something else.'

What's a human being without a story?

I turn on my chair and look my eyes into the left eye of every person in the bar. They are afraid of me. They think I am the devil. They always want more.

Outside, the cool-ball light is falling down on the mountain, Not-Really-A-Mountain, that's snagging us here. Making us think that what we're doing is what we're doing.

'If you're the devil, then it's not me telling this story,' I say.

'That's it, that's how the story begins,' a woman says. They step closer.

*

I run past the Shed, through the gate, and head toward Chinatown along the old wire fence until Hot Creek. Three jumps across Hot Creek on the rocks that I placed just so. Then on up running past the jailhouse with the door always open and nobody in the jailhouse except on Saturday night, running up to Dr. Ah Fong's, through Chinatown, to the cemetery.

Leaning against the big Douglas fir, the field to sunset green only for about a week and the rest of the time golden.

Running up to the hot springs, coming to the edge, where the earth goes down. In the pool, sun through the falling water, killdeer rainbows.

Up at the nest, throwing myself off the big granite rock into the air, flying through the blue sky into deep blue green grey black clear water, getting out fast, standing naked in the sun, panting, heart beating.

Back into town running, the buildings all falling over, crumbling onto themselves, becoming dust. The Mormon school, the Mormon churches – the white one, the green one, and the brick one empty, boarded up. Ida's Place gone, the post office gone, Stein's Mercantile fell over, North's Grocery burned, Thord Hurdlika's rock house another tombstone, Damn Dave's still standing although leaning due east. Goats living in Doc Heyburn's clean white office. American flag not flying anymore – lightning hit the pole. Horse trough's still there, and the red-handled spigot.

William B. Merrillee's mill three stories of rotting wood and rusty iron.

The Dry House only the tin roof.

Gold nowhere to be found.

Up on Not-Really-A-Mountain, I crawl down the granite rocks and walk through my meadow, straight to the edge. The purple flowers that stick up are blooming, and the Indian paintbrush, and the yellow ones. On the rock, on the edge that sticks out the farthest, a gust of wind hits me. I stand myself into the circle I have drawn on the rock, where I promised, so long ago, to free myself of woman's hole.

Truth is, the world is, Mother Earth is, woman's hole. Truth is, we're all stuck in that hole, men or women, stuck in our own hole, in each other's.

Human-being story, knowledge becoming understanding, doing our best to get free.

I look over the edge. You can see everything – the mountains up and down, jagged, rolling, to the horizon. Snow on some even in August. Gold Hill, and Gold Bar – not the town itself but the valley of it. Devil's Pass. You can see Excellent down there – what's left.

Without gold, Excellent only darkness in wilderness – darkness; that is, except for one circle of light: the Solo Lounge light.

The wind gusts strong and picks me up. Flying owl, I glide down past the sandstone flickers of moon, past the special breed of buffalo clouds, moon full in the blood of ornithological I, over the river, the fog on the river, across Pine Street, to the window. To the pernicious blue neon moon. Forever the breath, the breath within breath, the heartbeat. I perch at the window.

Moves Moves – the thrust, that without, we're nothing.

I stand outside and watch.

'Come take a trip in my airship and we'll visit the man in the moon,' the men and the women sing – every sorry one of us sings – us congregated at the piano, glorious, arms folded over one another's shoulders, body to body, leaning hard, reaching out to the someone else there.

Human beings in a bar, a family, laughing our fool heads off. Light in darkness.

'Sing the jubilee; everybody free. / Welcome, welcome, 'mancipation!'

PO BRONSON

Bombardiers

THE HILARIOUS, ELECTRIFYING NOVEL THAT DOES FOR
MONEY WHAT *CATCH-22* DID FOR WAR

'It makes as much sense as *The Name of the Rose* written by the Marx
Brothers, but far more chaotic . . . The prose explodes with the force of a
volcano, the dialogue is as flashy as a firework display, and the characters
are as relentlessly driven as motorcycles on the wall of death'

Time Out

'Required reading for politicians and financiers, in the hope that it will
make them think twice about the way they're mortgaging America's
future. Required reading for everyone else, just because it's so much fun'

Kirkus Reviews

'*Bombardiers* ranks with *Liar's Poker* as a portrayal of the craziness of
investment banking in its money-junkie phase'

Tom Wolfe

'The most entertaining depiction of greed and dishonesty on Wall Street
ever to see print . . . outrageous'

Business Week

'This is a wonderful novel. You will never invest again'

Mario Puzo

ALBERT FRENCH

Billy

The tale of Billy Lee Turner, a ten-year-old boy convicted for the murder
of a white girl in Mississippi in 1937, illuminates the monstrous face of
racism in America with harrowing clarity and power. Narrated in the
rich accents of the American South, Billy's story is told amidst the
picking-fields and town streets, the heat, dust and poverty of the region
in the time of the Depression. Albert French's haunting first novel is a
story of racial injustice, as unsentimental as it is heartbreaking.

'*Billy* may be the best first novel by a black author since Toni Morrison's
The Bluest Eye in 1969.'

Time

'I kept trying to think of a writer who has done a better job of capturing
clear, powerful and authentic language, the landscape, the people . . . the
air itself. I kept searching for comparisons and I kept coming up with
masters of the art, from Aeschylus to Ernest Gaines'

David Bradley

'*Billy* is a book that will stay with me in my dreams'

Tim O'Brien

LARRY KRAMER

Faggots

'The liberation of sexuality from the bonds of Moralism has left in its wake a crying need for principled, intelligent, vigorous explorations of how a genuine morality can be introduced to our newly-minted freedom. This exploration is a central part of Larry Kramer's historically significant literary work, of which *Faggots* constitutes an important beginning and a key. As a documentation of an era, as savage and savagely funny social parody, as a cry in the wilderness, and as a prescient, accurate reading of the writing on the wall, the novel is peerless and utterly necessary. It is brilliant, bellicose, contemptuous, compassionate – and as true of everything Kramer writes, behind its delectable, entertaining, sometimes maddening harshness is a profoundly moving plea for justice and for love. There are few books in modern gay fiction, or in modern fiction for that matter, that *must* be read. *Faggots* is certainly one of them.'

Tony Kushner

'True comic brilliance – a vicious Swiftian satire that, like all satire, contains a strong moral voice'

New York

'I hope the gay community won't lose its sense of humour about this book. *Faggots*, for all its excesses, is frequently right on target and, when it is on target, is appallingly funny'

Edward Albee

'Prophetic. *Faggots* chronicles the high/low point of gay hedonism and outraged so many because it dared to rain on the gay parade and point out that the "yes" of gay culture is not necessarily any more liberating than the "no" of the straight world'

Mark Simpson, *Guardian*

'A book of major historical importance – the first contemporary novel to chronicle gay life with unsparing honesty and wild humour. Larry Kramer has changed the way we think about gay men. He is one of our great humanists'

Erica Jong

'Larry Kramer has all the audacity, zaniness and, yes, even the wisdom of a Voggegut . . . I laughed from the opening page . . . I wish I could have written the damn thing'

Frederick Exley

'Larry Kramer is one of America's most valuable troublemakers. I hope he never lowers his voice'

Susan Sontag

SUSAN MINOT

Folly

'This is the story of Lilian Eliot, whom we first encounter as a teenager in 1917 Boston, following her through a tormenting wartime romance and a difficult marriage into a hard-earned kind of peace. It is not foolishness that Minot writes about but the growth of wisdom, in a style so simple it's like water: you can see into its depths'

Elle

'The first time I read *Pride and Prejudice* I couldn't wait to read it again, and that's how I feel about *Folly*'

New Woman

'An enchantment from start to satisfying finish'

Sunday Telegraph

'Susan Minot floats a delicious social comedy on an ocean of private pain and desolation'

Times Literary Supplement

'Henry James and *Brief Encounter* crossed with Jane Austen: a rare book. She writes like an angel'

Daily Mail

A Selected List of Titles Available from Minerva

While every effort is made to keep prices low, it is sometimes necessary to increase prices at short notice. Mandarin Paperbacks reserves the right to show new retail prices on covers which may differ from those previously advertised in the text or elsewhere.

The prices shown below were correct at the time of going to press.

☐	7493 9574 5	**Continental Drift**	Russell Banks	£6.99
☐	7493 9526 5	**Rule of the Bone**	Russell Banks	£5.99
☐	7493 9667 9	**Bombardiers**	Po Bronson	£6.99
☐	7493 9739 X	**Made in America**	Bill Bryson	£6.99
☐	7493 9767 5	**A Good Scent From A Strange Mountain**	Robert Olen Butler	£5.99
☐	7493 9628 8	**Faith in Fakes: Travels in Hyperreality**	Umberto Eco	£6.99
☐	7493 9797 7	**Nude Men**	Amanda Filipacchi	£5.99
☐	7493 9771 3	**Billy**	Albert French	£5.99
☐	7493 9663 6	**Holly**	Albert French	£5.99
☐	7493 9059 X	**Faggots**	Larry Kramer	£6.99
☐	7493 9527 3	**Other Women**	Evelyn Lau	£5.99
☐	7493 9896 5	**Nothing But Blue Skies**	Thomas McGuane	£5.99
☐	7493 9611 3	**Folly**	Susan Minot	£5.99
☐	7493 9505 2	**The Moviegoer**	Walker Percy	£6.99
☐	7493 9141 3	**Vineland**	Thomas Pynchon	£6.99
☐	7493 3602 1	**The Joy Luck Club**	Amy Tan	£5.99
☐	7493 9678 4	**Suspects**	David Thomson	£6.99

All these books are available at your bookshop or newsagent, or can be ordered direct from the address below. Just tick the titles you want and fill in the form below.

Cash Sales Department, PO Box 5, Rushden, Northants NN10 6YX.
Phone: 01933 414000 : Fax: 01933 414047.

Please send cheque, payable to 'Reed Book Services Ltd.', or postal order for purchase price quoted and allow the following for postage and packing:

£1.00 for the first book, 50p for the second; **FREE POSTAGE AND PACKING FOR THREE BOOKS OR MORE PER ORDER.**

NAME (Block letters) ....

ADDRESS ....

....

☐ I enclose my remittance for ....

☐ I wish to pay by Access/Visa Card Number

Expiry Date

Signature ....

Please quote our reference: MAND